MONSTERS, WEAK AND STRONG

The troll balanced on the limb of the tree and looked down at them. There was a rope about his neck, with the other end tied to the limb. "Stand back," he shrilled. "Make no move to save me. I have nothing left to live for. My bridge—"

He jumped. His feet hit the ground, and a good length of rope lay on the ground beside him.

"He bungled it," Harcourt said, feeling disgust at a badly done job. "He miscalculated the span of the rope."

Yolanda screamed. "Dragon!"

Harcourt spun about, sword out of its scabbard and in his hand. He saw a monster dragon sweeping in upon them. It was coming in fast, tilting to avoid the tree under which they stood. The taloned claws were reaching for him, and the cruel, beaked head was darting forward . . .

Also by Clifford D. Simak
Published by Ballantine Books:

Where the Evil Dwells

Clifford D. Simak

A Del Rey Book

Ballantine Books · New York

A Del Rey Book
Published by Ballantine Books

Library of Congress Catalog Card Number: 82-6839

ISBN 0-345-29751-2

Manufactured in the United States of America

First Hardcover Edition: September 1982

First Paperback Edition: September 1983

Cover art by Michael Whelan

One

Harcourt saw the dragon while he was riding home from the morning's hunt. It was flying down the river, a flapping dishcloth of a thing, its snakelike neck stretched out, as if the head and neck were striving mightily to haul the heavy body through the air. The long, twisting tail trailed along behind.

He pointed it out to the Knurly Man, who was riding beside him, leading a third horse that was loaded with the hart and the boar brought down earlier in the day.

"The first dragon of the year," Harcourt said.

"We seldom see them now," said the Knurly Man. "There are not many of them left."

That was right, Harcourt thought. There were not many of them left this side of the river. Most of them, over the years, had moved to the north. There, it was generally believed, they were working with the Evil, acting as scouts to spy out the movements of the cloud of barbarians who were hovering hungrily on the fringes of the Empty Land.

"There was, at one time, a rookery of dragons just up the river," Harcourt said. "There may be a few of them still there."

The Knurly Man chuckled. "That was where you and Hugh tried to catch the dragon."

"It was only a baby dragon," Harcourt said.

"Baby or full-grown," said the Knurly Man, "a dragon is nothing to be fooled around with. I guess you found that out. Where might Hugh be now?"

"I'm not sure," said Harcourt. "Guy may know. The last I heard, he was somewhere in the wilds of Macedonia. The factor of a trading post. We'll drop the hart off at the abbey. The boar is all we need. Those little, scurrying monks of Guy's seldom get a chance at honest meat. Guy does, of course. I think he visits the castle as often as he does because

1

of the table we set rather than the company he finds. I'll ask him what he hears of Hugh."

"Pompous as he may be," said the Knurly Man, "I like the Abbot Guy."

"To me," said Harcourt, "he is an old and valued friend. He and Hugh are brothers, and I can't count the times, in early years, when he extricated Hugh and me out of the scrapes we were always falling into. I used to think it was because he was Hugh's older brother, but now I know that he would have done the same for me if I had been in a scrape alone."

They came out of the woodland into plowland, green with the springing of the wheat, following a narrow cart track that ran between two fields. A lark went sailing up from the wheat, arrowing high into the sky, trailing behind it the trilling of its song.

Straight ahead, but still some distance off, could be seen the two round towers of the castle. It wasn't much of a castle, Harcourt reminded himself—not one of the fancy structures that had been built by lords of great wealth in centuries past. But it was home to him and it was all that a castle should be. Seven years ago, it had stood off attack when the Evil came swarming across the river to strike the abbey and the castle. They had sacked the abbey and, for three days and nights, had mounted an assault against the castle. The price, however, had been made too high for them, and finally they had pulled back and retreated across the river to the Empty Land. Harcourt had been a young man then, and he remembered, thinking back, how the castle's men had stood upon the wall and cheered as the Evil had broken off the siege.

To the right, at the head of a ravine that ran down to the river, rose the soaring spires of the abbey. Rising ground hid the rest of the structure, with only the spires thrusting up above the heavy growth of trees that covered the ravine and the river hills.

"Your grandfather was saying just the other day," the Knurly Man said, "that your Uncle Raoul had been gone too long. He said it as if he never expected to see him again. This last long absence has taken too much out of the old man. He worries a lot about that wandering son of his."

"I know he does," said Harcourt. "Uncle Raoul left shortly after the raid."

"I told your grandfather he would be back. One of these

days, I told him, he'll come walking in. I wish, though, that I could be sure of that."

"In this world," said Harcourt, "you can't be sure of anything."

From a distance, the twin spires of the abbey, in all their airy delicacy, had given the hint of a soaring structure of great majesty. Close up, that impression vanished. The spires retained their fragile beauty, but the supporting structure, while adequately solid, showed the signs of age and careless maintenance. The soot of wood fires, the verdigris of weathering copper, the soggy juices of fallen leaves, lodged in a hundred nooks and crannies and never cleared away, colored the masonry with unsightly stains and blotches. Here and there the very stones themselves were chipped by ice and sun. The entire building had a ramshackle look about it.

In the courtyard chickens ran about, clucking and scratching. A bedraggled peacock strutted ridiculously, fanning out a tail from which half the plumes were missing. Ducks waddled companionably and geese ran hissing. A half-grown porker, twirling its tail energetically, rooted with determination at a clump of weeds, seeking to uproot them.

The approach of Harcourt and the Knurly Man had been noticed. Monks tumbled out from everywhere and ran toward them from all directions. One of the monks seized the bridle of Harcourt's mount, and another moved toward the Knurly Man.

"No need," said the Knurly Man. "I'll not be staying. I'll take the hart around to the kitchen, then continue to the castle. We'll want the boar for supper, and it will take some time to cook him."

The monk holding Harcourt's horse said, "A bait of oats for the animal and a drink of water."

"That will be fine," said Harcourt. "I thank you for your courtesy."

He dismounted, and the monk led the horse away.

Hurrying around the corner of the abbey came Abbot Guy, a massive man who towered above the others. A black brush of beard offset the nakedness of his tonsured poll. Clear, blue, sparkling eyes looked out of the beard as if from ambush. His cassock was hitched up at the belt. Bare legs and feet showed beneath its hem. The feet, Harcourt saw, were unwashed, although why he noted that he did not know. Few people, even churchmen, paid much heed to soap and water.

"Charles," the abbot shouted, "it's good to see you."

Harcourt shook his outstretched hand. "Abbot, you haven't been to see us for a week. You know the castle is yours whenever you may come."

"Details," the abbot said in his booming voice. "Always and forever, details. If it's not one thing, then it's another. Always something to steal away one's time. These dolts of mine must be told everything they do—not only what to do, but how to do it and sometimes even why. Once at it, they do it willingly enough, but they must be told. I lead them by their hands, I wipe their noses for them, every one of them."

The watching monks grinned in tolerant good humor.

"Well, come with me," said the abbot. "We'll find a place where we can sit and tell one another bawdy tales, without all these people listening, endangering their souls by hearing all our dirty talk. Not to mention shirking the chores to which they have been set. I see you brought some venison."

"The castle needed fresh meat, and I was not busy for the day."

"Yes, I know. I know how it goes. Salted beef and pickled pork, after a time, grow weary to the palate. We have some fresh garden greens we'll send home with you."

He grabbed Harcourt by the arm, and the two of them walked around the corner of the abbey, heading for the abbot's tiny house. They ended up in a small room, its walls covered by faded, tattered tapestries.

"That chair over there," said the abbot. "The special chair for old friends. Also for distinguished guests, of which there have been none for years. We live, Charles, in a forgotten corner of the Empire. No one ever comes, not even passing through."

He started rummaging in a closet. "There is a special bottle," he said. "I am sure there is. I hid it away. Now if I can only find it."

He found it and came back with it and two glasses. He handed one of the glasses to Harcourt and sat down in another chair, legs spraddled, working on the cork.

"Your wheat is growing well," said Harcourt. "We rode through the field."

"So I'm told," the abbot said. "I have not been out to see it. It is this job I have."

"It's more than a job," Harcourt told him. "It is an honorable and holy calling, and you are doing well with it."

"If that should be the case," said the Abbot Guy, "wouldn't you think the Church would confirm me in my post? Six years an acting abbot. Not an abbot yet. I tell you, Charles, the way that things are going, I may never be an abbot."

"These are parlous times," Harcourt reminded him. "All is haphazard and uncertain. The barbarians from Hither Asia still pose an ever-present threat. The Evil still stands across the river. There may be, as well, other circumstances of which we are not aware."

"And we are the ones," the abbot said, "who, out here on the frontier, hold the shield for both the Church and the Empire. Occasionally, you would think, they should give some thought to us. Rome should pay us some attention."

"The Empire has fallen on bad times," said Harcourt. "There have been bad times before. But Rome persists. Since the founding of the Republic, if we can trust our history, it has persisted for more than two thousand years. It has its times of glory, it has its periods of weakness. There are times it huddles, as it huddles now, its frontiers pulled back, its economy crumbling, its foreign policy fumbling . . ."

"I have no quarrel with that," the abbot said. "Rome has been weak before; there was a time or two it tottered; but, as you say, it continues to persist. It has staying power. I, with you, trust that it will be great and strong again, and the Church strong with it. My worry is that its recovery will take too long a time. Will it and the Church gain strength soon enough for me to be confirmed in my abbacy, the Empire strong enough to provide the legions to protect this and other frontiers? Someday, some century, a great statesman will arise, as great leaders have come to turn the tide before . . ."

"It is not always great leaders," Harcourt told him. "Sometimes it is sheer circumstance. In the fourth century, the Empire came very near to splitting into east and west. While our historians do not all agree, it seems to me quite evident that the Evil saved the Empire then. The Evil had been there before, of course. Its presence was well known, but up until that time it had been a nuisance only, scarcely more than that. It became more than a nuisance when it attacked in force, without notice, all along the borders, reacting to the pressure of the barbarian hordes that forced it east and south. To turn back the invasion of the Evil called for the full capability of the Empire. There could be no thought of division then; fighting for their lives, the factions had to stay together. And out of that grew a stronger and a greater Rome."

The cork came out with a bang.

"There!" the abbot said. "I finally got it. Please hold out your glass. I cannot understand why I always have so much trouble with a cork. There are those who just nudge it gently."

"You're all thumbs," Harcourt told him. "You always were all thumbs."

The abbot filled his visitor's glass, then filled his own, set the bottle on a table within easy reach, and settled back, sprawling in the chair.

Lifting his glass, he said, "Appreciate this, please. It is almost the last of the special vintage. There may be a few more bottles, no more than a half dozen at the most. And to think—at one time we had five barrels of it."

Harcourt nodded. "Yes, I recall. You've told me the sad story several times. You lost it in the raid."

"That's right. We lost almost everything we had. Our beloved abbot slaughtered and many fine brothers dead, others scattered, hiding in the woods. Our outbuildings burned, the abbey sacked, everything of value taken. The cattle and the poultry either butchered or driven off. Granaries emptied. The smokehouse stripped. They left us to starve. Had it not been for the charity of the castle . . ."

Harcourt interrupted him. The catalogue of the abbey's losses, as conjured up by this abbot, had no end to it. "We were lucky," Harcourt said. "We were able to drive them off."

"You more than drove them off," the abbot told him. "You put the fear of God in them. There have been no further raids since that day of seven years ago. You taught them a lesson they have not even now forgotten. Oh, now and then, some minor forays, easily beaten off, mostly by the Little Folk, who apparently know no better. Elves and brownies and fairies, and the fairies are the worst of all. They can't hurt us much, but they do play shabby tricks. I'm certain it was the fairies who soured our store of new October ale last autumn. We have a good brewmaster. He's been making beer for years. You can't tell me the fault was his. The thing about the fairies is that they can sneak up on you. I sighted a flock of them the other day, but they went winging past."

"By the way," said Harcourt, "we saw a dragon just an hour or so ago, while we were returning from the hunt."

"Whenever I hear someone mention a dragon," said the abbot, "I always remember the time when you and Hugh tried to catch one."

"I know," said Harcourt. "All the people I know remember

that, to my continuing embarrassment. What they forget is that Hugh and I were only twelve years old at the time and had not a lick of sense. We found this baby dragon that had fallen from its nest and was scrabbling around at the foot of Dragon Crag. The older dragons knew it had fallen and were making quite an uproar about it, but they couldn't reach the youngster because of the heavy growth of trees. When Hugh and I saw the little dragon, all that we could think was how great it would be to have a baby dragon for a pet. Not thinking, of course, of what we'd do with it once it had grown up."

"You roped it, didn't you?"

"Yes. We hustled back to the castle and got two lengths of rope and came back, and the dragon was still there. We figured we'd get two nooses around its neck and thus could control it. I got the noose of my rope over its neck, but there was a lot of loose stone and other rubble on the hillside, and Hugh fell down and couldn't throw his noose. The baby dragon started after us, and we knew then that we'd better get out of there. Both of us dropped our ropes, and even then it was a close thing. It was only by the grace of God that Hugh managed to escape that raging little dragon."

"My father, God rest his soul," the abbot said, "when he heard of it, fair whaled the tail off Hugh. I tried to talk him out of it. I said it was just a boyish prank and a part of growing up. But he wouldn't listen to me. He grabbed hold of Hugh with one hand and a paddle with the other . . ."

"What incensed grandfather the worst, I do believe," said Harcourt, "was the loss of the ropes. He lectured me on how hard rope was to come by, and he told me how feckless I was and how I'd never grow up to be a man. By the time he got through with me, I was crawling on my belly. I think he wanted to give me a licking, but he didn't. I wish he had; it would have gone easier than the things he said to me."

"Thinking of it," said the abbot, "I've often wondered if there is a dragon out there somewhere, flying around with your rope still hanging about his neck."

"I've often wondered, too," Harcourt said.

"It's been a long time since I have seen a dragon," said the abbot. "And I can't say I'm sorry for it. Dragons are a scaly lot. And you can't get at them. They swoop down and strike, then flap up into the air again, and you haven't got a chance of getting back at them. I remember how one of them would come sailing down and grab a cow, flying off with the poor beast in its grip. I always felt so sorry for the animals they took. The dragons never bothered to kill them; they just hauled them off. I saw one once that grabbed two pigs, one in each of its claws, which took a bit of doing, even for a dragon. I never will forget the squealing of those shoats. Pigs are the squealingest things there are, and those two porkers, dangling from the dragon's claws, must have set the record as the loudest in all of Christendom. I ran along, shaking my fist at the dragon and yelling words after it that now, as a churchly man, I could not repeat for fear of the injury I might inflict upon my mortal soul. But now there are fewer dragons, and the ogres and the trolls and others of the larger kind of Evil do not cross the river. Only the fairies and the elves and some of the smaller goblins ever come across, and we can cope with them, for they are only pesky rather than being downright dangerous."

"The Evil is caught between two fires," said Harcourt. "The barbarians to the east and north of them and the legions to the south of them. Although why they should fear the legions I don't know, for the legions are pulled far back from this frontier and perhaps from all the others. Pulled far back, I would suppose, because of the stupidity of Roman politics. It may be us the Evil is afraid of, although that's hard to comprehend. I don't mean us alone, but all the other forts and castles strung along the river."

"It may be true, however," said the abbot. "Seven years ago they overran this abbey—quite easily, I might say, for your average monk is not a fighting man—and some other religious communities and a number of unfortified or poorly fortified homesteads, but castles up and down the river generally held against them and inflicted painful damage on them. They took Fontaine, of course . . ."

He stopped speaking, and for a moment there was an embarrassed silence.

Then he said, "I am sorry, Charles. I should not have mentioned it. But my big mouth runs on and on, and I cannot seem to stop."

"It's all right," said Harcourt. "The memory has grown hazy with the years. It no longer hurts. I've learned to live with it."

Although, he told himself, that was not the truth. It had never grown hazy with the years, and it still did hurt, and he'd not learned to live with it.

He still could see her in his mind as he had seen her that

last time of all—that May morning with the spring breeze blowing a strand of her golden hair across her face, her lithe body limned against the blueness of the sky as she sat her horse to say goodbye to him. The hair, wild in the wind, had blown across her face and shielded it from him, so that now he could not remember the shape her face had taken.

He would have sworn, at one time, that he would never forget her face, that he did not need to see it, for he knew every feature of it; and yet, over the years, he had forgotten it. Perhaps, he thought, time was only trying to be kind to him, but he could have wished that it had been less kind.

Eloise, he said, talking to himself, if I only could remember, if I could recall your face. It had been a laughing face, he knew, a happy face, but he could not now recall the crinkle of happy laughter about her eyes, nor the shape her lips had taken when she smiled.

The abbot held out the bottle, and automatically Harcourt held out the glass. The abbot refilled his visitor's glass and added a dollop to his own, then settled back into the chair.

"Perhaps," he said, starting up where he had left off, "it is best the way it stands. It is a pattern that has gone on for centuries—as you point out, back to the fourth century. The barbarians to the east and north, we to the south and west, the Evil in between the two. The situation seesaws back and forth. Five hundred years or more ago the Evil pulled back, perhaps because the pressure from the barbarians lessened, and Rome extended its frontiers. Rome was strong in those days—it was then we had our short-lived renaissance. Whether the new awakening represented by the renaissance was killed by renewed onslaughts of the Evil is problematical; it might have faded out in any case. Something less than two centuries ago the barbarians surged forward once again, and the Evil, responding to their advance and needing living room, came roaring back at us. Rome was falling into decline again, and the legions were slogging back, with the refugees in flight ahead of them. The new frontier became our river, and so it has been since. But the point I am trying to make is that the Evil still serves as a buffer between us and the barbarians. Of the two, the Evil may be the easier to live with. We know them, we can predict to a point what they may do. For us it probably is better with the Evil across the river rather than the barbarians."

"I don't know about that," said Harcourt. "The barbarians are men, and we'd fight them as man against man, steel against steel. The Evil are nasty things to face. They come at you with fangs and claws. Their breath is foul against your face. There are no clean strokes. They are hard to kill. They hang on and on. I have had my belly full of them and their way of fighting."

The abbot leaned forward in his chair.

"We lost many fine brothers and almost everything we owned in that raid. But it's passing strange, and I am upset by it, for when I think of all we lost, one thing sticks in my mind. An item that undoubtedly was an insignificant possession. Perhaps you remember it. The little crystal prism that held a rainbow in it."

"I do remember," Harcourt told him. "I came here as a boy—I think that you and Hugh were with me."

"Yes, I recall. We were."

"One of the monks, I forget which one, took us into the sanctuary and showed the prism to us. There was a shaft of light shining from a window high up in the wall, and when he held the prism up so that it was struck by that shaft of sunlight, it blazed with all the glory of a rainbow."

"It meant nothing, really," said the abbot. "It was a mere curiosity, a conversation piece. Although, come to think of it, it could have been more than that. A piece of art, perhaps. It had been made by an ancient craftsman. Some said in Rome, others said in Gaul. Cut from a piece of the purest crystal, polished expertly. More than likely it was crafted centuries ago, probably during that now-vanished renaissance."

"I have often pondered," Harcourt said, "what the world might now be like if the renaissance had not been throttled by the rush of circumstance. It built this abbey; it built and created many other things in which we hold a pardonable pride. Eloise gave me a book of hours dating from that time. No artist today can do that sort of work."

"I know. I mourn it, too. The prism was a small example. The old abbot, the one who was killed in the raid, once told me that it was an expression of meticulous mathematics. What he meant by that I can't pretend to know. But no matter now—the prism's gone. For some time, I thought it might have been overlooked by the raiders. Perhaps, I told myself, one of them had picked it up and, not holding it to the light so that he could see the glory of it, had tossed it to one side as a worthless piece of glass. But, search as I might, I was unable to find it. Now I'm convinced that it was taken."

"It's a pity. It was so beautiful."

"Legend has it," said the abbot, "that there was another prism. Much larger than the one we had. Perhaps fashioned by the same craftsman. At one time, so the legend says, it was the property of a wizard by the name of Lasandra."

"I have heard the legend," Harcourt said.

"Then you know the rest of the story."

"Only that the soul of a saint was supposed to have been imprisoned by Lasandra in the prism. No details. Just that."

"The details," said the abbot, "if they are details and not simply pieces of disconnected legend, are hazy at the best. There is, I would suspect, a good deal of nonsense in all legends. But the story is that the saint, whose name, I regret to tell you, has been lost in the mists of time, tried to expel the Evil from this world into the Outer Darkness. That had been his intentions, but he messed up somehow, and there were some of the Evil left. He drove them through the gate, so the story goes, and slammed it shut behind them, but he'd not driven all of them. He missed a few. And the ones he missed, conspiring with the sorcerer Lasandra, trapped him and slew him; but before slaying him, they trapped his soul inside the prism. I tell you only what I have read in ancient documents."

"You mean that you have studied this legend?"

"There is little that can be studied. There may be more, but I do not know of it. There was a reason for the little study I've made."

"And the reason?"

"A whisper. Even less than rumor. A whisper only. The whisper says that, in some manner not explained, the Church wrested the prism of Lasandra from the Evil and kept it in holy reverence, but that it again was lost. How lost the whisper does not say."

"So the whole story could be no more than legend. There are so many legends that one cannot give equal weight to all of them. Many of them may be no more than simple-minded tales made up in intervals of idleness by some inventive mind."

"That could be true," the abbot said. "What you say is true. But there is further. Do you wish to hear it?"

"Of course I wish to hear it."

"Your family built this abbey. You know that, of course. But do you know that it was built on the site of a much older abbey, one that had been abandoned for many years before your family came here? Some of the scattered stones of the old structure still stand in the walls of this one."

"I had understood there had been an earlier building. I did not know it had been an abbey. Don't tell me . . ."

"But I will," the abbot said. "The whisper continues. It has one more gasp left in it. It says that the prism of Lasandra was housed in reverence in that old deserted abbey which was replaced by this one."

"And you believe that?"

"I fight against believing it. I tell myself that none of the story may be true. But I am tempted to believe. Charles, I am sorely tempted."

Someone knocked loudly at the door.

"Enter," the abbot called.

The door was opened by a monk. He said to Harcourt, "My lord, the miller's waif is here."

"You mean Yolanda?" the abbot asked.

"That is the one I mean," said the monk, sniffing just a little. "She carries word, my lord, that your Uncle Raoul has come home again."

Two

Hurrying around to the front of the abbey, with the abbot trailing behind him, Harcourt found the miller's waif, Yolanda, waiting for him, half encircled by a crowd of monks. Another monk was leading out his horse.

"What is this?" Harcourt asked Yolanda. "You say my uncle's home. How come that it is you who brings the word to me? If my uncle were home . . ."

"He's not home," she said. "He is not home as yet. He lies in my father's house."

"Lies in . . . ?"

"He is sick and weak," she said. "He was sleeping when I left. My mother tried to feed him, but he fell asleep before he could take the food. So I ran up to the castle—I, rather than my father, for he is lame, you know."

"Yes, that I know."

"The castle told me you were here. Knowing you would wish to know as soon as possible . . ."

"Yes, yes," he said impatiently. "It was kind of you."

"It will take men to carry him to the castle," she said. "Your grandfather said he would get together enough men to carry a litter up the river bluffs. When I left, he was cursing something dreadful because all the men were scattered, doing different jobs, and it would take time to bring them in."

The monk leading out the horse brought it up to Harcourt and stood holding the reins.

"If you plan to ride down the ravine to the miller's place," the abbot cautioned, "it would be well to exercise all care. There is a trail, but it is very rough and steep."

"I know the way," Yolanda said. "I can point it out to you. I can mount up behind you."

Now, for the first time, Harcourt looked squarely at her. She was dressed in a tattered robe, with its cowl pulled up about her face. Strands of flaxen hair straggled out from beneath the cowl. Her face was thin and pinched; her eyes were cornflower blue. Her hands, he saw, were rough with work. He had seen her before, had known of her and her strange story, but this was the first time he had really looked at her.

"All right, then," he said. "You get up behind me."

He sprang into the saddle, gathered the reins in one hand, and reached down the other to her. Her hand grasped his, and he was surprised at the strength he sensed in it. As the two hands clenched together, he heaved his strength against her and she vaulted up, settling astride the horse's back behind the saddle. The assembled monks sucked in their breaths in gasps.

Harcourt clucked to the horse and drew rein against its neck to guide it toward the ravine that lay beyond the back of the abbey. Turning in his saddle, he waved farewell to the Abbot Guy.

Yolanda tightened her arms about his waist. "Did you hear those nasty little monks?" she asked. "A little show of leg . . ."

He chuckled. "They are unaccustomed to it," he told her. "You must have some tolerance for them."

The trail that led down to the river and the miller's place was steep and winding, twisting its way around great boulders that in ages past had fallen from the cliffs that hemmed it in. At times it followed a rocky watercourse with the water barely covering the horse's hooves; at other times it plunged down sharp, steep slopes that the horse negotiated by sliding on set feet. In places the trail disappeared entirely, and Yolanda had to point the way.

"You say my uncle made his way to Jean's house," Harcourt said. "From whither did he come?"

"He came across the bridge."

"You mean he came from the Empty Land!"

"It would seem so," she said. "When I first sighted him, he was walking on the bridge, toward this side of the river, coming from the other. He was having trouble walking, and I thought at first that he was drunk. He fell a couple of times, but each time he managed to get to his feet and stagger on. I thought, how disgusting to be as drunk as that. Then I thought, what if he weren't? What if he should be hurt or sick? So I called out to Jean, my father, and he came running, hobbling rather than running, for that is the best that he can do. Together we got him to the house. At first my father did not recognize him, but before we got him to the house, he did recognize him. My father said he'd grown older; that was why at first he didn't know him. As soon as we knew who he was, I started for the castle with the word."

"Did he say anything to you? Did he speak at all?"

"He mumbled. That was all. He was dead upon his feet. He had been traveling on sheer nerve alone. He was unhurt. He had no wounds. He showed no blood. I made sure of that."

"You say he mumbled. Then he tried to talk."

"I don't think he was trying to speak. He was just making noises."

"And at first Jean didn't know him?"

"His hair is white," she said. "It had been black, only turning a little gray, when Jean had seen him last. To me, he looked an old man."

Uncle Raoul, Harcourt thought—he would be older now, for he had been gone for long, but even knowing how long he had been gone, Harcourt still remembered him as a strangely youthful man—youthful even when he wasn't. A youthful, powerful man standing straight and tall, a man who somehow did not belong on these acres, but in far and foreign places. How many times had he been home? Harcourt wondered and, trying to think back, could not estimate the number. Five or six, perhaps, but he could not be certain.

There had been times when Raoul had returned a failure, a man whose venture had finally come to nothing. There had, however, never been about him any sense of failure. He had always been quite frank in his admission of his failure, although he never spelled out what the failure was, acting as if it were of no importance that he failed. At times this strange, wandering uncle must have felt some disappointment and perhaps even bitterness, but he never showed it, and a failure never stopped him. Given a few weeks, or a few months at the most, he'd be off again. It had been possible, Harcourt remembered, to predict when he would leave. For some days before he left, he would be restless, straining against the leash to try some new adventure that had been hatched in his fertile brain.

There had been other times when he had returned successful, riding a splendid horse with costly trappings, dressed in new finery, and bearing wondrous gifts for all of them. But, successful or failing, he never talked about what he actually had done. He had talked of many other things, and from the sort of tales he told, it was often possible to guess where he might have been, that is, the area that he had visited, although there were never any clues as to exactly where. The family, of course, had wondered about the facts that were left untold, but they never asked, perhaps because they were afraid to ask, fearful that they might learn some shameful thing they would not want to know.

There had been one momentous occasion, Harcourt recalled, when his uncle had sought him out where the two of them could be alone and had talked to him as if he were talking to a man rather than a boy.

"Charley," he had asked, "I wonder if I could rent your eyes? Do you think you could maintain a sharp lookout in my behalf? I'll be watching, too, of course, but it would be better if there were two of us."

There had been a quality about it all that had hinted of a great conspiracy to which Harcourt had been made a partner, a tingling, throat-tightening experience that had made the world come bright.

"I may not be staying here much longer," his uncle had said, "but as long as I am here, I shall pay you handsomely, a golden besant for every day that you watch for me. You'll be watching for two men, traveling together. They'll probably come walking. You can tell it's them because one of them will limp. More than likely they'll travel the ridge road."

"Uncle Raoul, are these two men after you?"

"I would think they might be."

"If I see them, I'm to run and tell you?"

"That is exactly right. Will you take the job?"

"Of course I will."

"There is another thing. You must tell no one of this. Not your grandfather, not your mother, not the Knurly Man, not anyone at all. Do you agree to that?"

Harcourt remembered how fervently he had said that he did agree to it and how they'd struck the bargain. He had been of the age when a secret was a fascinating and exciting thing, and here was a big secret, not one of those piddling little secrets that one most often had to settle for.

"Then here is your first coin," his uncle had said to him. "Be sure that you don't lose it. Every day you watch, there'll be another one."

Harcourt remembered how suddenly rich it had seemed he was, for a golden besant was a princely sum, very seldom seen.

He had watched most faithfully for five days, after which there had been no further need of watching, for in the middle of the night of that fifth day his Uncle Raoul had left, saying no goodbyes. On each of those five days, he had given Harcourt a besant. The family made no comment on the uncle's leaving; it was to be expected; it was the way he ordinarily left.

With his uncle gone, Harcourt no longer kept a regular watch, but for the next several days he watched off and on. It turned out disappointingly; the two men never did appear.

Huge trees covered the steep hillsides, some of them crowding against the trail they followed. The great trees clung with massive roots wherever there was soil enough for them to find an anchor. Clumps of writhing juniper and twisted birch grew from ledges in the faces of the cliff.

Yolanda pointed to one of the trees that grew close beside the trail.

"That one is mine," she told Harcourt. "Jean has promised that when he finds the time, he'll cut it for me and skid it to the mill. It is a cherry tree."

Harcourt grinned, amused at the importance she placed on one tree among so many trees, at her calm, positive announcement that the tree belonged to her.

"What," he asked, "is so important about a cherry tree?"

"It's the best wood of all to carve," she said. "It is easy and true to work, but durable. The grain is good and it takes a ready polish. I'm going to make a carving from it for the Abbot Guy. He told me he needed a carving of a saint, and I will make him one."

"Of which saint?" Harcourt asked.

"All saints look alike," she said. "They all have stern and solemn faces and are dressed in pleated robes. I'll make a saint for him and let him name it what he will."

"You know the abbot? You have talked with him?"

"I am acquainted with him. I do not see him often. He came down to the mill one day last winter to talk with Jean on a matter of small business, and there he saw the carving I had done. It was then he asked me to carve a saint for him."

"I knew you worked in wood. Do you do much of it?"

"I work almost every day. My father built a shed for me to provide a place to work and where the pieces I make will be protected against the weather."

"It is a marvelous gift," said Harcourt. "Have you made some study of the craft?"

"No study and no teaching. Who is there to teach me? I feel it inside myself. I see within the wood a figure struggling to get out and I help it to get out. Or I try to help. If I had better tools, I might do better. The only tools I have are the ones Jean made for me."

A strange woman, Harcourt told himself—very strange, indeed. A waif with no known parentage, who had simply wandered to the miller's place and had been taken in by the miller and his wife. She had been fortunate in the place she had wandered to, for the miller and his wife had ached to have a child. Some years before they had had a son, but the son had died of a childhood ailment and there had been no other children, although they had kept on hoping that there might be one.

Sitting on a bench outside the mill, watching the river flowing past, the miller, he remembered, had told him how it came about.

"You can imagine how we felt," the miller had said, "when, one fine October morning, we found Yolanda sitting on our doorstep, playing with a new kitten that we had. She was, maybe, seven or eight years old. We had no idea where she had come from, and she couldn't tell us. We were glad that she had come to us and we took her in, fearful all the while that someone would show up to claim her. We made discreet inquiries, but it seemed no one had lost a child. She has been with us ever since. She has been a daughter to us."

Harcourt remembered asking, "You still have no idea where she came from?"

"We can't be positive," the miller had said, "but it is possible she may have come from the Empty Land. There still are a few humans there, you know. Someone might have smuggled her across the bridge in the dead of night. To get her out of there."

"You have reason to believe this?"

"No," the miller had told him. "It is just a thought we had."

The trail grew less rough. The incline of the bluff began to level off. Looking over his shoulder, Harcourt saw the stark thrust of the limestone cliffs they had traveled through. To his ears came the muffled roar of the mighty river.

And there, through the trees ahead, was the bridge, a massive timbered structure set on great stone piers. It had been built by a long-forgotten legion that had toiled here when all the land about had been a howling wilderness.

Instinctively, not meaning to, surprised when he did it, Harcourt lifted an arm in silent tribute to those engineers of so long ago.

Three

Harcourt's uncle lay on a pallet in the miller's kitchen, a sheepskin covering him, pulled up to his chin. His hair and beard were white, his face bony, no more than a skull with the skin pulled tight over it. He was asleep; the closed eyelids had the look of thin parchment.

"He's been like that ever since Jean carried him in," said the miller's wife. "Never in my life have I seen a man so bone-tired. Jean propped him up and I tried to feed him soup, but he drifted off to sleep with the spoon still in his mouth."

"Where is Jean now?"

"He started up the trail to see if he could be of help. I begged him not to go, for the trail is steep. Did you not meet him on the way?"

"No," said Harcourt. "He probably went up the castle trail. We followed the trail from the abbey. Yolanda learned that I was there and ran there to tell me. My grandfather will be sending men to take my uncle home."

"You can leave him here," said the miller's wife. "He's causing us no trouble, and it would be a shame to wake him. Let him get his rest. Poor man, he must have been through a lot."

"That's kind of you," said Harcourt, "but my grandfather's waiting up there at the castle. I think he had given up ever seeing my Uncle Raoul again. He's been gone so long this time and no word of him. Not, come to think of it, that there was ever word the other times he went. The old man will count the hours until he lays eyes on him again. And there's my mother, too. She's probably bustling around to fix a chamber for him and to cook the food he likes . . ."

"Does your mother still stay well?" the miller's wife asked. "And the old gentleman? You've all been so kind to us. Your grandfather, I remember, sent quick word to us when the Evil crossed the river. It gave us time to reach the protection of the castle . . ."

"Jean paid back any debt he might have thought he owed us for the warning," Harcourt said, rather shortly. "He fought bravely on the wall. That's where he took his hurt. We needed men like him."

Yolanda came across the kitchen with a tall mug in her hand.

"Please, my lord," she said, "poor as it may be, a draught of ale."

"Never poor," said Harcourt. "If my memory serves me right, Jean brews a splendid ale."

He took the mug from her and tipped it to his lips. He had been right. Jean did brew a splendid ale.

He looked closely at his uncle, who was still sleeping. Raoul muttered as he slept, and one arm twitched nervously.

"It may be a little time until the men from the castle arrive," Harcourt said. He turned to face Yolanda. "I wonder if you'd be so kind as to show me the work that you are doing?"

"My lord," she said, "I'd be honored to."

He drained the mug and set it on a table, then followed Yolanda out the door.

Outside, the westering sun shone pleasantly and warmly, its rays sparking off the river that slid boisterously down the land, talking as it went in that deep, confident tone that large rivers use. The faint, delicate perfume of wild woods flowers, blooming in the shade beneath the forest trees, flowed across the clearing in which stood the miller's house and mill. It was a pleasant place, Harcourt told himself. It would be good, he thought, to stay here for a while, watching and listening to the river and breathing in the essence of the flowers.

Yolanda guided him around the mill to a small shed down-river of the mill. The wall to the south side of the shed went up only halfway to the roof, providing light for the interior.

"A projecting eave over the opening," Yolanda said, "pro-tects it from the rain and allows some circulation of the air, which is necessary for the seasoning of the wood."

She opened a door and, standing aside, motioned him in. Harcourt stepped inside and stopped, astounded at what he saw.

Propped against the wall stood full-figure carvings, some of them only half-finished, others of them, to Harcourt's uncriti-cal eye, quite finished. On shelves stood carven heads, not only human heads, but also the heads of monsters he could not put a name to. Here and there were things other than heads—a rose entwined with a vine on a flat panel of wood, a few small horses, a cat and kittens, an ox pulling a cart, with a man walking and leading the ox. But mostly it was heads.

"It's difficult to find good wood," Yolanda said. "Each wood has a quality of its own. Cherry and walnut are the best, although one must search to find good walnut trees. There is plenty of oak, but oak is hard to work, and it wants to split and check. Some of the softer woods are fine, but they do not take a polish."

At the end of one of the shelves stood a gargoyle, so ugly and misshapen that it was beautiful. Its snout spread across half its face, its ears were bat ears, its nostrils flared, the mouth was large and fanged, the lips were thick and flabby.

"What I don't understand," said Harcourt, "is how you can conceive some of the figures you have carved. This gargoyle, for example . . ."

"There are sculptured gargoyles at the abbey," she told him. "With the Abbot Guy's permission, I have studied them and some of the other figures that are scattered here and there, all through it."

"I suppose there are," said Harcourt. "I never thought of that. I've never really seen them. Just glanced at them is all."

"I look at them," Yolanda said, "and fix them in my mind. Then I make little changes of my own. I try to give them extra life. I try to make them real. That gargoyle you are looking at is a monster, but I tried to make him a living, breathing monster. I talked with him while I was shaping him and pretended he talked back, and I tried to make him look as if he could talk back."

The miller's wife stuck her head in the door.

"Your uncle's awake," she told Harcourt. "He tried to talk. He said some words, but he mumbled so that I could not make them out."

"I'll go see him," said Harcourt, starting for the door.

In the kitchen he knelt beside the pallet. "Uncle Raoul," he said.

The uncle opened his eyes. "Charley? Charley, is that you?"

"Yes, Uncle. I have come to take you home. Grandfather is at the castle, waiting for you."

"Where am I, Charley?"

"You are at Jean's mill. Jean, the miller."

"Then I'm across the river."

"You are safely across the river."

"I'm out of the Empty Land?"

Harcourt nodded.

"Good," his uncle said. "That is very good. Finally, I am safe."

"We'll carry you up the bluff trail to the castle."

The man on the pallet reached out to grasp Harcourt's arm with his clawlike hand. "Charley," he whispered. "Charley, I found it."

Harcourt leaned closer. "Don't worry now," he said. "Don't try to tell me now. You can tell me later."

"I found it, but I couldn't get my hands on it. There were too many of them. But I know where it is. I know that it exists. It is not just a legend. Not just a silly story."

"Uncle, what are you talking about?"

"The prism," his uncle whispered. "Lasandra's prism."

"You mean the one . . ."

"The one," his uncle said, "that prisons the soul of a blessed saint."

"But, Uncle . . ."

"I tell you I know where it is. I almost had it. I got to where it was. I would have had it, but . . ."

"Forget it now," said Harcourt, speaking more harshly than he had intended. "We can't discuss it now. We must get you home."

The miller's wife spoke from the door. "Here are the men from the castle. They are coming down the trail."

Four

Harcourt had heard the muted sounds of metallic clanking and raised voices when he still was some distance short of the end of the trail. When his horse reached the crest of the rise, he pulled to a halt and sat looking at the assemblage of armed men clustered in front of the castle. The milling crowd, he saw, was made up of Roman legionnaires. They were dressed in marching gear. Helmets, breastplates, and greaves shone in the sun of late afternoon. The pilums, the heavy, six-foot javelins of the legionary infantry, made ragged lines, slung across the shoulders of the men as they struggled to form themselves into marching lines under the shouted commands of their officers.

A mounted centurion, scarlet plumes floating above his helmet, urged his horse forward to meet Harcourt. As they came abreast of each other, the centurion raised his hand in brief salute. Harcourt answered with one as brief.

"We were told you'd be coming up the bluff, carrying an ill man in a litter," said the centurion. "So we waited until you had cleared the trail. We were told it was narrow and steep. You are Harcourt, aren't you?"

"Charles Harcourt, at your service, sir. And you?"

"Decimus Apollinarius Valenturian, commanding a company in this fragmentary cohort. I'm frank to tell you that we are understrength. This unit is designated a cohort, but it's not by half. The legion, these days, has fallen into doing everything by halves."

"Things are bad everywhere," said Harcourt.

"That is true," said Decimus, "and especially in Rome. We have a drooling idiot for an emperor and, if rumor's true, a woman for a pope."

"I had not known of that," said Harcourt, flustered at the news.

"It's a recent development," said the centurion. "By the time the news reaches out here through normal channels, it may no longer be true—outdated news. Communications have

22

broken down everywhere, and no one knows what is happening."

Harcourt wanted to ask more about the woman pope, but he was afraid to. He had a sneaking hunch it might be no more than a bad joke and best left alone. The drooling idiot as an emperor did not bother him. This was not the first time the Empire had been headed by a drooling idiot. It was nothing new.

"You're on patrol?" he asked the centurion.

"Something more than a mere patrol," the centurion told him. "We're on a reconnaissance into the Empty Land. The word is that the barbarians are edging in and the Evil is uneasy. If this is true, almost anything could happen. We don't know if the Evil can hold against the barbarians. If they can't, you can never tell about them. They could start lashing out in all directions."

"Your force," said Harcourt, "seems small for such a mission. Less than a cohort, did you say?"

"Take a look at them. Does it look like a cohort to you?"

"No, it doesn't. But, from the looks of them, good fighting men."

"The scum of the earth," the centurion said proudly, "and the meanest bastards alive. They are frontier-wise and nasty men in battle."

"Well, just a reconnaissance. You won't be picking fights."

"If the command were to be used rightly, that is true," said the centurion. "Quick in, quick out, to assess the situation. But our tribune won't let us do it that way. He is out for glory. He's apt to get us killed."

"It's been quiet for the last few years," said Harcourt. "Since the big raid, we've had no trouble. I've often wondered . . . Maybe you can tell me. When the Evil came swarming in on us and we were hip-deep in them, fighting for our lives, where was the legion?"

It was a sore point with Harcourt. For a long time it had festered in him.

"Sitting serenely in its camp," said Decimus. "It would have moved if you had folded."

"We didn't fold," said Harcourt. "All along the line we drove them back across the river."

"When you say there has been little trouble recently, I hope that you are right," said the centurion. "Maybe they won't make a move against us. But I won't be holding my breath. I believe this is your party."

Harcourt swung about in his saddle. "Yes, it is," he said. "They'll clear the trail in just a short time and it will be open to you. Thanks for waiting for us. It would have been a tangle if we'd met."

Six men carrying the litter were in sight, toiling up the final slope. Close behind them came the others, who had served as relay litter carriers.

"It's my uncle," Harcourt said. "He was taken ill."

"So the castle told me. I hope he mends rapidly."

Harcourt offered no further explanation, and the centurion asked no questions. Apparently, Harcourt told himself, my grandfather has told the Roman nothing. If the centurion had known that Raoul had come from the Empty Land, there would have been no end to questions.

The litter party went past, heading for the castle, the others trailing behind.

"We must get over the river before dark," said the centurion. "We are advised the bridge is in good repair."

"It's in good repair," said Harcourt, hoping that the pride he felt was not too much reflected in his words. It had been his family's responsibility for years to keep the bridge in good repair, and the family had never failed its trust. It was important that the bridge be kept in good repair, for it was one of the few bridges up and down the river.

The centurion swung his horse about, raised his arm, and brought it down sharply, shouting an order. The front company lurched forward, marching in line, two men abreast, armor clanking as they moved. Behind the company came two carts, pulled by bullocks, piled high with supplies; and behind the carts, the rest of the cohort.

Decimus pulled his horse over beside Harcourt's, and the two of them sat together, watching the men march past.

"They don't march too well," said the centurion. "They are a sloppy outfit, but good marching doesn't make good soldiers. They are the best there is. Every one a born cutthroat. They don't give a damn for anything except meat and drink and women."

They looked it. Never in his life had Harcourt seen such a bunch of renegades. The scum of the earth, the centurion had said, and they were all of that. A pack of wolves.

"You'll have to watch those carts on the way down," Harcourt warned the man who sat his horse beside him. "There are places where there's not much room."

"We'll get them down," the centurion said carelessly.

Harcourt looked over his shoulder and saw that the procession carrying his uncle was crossing the drawbridge into the castle yard.

The Roman held out his hand to him. "I hope we meet again," he said. "Perhaps, if we come back this way . . ."

Harcourt shook his hand. "Be sure to stop," he told the centurion. "We could have a drink together."

He sat and watched until the Roman had disappeared down the trail, then swung his horse about and proceeded at a steady pace toward the castle gate.

Looking at the castle's two squat towers, he recalled once again how, seven years before, the attacking Evil had been beaten off. And for no reason whatsoever, he remembered something else as well—how, at that time, the castle had had the services of a resident wizard who, after it all was over, had claimed the major credit for the victory. The castle no longer had a resident wizard, and just as well, he thought. After everything was over, his grandfather had booted the wizard out.

"I can't abide the rascal," his grandfather had said. "He sat mewling in his chambers, burning noxious-smelling substances and jabbering to himself, while the rest of us were up there on the wall fighting for our lives. It was our strong arms and our trusty blades, not to forget the good marksmanship of our archers, that drove off the enemy. But once the danger was all over, what did this fraud of a wizard do but come creeping from his lair, claiming all the credit. As long as I live, there'll never be another wizard in this castle."

The Knurly Man had tried to reason with the grandfather. "I grant," he'd said, "that the one you ran off was a most obnoxious type. But do you think it wise, old friend, to forswear all wizards? You can never tell when you might have need of one. Having got rid of this one, and rightly so, do you not think we should find ourselves a more likely one?"

"All wizards are charlatans," the old man had said. And that had ended it. There had been no wizard since.

Five

Harcourt's grandfather and the Knurly Man sat in front of the great hall fire. There also sat the Abbot Guy, who was sprawled on a bench, his back against the wall, his cassock shucked up, his muscular calves and dirty feet thrust out in front of him. The fire burned merrily, the huge stone chimney throat mumbling like a dreaming dog.

"When I saw the legionnaires," the abbot explained to Harcourt, "I came running over to find if there were aught that I could do, some assistance I might render."

Harcourt nodded in acceptance of the explanation, although he knew that the abbot had not thought of any assistance that he might give, but had come running through his sheer inability to keep his nose out of anything that happened.

"When your revered grandsire," the abbot said unctuously, "suggested that I stay for supper, I accepted gladly. There is nothing I relish quite so much as well-roasted, juicy pork."

Behind them, at the table where serving men had been setting out trenchers and cutlery and mugs, there was much scurrying about with tapers to light the candles placed upon the board.

Harcourt walked over and sat down beside the abbot, facing his grandfather and the Knurly Man.

The Knurly Man rose and stood before the fire. He was furred like a summer bear that had shed its winter coat, and all he wore was a white loincloth about his hips. He was a burly man, and now, looking at him, Harcourt realized with a start that he was not a man, not the same kind of creature as a human was. For years Harcourt had accepted him as his grandfather's friend and constant companion, never thinking of him really as a man, but as a living being that was entirely acceptable as a man, a person not to be remarked upon. Why now, he wondered, should he finally see the Knurly Man for what he was?

It was easy to see why he was called the Knurly Man. He *was* knurly. His shoulders were massive, but they were not put together quite like a man's would be. His arms were longer than human arms, and his head thrust forward rather than standing upright on his shoulders. He had no neck, or scarcely any neck. His legs were bowed as if he might be straddling something. Now, seeing the differences—or, rather, realizing the differences—for the first time, Harcourt was shocked that he should see them. For he loved this Knurly Man, even now, despite the differences. The Knurly Man had trotted him on his foot when he had been a babe and later, when he had grown a bit, had taken him on walks, pointing out to him the wonders nature held. He had shown Harcourt bird nests that, alone, unaided, he never would have spotted and had told him how to look for them. The Knurly Man had identified wild flowers that had been no more than pretty posies to the boy and had told him how the roots of one would cure one ailment and how the leaves of another, steeped into a bitter-tasting tea, would alleviate another. The Knurly Man had shown him the lairs of foxes and the dens of badgers. And, Harcourt remembered, everything that the Knurly Man had shown him, he had invested with an importance that no one else could have conjured up. When the walk had been done, the two of them would sit beneath a tree, and the Knurly Man would spin long stories so well and thoughtfully that the listening boy had believed in them and still remembered many of them.

The grandfather grumbled at the abbot. "You had best hold in your liking for pork. You're apt to starve waiting for it. Such running about and twittering I've never seen in all my born days. The women of this place have this wandering son of mine tucked into one of the choicest beds and have been carrying mulled wine and other dainties to him and holding his hand and ministering to him. It is enough to make one vomit."

"How does he seem?" Harcourt asked.

"There's naught wrong with him that twelve good hours of sleep won't cure, but they're so pestering him with goodies that he can't close an eye. Your mother is one of the finest women alive, but she sometimes overdoes her goodness."

The way the old man was running on, Harcourt knew, there was no sense in talking further of his uncle.

"What did the Romans want?" he asked. "Or were they just passing through?"

"Romans never just pass through," his grandfather told him. "They wanted grain for the horses and, for the men, hams and brined beef and sausages and whatever else they could lay their hands on. They loaded those two carts of theirs until the axles creaked. They gave me a voucher for everything they took, whatever good that is."

"You may have to go to Rome to collect," the abbot told him, "or, at the least, to the nearest legionary camp, wherever that may be. Thank the blessed Lord, they passed the abbey by."

"They well knew," the old man said to him testily, "that abbots are tightfisted. They knew that, being a loyal citizen of the Empire, and being unable to do otherwise, I'd give them what they needed."

"It seems to me," said the Knurly Man, "that you pay an exorbitant price for your citizenship, which in the end is worthless."

The old man made no reply, but asked Harcourt, "Did Raoul tell you what this is all about?"

"Not much. Very little, in fact. He tried to tell me, but I shushed him. He said he'd found Lasandra's prism."

The abbot jerked himself bolt upright from his slouching position. "The prism!" he blurted. "The very one we talked of this afternoon?"

"The same," said Harcourt. "The one that is said to have a soul caught in it."

Harcourt's grandfather came to the heart of the matter. "Did he bring it back?" he asked.

"No. All he knows is where it is."

"Always searching," said the old man. "He would never settle down. No sooner was one wild-goose chase finished than he was off on another of them."

"But you're glad to have him home, grandfather."

"Of course I'm glad. He is my only son. He and your mother are my only children—at least the only ones I know of."

The abbot said, "If Raoul is right . . ."

"On matters of great importance, such as this," the grandfather said, "my son is not a liar. He dresses some of his stories up outrageously to make for better telling, but if he says he saw a thing, you can be sure he saw it. If he says he knows where the prism is, then you can be sure it's there."

"A legend one cannot be sure of," said the abbot, rapidly mending fences, "but if a truthful man swears he saw the central object of a legend, then it is no longer legend."

"That is what my uncle said," Harcourt told him. "He said

it was no longer legend. That he knows it exists. That he knows where it is."

"In the Empty Land?" the Knurly Man asked.

"I suppose so. That is where he came from. He said he couldn't lay his hands on it because there were too many of them there. Too many of what he did not say."

"Ah, well," said Harcourt's grandfather, "he can tell us more fully of it later. Right now the boy needs rest and no one pestering him."

"But if it exists!" the abbot said. "Knowing it exists, then surely . . ."

"We know now that the prism exists," said the grandfather. "Surely that is enough. It sets our minds at rest . . ."

"But it holds the soul of a blessed saint clutched within it, and it rests in Evil hands."

"It wouldn't seem to me it would make much difference to a soul where it might be so long as it was prisoned."

"But it would," the abbot said. "A soul should not be in Evil hands. It should be among the most holy relics in all of Christendom. It should be lodged safely in the bosom of the Church, nourished by the prayers of a devout community, guarded against any harm that might come to it, safe against the time when it will be liberated on that final day of all and make its way to heaven."

"I suppose," the Knurly Man said dryly, "that you would be willing to afford it such sanctuary in the sacred confines of your abbey."

"I most surely would," said the abbot, falling almost eagerly into the trap the Knurly Man had set for him.

"And run the risk of the abbey, as the custodian of such a relic, becoming the most famous in all the Empire?"

"Alaric," Harcourt's grandfather sternly told the Knurly Man, "such a sentiment is unworthy of you. The abbot, I am sure, would not . . ."

He did not finish what he meant to say, for just at that moment Harcourt's mother, trailed by her ladies, came down the great staircase. At almost the same moment, the roasted boar, an apple in its mouth and sprigs of holly wreathed upon its brow, was borne to the table with a flourishing of trumpets.

Six

It was late when Harcourt finally retired to chambers. There had been much merriment at the table. His mother, especially, had done much chattering, full of the return of her brother to the family fold. His grandfather had been unusually silent, sitting at the head of the board, only growling an answer when, now and then, someone asked a question of him, drinking more heavily than was his wont. The abbot had said almost nothing, which was not his usual style. But that had not been so wonderful as it might have seemed, for during the greater part of the meal his mouth had been too full to admit of speech. The boar had proved good eating, and the abbot had done full justice to it, the grease running down his beard until it had shone in the candlelight. The rest of the company, however, had taken their cue from the mistress of the castle and had jabbered with her, making for an unusually merry meal.

Once in chambers, Harcourt found an extreme reluctance to go to sleep and, as he prowled about uneasily, came to understand what the trouble was. The uneasiness, he knew, came from what the Abbot Guy had said that afternoon about the fall of Castle Fontaine. At the time Guy had blurted it out, he had been too stunned to show his feelings and had, in fact, managed for some hours to go about his life as if the words had not been said, but it had been a heavy blow. Through all the years, his family had been careful not to mention the tragedy in his presence, and for this he had been grateful. The silence, he was sure, had helped him to forget to some extent. It had waited for this friend of his to include in his rush of words the event that he had been trying to banish from his mind. There had been times when it had faded almost to forgetfulness, but it had never gone away entirely. Eloise still lingered, waiting, in his mind.

He stopped his pacing and stood uncertainly in the center of the room, staring at the desk standing in the corner. Lifting the candle from the bedside table, he crossed the room to the desk, pulling the chair out from the desk and setting the candle on its top. Lowering himself into the chair, he opened a drawer to find the key and then unlocked the drawer it fitted—the bottom one on the left-hand side. Reaching in, he found and brought out the book. There was no trouble finding it; he knew exactly where it was. Laying the book on the desk top, he opened it and pulled the candle closer.

In the candlelight the sharp, bright colors of the painting, the marginal decorations, the ornate capital letters leaped out at him. Looking at them, he drew his breath in sharply, for all of it was far more beautiful than he had remembered.

Staring at the two pages to which he had opened the book, he sought the tenderness—the old, old tenderness he'd felt for Eloise all the years ago. Not the self-pity, not the sorrow or the bereavement, not the bitterness, but the tenderness, the upwelling of the sense of love. But he could not find the tenderness; it had faded, he thought, too far into time.

The book was old—probably centuries old. It dated from that now-forgotten renaissance when men, once again, after the darkness of long ages, had found beauty in their minds and souls. It had been in Eloise's family for years, coming into her hands from a dead grandmother. She had given it to him, a most unlikely gift, for no one had suspected that he might treasure the beauty of a book of hours. No one but Eloise—she had suspected it, and had given the book to him, a family treasure given to the man she loved, who loved her in return.

He tried to recall what she had said to him when she had given him the gift, what they might have said to each other, but he could not remember; it all was gone. It had been washed away, he knew, by his bitterness and grief. Sitting at the desk in the middle of the night, he finally came to know what his bitterness had cost him.

She had touched this book; her fingers had turned the pages; her eyes had seen what he now was looking at. She had treasured it, she must have treasured it, as her family had treasured it for centuries—and she had given it to him, this Eloise whose face he could not now recall, knowing only how her eyes had crinkled at the corners when she smiled.

He sat for a long time looking at the book, at the delicate miniature of a painting, showing serfs driving in the hogs, others climbing trees to pluck the fruit, still others building shocks of grain as the reapers went swinging down the field, and in the distance the faint shape of a castle, all spires and turrets and slender towers, not at all like this castle his family occupied.

The people in that day when the painting had been done had viewed the world through different eyes, had seen a brighter world and happier people; and he wondered if Eloise might have been thinking, perhaps, that the two of them, given each other, could together view the world through such eyes as had the ancient artist who had painted the swineherds driving in the hogs and the people climbing trees.

For a long time he stayed at the desk, with the candle flickering, looking at the book, not all the time really seeing the book, but looking, in his mind's eye, at what it represented, trying to remember once again what it meant to him. Then, finally, he closed it and put it back into the drawer, locking the drawer and putting the key back into the place from which he'd taken it.

It all was wrong, he told himself. It did not come true. His memory faltered, and he could not remember. It had gone from him, the sharp, poignant sense of the love that had lain between the two of them. He had been bitter for too long.

Arising from the desk, he strode to an armoire set against the wall and took from it a heavy cloak that he draped around his shoulders.

Halfway down the hall, he came upon his mother, who ducked out of an intersecting corridor, on her nightly round of making certain that everyone was tucked safely into bed. She had done this chore each night for as long as he could remember.

"Charles," she told him disapprovingly, "you should be in bed and fast asleep. Your day has been a hard one."

"I'm just stepping out for a breath of air," he said.

"You're exactly like your father, a brooding, introspective man no one understood. Even loving him as I did, I never understood him. I'm not sure he even understood himself. Perhaps that I did not understand him comes of the fact that we were too different people, he from this harsh northern country and I from the southern part of Gaul, a soft and gentle and, I might say, a civilized land, which this land is not. Although, to be honest about it, I was happy to follow him here. I would have followed him anywhere at all. No matter where he went, I would have gone. You are much like him, Charles, and you must guard yourself against black moods."

It was the first time in years that she had mentioned his

father to him, although he was sure there had not been a day in all that time that she had not thought of him. Of his father, Harcourt had no memory. Less than a year after he had been born, his father had been killed while riding on a hunt, an arrow through his throat. Although no one had ever told him so, he had often wondered if his father might have been the sort of man who would have the kind of enemies who would put an arrow through his throat. But whatever kind of man he might have been, now he lay in his tomb in the abbey, along with his father and his paternal grandfather and all the other Harcourts who had died since that distant day when the abbey had been built on Harcourt land and under Harcourt patronage.

Harcourt had grown up under the close supervision of his maternal grandfather, who had journeyed from the south to help Harcourt's mother handle the fief. He had brought with him the Knurly Man, and later on Uncle Raoul had shown up. Just what the position of his mother's family had been in the south of Gaul, Harcourt had never rightly known, although he had the impression that it had been a branch of a great commercial house. At one time, he recalled, his mother had been in the habit of talking at some length about the beloved country she had left—but about the country rather than the position of her family there. That she had not remarried after his father's death, Harcourt had later learned, had been the subject of much talk in the castles and the homesteads all up and down the river. She had remained unmarried, he had thought at times, not only out of the love and loyalty she felt for his father, but perhaps as well out of regard for her son, probably fearing that marriage to the wrong kind of man might compromise his inheritance. With his grandfather in the castle, there had been no need of another man to manage the fief. Through the years, until Harcourt had gained his competence, the old man had done as well by the fief as if the acres were his own.

"Don't stay out too long," his mother warned him. "Much as you may doubt it, in the arrogance of your youth, you do need your sleep."

The drawbridge was down. These days it was seldom raised, for there was little need. But the castle did maintain a good guard on the gate, sufficient men to raise it quickly if there should be need.

Old Raymond was at the postern gate that let out onto the bridge.

"Don't stay out too long," he cautioned Harcourt, "and don't go too far. I heard wolves just a while ago. A pack of them, I think. If it is air you want, why don't you just take a stroll along the wall?"

Harcourt shook his head. "This time of year wolves do not attack. There's plenty of eating to be pulled down in the forest. The only time one must fear them is in the dead of winter."

Raymond grumbled at him. Harcourt paid him no attention; Raymond always grumbled at him. He was still grumbling as he crossed the bridge.

The night was dark. The moon rode low in the west, but was obscured by a bank of clouds. Other than for the western cloud bank, the sky was clear and the stars shone brightly.

He climbed the rise that would take him to the cart track that ran through the field of wheat. Walking up the rise, he thought back to that day, once the siege of the Evil had been lifted, when he had ridden out with a small, but well-armed, party to learn how their neighbors might have fared, for the raid, they felt certain, had not been limited to the Harcourt castle and the abbey, but more than likely had swept a broad front along a wide stretch of the river.

They had found all well until they reached Fontaine. There the Evil had broken through, and no life was left—not even a scuttering chicken. A gagging odor hung over the castle, and human bodies were scattered all about. Not only human bodies—there were others: ogres, trolls, even a couple of dragons, and other forms of disgusting and hideous life with which he and his party were less well acquainted. Fontaine had fallen, but the price the Evil had paid for the victory had been high.

The chore of collecting the dead humanity had been a grisly one, the attempts to identify the bodies mostly unsuccessful. Burial in a common grave had been the only answer, the only way the bodies could be handled after several days of lying in the sun.

The Knurly Man had come up to Harcourt. "This is not work for you," he'd said. "Let the others do it."

Harcourt remembered how he had shaken his head stubbornly. "No, she must be here and she must be found. She must be given separate burial, not thrown into a hole with all the others."

Guy, who had joined them when they had gone past the

looted abbey, also tried to reason with him, but he would not listen.

She had not been found, although Harcourt had known that not finding her did not mean she wasn't there. Many of the dead had been so torn and mutilated that they were scarcely recognizable as human. The maggots had been the worst—the maggots crawling on the dead.

So what was left of them had been buried in a common grave, Abbot Guy—who had not been an abbot then, but only a simple churchman—standing beside it and chanting the services for the dead while the others of them, scarves tied about their noses, shoveled dirt into the pit.

Harcourt reached the edge of the wheat field and swung about to face back toward the castle and the north. Why do I do this to myself? he asked himself. Why do I insist on living that day over again in all its racking detail in this place?

Why must he now walk the dark earth, thinking back—almost as if he fought to keep the agony alive, clinging to the bitterness, punishing himself for a guilt where there should be no guilt?

The castle was a black hump with only an occasional light showing. Beyond the river lay the Empty Land, a nighttime mass of darkness beneath the star-flecked horizon. Out there, beyond the river, laired the Evil. Out there somewhere was the prism of Lasandra, if his uncle were correct. Guy, he knew, even now, safe in his abbey bed, might be lying, still not asleep, dreaming of venturing out into the Empty Land to rescue it, to bring it back to the abbey and give it sanctuary, still nursing the thought that at one time it might have been sheltered in the forerunner to the present abbey.

Harcourt tilted back his head and looked up at the stars, and there, fixed in its place, was the Wain, the first of the constellations the Knurly Man had pointed out to him, the two stars that formed the back of the celestial cart pointing to the Great Star of the North, hanging just above the horizon.

"It lies always in the north," the Knurly Man had told him, "with the two stars in the Wain always pointing to it. Seek out that bright star on any night, and the directions will lie plain."

Suddenly he felt chilled. He had noticed no chill before. The chill had not come from the blackness of the night or from the northwest wind. The chill came, he knew, from inside himself.

He had gone as far as was necessary, and now he knew that

it had been necessary that he walk this darkened earth and, walking the blackness of it, think back. He had done that, and it was over now.

He set out briskly, heading for the castle.

Seven

The abbot arrived at the castle shortly before the breakfast hour and shared some bacon with the others before they all trooped up to see Harcourt's uncle.

Raoul was out of bed, sitting in an armchair, one of the few the castle boasted. He was wrapped in a great robe that at one time had been a splendid garment but now was the worse for wear, although still warm and comfortable. Someone had tried to comb his hair to make it lie down fashionably, but it had been uncombed too long to be manageable. Rooster tails stuck out all over his head, giving him a wild look.

Harcourt's grandfather growled at him. "How do you feel this morning? Did you get some sleep? Will you stay this time and not go running off again?"

"Father, you know those other times I could not help myself," said Raoul. "There was no reason for me to stay here. It wasn't my country; I just came to see you and Margaret—and Charley, here, of course. Charley and I are great friends. We get along together. You remember that time, Charley, when I hired you to watch and . . ."

"The rest of them don't know about that, Uncle Raoul," said Harcourt. "You asked me not to tell anyone, and I never did. Even after you left, I kept watching now and then. But the two men never came. Did you ever see them?"

"Yes, I did," said Raoul. "I saw them later on. They caught up with me."

"And?"

"I'm here," said Raoul. "Make what you want of that."

Harcourt's grandfather bellowed at them. "What is this? What is going on? Do you mean to tell me, Raoul, that you involved my grandson in some of your shady doings?"

"It was a long time ago," Harcourt told him. "I was just a

lad. He hired me to watch for two men who were following him. I wasn't to do anything about it. I was just to run and tell him."

The grandfather grumbled. "Well, it might have been innocent enough. But I don't like it, Raoul."

"I knew you wouldn't," said Raoul. "That's why I asked him not to tell you. But now to get on with my general defense."

"I'm not asking you to defend yourself."

"Yes, you are. You were always urging me to stay and put down roots. Root yourself in these solid acres, you would tell me. The thing is, they weren't my acres and neither were they yours. Except for you and Margaret, these are alien acres to me, as alien as any I have traveled."

"They are my acres now," Harcourt told him, more arrogantly than he had intended. "And I'm telling you you're welcome. I would like to have you stay. Why don't you settle down and stay? It would be a great comfort to grandfather, and we'll do all possible to make you feel at home."

His uncle looked straight at him for what seemed a long time. Then he said, "Charley, I may take you up on that. I'm not as young as I was at one time, and I might settle for a while. But it's not a promise," he told his father. "If I feel like going off again, I'll go."

"I know you will," his father said. "There'll be no holding you." He said to the abbot, "I must apologize for this unseemly family quarrel. It does not often happen. I'm sorry that you had to witness it."

"It was a quarrel," the abbot said smoothly, "that was filled to overflowing with deep family love. I am the one who should apologize for sitting in on it. I intruded most obnoxiously. I can only say that I am here because of my deep concern for what Raoul found in the Empty Land."

"What did you find?" the grandfather asked of Raoul. "Charles said that you told him you found the prism of Lasandra."

"I did not actually find it. I located it. I did not see it and I did not lay my hands upon it, but I am convinced I know where it is. I could not get to it because its defenses were too formidable for a lone man to wriggle through."

"You're sure it's where you think it is?" the abbot asked.

"I'd stake my life upon it."

Harcourt's grandfather nodded sagely. "That is good enough for me. My son must be certain of it to stake his life upon it. Would you mind telling us, Raoul, how you were led to it, how you know where it is?"

"I would be willing, but without the use of names. I will not speak the names, for there is danger in even knowing there is such an object. I first was given evidence of its existence when I happened to be in Constantinople. I had known the legend, of course, as does almost everyone. But this was the first time that anyone had sworn to me there was actually such a prism. I asked my informant how he knew, and he explained it to me, although I suspect not fully. Even so, the story was a tortuous one, and I'll not attempt to repeat it here. As you can well imagine, I was intrigued by the story, which had the ring of truth in it, and thereafter I kept my ears open for any further word, discreetly probing where I deemed it safe to do so. I heard many wild stories, of course, in most of them not a grain of truth. Then, of all places, in Hyrcania, on the southern Caspian shore, in a hermit's cell, I was shown a parchment that gave a place name, and that place name, I later learned, was in our Empty Land. But the point is that the parchment agreed in almost every detail with what I had been told in Constantinople. And the parchment had been written only forty years or so after the prism had been deposited in the Empty Land—at a time, I might add, when the area across the river was not the Empty Land, but a Roman province. The parchment may have been based upon information that was secondhand, although its wording indicated it was not. I was satisfied that it was an account that had not passed through many mouths, subject to error and exaggeration with each repetition."

"Even so," Harcourt's grandfather asked, "what in the world compelled you to go in search of it? To risk your life to go in search of it?"

"I've risked my life for lesser things. Usually for objects that would do no more than enhance my material existence. But here, finally, was something that might benefit my spiritual condition. There comes a time in every man's life, usually much too late in life, when he shifts to a concern for his soul rather than his purse."

"That I can understand," said the old man.

"I did exactly that," said Raoul, "and I reached the place name that I had been told. Only to find it was not there. It was in another place."

"How could you know that?" Harcourt asked.

"I was told. There was a man who told me."

"A man? In the Empty Land?"

"There are a number of humans still in the Empty Land.
There were those who could not flee or did not flee when the
Evil was forced back by the barbarian pressure. Ahead of the
retreat of the Evil, the outnumbered Roman legions came
reeling back, the refugees fleeing with them, leaving everything they had behind them, running for their lives with horror nipping at their heels. All, however, did not flee—there
remained behind stubborn souls or silly souls or trusting souls,
perhaps trusting in the Lord. Many of those who remained
behind must have died, but some hid in the fens or in other
places, and these few lived, or at least some of them lived.
Their descendants still live on. Plus, I would imagine, other
simple ones—simple or brave, I do not know—who over the
years have gone back to that goblin-haunted land, perhaps
driven by many different reasons. Humans live there still,
keeping their heads down, hunkering low, tolerated by the
Evil, who, I suspect, find some quiet amusement in them. It
was one of these, an old priest—at least he claimed to be a
priest, although I'm not sure he is—who was hiding in an
abandoned, ruined cathedral, who told me the prism was not
in the cathedral, where I thought it was, but in another place,
some distance farther on. We sat the night and talked, and he
pleaded with me to secure the prism and return it to Christendom. He did all he could to help me. At times it was difficult
to understand him, for he had lost four front teeth, two low-
ers, two uppers, which made a horrifying gap. He hissed
continually while he talked. He would have gone along to help
me, but was unable to. He is old and feeble, and he did not
have the strength."

"You found this other place?" the abbot asked.

"I finally found it. I tried to get in and almost lost my life
in trying. It is too well guarded for one man alone. I could not
even get too good a look at it. The priest told me it was an
ancient palace. I doubt it is a palace. More likely an old
Roman villa, one of those ornate structures built by powerful
and wealthy landowners. It sits in the midst of a great fenced
park, the park filled with trees and shrubbery running riot.
I'm certain the prism is there. The priest told me it is, and he
is a sincere and, I would judge, a truthful man, sharp and
alert despite his years. The fact that the place is so well
guarded argues there is something of great value there."

"How guarded?" the abbot asked.

"By sorcery. Necromancy, witchery, call it what you will. There are traps and dragons, ogres, trolls . . ."

"In the face of that, you tried?"

"I tried," Harcourt's uncle said.

"One man," said the abbot. "Could two men have done it? Could three? Could an army of fighting men?"

"Not an army. Least of all an army. If an army tried going through the Empty Land, it would be wiped out. It wouldn't cover ten leagues before it was wiped out. The only chance would be for a small party to go sneaking in. That is how I got as far as I did."

"For a small party of determined, resourceful men, there might be a chance?"

"A chance. A bare chance only. I would not make book on it."

Harcourt's grandfather asked the abbot sourly, "Do you propose to have a try at it?"

"I had thought of it," the abbot said.

Saying this, he looked hard at Harcourt. Harcourt shrugged. "I don't know," he said.

"It would be a noble thing to do," the abbot said. "A holy thing. A crusade for the Church."

"And for the glory of your abbey," said the Knurly Man.

"All right," the abbot said, "I might have thought of that, but not of that alone. It would be done as well for Holy Mother Church. And there is something else. A legend—well, not strong enough to be a legend, but a rumor, a rumor supported in part by some very ancient writing that I came across—that says the prism of Lasandra may have been housed at one time in that ancient abbey upon the foundations of which the present abbey here is built."

"You mean your abbey?" the Knurly Man asked. "The one of which you are the abbot?"

The abbot nodded.

"He is right in one regard, at least," the grandfather said. "In late years, with nothing else to occupy me, I have dug through the records of this fief. The abbey built by the Harcourt family was indeed built upon the foundations of a long-abandoned abbey. Much of the stone that had been used in it was quarried to build this castle. When the time came to build another abbey, it was erected on the foundations of the old."

"I had not known that," said Harcourt. "Not until yesterday, when the abbot mentioned it."

"You do not spend much time with the castle papers," said his grandfather. "You have other things to do."

"So you can see," the abbot said, "that I have something that amounts to a proprietary interest. Not that I am entirely convinced that the story is completely true. But there is a chance it might be."

"To me, an attempt to rescue Lasandra's prism," said the grandfather, "would seem foolhardy. Foolhardy for you to think of it, abbot. Foolhardy for you, Raoul, to have tried it."

"Yes, it was," Harcourt's uncle said. "I know that now. Starting out, I didn't."

"But you could tell us the way," said the abbot. "You could draw a map for us. Knowing what was ahead, we could travel faster, avoid danger points."

"Of course I could. But I don't know if I will. I am reluctant to. I don't want you on my conscience."

"Not even for the glory of God?"

"Not even," said Raoul, "for the glory of God."

"It would depend," said Harcourt, "on what direction we would have to travel."

"Straight west," his uncle told him.

"The Roman cohort that passed through yesterday," said Harcourt, "probably will strike north. It would be a diversion for us. The Evil forces will be pulled north by the cohort. They'll be watching the Romans. We could probably slip through."

"And when you reached the palace or the villa, whichever it is?" his grandfather asked.

"Then circumstances would govern us."

"Does all this mean you are thinking of going on this harebrained adventure?"

"Not really," Harcourt told him. "I was only assessing the situation. Thinking out loud, an exercise in mental tactics."

His uncle spoke hesitantly. "I had said I would not draw a map, would not help you. But there is another facet that I haven't mentioned. Charley, there is something that might be of personal concern to you."

"A personal concern? What is it?"

Raoul's face had a look of agony, or of indecision. "I am reluctant to voice it," he said, "because it could unduly influence you. And yet I feel I must. I could not live with myself if I didn't. I never could look you straight in the face again."

"For the love of Christ," said Harcourt, "out with it. Go ahead and tell me. It can't be all that bad."

"Perhaps not bad at all, but I still have great reluctance . . ."

"Go ahead and say it," the grandfather urged. "My grandson is a grown man. If it is something that concerns him . . ."

"When I was talking with the cathedral priest that night," said Raoul, "he mentioned a name. It seemed to me familiar, and then I remembered where I'd heard it. The name was Eloise."

Harcourt came to his feet in a single, upward surge.

"Eloise!" he shouted. "What of Eloise?"

"Charles," said his grandfather, speaking sharply, "please contain yourself. There is nothing gained by shouting." He said to Raoul, "What of Eloise? Eloise is dead, slain seven years ago. As you well know. It ill behooves you, in this house, to bring her name up lightly and without sufficient reason."

"There is just a chance she is not dead," said Raoul. "There are humans in the place the prism is. As an earnest of the truthfulness of what he told me, the priest said he knew the names of two of them. One of the names he spoke was Eloise."

Harcourt sat down limply and was surprised to find that he was trembling.

"It doesn't mean," his uncle said to him, "that it is your Eloise. As I said, it's just a chance."

It was a chance, Harcourt knew, that he could not pass up. As far as Eloise was concerned, there was no chance he could ignore. There was nothing that could stop him, not a thing at all, no sort of danger that could turn him to one side. If Eloise was still alive . . .

"She may be alive," he said. "We did not find her body."

"There were many bodies," his grandfather reminded him, "that we could not identify."

"Yes, I know," said Harcourt, "but if there's any chance at all . . ."

Someone standing beside him put a great arm around his shoulder and hugged him tight. He looked up and saw that it was the abbot.

"We'll go," the abbot said. "The two of us will go and bring back Eloise—and perhaps the prism, too."

Harcourt huddled in his chair. Before him the room was swimming, as if the whole of it had been plunged beneath water that had a running current.

He heard his uncle say, as if he were speaking from some distance off, "I'm sorry. I see I should not have mentioned

"No," the grandfather answered. "You would have been delinquent in your honesty had you not. For years the boy has brooded on it."

The room began to clear. The water went away, and the room and the people in it became solid once again.

Harcourt said, "I'm going. There can no one stop me. The abbot will go with me, for now both of us have reason."

"In this matter," said the grandfather, "we must be circumspect. If anyone overhears a word . . ."

"We can't keep it quiet," said the Knurly Man, "no matter what we do. This very place has ears. By evening there'll be rumors, not only in the castle, but throughout the neighborhood."

"There may be rumors," the grandfather said, "but the rumors won't touch on the crux of the matter. No one will know you're going till you're gone." He looked at Harcourt and asked, "You're certain that you want to go ahead with it? If you've had second thoughts . . ."

"No second thoughts," Harcourt said. "I'm going."

"You know, of course," said the Knurly Man, "that I'll be with the two of you. I could not let you go without me."

"I thank you for that," said Harcourt. "I had hoped you would, but I couldn't ask."

"It takes a weight off my mind," the grandfather said. "Two would be so small a party. I'd join you, much as I still think this is a harebrained scheme, but I'd be no addition to the force. My infirmities would slow you up."

So here they were, Harcourt told himself, trapped and committed to their action, not trapped by greed—the factor that trapped so many—but by their emotion and their piety. Piety, as a matter of fact, he thought, might be an emotion of the quieter kind. What he had thought of before as a rather silly venture, which his grandfather still believed to be a harebrained scheme, now seemed straightforward and commonplace, the kind of enterprise that anyone at all quite logically could be expected to embark upon.

"Three is enough," the Knurly Man was saying. "We have to travel fast and keep out of sight. We won't be traveling on the roads; we'll make a point to keep well off them."

"The old Roman road," said the abbot, "strikes straight west. We'll keep south of it."

"Are you certain," the grandfather asked, "that you don't

want a few good men-at-arms? We could pick the most reliable."

"They'd not have their hearts in it," said Harcourt. "They'd be running scared. They'd do a lot of bitching."

"In any case," said the Knurly Man, "we'll not be inviting fights. We'll duck encounters of any kind at all. We'll travel light and fast, carry our own provisions. We may be gone only a short time."

"And when you reach the place where the prism is?" Harcourt's grandfather asked.

"It won't hold us up for any length of time," Harcourt told him. "Either we get in or we don't, although I'm determined that we do. In either case, we won't be around for long."

"Raoul will draw you a map," said the grandfather, "before the day is done and will go over it with you. If you're going, you can't wait around too long. In a day or two, the country will be seething with rumors, and somehow or other the rumors will get over the river. You have to cross the river before the Evil knows you're on your way."

"Which means we can't use the bridge," the abbot said. "Someone would see us. Word will get out we're gone, but if we can slip across without being seen, no one can know exactly where we've gone."

"The miller has a boat," Harcourt said, "and he knows the river like his own backyard, even in the dead of night. He could drop us down the stream and over on the other side, well below the bridge."

"That's a good idea," said his grandfather. "Jean is one who can be trusted. He'll keep his mouth shut. Charles, why don't you ride down and arrange it with him?"

"I say we should leave tonight," said the Knurly Man. "The longer we wait . . ."

"That's right," the grandfather said. "You'll leave tonight."

Eight

Jean, the miller, and Yolanda were sitting on a bench before their cottage when Harcourt came riding down the trail. Yolanda was playing with a half-grown kitten, and the miller was splicing a rope. At the sight of Harcourt, both came to their feet and stood waiting for him. He dismounted, tied the horse to a tree, and walked up to them.

The miller touched his forelock. "My lord," he said, "you are welcome. How is your uncle this morning?"

"My uncle is fine. Very much himself. I have come to ask a favor."

"No matter what the favor, it shall be done."

"There is about it a matter of confidentiality," said Harcourt. "Nothing must be said."

"My lord," said Jean, "you can trust me with your life."

"Just possibly it might come down to that. So much as a whisper . . . and that, Yolanda, applies to you as well."

"It applies to all of us," said Jean. "To myself, Yolanda, and my wife. You can trust us all."

"Yes," said Harcourt. "Yes, I believe I can."

"What, my lord, is this thing?"

"I must go into the Empty Land. I and two others. It can't be known we are going there. We cannot cross the bridge. Someone would see us, and the word would be out."

"I could drop you down the river in my boat, over to the other side," said Jean. "After nightfall. In the dead of night. I know the river and . . ."

"That's what I came to ask," said Harcourt. "And nothing said of it. You are to be back well before dawn so no one will see you."

"If you're going to the Empty Land," said Yolanda, "I am going with you."

Harcourt turned on his heel to face her. "No, you're not," he said.

"Yolanda!" said Jean, protesting.

Yolanda's cowl had fallen from her head, and the flaxen hair hung all about her shoulders. Her jaw was set.

"The boat is mine," she said. "Jean gave it to me. I used it more than he did. He almost never used it. So he gave it to me. And, besides, I have been in the Empty Land. I know the Empty Land. You'll need someone who knows it."

"I know you go to the Empty Land," said Harcourt. "Or so rumor said. I wondered why you did. I could not believe it. Jean, how could you let her?"

"My lord," said Jean, "there was no help for it. There was no stopping her. We talked with her about it. She would give us no reason. She would tell us nothing. We were afraid of losing her if we protested too much. And we were afraid of rumor."

"It was only," Harcourt said, "the very smallest rumor. It was whispered to me in confidence. It is not a general rumor." He said to Yolanda, "I could take the boat, you know. With or without permission."

"I know you could," she said coolly. "But then you could not be sure of the silence of this family."

Jean stepped toward her, face white with anger, hand lifted.

"No," Harcourt said sharply. "No, not that. Why would you go with us?" he asked Yolanda.

"This family," she said, "has been here almost from the time that Harcourts were here. Its men have marched in your armies, fought by your side, helped protect this land for centuries. Now it is my turn."

"And if you came, what could you do for us?"

"I could scout out the land. I know the dangers there. I am handy with the bow; I could bring down game. I could hunt out fruits and other edibles. I would not be a burden. I'd not be in the way."

"The impertinence!" Jean sputtered. "The impertinence of her. My lord, I cannot tell you . . ."

"No need to apologize," said Harcourt. "What do you think of it?"

"Think, my lord?"

"Of her going with us?"

Jean gulped and said, "Everything she told you is true. She could do all she said. She could spy out the land. She has a way of seeing things that other people miss. I do not think she should go. I'd be nervous at her going. I don't know what has gotten into her. But she could be a help to you. Better than any man I know. Although, if you need others . . ."

"We need no others," Harcourt said. "There must be few of us. We must move swiftly and quietly."

"Lame as I am, I could not move too swiftly. But I have a good right arm and I can draw a bow."

"No, thanks, old friend," said Harcourt. "None of us may return." He said to Yolanda, "You know that, of course. You place your life in peril."

She replied quietly, "I know that, my lord."

Harcourt looked at her squarely. "I like it not," he said.

And yet, he told himself, she could be valuable. She knew the land and seemed capable. Somewhere along the way she might tilt the balance in their favor in a situation where there was slight margin between success and failure. God knows, there'd not be many of them. He could use another.

And the worst of it, he thought, there was no time at all to ponder a decision.

Looking at her, he made up his mind. "Be ready," he said. "We leave once it is fully dark. Jean, you'll row the boat?"

"I'll row the boat," said Jean.

Nine

Harcourt lay flat upon his belly in the thicket at the edge of the forest and watched the unicorns at play. He had never seen a unicorn before; he had read of them and listened to endless tales about them, but he had never seen one. And they were, he thought, as beautiful as he had been told they were. Abbot Guy lay to the left of him and Yolanda to the right, with the Knurly Man beyond Yolanda, the four of them stretched out in a row, hiding in the thicket, staring at the unicorns. The abbot, Harcourt was sure, like himself, had never seen a unicorn before. It was fairly certain that Yolanda had, he thought, although she seemed to be as fascinated as the two of them. The Knurly Man he didn't know about; the Knurly Man might have seen unicorns, for the Knurly Man was a mystery, and no one could tell about him.

The unicorns were gamboling in the clearing—that is, most of them were gamboling. One stood quietly by himself and two were lying down, but the rest of them were frisking all about the clearing. The standing one and the two that were lying down, Harcourt told himself, probably were older animals and had left all play behind them. The others gamboled in the grass, running, chasing one another, taking little hops and leaps, posing for anyone who might chance to see them in all their shining glory. All of them were white and sleek and smooth; they looked as if a stablehand had groomed them just an hour or so before. Their twisted horns glittered in the noonday sun.

There were no fairies with them. Yolanda, racing out ahead of them to scout the way, had come racing back to report the herd of unicorns. But if you want to have a look at them, she'd told them, be careful not to show yourself. "Where you find unicorns," she said, "you often will find fairies, for fairies simply dote on unicorns. I don't know why, nor does anyone. But it's true that when you see unicorns, you must watch out for fairies. Keep well under cover and be careful. Fairies are little tattletales; if they should catch sight of us, they'll be off like arrows to spread the word to anyone who listens."

So, taking Yolanda's warning well to heart, they had sneaked up on the unicorns very cautiously. Harcourt had never heard, in all the wild stories he'd been told, that fairies and unicorns were friends, but he took Yolanda at her word, and so, apparently, did the other two, for they crept as cautiously as he. He found himself wondering once again about this strange woman, a waif who came out of nowhere and had been taken in by the miller and his wife, a shaper of exquisite wooden statuary who could see a form captured in a tree and bring it out to life. Why, he asked himself, should she be so taken with the Empty Land? Was it that she had come from this land and still held with it some strong bondage that pulled her back to it? Could it be that her subconscious roots were deeply and intricately entwined with the life of the Empty Land? Was this her ancestral home?

There was no reason in the world, he told himself rather sheepishly, why the four of them should go creeping through the woods to see unicorns, or even unicorns and fairies. God knows, across the river they had seen more fairies than they wanted to. Fairies were pesky things to have around, but there wasn't much that one could do about them. It was senseless, he told himself, the thing that they were doing, for neither unicorns nor fairies had anything to do with their being there. But as soon as Yolanda had told them there were unicorns ahead, there seemed to be no question that they simply had to see them.

The venture so far had gone well, without a single hitch, unless this sightseeing diversion to see the unicorns should turn out to be a hitch.

Jean had taken them somewhat farther down the river than he had intended, for the weather had been fine and the river smooth. The night had been dark, but the stars that were sprinkled overhead and a sickle of a moon deep in the western sky had provided enough light for them to see where they were going. The miller had landed them on a pebble beach on the northern shore, a beach that marked the end of a deep ravine that came slashing down between two high, steep, heavily forested hills. Here, on the northern side of the river, were none of the precipitous cliffs that rose on the southern shore, but the hills were as high, or higher. Once landed, they had followed the ravine through the heavy woods; well into the forest, with all light from the sky cut off by the heavy foliage, they had to wait for the first predawn light before they could continue.

Following the ravine, Harcourt had caught the first sense of mystery and of menace, the bone-deep feeling that this was not familiar ground, that they had moved into a wraith-haunted country where they were strangers and unwelcome. He tried to isolate some reason he might feel so, railing silently at himself for letting his imagination run away with him. This country, he told himself, was no different from the land that they had left. The crossing of the river could not bring about such change. And yet the sense of change persisted. The brooding menace lurking in the darkness did not go away. When the darkness deepened underneath the heavy forest trees that shut out the light of dim moon and glittering stars, he crouched down with the others and waited for the faint light of first dawn. Crouching, he kept alert, peering into the darkness to detect the darker shape that might be moving in it, although how, in this total lack of seeing, he could have seen a darker shape—or how, in fact, anything could be darker—he could not imagine. He heard faint sounds, slitherings and crawlings, and held himself taut against them. Nothing happened. One slithering would end and there'd be silence for a time, then another would start and he'd tighten up again. It was an agony such as he had never known before. The worst of it was that he had to crouch and take it. There was nothing he could do. There was nothing he could strike against. And he could not warn the others, for they might not be feeling it and he would only frighten them. Am I, he asked himself, the only trembling coward among us?

With the coming of first light, some of the fear evaporated. Now he could see if something crept up on them; seeing, he could face it. There was nothing to see but the mighty trees that crowded all about them and loomed over them, their massive boles covered with thickly grown moss and lichens, lending them a hoary look. The somber sense of haunting still remained. They found themselves speaking, when they spoke, in whispers, for the silence underneath the trees was so hushed and heavy that it seemed irreverent to break it.

They struggled up the hill. Forest duff lay thick beneath their feet. For centuries leaves and broken bits of branches and chunks of scaling bark had fallen on the forest floor and stayed there. In time, the lower layers of the accumulation had been transformed into forest mold, but that took years, and while the lower layers were turning into mold, the top layers continued to build up.

As they climbed, Harcourt wondered if other feet than theirs had ever trod this ground. It was wild country, this land close to the river, and of little use to anyone; there would be scarcely reason for anyone to come here.

Finally, after half an hour of climbing, the heavy growth of crowding trees thinned out, and they moved in more open country, although there still were trees. The menace fell away, but it did not fade away entirely. They still moved through another country.

And now here they were, the four of them, lying on their bellies, well screened by the heavy growth of shrubbery that grew at the forest's edge, watching the unicorns at play in a parklike opening in the woods, just beyond the crest of the river hill they'd climbed. Beyond the crest the ground sloped down, and beyond the parklike opening, heavy woods closed in. The open piece of ground, Harcourt thought, might at one time have been a field that a now-vanished settler had chopped out to make a farm. At the far end of the opening he had glimpsed an irregularity that might have been the ruins of a farmhouse. But, looking at it again, he could not be certain. Should it be an abandoned farmstead, it would not be unusual; in this land there would be many such ruined structures, marking spots where humans had settled in to make a life for themselves, then had been forced to flee and leave it all behind them when the Evil had come surging back.

The unicorns were still playing, but there had been a change. They were playing differently. Suddenly a small group of them wheeled and raced toward the far edge of the clearing, swinging wide and then sweeping back. Ahead of them a dark figure fled, running for its life. Harcourt strained his eyes, squinting for better focus. A bear or a man? He could not be certain.

The other unicorns had stopped their gamboling and were watching, heads lifted high, their slender, spiraled horns shining in the sun. Then, as if by a given signal, they all started trotting, encircling, and closing in on the fleeing thing. Then they were on top of it, rearing, chopping down with knife-sharp hooves.

Harcourt surged to his knees, but his bow, which he had stuffed into the quiver on his back, caught on an overhanging branch and threw him off his balance. A hand closed on one of his wrists, jerking it out from under him, and he fell back to the ground.

"Keep down," said Yolanda, her hands still gripping his wrist. "For the love of God, keep down."

"But that's a man out there!" Harcourt protested.

"I thought it was a bear," said the abbot. "I could swear it was a bear."

"Man or bear," Yolanda said, "there is nothing we can do for it. They are chopping it to ribbons. They'd do the same to us. Trying to help it, we'd only risk our lives."

"It's beyond all help," the abbot said. "They are tossing it."

Above the tossing horns, something was thrown into the air, but there was no way to make out what it was. It was a ragged blackness, disjointed, flapping grotesquely as it rose and fell. Then it was down again, and the encircling ring of unicorns reared and fell forward, slashing with their hooves. Whatever lay upon the ground was being sliced to tiny pieces.

Gorge rose in Harcourt's throat. Such beauty, he thought, such incredible, shining beauty, and all that beauty no more than a mask for this viciousness. Evil, he thought—all in this land was evil.

He rolled over on his side to disentangle the bow from the branch on which it had caught. A bow, he thought with some distaste, was a clumsy thing to carry. All four of them carried bows. It had been only after long consideration that he had decided he also would carry one. He disliked the bow; it was a coward's weapon. A good bowman, from a safe distance, could shoot down a group of valiant swordsmen before they could come to grips. To Harcourt, this went against the grain. But a bow, he finally agreed, was an efficient weapon, and with his band so small and the odds so great against them, he finally had come to the opinion that it made good sense for them to have four bows. He was the only one among them who carried a sword, probably the only one who could handle one. The Knurly Man's weapon was a short battle-axe, and Yolanda had only her bow and a dagger, while Guy, the great oaf, packed a mace on the ground that since he was a churchman and an abbot, he was forbidden to spill blood. The distinction, it seemed to Harcourt, was so fine as to be ridiculous. Yet it was a rule that no churchman could carry an edged blade, and his old friend the abbot would have it no other way. Perhaps, Harcourt told himself, it made no great difference. A mace could kill as easily, although perhaps not as cleanly, as a sword.

The bow disentangled, he started to back out of the thicket. But before he could do more than make a wiggle or two, the abbot nudged him with an elbow. Undoubtedly he had meant to nudge him in the ribs, but since Harcourt was backing up, the elbow nudged him in the head, a nudge that was somewhat stronger than need be, and it set his ears to ringing.

He turned his ringing head to see what was going on. The abbot had his head flung back, staring at the sky with one finger pointing upward. Looking in the approximate direction of the pointing finger, Harcourt made out three flapping dishrags in the sky.

Three dragons. There could be no mistaking that dishrag flapping. Three dragons heading for the clearing. This was the second time in a few days that he had sighted dragons, and it was, as far as he was concerned, twice too often. He hated the scaly things. They swooped down and made a pass at you, then zoomed back into the air, out of reach—that is, if they missed you. If they didn't miss you, you were dead, or worse than dead.

Out in the clearing, the unicorns had seen the dragons and were running for their lives. Harcourt had never heard that dragons preyed on unicorns, but seeing the frantically fleeing unicorns, he knew very well they did. Pigs, cattle, people, unicorns—they all were meat to dragons.

The unicorns, after the first wild flurry of running, had bunched together and were heading straight toward the thicket in which Harcourt and the others hid. In fascination, unable to move, he watched them come, the hurtling white bodies, the driving legs and the polished hooves, the tossing, spearlike horns. He was unable to move, but there would have been no use in moving. Tangled as they were in the thicket, Harcourt knew it would be impossible for them to get out of it in time. The unicorns would be on top of them before they could free themselves.

The dragons were dropping, plunging on the herd. Ungainly as they might be while flying, they were like lightning bolts when they dropped upon their prey, wings folded, necks stretched out, claws thrust forward in a striking position.

Harcourt tried to flatten himself against the ground, locking his hands over his head.

Then the unicorns were upon them. In front of Harcourt, inches away from his shoulder, a hoof came plunging down, cutting deep into the earth, spraying dirt across his face. Another hoof caught him in the right leg, barely grazing it. A unicorn loomed in front of him, squatting down in preparation for a mighty leap. It leaped and went sailing over him. Out in the clearing, something squealed, a heart-rending, terrified sound; then the last of the unicorns was past.

Harcourt jerked his head up and saw two of the dragons, wings open, sailing up to clear the trees. The third dragon was a little farther off, beating its wings frantically to clear the ground and raise itself, wheeling desperately to angle away from the trees. From its claws hung the limp body of a unicorn.

And something else—from the stretched-out neck of the dragon that had bagged the unicorn trailed a rope, some ten feet of rope, with the loose end frayed, the noose still encircling the neck.

Harcourt reached out and grabbed the abbot's shoulder. "Do you see that?" he shouted. "Do you see the rope?"

"So help me Almighty God," the abbot said, "I do."

"It couldn't be," Harcourt said, his voice shaking.

"It has to be," the abbot told him. "Who else but you and Hugh would be fools enough to try to rope a dragon?"

The dragon with the rope and the unicorn had cleared the trees and was flapping off. The grassy opening in front of the thicket was empty. The rope on the dragon streamed out, almost parallel with the body as the dragon picked up speed.

"Is everyone all right?" Knurly asked.

"I am," Yolanda said. "I wasn't even touched."

Hurriedly, all of them crawled out of the thicket and regained their feet. They stood, looking at one another, still not quite believing what had happened.

"We were lucky," said the Knurly Man.

"God watched over us," the abbot declared. "I take this as a sign that we're under His protection."

"It was a foolish thing for us to do, to start with," Harcourt said sourly. "Crawling into a thicket to gape at some silly unicorns."

There was no sign of the unicorns. By this time, they would be deep into the forest, probably still running.

Yolanda was unruffled, acting as if nothing at all had happened. Her robe hadn't been dirtied by their having been run over by the unicorns; not a hair of her head was out of place.

"How about that man out there?" Harcourt asked.

"I don't think it was a man," said Knurly. "Like the abbot, I took it for a bear."

"But should it be a man," the abbot said, "it would be only meet if we tarried long enough to say a few words over him. The comfort of the Church ..."

"If you could find enough of him to say your few words over," Knurly said.

"Much as I hate to say this, abbot," Yolanda said, "I think that Knurly's right. We should waste no further time. We should be getting on."

"I'm certain it was a man," Harcourt told them. "It seems unchivalrous and ungodly to do nothing for him. Even in his death, we should do something for him."

"Charles," said the Knurly Man, "you're out of your everlasting mind. You've seen men die before. You have seen them die and have walked away."

"Yes, but ..."

"Reluctantly, I must agree," the abbot said. "Much as it saddens me, it may be best to walk away. And, anyhow, I think it was a bear."

They headed west, following the crest of the hill. The walking was fairly easy, and they made good time. Yolanda disappeared, scouting out ahead. No one marked her going. One minute she was there, and the next time they looked, she wasn't.

"I'm getting hungry," the abbot complained. "We haven't eaten since last night. How about our stopping and having a bit of cheese and bread?"

"Dig it out of your pack," said the Knurly Man, "and eat it while you're walking."

"I don't eat while I'm walking," the abbot said. "Walking joggles up my stomach and I catch a colic."

"We can halt for the night in a couple of hours or so," said Harcourt. "The sun is getting well into the afternoon. We've made good time; we could have done much better if we'd not allowed the unicorns to delay us."

The abbot grunted at him in some displeasure, but he kept

on going, hurrying every now and then to keep up with the
other two. An hour or so later they came to a point where the
ridge on which they had been walking plunged down into a
deep valley. Wispy fog hung over the valley. Through the fog
could be glimpsed small lakes and sparkling tongues of water.
The valley was wide; the distant hills on the other side of it
shone a chalky blue in the light of the fading day.

"A fen," the Knurly Man said in some disgust. "I hope we
can find a way around it. Fens are nasty things to travel
in."

"A small one, however," the abbot told him, "and, it would
seem to me, somewhat displaced. Most fens are found in flat
country, not tucked among the hills."

"You find them," said the Knurly Man, "wherever water
can collect and spread out across the land."

"Perhaps we should reconsider," said the abbot. "It might
be a good idea if we struck north until we found the Roman
road. The Romans are good engineers. Their roads have little
grade to them. It would be level walking and no blundering
through thick forests or floundering through fens."

"On the Roman road," said the Knurly Man, "we'd all be
gobbled up before the day was done."

Harcourt heard a rustle of leaves behind him and turned
quickly about. Yolanda stood just a few feet away, peering
out at them from under the cowl of her robe.

"Gentlemen," she said, "I have found a camping place
nearby, with a lively spring of water close at hand and a
young buck hanging in a tree."

The abbot spun about. "Venison," he croaked. "Venison,
and here I was, thinking of eating cheese and bread."

"Follow me," said Yolanda, and they followed her to the
camping site she'd chosen, with a spring nearby and a young
buck in a tree.

Well before dark they were settled in, with a campfire blazing, a supply of wood hauled in, and generous cuts of venison
broiling on a bed of coals.

The abbot sat with his back bolstered against the trunk of a
mighty tree, his hands clasped about his middle, the great
mace lying close beside him. He sniffed the aroma of the
cooking meat.

"This," he said, speaking comfortably, "is a perfect end to a
day replete with high hills to be climbed, with unicorns and
dragons. The smell of venison makes up for all the trials we've
faced."

"There is a fen ahead," the Knurly Man said to Yolanda. "Do we have to cross it?"

"No, we don't," she replied. "We can go around it."

"Praise be the Lord," the abbot sighed. He said to Harcourt, "This guide we have is worth her weight in salt."

When the steaks were done, they ate, broiled more steaks, and ate them as well. The abbot's bushy beard, when he could force himself to eat no more, was shiny with the grease.

They lounged about the fire, full of meat, pleased with themselves. The abbot found a bottle of wine in his pack and passed it around. By now full dark had fallen. Night birds called from the fen. A light breeze muttered in the treetops. Everything was pleasant—far more pleasant, Harcourt told himself, than it should have been. Despite the euphoria of the meal and the relaxation after a hard day's trip, he found himself suspicious and even a little apprehensive about all the pleasantness. This was hostile land and should not be so pleasant.

He looked across the fire at Yolanda, who sat cross-legged on the ground. Her face had taken on a softness that she had not shown before. It might be, Harcourt thought, no more than a trick of the flickering firelight. She was easy with herself, and of all of them, he surmised, she would be the one who'd know if there were any lurking danger.

The abbot heaved himself up and threw more wood upon the fire.

"Should you be doing that?" Harcourt asked. "It might be better, now that the meat is cooked, to let the fire die down. It might be best if we went without a fire."

The abbot guffawed at him. "There you go again, in one of your black moods. Why can't you settle down like the rest of us and enjoy a full gut? We're no more than on the fringe of the Empty Land, and danger is unlikely."

"There were unicorns and dragons."

"The unicorns are long gone," said the abbot, "and the dragons, too. I don't see . . ."

He stopped talking, suddenly tense.

Harcourt straightened from his lounging position. "What is it, Guy?" he asked.

"I heard something. A rustling of some sort."

Then they all heard the rustling and were on their feet. Harcourt's hand went to his sword, but he did not draw the blade, for the rustling was no longer there. They stood, all four of them, and waited for the sound.

Perhaps only a bird, Harcourt thought, changing its position on a branch, or a tiny, furry creature that scurried in the fallen leaves.

The abbot stooped and picked up his mace.

Harcourt walked around the fire to stand beside Yolanda. "What did you hear?" he asked.

"What the rest of you heard. A rustle. There is something out there."

The new logs that the abbot had thrown on the fire now caught and flared up suddenly, and Harcourt saw what had caused the rustling—a scabrous mound of filth that had risen, and was rising still, beneath the monstrous oak that stood to one side of the campfire. As it rose, it sloughed off leaves and forest mold, dead twigs, the bones of animals that had died, living plants, and moss. It was of the soil itself, a creature of the forest floor, but it was moving and alive. It fouled the air with a released rottenness, and an evil flowed out from it, an evil so thick that one could feel its physical impact; the rottenness was so foul that it made one stagger and seized one by the throat with a choking, strangling grasp, as if the foulness had fingers that could reach out and clutch.

Harcourt stepped back a pace, driven back by the strength of the evil and the solidity of the fetor. His sword rasped as it came out of the scabbard, and the firelight made its burnished steel seem red, as if with blood. But the thing that rose before them, underneath the oak, would have no blood, no red and honest blood, Harcourt told himself. Cut, it would exude green ichor or a flood of inky ooze, but no honest blood. Looking at it, he thought that for an instant he had caught the gleam of protruding fangs and claws, although if they were fangs or claws, they were most strangely placed; they might be no more than splintered bones or slivered stone that had lain embedded in the forest floor.

It continued rising from the litter, from the decaying leaves, the decaying bones, the sloughed-off bark, the broken twigs, the dung of birds and other forest denizens, the molted feathers, and it was given a further semblance of life by the firelight that danced across it. The evil flowing from it became stronger and the gagging rottenness thicker. Harcourt choked, half from the rottenness, half from the horror-ridden anger that such a thing as this would dare exist, could dare to rise and intrude into a comparatively clean and decent world. He took a quick step forward, but the abbot was there before him. In a single, fluid motion, the churchman heaved the

heavy mace high above his head in a two-handed grip and
brought it down upon the mound of filth. The mound
squashed at the impact. It made a gurgling sound, and gobbets
of it squirted out; the dark brown stench of it was worse by
far than it had been to start with. Harcourt took two more
steps, lurching forward, but before he could reach the abbot's
side, he doubled over, bent in the middle, retching, vomit
bitter in his throat and mouth, tears streaming from his eyes.
The foulness of the shattered mound washed over him, and he
made unconscious clawing motions with his hands, as if he
were swimming in it. By a superhuman effort, he straightened
and saw that the mound was gone, but that the abbot stood
where it had been, the mace rising and falling, up and down,
as the abbot beat at the squirming fragments of what once
had been the mound, whooping with laughter while he beat at
the quivering noisomeness.

Harcourt tried to call out to the abbot, but the words
choked in the bitterness of his throat. Finally they broke free.
"Guy, get out of there!" he shouted. The abbot paid him no
attention, but kept on beating at the fragments. Harcourt
staggered forward and seized him by the arm, tugging at him.
"For God's sake, man, stop. There is nothing left."

The abbot, between his hoots of laughter, shouted back,
"By the time I get through with it, there'll be nothing left, less
than nothing left."

"Damn you, come to your senses," Harcourt bellowed. "We
must get out of here. We can't stay; we have to get away. This
place is so fouled with stench, there is no living with it."

Reluctantly, the abbot turned about and went back to the
fire with him. Yolanda stood to one side, a scarf she had worn
about her throat wadded up and pressed tightly against her
nose and mouth. The Knurly Man was gathering up their
packs.

"Come on," he urged. "Come on, we must leave this place."

Harcourt grabbed two of the packs and slung them over his
shoulder. He pushed the abbot ahead of him.

"Now you've done it," the Knurly Man scolded the abbot.
"Now you've really done it."

"But the evil of it," the abbot protested. "Did you not feel
the evil of it?"

"You do not beat a polecat to death," said the Knurly Man.
"When one shows up, you quietly leave or carefully walk
around it."

"But I killed it. It needed killing."

"That thing you can't kill. It's one thing that doesn't die. You hope it goes away."

They plunged into the nighttime woods, downhill toward the fen, proceeding carefully. Occasionally one of them collided with a tree or tripped over a fallen branch, but still they continued, making careful progress.

Harcourt heard the faint wailing when they approached the edge of the fen. He halted in his tracks and listened. The sound came from far away. It was muted by distance and whipped by wind, but it was a wailing. He was sure of that. Something out in the fen was wailing.

"What is that?" he asked.

"Lost spirits," said Yolanda. "Lonely spirits wailing in the fen."

"Spirits? You mean ghosts?"

"This land is filled with ghosts. So many died unshriven."

"I'd never thought of it," said the Knurly Man, "but that could be a fact. Many fled when the Evil came back into the land, but not all of them escaped. Many were trapped. Others hid or tried to hide."

The wailing had faded away. They stood for several minutes and, not hearing it again, continued down the hill. In the pale, sickly moonlight, the fen was an eerie place, a sketch in black and silver. The water was silver, the reeds and bushes a different shade of silver, and the shadows black. In front of them stood a small pool of water, flanked on each side by waving grass. A narrow, sandy shore ran up from the pond.

They stood and listened for the wailing and heard it once again, still far off and faint. Then it faded out, and there was only a haunted silence.

"The stink is still with us," said Harcourt, "but more bearable."

"We still carry it with us," said the Knurly Man. "In a day or two it will wear off. We can get rid of some of it by taking a bath and washing our clothes."

"But what was it?" Harcourt asked. "I've never seen its like, nor even heard of it."

"It would be strange if you had," said the Knurly Man. "Very few have ever heard of it. It comes from ancient times. It is an elemental. It is of the earth; it generates in the earth and comes from the earth. It is a thing that rises from dead matter. It is not of the Evil. It was here long before the Evil was. At one time, so the stories go, there were many of them, but there no longer are. I had thought that they were gone from earth, that there'd never be another. But in a place like this . . ."

"You say few people have ever heard of an elemental. And yet you have. You knew of it."

"The old stories of my race," said the Knurly Man. "That is how I knew of it."

"Your race?"

"Certainly," said the Knurly Man. "You've never mentioned it, of course, nor has anyone, but you know that I'm not human."

"I'm sorry," Harcourt said.

"No need," said the Knurly Man. "I'm as good as any human."

"Let's start washing up," the abbot suggested. "Then we should try to get some sleep. We're very short on sleep."

Saying this, he walked out into the pool until he was in the water up to his middle. Stooping down, he cupped water in his hands and began scrubbing his face and clothes.

"We'll have to set a watch," Yolanda said.

"I'll take the first," said Harcourt.

"And I the second," said the Knurly Man.

Measuring the time he spent on watch by observation of the stars, Harcourt woke the Knurly Man, who stumbled, grunting, to his feet.

"How is everything?" he asked.

"All is well," said Harcourt. "Some rustling in the woods, but not the kind of rustling we heard back there on the hill. Probably just small animals. There has been some wailing in the fen, but that is all."

"All right," said the Knurly Man. "Get into your blanket and try to catch some sleep."

Harcourt lay down and wrapped himself in the blanket, but sleep was hard to come by. For a long time he lay, looking up at the stars and thinking. I'm not human, the Knurly Man had said, and that was the first time that he, or anyone, had said it. My race, he'd said, my race are the ones who knew of the elementals, speaking as if, at one time, there had been many elementals. Not the Evil, he had said; they came before the Evil. He, Harcourt, had never heard of a race of Knurly Men; as far as he knew, there was no more than one Knurly Man, although if he'd thought of it, he surely would have realized that at one time there must have been other Knurly Men. The elementals, then, were old, for the Evil was an ancient evil, and the elementals, the Knurly Man had said, came before the Evil. There were not many elementals now, he'd said, hinting that he was surprised there should be any left. And if that were true—if the elementals and the Knurly Men had lived in this world together—then both of them were ancient, and the chances were that there were few Knurly Men left, as well as few elementals.

When he got home again, Harcourt told himself, he would have to ask his grandfather about it, although it would be a touchy subject to bring up. His grandfather, he knew, might recognize the sincerity of the question and answer it, although perhaps not completely, or it was just as possible that he would fly into a rage. For years his grandfather and the Knurly Man had been close companions, and the two of them held great loyalty to each other.

Thinking thus, puzzling and debating with himself, he finally fell asleep. The abbot wakened him, roughly shaking him by the shoulder.

"Get up," he said. "There are more of them out there. The woods are full of them. They have us surrounded."

Harcourt sat up, dazed. "What has us surrounded?"

"The stinking mounds," said the abbot. "I would have gone out and taken care of them, but Knurly raised so much hell about the first one, I thought I'd better not."

The sky, Harcourt saw, was getting light.

Yolanda, wakened by the abbot's bellowing, came out of her blanket; the Knurly Man sat up, blinking.

"What's going on now?" he asked the abbot. "Why can't you be quiet?"

"The mounds have us surrounded."

The Knurly Man leaped up. "Are you sure of that?"

"Sure," the abbot said. "There is a line of them behind us, extending down to the edge of the fen on either side of us. They've got us hemmed in. I didn't hear them this time. They were very quiet about it. I saw the first one when it got light enough. Before I said anything about it, I made sure."

The Knurly Man turned to Yolanda. "You said we could skirt around the fen. Is it impossible to cross it?"

"Perhaps not impossible. I've been told there is a path. It wouldn't be easy. We'd have to do some wading. But I think we can get across."

"That's mad!" the abbot cried. "We can break through these things. We can go around the fen."

"You might be able to break through them," said the

Knurly Man, "but I wouldn't want to try. You don't know a thing about them."

"But you do and you said . . ."

"I don't care what I said," the Knurly Man told him. "We go across the fen. If we do that, I doubt they can follow us."

Ten

The spirits were closing in on him again—even in the daylight they were closing in. Harcourt could not see them, although at times he thought he could—a slight waver in the air, like the waver of heat on a blistering summer day, shimmering above a field of ripe and golden wheat. But they talked to him; they talked incessantly. Most of the time he could not make out what they said, but at times he thought he could. Mostly their words were just a mumble, the kind of blurred buzzing that he had often heard when he had passed a closed door behind which his mother and her women spent an afternoon of sewing, but doing much more jabbering than they were doing sewing.

Harcourt waded through waist-deep water with the bottom mud sucking at his boots. The others trailed along behind him. The spirits yammered at him. Swarms of insects spun about his head, and every so often he raised his hands and waved them in hopes of driving the insects off, but they paid no attention to his waving hands—they kept on spinning about in a swirl of buzzing wings shining in the sunlight.

He came to a hummock that he had sighted some distance off and had been heading for ever since. Coming to it, he braced his arms on the solid ground and hauled himself upon it, not getting to his feet, but lying prone to regain his breath. Yolanda was the next in line, and when she reached the hummock, he held out a hand and boosted her up on the ground beside him. The Knurly Man was not far behind Yolanda, and behind him came the abbot, red of face and panting, forcing his heavy body through the muck and water. One by one they came up, and Harcourt held out a hand to each of them and helped them to dry ground.

Once they reached the hummock, they sat side by side in a sodden, solemn row, not doing any talking, too out of breath to talk. They were wet to the skin and spattered with mud and somewhat out of sorts.

"I never bargained for anything like this," the abbot finally said. "I had known, of course, that there would be a lot of walking, and I'm not adverse to walking. But wading through a mucky place like this is not my idea of adventure. This is plain hard work."

"We probably would not be doing it," said the Knurly Man, "if you'd let the mound alone. But no, nothing would do but you had to go out and beat it to a pulp."

"Those other mounds back there," said the abbot, "were not, I am convinced, duplicates or offspring of the mound that I took care of. You can't tell me the fragments that I left behind could have come scuttling down the hill, each of them forming a new mound to entrap us."

"I don't know about that," said the Knurly Man, "although one cannot be certain. In my day I have heard strange and awesome tales about the doings of the mounds. Yonder hill may have been a favored spot for them, with many of them forming. It might have taken years for all of them to come to life, but when the word went out . . ."

"The word went out?" the abbot asked.

"Yes, the word, perhaps, that an enemy was about and had fallen on them. So they gathered for revenge, hurrying their time . . ."

"Revenge," the abbot snorted, lifting the mace and thumping it on the ground. "If you'd turned me loose, I'd have given them fair reason for a vengeance."

"That's all done and over with," said Harcourt. "Why don't you two forget it?" He said to Yolanda, "Just ahead of us, on what appears to be an island of fairly solid earth, I thought I saw a continuation of our path."

She was delighted with the news. "Then there really was a path and we didn't miss it. When it came to nothing, I thought we might have taken a false trail, extending only for a short distance, and that there might be no path at all. But if you are right, there is one. The path was only drowned, and now we pick it up again."

Harcourt shrugged. "We may lose it a dozen times again, for this is treacherous land. But we'll keep going on. How far do you think we've come? Are we halfway across, perhaps?"

"I don't think so. Not quite halfway as yet. It would be nice if we could get across before the fall of night."

"Maybe we can," said the Knurly Man, "if we steadily keep at it. If we didn't have to stop to rest and engage in idle chatter every time we reach a piece of solid ground."

"If we do not rest occasionally," the abbot told him, "we'll not make it across at all. A man must take a moment every now and then to build up strength for his next assault."

"You," said the Knurly Man, disgusted, "are the biggest and strongest weakling I have ever come across."

"I've always liked you, Knurly," said the abbot. "Funny as you look, I've held respect for you. But hard doings bring out a streak of meanness in you I've never seen before . . ."

"Now let us stop this bickering," said Harcourt. "The both of you. We're in this together and of our own free will. No one shoved you into coming."

"What I want to know," said the abbot, "is why we have to wade this fen. The four of us, together, could have broken through the ring of mounds and gone on dry land around it. After all, the mounds couldn't have done much to stop us. The one at the camp—I just stepped up to it and mashed it flat."

"I think that might be a fair question," Harcourt said to the Knurly Man. "I've been doing some wondering myself. We took you at your word, of course . . ."

"It is a fair question, and I'm glad to answer it," said the Knurly Man. "The one at the camp had no way of knowing what kind of maniac it faced. It never had a chance. This solid, solemn Christian just walked up to it and let it have twenty pounds of iron and . . ."

"What was I supposed to do?" the abbot asked. "There it sat, stinking up the place and pouring out its evil."

"I tried to yell a warning," said the Knurly Man, "but I was too late. I would have stopped you if I could have, but when it was done, it was too late to do anything about it. The only reasonable action then was to get away. And I must say, as well, that never for a moment did I consider that other mounds would come surging from the ground and move in to besiege us. This, since I knew the history and the nature of the mounds, was unthinkable. I call them mounds because that is what you call them, but there's another name for them, a historic name . . ."

"You talk a lot," the abbot said, "but you don't tell us

anything. Tell me now, in as few words as possible, why we couldn't have broken through the ring of mounds."

"There's a bare chance that we could have," said the Knurly Man, "a bare chance only, but probably at a terrible cost. You felt the evil in them."

"Of course we did," said Harcourt. "All of us felt it. It and the stench. I don't know which it was, the evil or the stench, but it buckled me. I tried to reach it . . ."

"It didn't buckle me," said the abbot.

"That's because you have no sensitivity," said the Knurly Man. "You talk loudly of souls, but you have no soul, and what is more . . ."

The abbot came to his feet, raising the mace. "You can't talk like that to me!" he shouted. "You can't say . . ."

"Sit down!" said Harcourt, his voice icy. "And put down that goddamn mace. We three will be gentlemen even if it kills us."

Grumbling, the abbot sat down, but he kept his mace in hand.

"And now," Harcourt told the Knurly Man, "give us the answer to the question, with no side remarks."

"The answer," said the Knurly Man, "is that we are dealing with a creature that is unlike anything living in this world. It comes from and has its roots in the rawest common denominator of nature. And nature, when you think of it, is cruel. Cruel and uncaring. Nature has no love; it cares not what happens to anyone or anything. There is no way in which it can be appealed to. You live according to its rules. Make one small mistake and it kills you, carelessly it kills you. The definition of evil is the lack of love. A thing cannot be truly evil except that it feels no love, perhaps doesn't even suspect the concept of love. The truly evil may not even love itself. The mounds do not ask for life; life is thrust upon them by some unknown, mysterious alchemy found in the dead and dying matter of the soil. They may even resent life, angered and dismayed by their forced emergence into a world they never asked for. Are you beginning to understand what we are dealing with?"

Harcourt said soberly, "Yes, I think perhaps I do."

"If we had attacked the mounds back there," said the Knurly Man, "they probably would have killed us before we could come to grips with them. They would have over- whelmed us by the evil that is in them, or strangled us with their stench, or poisoned us with the poison they have stored up inside themselves, or perhaps in any one of a dozen other ways. They would have known about us and been waiting for us. I can give no better answer, for there is no precise knowledge of the mounds. No one can claim to be an expert on the mounds. Before you can become an expert, you are dead."

He paused and looked around at the others. "Does that satisfy you? Is that sufficient answer?"

None of them said anything.

"Their favorite place for hatching," said the Knurly Man, "if you can call it hatching, is in the forest floors, in undisturbed areas where thick layers of forest debris have lain for years, supplying whatever unknown factors that bring about the hatching. That land back there in the forest probably has been undisturbed for uncounted centuries. The situation we ran into is one that I've never heard of. Even the wildest legends of my race do not tell of a great number of them coming into being all at once. I think the attack upon the first one forced the others to emerge before their time. How they could have known of the attack I do not know, cannot imagine. Our legends do not say or even hint that they can talk with one another."

"But they can't reach us here?" Yolanda asked.

"I doubt they can. While they can move, and at times, I would suspect, rather rapidly, they tend to stay near their place of birth. My guess is that they will not leave the forest. I doubt very much they'll venture into the fen."

He shook his head. "As you can understand, this is a shock to me. They come from ancient times. Once, so the olden stories say, there were many of them. But as the forests were cut down and plows put in the ground, they became less and less. As their habitats were destroyed, there were fewer of them. I would have told you, had you asked me, that there were no more of them, that they were simply stories from the past, that they had become extinct."

"No one would have asked you," Harcourt said, "because no one knew of them and you never mentioned them."

"There are many things," said the Knurly Man, "that I never mention."

Saying this, he heaved himself to his feet. "Shall we go on?" he asked. "Charles, I think you mentioned that you had seen a path ahead."

"Yes," said Harcourt. "I'll take the lead again and travel toward it. An island with a group of trees standing at one end of it. Because of the grass and reeds, it can be seen only every now and then. This hummock appears to be of small area, but the island where I thought I saw the path seems to be somewhat larger."

"Has anyone else been bothered by all the whispering and yammering?" the abbot asked. He said to Yolanda, "I think you said that they are spirits."

She nodded. "That is what they are. Or are said to be. The uneasy ghosts of people who died outside the pale of Holy Mother Church. They wander here and in many other places. Many human refugees may have died here, hiding from the Evil."

"Is there naught that can be done for them? No way to give them peace?"

"I do not know," Yolanda told him. "I only know they're here. I have never talked with anyone about them. Of course, I sorrow for them, as any Christian would."

"You might try," the Knurly Man said to the abbot, "sprinkling a squirt or two of holy water on them."

The abbot grunted at him disrespectfully and clambered to his feet. He tucked up his cassock. It was muddy at the hem and waterlogged and dripping.

They started out again, crossing the hummock, which, as Harcourt suspected, was only a small area lifted above the water of the fen. Reaching the edge of it, he plunged into the water again, the others following.

The water was not deep, in places only ankle-deep, at the most no more than waist-deep. The bottom was slimy, slippery mud, and in places fallen tree trunks and heaps of stones were embedded in the mud. It was necessary to proceed slowly, feeling out the way, alert against obstructions that might trip one up.

Occasionally they came upon stretches of open water, but more often they followed narrow, meandering lanes of water lined by tall reeds and grasses. Dead trees protruded from the fen, skeletons of trees that had died long before, when the conditions had come about that made possible the forming of the fen.

When they had stopped on the hummock to rest and talk, the spirits had drawn away or, at least for the moment, had fallen silent. Now, out in the water again, they came back and resumed their whispering. Harcourt tried to shut his ears and mind to them, but that was difficult to do, for they pressed themselves upon him and kept up a continual murmuring.

At first he had felt twinges of horror at their mumbling and did not feel ashamed of it, for there was inherent in ghosts of any sort a vague uneasiness, if not a forthright fear. A man, he thought, comforting himself, would be less than human if he could accept a ghost as something of not too great importance. But after hours of listening to them, the tinge of horror and the initial uneasiness had given way to annoyance. They had become pests, still capable of inspiring horror, although more pest than horror, and since there was nothing else that could be done, he tried to shut them out. But no matter how strong a man's willpower might be, he could not shut them out entirely. They pressed in too close, their voices too insistent, for him to shut them out. There were times when he had the impression that ghostly fingers were clutching at his arm in an effort to detain him, but that, or at least he so told himself, was no more than an aroused imagination.

Mostly it was gabble, but at times it seemed that he could distinguish words or phrases, although, once again, he was never certain if he heard them or if it was no more than words and phrases that he conjured up unconsciously. "Go back," they'd say, or seem to say. "Go back, danger lies ahead." A warning; at other times it was a plea. "Help us. For the love of God, have mercy on us. Have pity. We exist in this shadow world between life and death, neither alive nor yet decently dead. Lacking help, we'll stay in this wise forever." Never in that form, of course, never spoken all together, but words and phrases that spelled out to the plea, that ran together in his mind and put themselves together.

Behind him, the abbot bellowed, "Down! Everyone down and hide!"

Instinctively, without knowing why he should get down and hide, Harcourt hunkered in the water, crouching close against the tangled wall of reeds that hemmed in the channel he had been following. Scrooching around, he looked back and saw that all of the others were hiding, too, like chickens in a barnyard squatting down and freezing motionless when a hawk sailed overhead. The abbot, at the far end of the line, was motioning toward the sky. Looking up, Harcourt saw them, three dishrags flapping against the blue, flapping easily, not going anywhere, but circling the fen, alert to any prey that they might spot. They were flying high, so high that they were little more than moving dots imprinted on the sky.

Dragons, he told himself, three hunting dragons, perhaps the same three that had attacked the unicorns. He looked hard in an effort to see if one of them might be trailing a rope noosed about its neck, but they were too far away to make out any detail.

Time passed, and still the dragons circled. Once they dropped lower, but after a while beat their way up again. Watching them, Harcourt cursed silently. Precious time was being wasted; the dragons were holding up their crossing of the fen. It was essential that they get through this treacherous stretch of watery wasteland before the fall of night. The way events had been going—hiding in a thicket to gape at unicorns, hiding in a fen from dragons—it would take forever to get where they were going.

Back there in the castle, they had assumed they knew what they would face—a simple matter of ogres and trolls and dragons and others of the Evil—but now he knew that the Empty Land was no simple matter. In a short span of time, they had encountered two other factors they had not known or imagined: the mounds in the hills and the spirits in the fen. How many other surprises awaited them in the leagues ahead? Wondering, he fretted at delay.

The spirits, now that he had halted, came in even closer and in greater numbers. Their yammering filled his brain to the exclusion of all else. The words, if they were words, meant nothing.

Then there was one word that did mean something to him, one word that he recognized.

Eloise!

He straightened up when he heard the word and screamed aloud, "Eloise! What of Eloise?"

The abbot bellowed at him. "Get down! You damn fool, get down!"

He got down. For the moment he'd forgotten, but at the abbot's bellow he got down, hiding once again, looking up to see the dragons. They still were there, tiny dishrags flapping against the sky.

Eleven

Finally the dragons went away, flying off toward the east. Whether they had been searching for the humans or were only out on a hunting expedition, there was no way of knowing.

Harcourt did not see them go; he had not been watching them. He huddled in the watery channel, pushed partway into the wall of shielding reeds that flanked the channel. He crouched there, with one word ringing in his brain: Eloise! Eloise! Eloise!

And all the time the cloud of unseen spirits, unseen except that every now and then there was a shiver or a quiver in the air, not really seen, but marginally detected on the far periphery of his vision—the cloud of unseen spirits had crowded in upon him, spinning all about him and yammering as they spun. He tried to talk with them, shouted at them, talking and shouting in his mind, saying not a word.

Tell me, he shouted, tell me of Eloise; what is the word of her? He realized with a shock that if there were word of her in a place like this, yammered by the gabbling spirits of the fen, he would shrink from it. Unclean, he thought, unclean! Eloise could not be here, he did not want her here. There could be no way that she could be here, for if she'd died, she had not died here, but at Castle Fontaine across the river.

The questions and the wonder numbed him, and he crouched, withdrawn within himself, divorced from reality, from the blazing sun, the stinking water, the rustle of the grass and reeds, the menace of the circling dragons.

He did not want her here, in this stinking morass. Did he want her anywhere? And at the unbidden thought, sneaking from deep inside his consciousness, he stiffened, aghast that he should think it, that any part of him should think it, that even that unsuspected, unknown part of him that lurked deep inside himself should think it.

He could no longer recall her face; the wind always blew the strand of hair across her face. And when he had looked at the book of hours, he no longer could recall the words she'd spoken when she had given it to him; he could no longer see her fingers turning the pages. She had drifted from him, she had receded into the distance with the years. My God, he told himself in horror—for the love of God, I have forgotten her.

Dear God, he prayed, do not let her be here. Do not let her speak here to me. If she were here and I met her here, I would recoil from her, and that would break her heart and mine. We cannot meet in a foul place such as this. When we meet again, if we do meet again, it must be in a fair and pleasant place, a meadow with many blooming flowers blown in the wind. Not here, God, not in this sort of place!

The abbot's shout aroused him. "Charles, let's go. Lead on, my friend. The dragons are no longer with us."

He rose to his feet, as if in a dream, as if jerked out of troubled sleep. He canted back his head and looked about the sky. There were no dragons circling. Mechanically, he lurched forward, following the channel, and there, with the channel ending, across a placid lake of shallow water, lay the island he had sighted, with the clump of trees at its end and a path that led up from the water's edge to skirt the clump of trees.

The abbot came splashing through the water, passing Yolanda and the Knurly Man, to reach his side.

"The dragons cost us time," the abbot panted. "We'll not get across the fen by nightfall."

Harcourt looked at the sky and saw that the sun was far down toward the west.

"We'll do what we can," he told the abbot. "If we have to spend the night here, we can manage it."

"It's not going well," the abbot said. "It's not going well at all. We should be leagues from here, farther down the land."

"It will go better later on," said Harcourt. "I am sure of that. As soon as we reach dry land and some easy walking."

They plunged a little farther on, and Harcourt asked, "Do you think the dragons were hunting us? How could they know that we are here?"

"I don't know," the abbot said. "I have thought on it and I don't know anything at all. But it makes no difference. Hunting us or not, if they'd seen us, they'd have been down upon us."

"Could you make out if one of them had a rope about its neck?"

"No, I couldn't. They were too high. But the thought occurred to me."

"I have a feeling," said Harcourt, "that before all this is over, we'll see that dragon again. Face to face, perhaps. I intend to kill it."

"You're a romantic, Charles," said the abbot. "An incurable romantic. Despite your stodgy nature and your tendency to black moods, you're addicted to fantasy. Even in broad daylight, you are fantasy-addicted. Who else but you would have dreamed up the snaring of a dragon?"

"I mean it," Harcourt told him. "Every word of it. I feel it in my bones. I will face the dragon and I'll do my best to slay it."

"You think that it was written on that day of long ago beneath the frowning heights of Dragon Crag? That what was set in motion then must culminate here, somewhere in the Empty Land?"

"I don't know about that," said Harcourt. "I do not have your philosophic bent. I feel it in my bones, and that is all that I can tell you."

The walking was becoming harder, and the island that lay ahead seemed to be receding instead of getting closer. Harcourt looked down at his feet and saw that the water was little more than ankle-deep; he still was moving forward, although it seemed at a slower pace than he had before. The water, it seemed, had become thicker than any water he had ever known before, and the air, he saw, was different, too—a thicker, less transparent air.

"Guy!" he said, speaking almost in a whisper.

"Yes, I notice it as well," the abbot said. "There is something happening."

They plowed ahead, struggling to move faster, to regain their pace, but the world was very strange. The water seemed to have a sticky-molasses kind of quality, although that, Harcourt knew, could not be the answer; he was taking strides as long as he had before, and the distance that he covered was not commensurate with the stride. Ahead of him the island blurred and then came into focus, blurred again, and once more came into focus, although not as sharp and clear as it had been before. The spirits of the fen still mumbled every now and then, but the mumble was distorted and had a hollow sound, as if the mumbler had been mumbling in a barrel.

Off to one side, to the left-hand side—no, now it was the right-hand side—there was something watching them. Har-

court swiveled his head to the left and right and could not
see a thing except the fen that stretched to either side. And
yet, despite his seeing nothing, the feeling that they were being
watched still persisted—off there, somewhere to the left or
right, some monster squatted in the mud, grinning viciously at
what was going on, leering at them, mocking them.

They kept going ahead, although the pace was slow. The
island finally edged a little closer. Maybe, Harcourt thought,
when they reached the island, everything would right itself;
the old, safe, familiar world, the familiar air and familiar
water, would come into its own again.

And now, without even turning his head, he caught a
glimpse of the thing that sat to one side leering at them. It
squatted in the mud and water. Not all of it showed, and what
little of it did was indistinct and distorted, as if he were seeing
it through an imperfect pane of glass that did not pass the
light with any clarity, but broke it into shimmering, wavy
lines. The thing was mostly mouth and eyes, and there were
warts upon it, and it looked something like a frog, although it
was not quite a frog. He caught just a glimpse of it, and then
it was gone. He tried to bring it back, but since he did not
know how he'd seen it, he had no idea how to bring it back.
Why he wanted to bring it back puzzled him a bit, for it was
not a pretty thing to see. But he had to know, he thought,
what it was that had cast this enchantment on them—if it
were, in truth, enchantment—for until he knew, there would
be nothing he could do to break the enchantment chains.
Once again, he wondered how, just by seeing it, he could
know how to break free of it.

He did not mention it to the abbot, for the abbot more than
likely would not have believed him. The abbot, just a while
ago, had said that he was a romantic and much ridden by a
sense of fantasy. Although, he thought, what better place for
sensing fantasy than in the Empty Land?

They reached the island and climbed up its sloping shore
until they were on solid ground. Harcourt had hoped that
when they reached the island, there might be an end to what
was happening, but there was not. It was no easier to walk
upon dry land than it had been to walk in water. Under
ordinary circumstances, having reached dry land, he would
have sat down to rest for a moment, but he did not stop, and
neither did the abbot. He, as well as I, Harcourt told himself,
will not stop to rest until we finally are free.

Except for the small grove of trees at one end of it, the

island was barren and not an extensive stretch of land. There was a path, however, and they followed it until the island ended and another lakelike stretch of water loomed before them. Far in the distance what appeared to be a pile of white rocks thrust out of the water.

The moment they stepped into the water they knew the change. It was just water once again, and the air was clear. They could see that the further island, which was a pile of stones, was much farther off than it first had seemed.

The abbot made a slobbering sound, letting out his breath. "Thank Almighty God," he said, with more fervency in his voice than Harcourt had ever heard him express before. "We are finally out of the clutches of it."

They waded out a little farther and nothing changed. The world stayed normal. Then they turned about and saw Yolanda and the Knurly Man come stumbling down the bank and out into the water.

"Do you know what it was?" the abbot demanded of them.

Yolanda shook her head. "A small enchantment. That is all. I don't know where it came from."

"Just a slight tap upon the wrist," said the Knurly Man, "to remind us of what may lie ahead."

"We seem free of it now," said Harcourt, "and we had best forge ahead. I fear that the sun is too far down for us to reach the other side before the fall of dark. The best thing for us to do is to reach that rocky island and settle for the night."

"Two blessed days it has taken us," said the abbot, "to cover no more than two leagues of travel. At this rate, we'll never get where we are going."

"We'll get where we are going," said the Knurly Man, "because we must. And the rest of the way we'll not be traveling in a fen."

They set out toward the rocky island, no longer traveling in line, but all four of them abreast. The sun was down, disappearing behind the dark blue line of the western hills, and dusk began creeping in across the fen. Night birds began their crying and flocks of ducks swirled in the sky, seeking out their places of refuge for the night. Wraithlike mist rose off the water, hugging close against it, thrusting out wispy tendrils that slid along the surface. In the east a pale moon glimmered in the sky.

The spirits came crowding in again, and now Harcourt thought that at times he saw the forms of them, although he could not be certain if it were the manifestations of the spirits or only the wisps of swirling mist that he was seeing. Their yammering was the same as it had been before, mostly indistinguishable, but now and then that terrible, whining plea for help or the half-heard warning. No further word of Eloise—although by now he was not certain he had ever heard the name Eloise. It could have been no more than his imagination.

"I have never had an enchantment cast upon me before in all my born days," said the abbot. "I must say that it was an eerie feeling. Have any of the others of you ever felt such a thing before? I know you haven't, Charles, but how about the others of you?"

"I never have," said Yolanda, "although I recognized it for what it was. Instinctively, I think, for I had no previous experience that would have guided me."

"On two occasions in my life," said the Knurly Man, "I have been touched by enchantment, both of those enchantments much worse than the one we just experienced. This one was a feeble exercise of the wizard power. As if some wizard might have seized the opportunity to get in a touch of practice."

"I sensed as well," Yolanda said, "that there was no great intent in it. No wish to do us harm."

"My God!" the abbot said. "Do you mean to tell me that there are wizards squatting all about the landscape, waiting for travelers upon whom they can perfect and hone their powers?"

"In this Empty Land," Yolanda told him, "you must not be surprised at anything at all."

"You say this," the abbot said, "and yet you do not fear? Knowing this, you were willing to come with us as guide?"

"I do fear," Yolanda said, "but I have some trust in myself to recognize a danger in time so that something may be done about it. You know that at times I travel in this land."

"Yes, you told me that," said Harcourt. "I wondered why you might want to do it."

"I am not sure," Yolanda said, "that I can spell it out to you. But there is something here that appeals to me. A certain sense of aliveness and mystery that touches on my spirit."

They kept on toward the rocky island, which was drawing nearer. Finally they came upon it and clambered out on its rocks. From a distance it had looked white, and now they saw that it was white, indeed. The stones were marble-white, and most of them were large—it looked as if someone had dumped a gigantic cartload of the white stones in the middle of the fen. They lay in marvelous disorder, exactly as they would have looked if a cartload of them had been dumped there. Some of their surfaces were jagged, but others were straight and smooth, as if they might at one time have been chiseled into shape.

They sat for a time upon the stones and stared out across the stretch of water they had crossed. The dusk was closing in deeper, but they still could distinguish the island with the clump of trees, a dark smudge against the moonlit surface of the fen. Finally Harcourt stirred and rose to his feet.

"I think I'll climb to the top," he said. "From there, it might be possible to see the farther shore. We can be no great distance from the ending of the fen."

"I'll go with you," said the Knurly Man.

Climbing the rocks of the island, Harcourt told himself, must be somewhat akin to the climbing of the great pyramids of Egypt, which his Uncle Raoul had told him of many years ago, except that the climbing of the rocky islet might be a harder task, for the stones of the pyramid were set firmly into place, and here they had been dumped helter-skelter, with the blocks lodged at random against their fellows and some of them so insecurely balanced that they were a hazard.

Picking their way with care, he and the Knurly Man hauled themselves up the pile of stone. There were places where they had to sidle along before they could find a means of safer climbing. Little by little, they edged their way upward.

Finally, Harcourt saw that the smooth stone block tilting above him would be the last he would have to negotiate. Standing on his tiptoes, he reached up with his hands and grasped its top with his fingers. He hauled himself up its face, found a foothold in an irregularity, and heaved himself up, getting his elbows on top of the rock. Grunting, he hauled blindly at his body and finally managed to get a leg across the stone. Rolling, he gained the top of the block and was about to swivel around to reach down a hand to the Knurly Man when he saw what faced him.

It was a skeleton—at first he thought it to be a human skeleton, then knew almost instantly that it wasn't. It was affixed to a stubby cross, the base of which was thrust into a crevice between two stones, the cross canted toward him so that it seemed as if the skeleton were lunging at him, frozen midway in its lunge.

Looking at it, he gulped in sudden terror. The bones

gleamed whiter than the stones, and the even whiter teeth in the gleaming skull grinned at him with a sullen malevolence. The skeleton, he saw, was bound to the cross with chains, bound so tightly and so closely that most of the bones still remained in place. The skull was intact, the lower jaw still hinged, the rib cage intact as well. The finger bones had fallen from one hand and, except for a couple of the fingers, still remained intact upon the other. The spine, somewhat skewed out of shape, sat upon the massive pelvic structure.

"Charles," came the voice of the Knurly Man, "reach down a hand to me. I cannot get a grip."

Harcourt swung around, thrusting his head over the edge of the block and reaching down a hand. The Knurly Man grasped it and, as Harcourt heaved, came swarming up. The Knurly Man started to get to his feet and stopped in a crouch, his head canted up to stare at the skeleton on the cross.

"What have we here?" he asked.

"Not human," Harcourt said. "At first, I thought it was."

"An ogre," said the Knurly Man. "As I live and breathe, an ogre. And a damn good place for him."

He rose to his feet, Harcourt rising with him. Together they walked closer to the cross.

"Do you think he was alive . . . ?" Harcourt asked.

The Knurly Man interrupted. "Alive? Of course he was alive. Why go to the trouble to chain a dead ogre to a cross of cedar? Here, Charles, you gaze upon an act of retribution. Here came to its end an Evil One that in its time must have done great harm to the human race. Here the score was evened, or partially evened. He did not die as your Christ died, hanging on His cross. The body of the ogre was supported by the chains, and death did not come as a result of bodily tensions, such as was the case in other crucifixions. This one starved to death. This one hung here until he died of hunger and of thirst. Of thirst, most likely."

"But the savagery. The ruthlessness . . ."

"Undoubtedly those who performed this deed had reason for their savage ruthlessness."

"I still do not like to think of it," said Harcourt. "A quick death by a sword stroke—that's one thing. This is quite a different matter. It shows a rabid hatred."

"The humans in this land," said the Knurly Man, "might have had reason for their hatred. They came by it the hard way."

"What do we do about it?"

"We do not a thing. We leave it hanging here. What would you propose—a Christian burial?"

"Well, no, not that."

"Then let it go. Let it stay, grinning at its death."

"I suppose it's just as well."

The Knurly Man swung around, away from the cross and skeleton, looking toward the west. He pointed. "There. We've found out what we came to learn. The end of the fen is only a short distance off. Look and you can see it."

Twelve

After an uncomfortable night on the rocky isle, they crossed the last stretch of the fen at first morning light, reaching dry and open ground, with the blue of the hills looming to the west.

Except for a few catnaps, Harcourt had not slept at all. The fen, once full night had fallen, had become a nightmare. The spirits wailed and moaned and at times could be seen, although there was always doubt whether what was seen were white-garbed spirits or simply drifting mist floating all about. Night birds had cried, and a short distance to the east something seemed to be thumping on a drum. Harcourt lay awake, concentrating on this sound, trying to make up his mind whether it was a croaking or a drumming. He told himself, and tried to fight the feeling off, that it was the croaking of the wart-covered, froglike thing that he had glimpsed, or thought he'd glimpsed, when the enchantment spell still held. He could never quite convince himself it was, for while at times it sounded like a croaking, there were other times he could have sworn that the sound was the beating of a drum. Although, he asked himself, who would be squatted in the fen, in the middle of the night, beating at a drum?

When they started out in the morning, the edge of the fen had been marshy for a little distance, then became solid land. They strode along rapidly, glad to be out of the marsh, heading for the line of hills. Yolanda raced ahead of them and soon had disappeared. More than likely, Harcourt thought, she was out to search for the easiest path by which they could climb the hills. He marveled at her agility and strength.

On occasion Harcourt found himself craning his neck to examine the sky. The dragons had made more of an impression on him than he had thought. Except for a few hawks sailing overhead, the sky was empty. The dragons, it appeared, were not about.

They walked through heavy grass speckled with meadow flowers in full bloom. The hills lost the blue of distance and became tree-clad heights, rising not quite so high as had the river hills.

The abbot, who was somewhat in advance of Harcourt and the Knurly Man, dropped back to walk with them. He had regained his normally high spirits.

"Now we are making time," he said. "Perhaps, given some good luck, we can make up the delay caused us by the fen."

"We'll have good days and bad," said the Knurly Man. "It is my expectation that along the way we'll meet with more delays."

"But nothing," said the abbot, "quite so terrible as the fen."

In a couple of hours they were approaching the upsweep of the hills, and there they found Yolanda waiting for them.

"Let us turn slightly to the north," she said. "I have found a winding valley that will lead us through the hills."

"Soon," said the abbot, "we should halt to eat. We had no more than a nibble of cheese and a mouthful of bread before we started out this morning."

"Do you never think," the Knurly Man asked, "of anything but that enormous gut of yours? If you had your way, we'd be halting every half a league to have a bite to eat."

"A man travels on his belly," said the abbot. "I have always taken care to pay attention to mine and to treat it well."

"Once we reach the valley," Yolanda promised him, "we'll find a place where we can stop and eat. There is a small stream running through it and groves of trees."

They found the valley and, leaving the grass, went up it to a pleasant willow grove beside a stream of laughing water that went dashing down its stony course to flow into the fen. The grove where they stopped to eat was no more than a clump of willows, but on the two hillsides that rose on either side of the valley the trees were oak and maple, beech and birch. A short distance up the valley the hillsides began pinching in, so that the stream ran in a narrow ravine. Walking here was difficult at times.

The valley kept on and on, burrowing into the hills. The ravine became narrower, and the heavy forest of the hills moved down until the trees arched above the stream, which had by now become little more than a trickle of water. A trail of sorts ran along the stream, at times crossing from one side to the other, and while it was better than no path at all, it was rough and twisting, filled with humping roots and half-buried stones. In late afternoon, they came to a path that branched off the main trail and went slanting up the hillside. When she came to it, Yolanda stopped, peering up the path.

"Stay here and wait for me," she told them. "I'll be back in just a moment."

Glad to halt and rest, they waited while she went bounding up the trail.

"The child never gets tired," said the abbot. "She runs and leaps like a zany goat, and she could keep it up forever."

Harcourt, standing on the path, felt the somberness of the forest. It crowded in upon them, as if intent on smothering them. Except for the tinkle of the water in the tiny stream, running on its rocky bed, and the soughing of the wind in the higher treetops, there was no sound.

Yolanda came running down the path. "I have found a place to spend the night," she said. "A cave. There has been someone living there, but he is not around. I do not think that he would mind."

"How could you possibly know that?" asked the Knurly Man.

"I do not know," she said. "I only think and hope."

"Perhaps," said the abbot, "we'll be up and away before anyone returns. Whoever he may be may never know that we were there."

They climbed the path and came to the cave. It was a fairly small one, shallow, not reaching back into the hillside for any distance. Out from its front extended a wide platform of level stone, which continued inward as the floor of the cave. On this platform, outside the opening of the cave, was a small firepit, with dead gray ashes and blackened chunks of half-burned wood. In one corner of the cave, blocks of wood propped up a rude pallet. Three pans and a movable cooking spit were stacked against the far wall. A neat pile of dry firewood stood ranked just inward of the cave's mouth. Next to the pans and spit, leathern bags were piled carefully on a platform of flat stones.

Stooping to keep his head clear of the cave's roof, the abbot ambled in and sat down on the pallet.

"By all means," said the Knurly Man, "make yourself at home."

"And why should I not?" the abbot asked. "If he be an honest man, our unknown host would want his guests to make themselves at home."

"There is a question in my mind," said the Knurly Man, "whether we are guests."

"That question you can put to rest," said a voice from the path below them. "You are indeed my guests and most welcome ones."

They turned about to see who had spoken to them. He was a small man, his face tanned by the sun almost to blackness, smooth-shaven, but with bristly stubs of whiskers showing. His eyes squinted at them, eyes that were accustomed to squinting against the sun, with tangled nests of crow's-feet at the corners. He carried an empty pack slung over one shoulder, although his shoulders were humped and thrust forward, as if he were accustomed to carrying a full and heavy pack. In one hand he grasped a pilgrim's staff. He was barefoot and his trousers were in tatters; a sheepskin vest with the wool side out covered his upper body.

"I'm Andre the peddler," he said, "and this is my humble home. You are the first visitors who have ever honored me in all the years I've been here, and I am glad you found me."

He came trudging up the path until he reached the stony platform. There he stopped and carefully looked them over.

"We are travelers," Harcourt told him, "just passing through."

The peddler put up a hand and wiped his face. "This is passing strange. We have few travelers in these parts. It is not a pleasant land."

"I am Charles, of Castle Harcourt just across the river. We seek my uncle, who is missing. We have reason to believe he is in the Empty Land. Perhaps you have some word of him."

The peddler shook his head. "I have no word of him. Not a hint of him. It is foolishness to wander here."

"My uncle," Harcourt told him, "is a foolish man. He always has been so."

"Well, for the moment, let that be," the peddler said. "You will spend the night. Longer if you wish. I will start a fire . . ."

"No," said the Knurly Man. "I will start a fire, and that great lout sitting on the pallet will go out to gather wood to replenish what we use. Should we augment your woodpile to a slight extent, it will be no more than poor payment for the hospitality that you offer."

"In a small pool just below where your path turned off," Yolanda said, "I noted swimming trout. I'll go and do my best to catch some fish for supper."

The peddler smiled. "Such obliging and helpful guests I have never heard of. Any host would be glad to have the four of you drop by." He said to Harcourt, "Your servants are well trained."

"They are not my servants," Harcourt told him. "They are friends of mine. The so-called lout who is leaving to gather wood is an abbot, and while he may do the chore most grudgingly, he nevertheless will do it."

"You are fortunate," said the peddler, "to have friends such as these."

"I think so, too," said Harcourt.

He did not like this man or trust him. The peddler had a foxy look about him and was just a shade too smooth. With this man it would be well to guard one's tongue. There was, on the surface, nothing that Harcourt could put a finger on, but when he tried to reason with himself, the feeling still persisted.

The peddler dropped the pack he carried on the foot of the pallet. Reaching into it, he brought out a handful of trinkets and dumped them on the blanket that covered the bed.

"My prices are not high," he said, "and I dicker quite a lot. I do not ask too much and I do not get too much, but, all in all, I manage."

There was an ancient copper coin, a length of broken necklace chain, a polished agate, a ring green with corrosion and a red stone set in it, a spear point of bronze, also green with age, and other odds and ends.

"The people know me," he said, "as a doddering idiot, not quite together in the head, a harmless man and a truthful one, too stupid to be more than truthful. They are not afraid of me; some of them may even trust me. I am safe in my wandering. I am welcome as the bringer of fresh tidings, of all kinds of news and gossip, sometimes even scandal, and when my supply of tidings may be slightly short, I spend a little time while I'm trudging along, to think up a sufficiency of it to titillate my clients."

"The people whom you deal with," Harcourt said. "Exactly who are they?"

"Why, just people, that is all. Oh, I see what you mean. Well, I tell you the truth. They are both humans and the Evil Ones. I make no distinction between the two of them. A sale to one of them is as profitable to me as a sale to the other."

"In which case," said Harcourt, "perhaps you can be of some help to us. That is, if you are of a mind to be."

"Certainly I am of a mind to be. I help everyone who asks."

The Knurly Man had a good fire going in the pit on the flat platform of stone beyond the cave mouth, and the abbot had brought in an armful of wood and was leaving to scrounge a second.

"After we have eaten," said the peddler, "we can sit around the fire and talk. You can ask me what you will."

And that was fine, Harcourt thought. But how much of what he told them could they believe?

"We'll be grateful," he told the peddler solemnly, "for any information that you can provide us."

Yolanda came up the path with a string of trout, and she and the Knurly Man sat beside the fire and began cleaning them. The peddler brought a skillet and a jar of cooking grease, and about that time the abbot came in with his second armload of wood and stacked it on the pile. He sat down heavily beside the fire.

Looking at the fish, he smacked his lips. "Good and fat," he said, "and fresh from the pool in which they swam."

"They are of excellent quality," the peddler told him. "When I find the time to catch them, I often make a meal of them." He studied the abbot. "From the condition of your cassock," he said, "it appears that you were mucking in the fen."

"We crossed the cursed place," the abbot said in disgust. "More than a mortal day it took us to plow our way across it."

"You could have gone around it," said the peddler, his tone implying that any sane man would have gone around it.

Harcourt cut off what the abbot was about to say. "There were special circumstances," he said, "that made it seem wise that we should cross it."

"Yes," said the peddler, "I can well imagine. At times special circumstances, as you call them, do have a tendency to arise. Especially in this place."

The fish were frying now, and they sat around and watched them fry.

"We have cheese and bread," Yolanda said, "and a slab of bacon. Perhaps a bit of bacon might enhance the trout."

"If you can spare it," said the peddler. "I trade for bacon now and then, but I've not tasted it for a month or more. There is nothing I would like more than a slice of bacon."

Yolanda cut several slices of the bacon and nestled them in the pan with the frying trout.

Sitting about the fire, they ate their meal. When it all was done, the peddler said, "You mentioned that you wished some information. What is it that you want? I suppose you might like to know what may lie ahead."

"That is right," said Harcourt. "We travel to the west. We have heard of an ancient cathedral that lies in that direction."

The peddler bore a thoughtful look. "You have a far way yet to go," he said. "I have never been there. I have not seen this cathedral of which you speak, but I have heard of it. All I can tell you is that you must travel west and ask as you go along."

"But whom do we ask?" said the Knurly Man. "Not the Evil, certainly. Will we meet other than the Evil?"

"There are humans," said the peddler. "You'll find them in hidden and secluded places. The Evil know that they are there, but do not bother them. What do you know of the Evil?"

"I stood for days against them on the castle wall seven years ago," said Harcourt.

"Ah, yes," the peddler said, "those were hard days, indeed. But your ordinary Evil Ones are not always vicious. They have their cyclic periods. There have been times when one could have walked through this land unscathed, other times when even I will not venture out, but stay in hiding. They are stricken by periods of madness, and when the madness is all over, they sink back to their usual obnoxious attitudes, but do not kill you out of hand. Now, I would think, might be a bad time. A cohort of Romans is on the loose somewhere to the north, and that does not improve their temper."

"You have heard naught else of the Romans?" the abbot asked. "Only that they are somewhere in the north?"

"A skirmish or two. Mere glancing blows, the kind that happen when small bands of enemies accidentally collide. Nothing serious."

"Then there is a chance," said Harcourt, "that nothing

serious will happen. The cohort is out on reconnaissance—that is all. The Romans are not looking for any confrontation."

"That could be true. I hope it is the case. Most of the Evil are massed along the far frontier lines, keeping ward against the invading barbarians—who, by the way, have not engaged in much invading recently, but are restless nonetheless. Raids by small bands of horsemen, but no large movements."

"Are there any points of danger that we should be aware of?" the Knurly Man asked. "Any areas that we should skirt around? Whatever in this wise you can tell us would be valuable."

"Some leagues to the west, beyond a rather large river, is a valley inhabited by harpies. They move around in their hunting, but stay fairly well in one sizable stretch of land. Once you cross the river, you must be alert for them. They are ugly creatures."

"Any dragons?" the abbot asked.

"You never can tell about dragons," said the peddler. "They can be anywhere. Always make a close survey of the sky before you venture out into open spaces. As much as possible, stick close to the trees. They can't get at you when you are among trees. Watch out for bridges. Trolls are partial to bridges. But you know that, of course."

"Yes, we do," the abbot said.

"You might ask, as you go along and have the opportunity, about a certain well. An ancient well, said to be at one time a place of pilgrimage. The legend is that if you bend over the crumbling stone wall that encloses it and look down into the water, you may be able to discern the future reflected in the water. I do not guarantee this. I am inclined to have my doubts. But the stories that are told of it are very interesting, and I have heard many of them."

"We'll ask about it along the way," Harcourt said, speaking carelessly.

The fire had burned down and the night was creeping in. The treetops on which the cave looked out swayed gently in the wind. The east was flushed, signaling the rising of the moon.

The peddler rose from where he sat and went into the cave. There he rummaged in one of the leather sacks that were piled atop the stone platform. He came back to the fire with an object in his hand. The firelight glinted on it when he handed it to Yolanda. It was a thing of beauty, or seemed to be when the firelight caught it. It flashed with iridescent color and its shape was strange—a spiral with a flaring horn at one end.

Yolanda turned it around and around in her hands, trying to make some sense of it.

"What is it?" she asked. "It's beautiful, of course, but what could it be?"

"It is a seashell," said the peddler, "brought from a distant ocean. It still carries the sea within it. Put it to your ear and you can hear the sea."

Unbelievingly, Yolanda placed the fluted horn against an ear. Her eyes widened as she listened, and her mouth dropped open. She listened for a long time while the others watched. Finally she took it from her ear and handed it to the abbot, who, after twisting it about to examine it more carefully, put it to his ear.

"Almighty God," he shouted, "it does carry the sea, or what I judge must be the sea, for I've never seen a sea. Like the roaring of great waters."

The peddler laughed in a rather wicked way. "I told you so. Did you not believe me?"

"Things of great wonder I do not believe," the abbot said, "until I have the proof in hand."

He passed the shell to Harcourt, and when Harcourt lifted it to his ear, he heard the roaring—as the abbot had said, like unto the roar of mighty waters.

He took down the shell. "I do not understand," he said. "How could a shell like this carry and retain the sound of the sea within it? Even carried many leagues from the sea, how could it retain the sound?"

The Knurly Man reached out and took the shell from him, but did not put it to his ear. "It is an old wives' tale," he said. "The sound you hear is not the roaring of the sea. It is something else. I have no explanation for it, nor, I suppose, does anyone. But it's not the sea you hear."

"Pray tell me what it is, then," said the peddler.

"I have told you," said the Knurly Man. "I've told you I don't know, which is as honest an answer as you're likely to come by. But I can tell you that it is not the sea."

He handed the shell to the peddler, but the peddler shook his head. "Don't give it to me," he said. "Give it to milady. It is a gift for her."

Thirteen

The next morning they got a late start. The peddler seemed loath to let them leave. He sat at the breakfast fire and prattled at them, but told them nothing of what they wished to hear. When questions were asked him, he either claimed no knowledge or launched into a wild tale that, on the face of it, was myth.

Finally, however, they were able to break away and went toiling up the narrow valley, following the twisted path. The sun had passed its zenith before they reached the crest of the range of hills. Here the forest was more open than it had been along the stream.

They halted briefly to eat from their packs, not bothering with a fire.

"I had hoped," said the Knurly Man, "that the peddler might have been some help to us. But he was not, and that is strange. He must travel widely in this country and in his wanderings must learn of many things."

"I did not trust the man," said the abbot. "Even had he told us of anything that might have been of value, I would not have trusted him."

"He told us nothing," said the Knurly Man. "He babbled about a flock of harpies, but gave us no specifics. He read us a primer lesson on how to avoid dragons and told us to be wary of bridges for fear of trolls."

"I did not trust him, either," Harcourt told them. "He had a foxy look."

"And the folk tale that he told us about the seashell," said the Knurly Man. "As if it were the truth. I can tell you that it is not the truth. I have seen the sea and have listened to it, and the sound within the shell is not the voice of the sea."

"He did tell us," said the abbot, "that the cathedral lay somewhere to the west. But that we already knew. We should have asked him about the villa, or the palace, whatever it may be, where the prism lies."

Harcourt shook his head. "That we should not have asked.

87

That could give away our game. As far as he or anyone else may be concerned, we are only looking for my errant uncle."

After they had eaten, they went on, following the crest of the ridge.

"It will carry us north," Yolanda told them, "but perhaps not too far. Following it, we may find easier land to travel."

They went into camp shortly before the fall of night. After the evening meal was over, Yolanda sat to one side, by herself, with the seashell held against her ear. After a time, Harcourt got up from where he was sitting and went over to her, crouching down beside her.

She took the seashell from her ear and placed it in her lap.

"You are fascinated with it," he said, "by the sound of the sea inside it."

She smiled at him. "Not by the sound, although the sound is strange and haunting. It is not only that. When I listen, it seems to me that there is someone talking, that back of the sea sound, beyond the sea sound, there is a voice that tries to tell me something."

"Magic?" he asked. "A magic voice?"

She frowned, considering what he'd said.

"What is magic?" he asked. "Can you tell me what magic is?"

"My lord," she said, "you ask me riddles."

"I had not meant to do so. I had thought that you might be able to tell me what magic is. It is a word very often used. It falls easily from the lips—a glib explanation when there is no other."

"And you thought you might find the answer from a simple lass. One who wanders occasionally in the Empty Land and is unable, or unwilling, to say why she wanders there. One who can see a shape within a tree . . ."

"I had not thought that at all," he said. But, he told himself sheepishly, that had been exactly what he'd thought. "If I have offended you . . ."

"You have not offended me," she said.

She lifted the shell from her lap and put it against her ear once more. Harcourt, taking this as dismissal, went back to sit beside the abbot.

The journey was going smoothly, he thought. They had had their trouble with the forest mounds and their trouble in the fen, but had faced no actual menace. There had so far been no evidence of the Evil, no hint that the Evil as yet had guessed that they were here. And that, of course, had been exactly what they'd hoped, but that hope, he knew, had not been realistic.

"Guy," he asked the abbot, "do you have the feeling that events are going just a bit too smoothly?"

"Yes, the thought has occurred to me," the abbot said, "but I am glad they are. This, however, is only the fourth day of our travels."

"Perhaps I worry unduly," Harcourt said, "but I have a prickle at the nape of my neck, a funny tingle in my shoulder blades. As if I could feel the eyes that are watching us. Tensed, ready to jump."

"I recognize the feeling," the abbot said, "but I try to put it down. I do not borrow trouble. I'm happy as it goes."

"Yolanda thinks that she can hear a voice in the shell. A voice that is drowned out by the roaring of the sea."

"A young girl's fancy," said the abbot.

"I know. That's probably it. But I do not trust the peddler. I do not like the shell."

The abbot laid a beefy hand on Harcourt's shoulder. "Steady on," he said. "Do not borrow trouble."

The next day the ridge that they had been following pinched out, and they came to a small plateau that bordered the river hills. It was a land of gentle swales but no steep heights to climb, and they turned west again.

"We've moved too far north," said Harcourt. "It might have been better if we'd stayed with the hills."

They had halted for a rest, and at Harcourt's words, the Knurly Man pulled from his belt pouch the map that Harcourt's Uncle Raoul had drawn for them. He spread it out, and the others leaned over his shoulders to have a look at it.

"It's hard to make out," said the Knurly Man. "The scale is not true to distance, but I make it that we're about here." He laid a finger on the map.

"If you are right," said Harcourt, "we're still a safe distance south of the Roman road."

"The map's no good," Yolanda said. "It does not show the fen."

"More than likely," Harcourt told her, "my uncle did not know about the fen. He probably crossed the country north of it."

"The cathedral is still a long way off," said the abbot, "but it would seem that it lies due west of us."

"Then," said the Knurly Man, "that is our answer. We keep on going west."

He folded the map and thrust it back into the pouch.

The plateau was less densely wooded than the hills had been. The forest was thinner and the trees were smaller. At times they came on small openings, short distances of unwooded land. Some of these may have been the sites of abandoned homesteads, but they saw no signs of buildings. They crossed the openings at a rapid pace, keeping a watch for dragons, but there were no dragons.

Occasionally they crossed small brooks wending their way into the river hills. The day was fine and sunny, not too warm, and with no clouds in the sky.

Yolanda, as was her custom, walked some distance ahead of them, but kept within their sight. Shortly after noon they caught up with her. She was waiting for them.

"Is something wrong?" asked Harcourt.

"I smell smoke," she said. She pointed. "I think it is down there."

"It could be humans," said the Knurly Man. "The Evil are not great ones for fire. They do not cook their meat."

"We'd better spread out," said Harcourt. "And, for God's sake, move with caution and keep a sharp lookout. If there are humans, we don't want to scare them off. We need any information they can give us."

"And if it's the Evil," said the Knurly Man, "we want to spot them before they see us."

They spread out and moved cautiously and slowly down the slope that led to the ravine Yolanda had pointed out. Halfway down, Harcourt caught the acrid scent of smoke. Yolanda had been right; there was a fire down there. Bending low, he crept down the slope, swiveling his head from side to side to sweep the terrain.

A guttural sound halted him in his tracks. He glanced to the right, from which the sound had come. The Knurly Man was crouched low against the ground. When he noticed Harcourt staring at him, he pointed, and Harcourt, looking in the direction the Knurly Man had indicated, saw the thin, faint blueness of drifting smoke.

He raised his hand and made a motion to go forward. Keeping low, he worked himself slowly down the slope. Glancing to his right, he saw that the Knurly Man was also moving, and just beyond him, the abbot. He could not see

Yolanda. Damn the girl, he thought, where is she? Is she always on her own? Then, on his left, he saw her, well ahead of them, flitting from one tree to another, a sense of motion only, blending with the background.

He scurried forward a few paces, then stopped, freezing against the ground. The fire was down there, in the floor of the ravine. A mean hut stood beside a small stream that went foaming down the cleft between the hills. A wood structure straddled the stream. A mill, he thought; for the love of God, a mill! The mill wheel flashed in the sunlight, its blades dropping a spray of water as it turned. On the superstructure, above the wheel, a wooden cage rocked back and forth. There was something in the cage, but he could not make out what it was. Irritated squalling came from the cage, but whether the sound came from the cage or from the thing inside the cage, he could not be certain.

A man knelt beside the mill wheel, working with a mallet and a chisel on a block of wood. He appeared to be an old man, for his long hair, falling over his shoulders, and his beard, falling down his chest, were white. He kept on working with the mallet and the chisel, apparently unaware that he was not alone.

Harcourt examined the scene closely. There was no one else about, no one he could see. Someone might be in the hut, he knew, but there was no one else in sight. The kneeling old man kept on working on the block of wood.

Harcourt rose to his feet and, walking softly, began to approach the kneeling man. But the abbot, he saw, had beat him to it. He was striding across the little plot of level ground that formed the floor of the ravine, moving, huge and massive, with a stately, churchly tread.

The old man dropped the chisel and the mallet, leaping to his feet. Staring at the abbot, he stood poised, ready to take to his heels. Then, suddenly, it appeared to dawn upon him who the cassocked, bare-polled man might be, and he sprang forward, racing for the abbot. He skidded, falling to his knees, clasped hands held piously on his breast. In a piteous tone, he bleated, "Bless me, Father! Bless me!"

The abbot raised a hand in blessing, mumbling Latin, making the sign of the cross, then reached down and lifted the man to his feet.

"I never thought I'd live to feel the touch of Mother Church again," the old man quavered. "I thought I was lost forever. I thought I was forsaken."

"The Good Lord," said the abbot, "never forsakes His children."

"But I took precautions," said the old man. "Perhaps in dismal ignorance. But I improvised."

"How, my son, did you improvise?" the abbot asked gently.

"Well, I had the bird, you see, the parrot."

"How in the world, in the Empty Land, did you come upon a parrot? Did you say a parrot?"

"Yes, Father, a parrot."

"And would you tell me, pray, what a parrot is? I've heard of many birds, but never of a . . ."

"A parrot," said the Knurly Man, "is a jungle bird, found deep in southern climes. It is picturesque, all green and blue and red, and it is capable, if rightly trained, of aping human speech."

"Indeed, that is right," said the old man, "but it requires much patience, and there are times one fails. I tried to teach it the Lord's Prayer, but that was beyond its capability, and, failing in that, I tried Hail Mary, but I failed in that as well. Finally, the best that I could do was to teach it 'God bless my soul,' but the silly bird runs all the words together . . ."

"God bless my soul," said the flabbergasted abbot. "You mean you taught the bird to mouth 'God bless my soul'?"

"Father," the old man pleaded, "it was the best that I could do. I tried the Lord's Prayer and Hail Mary, but . . ."

"And for what purpose?" asked the abbot.

"Why," said the old man, astonished at the abbot's failure to perceive his purpose, "I thought that I should have someone interceding for me, and since I did not have someone, I thought a bird would do. The bird, I told myself, would be better than nothing. Father, do you not agree?"

"I'm not certain that I do," the abbot said sternly. "It would have been far better if you, yourself . . ."

"But, Father, I did. I'm most faithful in my prayers. I fair wear myself out in the saying of them."

"Why, then, the bird?"

"Father, certainly you must see. I thought the bird would provide me an extra margin. And I need, surrounded as I am by vicious evil, all the margin I can get."

The Knurly Man asked, "Is that the bird in the cage?"

"Yes, good sir, it is."

"But why in a cage? If you freed it, it wouldn't fly away, would it? And why in a cage hung above the mill wheel? Certainly you could find a better place to hang it."

"To appreciate why it is there, you must know something I will tell you. That stupid bird will only say 'God bless my soul' when it is upside down, when it is hanging upside down upon its perch."

"And why is that?"

"Forsooth, sir, I do not know. I only know it is the case. So there was but one thing I could do. I had to devise a way that would ensure that the bird would be upside down at periodic intervals. So I built a cage with one perch only in it. Then I built the water wheel and attached the cage to the motion of the wheel. As the wheel goes round, so also does the cage, which means that at each spinning of the wheel, a part of the time the bird is upside down."

"But the cage is not going around now," Yolanda pointed out. "The wheel is going round, but the cage is not."

"That, alas, is because a sprocket that drives the cage is broken. It split quite in two. I am now engaged in fashioning a new sprocket. As soon as I have it finished, the cage will go around again."

"How long have you been here?" Yolanda asked.

"I cannot count the years. I was a young man when I came here."

"The bird came with you?"

"Yes, the bird came with me. We've been together long."

"You mean that all these years the bird has been going round in the cage? You, sir, should be ashamed of yourself."

"Not all these years," the old man told her. "It took me years to teach him to say 'God bless my soul.' Before I could accomplish that, I had to unteach him the words that he did know. I obtained him from a sailor, and the words the sailor had taught him would have made a strong man blanch."

"What I can't understand," said Harcourt, "is why you ever came here. No man in his right senses would come to the Empty Land."

"I beg your pardon, sir," said the man, "but you are here, aren't you?"

"With us," the abbot said, "the matter is quite different. There is a purpose in our being here."

"I also had a purpose. I envisioned myself as a missionary to the Evil here. I told myself that I had the stamina and capability to become a holy man. I thought that I had within myself the fortitude to become a martyr, if martyr I should turn out to be."

"But you did not become a holy man. You achieved no martyrdom."

"I was weak," said the old man. "My courage failed me. I could not go through with it. I tried to leave, I tried to run away, but they would not let me, and . . ."

"Who would not let you?" the abbot asked.

"The Evil would not let me. They would turn me back when I tried to run away. So I found this hidden place and hunkered down in it, and I tried to build a wall of devotion and of prayers to protect my craven body and purify my soul."

"You quit trying to get back to your own people? You just hunkered here?"

"No. Many times I tried to leave, and still they wouldn't let me. I had thought that I was hidden, but I wasn't. They found out I was here, and each time I tried to leave, they turned me back. Sometimes it would be an ogre or a troll that turned me back, sometimes a harpy, sometimes something else. They never tried to hurt me; they just turned me back. They played cat and mouse with me. They snickered at me even as they turned me back. They crouch there atop the hill and they chuckle at me. They only chuckle; they never laugh aloud. They never intrude into this ravine; they stay upon the hilltop. I see them sometimes, but not often, but I hear them chuckling. On the day they come down here, that will be the end of me. They'll come only when they are tired of playing cat and mouse with me, and then they will kill me."

"You spoke earlier of a wall that you tried to build, a wall of piety. This chattering parrot was part of your attempt to build the wall?"

"I did my best. I worked with what I had."

"You trained the parrot to recite 'God bless my soul.' What good could that have done you? The parrot, on the face of what you've told us, was asking God, not to bless your soul, but his. 'My soul,' it would say, not 'my friend's soul,' not 'my owner's soul,' not 'this human's soul.' Even you must realize that is ridiculous. A parrot has no soul."

"I intended," said the man, "that he be interceding for me. I had to make it simple. I had trouble enough teaching him the words I did without making what I meant explicit. I think that God must understand."

"So help me," said the stricken abbot, "I have never heard the like."

"Clearly the man is mad," said the Knurly Man. "A rational man would never think to be a missionary to the Evil. To the pagan, yes. Even to the infidel, for there could be some hope for him. But to the Evil, never. The Evil stands for everything we're not, be we Christian, infidel, or pagan."

"Mad I may be," said the man, "but each one to his madness. I have followed my own light. I have no apology to make."

"In error and unrepentant," said the abbot. "In error in so many ways, including, first of all, no clear understanding, even now, of what you did. My son, you have much to answer for, many tears to shed . . ."

"Hold up a minute, Guy," said Harcourt. "Where lies your Christian charity? This man represents the very people of whom you must be most forgiving. There must be some good in the man, if no more than simple courage, who could for years live huddled in this place."

"And what is more," said the Knurly Man, "he might be of some service to us. What would you say," he asked the man, "if we help you? Would you be of help to us?"

"Quite willingly," said the man, "but in what wise could you be of help to such as I?"

"You have said that you are not allowed to leave this place, that the Evil will not allow your leaving, that when you try to leave, they always turn you back. Well, you can leave with us. We'll offer you protection and . . ."

"You mean leave this place?"

"That is what I mean. That is what you want. You have tried to leave . . ."

"It's the one safe place I have," the man protested. "Here they let me be. They watch me and they chuckle at me and they mock me, but so far they've done me no harm. If I went with you, that protection I enjoy here would be gone, and furthermore, by going with you, I'd bring their full wrath down upon you and . . ."

"All right, then. If you don't want to leave, we can be of help in another fashion. Milady is skilled in the working of wood. She can make the sprocket that you need to make the cage go round. She can do it with dispatch and very workmanly."

"That, indeed," said the man, "would be of help to me. I can manage it myself, but at great labor and inexpertly."

"In return," said the Knurly Man, "you can tell us of the country toward the west. We travel in that direction and have little knowledge of it."

The man shook his head. "That I cannot do. As I have told you, I have not left this ravine in many years, have not been allowed to leave. I know nothing of what may lie around me."

"Well, there is another idea gone to pot," said Harcourt.

"This one and the peddler," said the abbot. "Neither of them worth a damn to us."

"Even so," said Yolanda, "out of charity, I'll carve the sprocket for him."

Something happened. Harcourt did not see it happen, but he knew the moment that it happened, and so, apparently, did all the others of them. The place seemed to change abruptly, and there was a quality about it that had not been there before. All of them, no matter what they had been doing, stiffened into stark postures; whatever sound there had been stopped, and a silence fell upon them, as if they had been cut away from all the world.

It was only for a moment—perhaps no longer than a heartbeat, certainly no longer than the drawing of a breath—but whatever it was played strange tricks with time, for it seemed much longer than a heartbeat or a breath.

The old man was the first of them to recover. He let out a bleat of fright and leaped up in the air, turning his body even as he leaped. When he hit the ground again, he was headed in the opposite direction, and even before his feet hit, he was running. When his feet did hit, he squirted out of sight, running down the ravine in a frenzied rush.

Harcourt, as if some sixth sense warned him where to look —and perhaps it did, although he could not remember later if it had—swung about and saw the ogre. He was well out of the trees and halfway across the clearing, moving forward with a shambling walk. He was black and huge, gross of face and body, and extremely fat. His bulging belly hung down so far as to half obscure his dangling genitals. He had not a stitch of clothes upon him. His barbed tail switched behind him.

Harcourt's hand went to his sword hilt, and there was a harsh scrape of steel as he began the draw.

"Put away your blade," the ogre told him, still shambling forward as he spoke. "I have no designs upon you. There is no need for us to go at one another."

Harcourt shoved the sword back into the scabbard but kept his hand upon the hilt.

The ogre squatted down upon the ground. "Come," he said, "let us sit down and reason together. We may find much benefit for all of us in a time of open chatter. And tell that devoted churchman to lower that hefty mace of his." He turned his head toward the Knurly Man. "You're the only one of sense among them. You made no movement toward your axe. Even the fair young lady had an arrow nocked."

"Sir Ogre," said the Knurly Man, "had there been need of the axe, I'd have had it in that overgrown gut of yours before you could count to one."

The Ogre chuckled. "I have no doubt of that. I have no doubt at all. I've heard stories of you or of others very like you."

Harcourt stepped forward and squatted down face to face with the ogre. It was aged, he noticed. It had appeared all black at first glance, but now Harcourt saw a scattering of gray hairs upon the shoulders and the chest. The fangs that extended from its upper jaw were yellowed, and the ogre lacked a left hand. The forearm came down to a blunt termination and was capped with a cup of metal, bound upon the arm. On the one remaining hand, triangular, razor-sharp claws extended, yellowed with age as well.

"I'm Harcourt," Harcourt told him, "from south of the river."

"I know who you are," the ogre said. "I knew from the very start. Your face is one I will not forget. Seven years ago, I faced you on the castle wall." He lifted the handless arm. "I owe this to you," he said.

"I don't recall," said Harcourt. "Much of what happened took place in a blur. Much of the time we were hard beset."

"We would not have fought at all," the ogre said, "if we could have controlled our young bloods. We cannot control them yet."

"You sound like a man of peace."

"Not a man of peace," the ogre said. "I hate you and all others like you as much as it is possible for one thing to hate another. Willingly I would rip your throat out. But prudent policy forbids me the pleasure of it."

"I and my fellows are no threat to you," said Harcourt. "We are on a simple mission. Once it is accomplished, we will leave. We seek my uncle, a most foolish man who, we learn, has intruded into the Empty Land for reasons that we do not know. Once we have found him, we'll go home. We seek no confrontation."

"We know of your uncle," said the ogre. "A most slippery one. He escaped us—how, we do not know. I would have thought that by now he would have made his way across the river. He messed into something that was none of his concern. I hope you have, for your sake, no such inclination."

"None at all," Harcourt said piously. "I know not what you mean and I do not want to know."

"I must warn you most solemnly," said the ogre, "that if you do not sincerely mean what you are saying, it will be the end of you—not only you, but all of you—this sanctimonious abbot who trails along with you, the atavistic being that you call the Knurly Man, even the maid, who, I understand, is half of our world, half of yours. We'll not do it prettily, I can assure you. There will be entrails scattered all about."

"Now you are threatening us," said Harcourt, "and I cannot let that pass. If you have an overwhelming hankering to do some entrail scattering, I'll be glad to afford you the opportunity. Just you and I together."

"Nay, nay, my good fellow. That is the last thing I would think of at the moment. Why do you persist in your belligerency?"

"I persist in it," said Harcourt, "because you, yourself, have been more than commonly loose-lipped in that regard."

"The truth is," said the ogre, "that this is a bad time for you to be here. You couldn't have chosen a worse time. There is a ragtag of stupid Romans staggering about the landscape. The very fact of their being here has aroused violent antagonism against all humans."

"I had understood there were Romans here," said Harcourt. "I could have hoped they would not come. But since they are here, there is little I can do about it. Even had I known about it, I could not have stopped their coming."

"You lie most prettily about the Romans," said the ogre. "Nay, keep your blade in sheath. There is no need for you and me to contend. But I am sure you knew about the Romans before they came tramping in. You could not halt their progress or intentions, that I am sure, but you did know about them. And I suspect there is more to your coming here than looking for a footloose uncle, though that I will not charge you with. But in the name of peace, do nothing to stir up the animals. That is all I ask of you."

"I sense," said Harcourt, "that you are actually of good will. And since you know my name, I'd be honored to know yours."

"My formal name," said the ogre, "is so grandiose and so

complex that it is ridiculous. Among my acquaintances I go by the name of Agard."

"I thank you for telling me," said Harcourt. "Next to knowing the name of friends, it would seem important to know the names of enemies."

"We cannot speak, of course, as friends," said the ogre, "but we can act, for the moment, like honest gentlemen. I came to let you know that we are aware of you and shall be watching you. Unless you transgress too greatly, we shall offer you no harm. Or, rather, perhaps, I should say that I'll do my utmost to see you're not offered any harm. Right at this time the last thing that I need is an event that will whet the passions of our young bloods. If only these fumbling Romans can be herded out of here without a bloody incident, I shall be well pleased. We have the barbarians to the north and east; I would just as soon avoid Roman legions hacking at us from the south. A minor massacre involving the four of you would serve to heat up the temper of our intemperate youngsters."

"I suppose you are working around to warning us out of the country."

"To be frank with you, I'd be greatly obliged if you did pick up and go. But I don't suppose I can persuade you on that score."

"Well, you see," said Harcourt, "there is this uncle of mine. I have great regard for him."

"Then find him quickly and get out. For my sake and for your own, accomplish it as circumspectly as you can. We have trouble enough without you stirring up a storm. Keep as clear as you can of trouble. Stay well south of the Roman road. Do not push your luck. And don't stay around too long."

"That is our intention," said Harcourt. "Not to stay around too long. In a few days either we'll have word of my uncle or we won't. In either case, we'll soon be gone."

"Well, then," said the ogre, "since we understand one another, I'll be on my way. You know, of course, that this visit with you is no evidence of good will on my part. I do it entirely for my selfish reasons. I want to keep the country calmed down so there'll not be a wholesale killing of the Romans; we do not want the Empire on our back. You can thank pure politics for the saving of your skins."

"I know all that," said Harcourt. "And while I enjoyed this conference with you, I would hope we do not meet again."

"So do I," the ogre said. "I hope it most fervently."

He rose to his feet and, deliberately turning his back on them, walked shambling up the hill. They watched him until he was out of sight.

"Exactly what was that all about?" the abbot asked.

"I'm not sure," said Harcourt. "Knowing the Evil, we are quick to ascribe nefarious motives to them. But in this particular case, I am half inclined to put some faith in what he told us. He is old, probably an elder statesman of his people. And he is in a bind. He's got trouble enough in the north and east without more trouble from the south. I don't know if roughing up the Romans would bring him new trouble from the south. God knows, the legions are not what they were at one time, but you never know about the policies of Rome. You would think the Empire might value the Empty Land as a buffer against the vandals, but, as I say, you never know . . ."

"Now we know the Evil are aware of us," said the Knurly Man. "They may have been watching us for the last couple of days. There are only four of us. If they were of a mind to and were willing to take losses, they could kill us any time they wish."

"They are playing cat and mouse with us," Yolanda said. "Snickering at us. As they did with the old man. If they'd been about to kill us, they'd have walked in here and killed us. Perhaps they could have done it at any time in the last three days."

"I suppose the safest thing for us," the abbot said, "would be to cut and run. They'd probably not try to stop us. But I'm disinclined to do it."

"So am I," said Harcourt. "We, all of us, should be scared enough to do exactly that, but for some strange reason I'm not scared. I've never had good sense."

"Neither have I," said the Knurly Man. "I think we should go on."

"I wonder," said Harcourt, "what happened to our man. He took off as if hell were gaping for him."

"He probably hasn't stopped running yet," said the Knurly Man. "This time he may really get away."

"Awrrk!" the parrot shrilled.

"We can't linger here," the abbot said. "I don't think we should. We should be looking for a defensible position where we can hole up for the night. What do we do about that bird? What if its master decides to keep on going?"

"We let it out," Yolanda said. "We can't leave it caged, to starve."

With no further word, she strode to the mill and scrambled up the superstructure. Fumbling for a moment with the cage, she found the peg that closed the door and pulled it. The parrot, coming out, flapped to the top plank of the superstructure and there strutted back and forth, grumbling to itself.

Yolanda scrambled down. "He can manage for himself," she said. "He'll find seed and fruit to eat."

"Awrrk," the parrot said.

"It's a handsome bird, it is," said the abbot. "More showy than our peacocks."

The parrot flapped up into the air and dived toward the abbot. Startled, the abbot ducked to get away, but the parrot landed on his shoulder.

"Godblessmysoul!" it chortled. "Godblessmysoul. Godblessmysoul."

Amused, Harcourt said, "I thought it only said that when it was upside down."

"It is overwhelmed by the sanctity of our abbot friend," said the Knurly Man.

The abbot twisted his head around to look at it. The parrot clicked its beak, half playfully, barely missing his nose.

"Abbot," Yolanda said, "it has taken to you. It recognizes you as the one kind man among us."

"Milady," the abbot said severely, "I would take it kindly if you did not slander me."

Harcourt heard the faint rustle in the heavy bushes that flanked the near side of the ravine. He jerked his head around and saw the body flying through the air. It dangled limply as it flew, its arms flapping, knees jerking, head flopping. It landed with a soggy thud, slowly sinking in upon itself. Looking down at it, Harcourt saw the long white hair, the long white beard. There could be no doubt the man was dead.

Harcourt's hand went to the sword hilt, jerking free the blade. There was nothing in the bushes, nothing anywhere. The ravine drowsed in the sun of early afternoon. In the quietness he heard the faint buzzing of a fly.

"So he didn't make it," said the Knurly Man. "This time they didn't turn him back."

From the bushes on the hillside something chuckled throatily.

Fourteen

They fled west, looking for some spot where they could hole up for the night.

"A cave," the abbot panted, hurrying along beside Harcourt, "a clump of boulders, almost anything at all. Where we can place our backs against protection and need only face the front."

"There may be no need," said Harcourt. "They may not be following us." Although, if the prickling hairs at the nape of his neck meant anything, they were.

"But the old man—they killed the old man and threw him at our feet."

"Perhaps only as a warning. To underline the warning of our ancient ogre."

"With my back against a wall, a wall of any sort," the abbot said, "I'd face an army of them."

"Hush up," said the Knurly Man. "Save your breath for travel. Yolanda is out scouting. She'll find something for us."

They traveled at first through woodland that, as they progressed, changed to heavy forest, huge majestic trees that formed a massive canopy, shutting out the sky, shutting out the world. They moved in a hushed gloom. There was no song of birds, no scurrying of small animal life. The parrot rode on the abbot's shoulder, hunched in upon itself, apparently subdued by the silent world through which they made their way.

It was sheer bad luck, Harcourt told himself, that they should be so soon discovered by the Evil. It had been his hope that, taking a route well south of the Roman road, they could reach the cathedral, perhaps beyond the cathedral, without the Evil becoming aware of them. But that, he now knew, had been foolishness. What had made him think so, he could not now imagine. Somehow they would have to break free of their followers, if there were followers. There had so far been no sign of them, but he was certain they were there. They had been all around the old man's ravine, and there his group had walked into them, as if into a trap, well baited. Although if what the ancient ogre had said was true, they had been known to the Evil well before they had reached the ravine.

"It seems wrong to me," the abbot said, "that we did not pause long enough to give our old man a decent burial."

"There was no time," the Knurly Man told him, "for mummery of that kind. He was dead, and nothing further could be done for him."

"I did the best I could," the abbot said.

"You wasted time," said the Knurly Man, "mumbling over him and making cabalistic signs . . ."

"They were not cabalistic signs, and you know they weren't."

"Shut up, the two of you," said Harcourt. "Cease your squabbling."

They ceased their squabbling.

The sun was an hour or more from setting, but the forest was growing darker, and where there had been no wind, now a strong wind sprang up. The great trees moaned as they bent before it, and there were leaves and other small debris flying in the air.

"A storm," the abbot muttered. "Now, on top of all else, we are about to face a storm."

"Perhaps only a few gusts of wind," said the Knurly Man. "As yet no rain is falling. Even if it does, it will not be the first time we have been rained upon."

They held doggedly to their course, bowing against the occasional gusts of wind. Here, on the forest floor, they were protected against the full brunt of the gale. Finally the heavier gusts of wind died down and the forest stopped its moaning. Through the trees ahead they saw occasional streaks of lightning, and from afar came the faint rumbling of thunder.

Quite suddenly, the forest ended, and they came out onto the shelving bank of a river. Yolanda was waiting for them there.

"I could not find what you wanted," she said, "but there is an island in the river. That may serve our purpose."

"That is far better than nothing," Harcourt said. "If the ogres come, we can see them come."

"It is a strange island," she said, "unlike any I have ever seen before. It is a cypress island."

"A cypress island?" Harcourt asked.

"An island covered by cypress trees. Even more gloomy than this forest."

"There is little cypress in this land," said the abbot. "Only a few here and there, imported in the older days from another land."

"It's all we have," said Harcourt. "Make what you will of it, it is all we've got." He said to Yolanda, "We are grateful that you found it."

The river, while not as great as the river that formed the boundary of the Empty Land, was still of a respectable size. It flowed slowly and with dignity through the heavy forest that lined either side of it. In the black sky that loomed beyond the river, the lightning continued to flash and the thunder rumbled.

"It can be waded," said Yolanda. "In its deepest, it came no higher than slightly above my middle."

The Knurly Man laid his hand on Harcourt's arm. "I seem to know this place," he said.

"How could you?" Harcourt asked. "You've not been here before."

"That is true, but I find it in my memory. The island, the shape of the trees, perhaps the very river. It all comes back to me, and yet I can't tell where it comes from. As if from very long ago. It comes from ancient roots. Perhaps it was not I who saw it, but someone else."

"Ancestral memory," said the abbot. "There are those who say there is no ancestral memory and others who say there is. It is a question of deep philosophy."

"Until this very moment, I have never heard of it," said Harcourt. "Are you sure it's not just something that you now thought up?"

"No, it's not," the abbot said stiffly. "It is in the literature. I have read of it."

"Well, then, what are we going to do about it? Are we going to seek refuge on that island, or do we cross the river and go stumbling on? On the island we'll at least be able to see or hear the Evil before it comes piling in on us."

"As to that, there is no question," said the abbot. "We'll take refuge on the island."

"What have you to say?" Harcourt asked the Knurly Man.

"The island," the Knurly Man replied.

"Yolanda, you've been strangely quiet."

"I told you," she said. "It is a strange island, strange in disturbing ways. But, as you have said, it is all we have."

Harcourt stepped into the stream. The flowing water tugged gently at him. The dark storm cloud in the west had blotted out the little daylight that was left. High above the trees on the farther bank, the lightning snarled and crackled, and the thunder now was a never-ending rumble. The gusts of wind that had preceded the storm had died away, but now new gusts were sweeping in to ruffle the surface of the river.

Walking beside him, Yolanda said quietly, "Once we reach the island, there'll be shelter."

"Shelter?" Harcourt asked. "You had not mentioned it before. What kind of shelter?"

"A building back among the trees. I don't know what kind of building. I hesitated to say anything about it. It's so old and sinister."

"Old and sinister it may be," said Harcourt, "it still is shelter from the storm."

In the gloom of the cypress woods, he told himself, any kind of building, even the most commonplace, would acquire a sinister look.

At midstream the water came up almost to his waist, then the bottom began shelving upward toward the island. He looked back and saw that the other two were following. The parrot that rode the abbot's shoulder had its claws dug deep, huddling against the threat of the storm.

Harcourt and Yolanda reached the island shore and stood for a moment, looking at the trees, waiting for the abbot and the Knurly Man.

"Does it seem to you," Harcourt asked, "that these trees are planted trees? Planted in rows. As if someone planted them."

"Yes, it did seem so to me. I told myself that I was confused and imagining it."

"I don't think you imagined it. I think they are. Where lies the shelter that you spoke of?"

"Up that way." She pointed up an avenue formed by the methodically placed trees.

"Then let us find it," said Harcourt. "The storm is about to break."

He turned and waved to the abbot and the Knurly Man. "Come on," he shouted to make himself heard above the thunder. "This way to shelter."

Not waiting for them, he started down the avenue formed by the trees, Yolanda trotting along behind him.

The gloom among the trees had deepened. Only the flashes of lightning, which were continuous now, lighted their way.

In the flicker of the flashes, Harcourt caught a fleeting glimpse of the shelter. He had expected that it might be no more than a small tumbledown hut. It was no such thing. It

was not small and it was not tumbledown. It was massive—
great blocks of stone that appeared black in the lightning
flashes, piled atop one another, the top of the structure lost in
the trees. Two great monolithic blocks of stone, with a third
as massive bridging them, outlined a doorway. In the flicker
of the lightning, Harcourt imagined that he saw hieroglyphic
scrawlings carved into the stone, but the flicker each time was
too brief for him to make them out.

A stone-paved area lay in front of the gaping doorway, and
he went across it to stand beneath the arch. Yolanda was
beside him, and the other two came up to them; all of them
stood in the doorway, looking back the way they'd come.
Under the mauling of the wind, the cypress trees whipped
about, a tortured mass of fluid motion. As they watched, the
rain came down, suddenly released, solid sheets of water that
marched in waves across the trees and spattered on the terrace
before the door, driving spray against them.

Watching the lashing trees, Harcourt caught sight, during a
brief moment of lightning flare, of a mass that towered above
them, weaving like a monstrous snake standing on its tail and
swaying to the violence of the storm, but swaying, so it
seemed to him in the split second that he glimpsed it, not to
the storm, but to a music of its own.

"Did you see that?" he shouted to the others to make himself heard above the howling of the wind and the booming of
the thunder.

"I saw nothing," the abbot shouted back.

"Let's get inside," said Harcourt. "We'll get wet standing
here."

Whether the others heard him in the tumult of the storm he
could not be sure, but he moved back deeper into the doorway; as he did he saw a thin slit of light to his left. Puzzled,
he moved forward cautiously, and as he shuffled ahead the
band of light grew wider. It was a dim light—even in the
darkness it was dim, and was not, he knew, either candlelight
or firelight. It had a green softness to it, akin to the soft glow
of foxfire that one often found in a rotting stump or log.
Looking at it as it widened, he understood; the doorway did
not lead directly into the structure, but after a short distance
changed its angle sharply.

He came to a halt and stared at the broader band of light,
trying to make out what lay beyond it, but was unable to. He
could make out certain vague shapes, but they were so fuzzy
in the softness of the light that there was no telling what they

were. The other three were clustered behind him, but none of them said a word. The abbot finally lumbered forward to stand beside him. "What is it, Charles?" he asked.

They had left the noise of the storm behind them, and while the rumbling and the crashing of the thunder could still be heard, the sound was not so loud as to drown out words spoken at a normal pitch.

"I do not know," said Harcourt. "I'm going in to see."

He slid the sword out of the scabbard and held it ready in his fist. When he moved forward toward the light, the abbot stepped along beside him.

"It's wondrous strange," the abbot mumbled. Harcourt did not answer. But, he told himself, it was wondrous strange, indeed.

They came to the end of the angled entryway and, laid out before them, they saw a widespread expanse of space, so large that there was no seeing to the end of it on any side. It was too large to be a room or a hall; it looked like a world that was sufficient unto itself. It was a dead world, or seemed a dead world. Nothing stirred within it. There was no apparent life or living thing in this world that held room enough for thousands. There was a dustiness about it and an emptiness, an emptiness despite the fact that furniture, or what appeared to be furniture of a sort, stood scattered all about. What could have been an altar was facing them, a short distance off. An altar, but not the kind of altar that was in the abbey church at home. Why, Harcourt asked himself, did he think it was an altar?

Fascinated, but fearful, terror-stricken by this great unknown, he moved out into the room and halted. Turning to face the others, he saw that there was no doorway. They had come through a doorway, but now it was gone. Where it had stood, a faceless mass of piled stone blocks rose up to be lost in the immensity of the place.

The faces of the stones were covered with twisting hieroglyphics, like unto the ones he had thought he'd glimpsed carved on the monolithic doorway as they had approached the building, scrawls that had been only half illuminated by the lightning flashes.

The terror that he'd felt came tumbling down upon him, and it was as if someone had reached out icy hands to touch him. That was ridiculous, he told himself, for there was nothing here. The room, if it was a room and not a world, was empty. It was old and gone to dust and there was nothing left.

He looked more closely at the hieroglyphics, trying to make out what they might represent, not what they meant or said, but what sort of forms they took, but that did no more than make the terror deepen, for if they represented anything, it was nothing he had ever known or seen. There was about them a primordial obscenity that set his flesh to crawling.

He heard a rustle in the room and whirled about, his sword half raised. But there was nothing there to rustle.

"Don't try to make them out," said the Knurly Man. "They still are here, but don't try to make them out. It's better if you don't."

"They!" Harcourt shouted, the shout echoing in the vastness of the place. "Who are they? Where are they? Show me where they are!"

The abbot, he saw, had the crucifix that hung from the rosary dangling at his belt clutched in his fist, half raised. The abbot's face was tensed in hard lines and his lips were moving, but no sound was coming out. The movement of the abbot's lips, Harcourt thought irrationally, appeared to show that he was mouthing Latin phrases.

The Knurly Man shouted at the abbot, "Put down that goddamn crucifix!"

Somewhere in the immensity of the room a voice cried out in an unknown tongue, and there were echoes of the unknown all up and down the place.

"It is an evil," Yolanda said. "It is a different evil from the one we know."

"There is no difference in evil," Harcourt said stoutly. "All evil is the same. Evil is evil, and that is the end of it."

He caught a glimpse of Yolanda's face. It was quiet and placid. There was about it, he thought, a certain holiness. The abbot, he saw, had dropped the crucifix, which now swung back and forth from the rosary at his belt.

First there had been a rustle and then the voice crying out in an alien tongue, and now there was the sound of wings, beating high above them, strong-pinioned, monstrous wings that beat the air, but beat in place, not moving off, not going anywhere. Shining in one far corner, a far corner in this place so huge that it had no corners, were gleaming eyes, outshining the foxfire light that filled the room, like eyes shining in the dark when there was no dark, and a slobbering that sent shivers up the spine.

"It is an evil," Yolanda said, "that came here when the

world began, a world unlike this world we know. It began when eternity was new."

The Knurly Man was walking forward toward the altar, not walking as he usually walked, not striding as he would along a forest trail, but shambling, and somehow he had changed, no longer the bowlegged Knurly Man, but a greater Knurly Man, an enlarged Knurly Man who, despite his shambling, moved with confidence.

"Charles, we are trapped," the abbot said. "The door is gone and we are trapped."

The sound of slithering came, the slither of a snake, and it must have been a large and long snake, for the slithering kept on; there seemed no end to it. There was a shadow on the wall, perhaps not on the wall, for there seemed to be no walls, but perhaps a shadow on the foxfire light, and the shadow was very like the massive thing, Harcourt told himself, that he had seen above the trees, swaying to its music, before the storm came down in all its fury.

He took a quick step toward the shadow and knew that the abbot had stepped along with him, the mace clutched in his mighty fist. And that was all right, Harcourt thought, that was resolute and brave, but what could a mace and a sword do against a dancing snake that threw its shadow on the wall?

A great, throaty voice shouted out in a gibberish that he did not know, a commanding, arrogant voice that flung a challenge against the world or room and whatever it might harbor—*Egong aud dunag aud . . . egholu amu auth d'bo . . . tor agna's unhl anc.*

"Almighty God," the abbot said, "it's Knurly doing all that howling."

Something they could not see was mewling somewhere to the left and another thing was scampering on many, many feet while the Knurly Man, his arms flung upward before the altar, kept bellowing in a tongue no man should have known or spoken.

"It waits and hides here for another time," Yolanda said, still speaking in a soft, unhurried voice. "For the end of this world, perhaps. Mayhap until the very end of time, when once again all will be in chaos."

The horror clamped down and came in close, as if it were intent on squeezing them—the horror of the thing that slithered and threw its shadow on the foxfire light, of the thing that mewled and the thing that slobbered. The most terrible feature of it, Harcourt thought, was that there would be no fighting back, nothing solid to fight against, nothing that sword or mace could touch. There was a loathsomeness in the very air one breathed; there was a crawling feeling on one's back, as if a million thousand-legged worms were racing up and down the spine. And out at the edge of the loathsomeness, at the edge of horror and helplessness, madness reared an ugly head and leered. Harcourt felt the urge to throw back his face and howl, tearing out his throat with howling, not trying to say anything, but howling like an animal that was trapped and frightened, with no way to break free.

Through it all the sonorous phrases—the phrases that meant nothing—came pouring from the throat of the Knurly Man, and Harcourt heard the abbot asking, in a strained voice fighting for control, "Yolanda, how do you know all this?"

"I do not know," Yolanda said. "I've only heard the whispers in the chimney corners in the dead of night. I've heard the olden stories, the tales that have been told forever. Tales of the Elder Ones who came from the farthest reaches of Beyond. I have only heard, but he knows." She pointed at the Knurly Man. "He knows and he holds them back. Hearing him, they cower back into their secret hiding places. For they are not as they were once. They now are weak and wait to build their strength against the day when they'll come out and prowl the world again."

God help us, Harcourt thought, if now they're weak, what were they in their day of strength?

They were massing now—he could half see, half sense the massing. He felt it with the raw endings of his nerves; he could smell the horror; he could hear the movement as they massed and got ready for the final assault that, when it came, would come suddenly, giving a man no opportunity to oppose it. Perhaps, he thought, it would be impossible to oppose it, for there would be nothing that one could strike against.

He strode forward, three long strides, to range himself beside the Knurly Man, lifting his sword and slashing it through the air, the sword stroke describing an arc of glitter in the greenness of the light. On the other side of the Knurly Man, Yolanda struck a stance, raising her arms and throwing back her head—and from the thrown-back head came an eerie chant that was as frightening in itself as the massing of the horror, a chant that seemed to have no words, but melded and became one with the words the Knurly Man was mouthing.

Far back in that enormous space that loomed in front of them, eyes gleamed with a fiercely golden light—more eyes now than there had been before. Some great monster was purring, and the silky, deliberate purr, like the purring of a million house cats, rumbled in the air. But behind the purring, laced into the interstices of the rumbling purr, were other sounds that were as chilling as the purr—the sliding sound of writhing wigglers that had no feet to walk on, the nervous chittering of crouchers huddling in the dark, the click-clack of scampering hooves, the wheezing and the slobbering of those who waited for a feast, tucking mushroomed napkins underneath their chins, and of the drooler that hunkered somewhere with thick ropes of saliva dripping.

The tension of fear grew, crackling in the place, and the menace mounted. Someone stirred beside Harcourt; when he turned his head, he saw that it was the abbot, crucifix gripped in one hand, his mace in the other. He said to Harcourt, out of the corner of a twisted mouth, "We may not get out of here, but we'll make the bastards smart."

"They're coming now," said Harcourt, for out of the corner of his eyes he saw the horror surging forward. In the face of Knurly's shouting and Yolanda's chanting, they were surging forward, for now they'd found the strength, and there was nothing that could stop them. He took a fresh grip upon the sword hilt and moved a step forward to face them. He saw the hate, the overwhelming, senseless hate, not in one great face, the face of horror, but in many faces that grew and then faded out of the forefront of the forward surge, fading to be replaced by other faces, each more repulsive and fearfully ridiculous than the ones that were replaced.

As the surge came rushing forward, rising higher as it came, like a mighty wave of water sweeping in upon them, with the tip of the wave curling over and forward as if it were a massive, fluid hand outstretched to grasp them, another voice rang out in the chamber, cutting through Knurly's thundering and Yolanda's chanting. The words were different from the words that Knurly mouthed, and as incomprehensible—although apparently not incomprehensible to the surging horror. As the sounds of them rang out, the advancing wave froze where it was, coming to a halt, and began flowing backward, retreating as a wave retreats when it has vented its violence on a rocky shore and is thrown back.

Silence fell. Knurly halted his thundering and Yolanda's chant ran down and the other voice seemed to have gone away. Harcourt looked around quickly to see whose the other voice might have been, but there was no other; there were just the four of them. The parrot, perched on the abbot's shoulder, squawked.

The foxfire light was fading and the gleaming eyes were gone. So were the purring, the slithering, the chittering, the slobbering. As the foxfire light faded out, there was another light. Looking up to seek its source, Harcourt saw the moon, almost directly above him, shining through a thin rack of fleeing clouds.

The moon, he thought—the moon couldn't be shining here, for it couldn't shine through all the masonry. But the masonry, he saw, was gone as well as all the rest of it. The building they had walked into was no longer there. Rather, they stood in the tumbled ruins of the building. Massive blocks of stone lay all about them, canted on one another. Great trees grew among the ruins; vines and bushes covered the nakedness of much of the fallen stone and, in the moonlight, shone with wetness.

"The rain has stopped," the abbot said, rather senselessly. "The storm has passed on to the east."

"Let's get out of here," said the Knurly Man, moving over to them, his voice husky with all the shouting he had done.

"What I want to know," said Harcourt, "is how you knew . . ."

"No time for that," said the Knurly Man.

Yolanda seized Harcourt's arm with both her hands, hauling him and guiding him out of the littered ruins. The abbot stumbled along beside them, stubbing his toes on fallen bits of debris.

Harcourt protested at Yolanda's help. "Tell me," he asked, "whose was that third voice? I looked, but there was no one there. Just the four of us."

"I looked, too," Yolanda said, "and there was no one. But I think I recognized the voice. I think it was the peddler's."

"The peddler's! The peddler is just a . . ."

"The peddler," said Yolanda, "is a wizard of very low repute."

"Of low repute?"

"Only," said Yolanda, "because he is careful not to flaunt his powers. He is a hidden wizard."

"But you knew him. Or you knew of him. You knew where he was to be found. You took us to his cave, pretending you only happened on it."

"I have known him," Yolanda said sweetly, "for the last few years."

By now they were free of the ruins, and Harcourt turned about to have another look at them. They looked, he thought, like any other ruin, any tumbled castle, any crumbling fort, except that there still hung about them the very stink of evil. Other ruins might be innocent; this one was not.

From a little distance off, the abbot called to them. "Will you come over here and see what I have found?" By the tenor of his voice he was fighting to be calm about what he had found, but not quite succeeding.

The abbot was standing to one side of the paved approach that had fronted on the great doorway to the building, and as Harcourt came up he saw the dark, huddled shapes that lay on the paving stones.

"Ogres," said the abbot. "A hell's brood of ogres."

They were dead, all of them, sprawled in frantic protest against their deaths.

"I count," said the abbot, "a baker's dozen of them. There may be others that I missed."

"So they were following us," said the Knurly Man. "Probably close behind us. Closing in on us. They'd have stormed in on us as soon as we had settled down for the night. So much for what that mealy-mouthed old ogre statesman had to say to us."

"There was one of the Elder—is that what you call them?— one of the Elder Ones out here before we went through the doorway," said Harcourt. "I glimpsed it—like a mighty snake, dancing on its tail."

"It need not have been that one," said the Knurly Man. "Everything was all tangled up—time and space and whatnot. No one could have known what was happening. It all was topsy-turvy; it never should have been."

"But you knew," said the abbot. "You knew something of what was going on. You stood up in front of that altar thing and you hollered at them and you held them back. And you told me to drop the crucifix. I never will forgive you. 'Put down that goddamn crucifix!' you yelled at me. You do not speak in that manner of a crucifix."

"Let's hold it down," said Harcourt, speaking sharply. "There'll be time later on for that sort of thing—later on there'll be time to yell at one another about altars and crucifixes and what should have been said and what should not. Right now we have dead ogres lying at our feet, and it seems to me we should remove ourselves from them as fast as we can manage."

"With the moon out and the sky clearing," Yolanda said, "we can get across the river and cover a league or two toward the west before morning breaks. What Lord Harcourt says is right; we should pay attention to him."

"I do not care!" the abbot shouted. "One does not call down damnation on a crucifix!"

The ogres had died rather horribly. There was not enough light to make out exactly what had happened to them, but it appeared to Harcourt that somehow they had been twisted out of shape, as if someone had tried to turn them inside out, but had been interrupted before the job was done. The sky was clearing, with the fleecy, fleeing clouds less thick than they had been only a short time before, but the moonlight still was tricky and did not provide good seeing. There was a clean-washed freshness to the air, the cypress trees now stood straight and tall, and everything was silent—there was no wind moaning through the trees. The storm had passed and the world was calm.

Harcourt asked Yolanda, "Have you got your directions straight? Can you lead the way? Straight across the river and onward to the west."

"That I can," she said. "Gentlemen, if you will follow me."

Fifteen

The first light of dawn found them at the foot of a high hill forested only halfway up its slope, the upper half of it bare of trees, strewn with a heavy boulder field.

The progress they had made during the night had been a brutal effort, wading the river, blundering through the wide river valley, studded with stretches of forest and, where there were no trees, thick grasses spotted with potholes and watery patches of marsh. Dead tired from lack of sleep and the heavy going, Harcourt forced himself to keep moving forward by the stubborn process of advancing first one foot and then the other. At times he was ahead of the abbot and the Knurly Man; falling behind, he would drive himself to hurry and catch up with them. Yolanda flitted ahead of them, never seeming to tire.

There was little talk. They were too tired and dazed to talk; they needed all their breath and energy to forge ahead.

There was a great deal to talk about, Harcourt told himself, many questions to be asked, but this was not the time for it. Later they would find the time. He attempted to mull over all that had happened, but his brain was too sluggish with fatigue to allow any consistent thinking.

When they paused at the first upthrust of the hill that had loomed ahead of them ever since the sky had grown light enough for them to see it, the sun still was far from rising. The first faint lightening of the east was brightening the land.

Harcourt looked up at the bare-topped hill.

"We should get up there," he said. "To the top of it. From there we could spy out the land, see if anything is following and what else may be going on."

"There's nothing following," said the abbot. "Those who followed are dead back on the island."

"Of that I'm not too sure," said the Knurly Man. "Some of them might have escaped and still be following."

"The heart was taken out of them," said the abbot. "After what happened back there, they'd have no thought of trailing anyone at all."

"The thing that sticks in my mind," said the Knurly Man, "is that the ogres, either those who escaped death back on the island, or those who could have come looking for them, may not be fully aware of what happened. They may think we are the ones who slew the ogres on the island and, in such a case, will be thirsting for our blood. I say we follow the suggestion made by Charles and get up on that hill."

"We'd be naked to the world," the abbot protested. "There are no trees to hide in."

"We can hide among the boulders," said Harcourt. "From down here they appear small, but I would judge that many of them are large."

"All right," the abbot said, giving in. "Although my aching muscles protest violently against it, we'll climb the hill."

They climbed the hill, bent forward to keep their balance, hauling themselves up by sheer strength and awkwardness, sometimes going on their hands and knees. The boulders, as Harcourt had estimated, were huge, some of them the size of barns or stables. The hill was higher than it at first had appeared to be. When they finally reached its summit, the entire area was laid out before them. The sun was a hand's-breadth above the horizon, and after last night's storm, the day promised to be fair.

The abbot collapsed, his back propped against a boulder. He said to Harcourt, patting the ground beside him, "You had best sit down here with me. You look no whit better than I feel."

"You always play out early," Harcourt said.

He would like to have sat down with his friend the abbot; he would like to have gone to sleep. He was afraid that if he did sit down, he would fall asleep.

"I've been watching," said the Knurly Man, "and there are no dragons. At least so far there aren't. If the Evil were hunting us, they'd have the dragons out. Or the harpies. Or other flying things."

"This should be about the area," Yolanda said, "where the peddler said we'd find the harpies, once we crossed the first big river. They may not use the dragons. Dragons are lazy things and don't like to fly too far. They may use the harpies."

"Let's have a look," the Knurly Man said to Harcourt. "The few steps to the very crest. Then I think, with one man watching, the rest of us can sleep."

The abbot had unshipped his pack and was taking food from it. He was busy chomping. He said, his mouth so full he could barely get the words out, "I never sleep on an empty stomach. Not if I can help it."

"I'll stand first watch," Yolanda said.

"No," said Harcourt. "I'll stand it. I can manage until noon, then I'll call someone else."

He could not afford, he did not dare, he told himself, to allow Yolanda to stand watch. And felt ashamed of himself for thinking it, for since the time they had entered the Empty Land she had served them well. But she had led them to the place of the Elder Ones, failing to warn them what it was, and she had joined the Knurly Man before the altar; she had been going into the Empty Land for years and she had known the peddler was a wizard. On the face of all of this, he told himself, it would be foolish of him to place any trust in her.

"No," he said. "I will stand the first watch and Knurly the second."

"I'm grateful to you," the abbot told him. "Although perhaps it is just as well. All the fiends of hell could not rouse me short of evening once I fall asleep."

The parrot squawked and, leaning forward from where he perched on the abbot's shoulder, stole a chunk of the bread the abbot was eating. Holding it in one claw, he started gobbling it.

"This bird is trying to grow onto me, to become a part of me," the abbot grumbled. "He has fair adopted me, and I'm not sure I like it, for he gives me nothing, except perhaps mites or fleas or whatever other vermin he may carry. Could I prevail upon someone to share him with me?"

"No, thank you," said the Knurly Man.

The parrot gulped down a beakful of bread and said, "Careful of the ogres. Careful of the goddamn ogres."

"That's the first thing he has said since we left the place we found him," Yolanda said. "Could it be significant?"

"He tells us only what to do with ogres," said Harcourt. "And we already know that. We are being careful of them."

"He apes speech only," said the Knurly Man. "He knows not what he says."

"However," said the abbot, "often out of the mouths of fools . . ."

"You're mad," the Knurly Man snapped. To Harcourt, he said, "Let's go up the step or two to the very top and spy out the land."

Lying side by side on the very top, they spied out the land.

After trending north for a short distance, the river angled toward the west. North and west, the river valley was a level grassland, with only occasional clumps of trees. To the south and the southwest lay thinly forested, rolling hills, none of them high. To the east were the heavily wooded hills they had crossed to reach the river.

"There's a small herd of unicorns almost directly north," said the Knurly Man, "moving about and grazing. I see nothing else."

"I see them now," said Harcourt. "I missed them before. A bit to the east of them is a small wolf pack."

They lay quietly side by side, only moving their heads to take in the land.

Finally Harcourt said, "It looks good. Nothing at the moment to worry about. I'll stay up here. Why don't you go back and get some rest? I'll rouse you around noon or thereabouts."

"Charles, you must have questions. About last night. I'm

reluctant to discuss them, for the moment, with the others, but you have the right to know."

"I have no right," said Harcourt. "I am curious, naturally, but I have no need to know. I'm just happy that you were able to do whatever it was you did. You held them off for us."

"I think," said the Knurly Man, "you have both the need and the right to know. You and I are family. Your grandfather and I have been friends for years, you and I friends since you were a toddler."

"I remember," Harcourt said. "You showed me birds building their nests and we watched them do it and you explained how they did it, wondering how a bird must think and feel about its building. Would it feel the same, we asked ourselves, as a man who built a hut—constructing a home and shelter against the elements? You showed me fox dens, and we hid silently and watched the little foxes creep out to play, wrestling and nipping one another like a troop of peasant kids wrestling and fighting underneath a tree while their mothers worked. You named all the trees for me and many of the plants and recited for me their virtues and their dangers."

"So you do remember," said the Knurly Man.

"I had no father," Harcourt said. "You and grandfather became joint fathers to me."

"Your grandfather knows some of what I am about to tell you," said the Knurly Man. "He knows I'm not a human, but he has extended to me all the friendship and the courtesy and, I could say, the love that he'd reach out to another human."

"I always thought of you as human," Harcourt said. "Until a short while ago, I never questioned it. Then, one day, I knew, and was surprised and guilty at the knowing. But while I might know, I still felt the humanness. That never changed. It will never change."

"I'm close to human," said the Knurly Man. "Maybe, in the last accounting, I am human, but not quite the kind of human that you are. My race preceded your race—how long we preceded you, I do not know. We are a long-lived people. One of us lives many times longer than your kind of people live. Why this is, I do not know. I've lived so long that I've lost all count of years. I never kept a count—for such as we, years are of little consequence. When I say the people of my race live longer than the members of your race, I mean a great deal longer. A thousand years perhaps, in some cases probably more than that. There is, as well, another peculiarity that is ours alone. We grow to maturity and live in maturity for our long span of life, but we do not age; before we age we die. Once we reach our allotted span, we do not sink into old age and senility. We die before we begin the long curve into the aging years. In this I think there is some benefit. We do not go through the agony of experiencing our bodies shrinking into a feeble semblance of their former states; we are not exposed to the indignity of a fading mind. Our memories stay with us, sharp and clear, to the very end. I have long memories, but I never speak of them, for it would be thought strange should I do so. And it's not only my own memories, but the memories of my race. Back there, at the island, the abbot put a name to it. You remember that I told you I had some memories of the island, not my memories, I said, but someone else's memories. And the abbot, catching at my words, said ancestral memories."

"You mean," said Harcourt, "that you carry with you the actual memories of your ancestors, of your father and grandfather and . . ."

"Much farther back than that," said the Knurly Man. "For my father and my grandfather carried ancestral memories of their own—how far back along the ancestral line I don't pretend to know. And some of those ancestral memories were passed on to me. Perhaps memories from a long way back. The important memories, perhaps, the ones that one should know, that might help one to survive or understand . . ."

"Then the words you said there on the island, the words that stopped and held back the Elder Ones . . ."

"I did not know I had them," said the Knurly Man. "They came to me. I was faced with a situation that called for them, and they came boiling up, out of some bottomless pit of ancestral memory. They made me understand, they helped me to survive."

"The words were ones such as I had never heard," said Harcourt. "You knew only the sound of them, not the meaning of them?"

"I knew the meaning, too. For a time, I think, I may have become, not myself, but some ancient ancestor who had stood against the Elder Ones, who had screamed at them the very words I used."

"You changed into another man? An old ancestor?"

"I do not know. There were a few moments when it seemed I had. It is something that in the future I will ponder on."

"Yolanda was the first to tell me what shape of things we

met. The Elder Ones, she said. She told me that they first came here when the world was new."

"How could she know?" asked the Knurly Man.

"She may be privy to many facts that are known in this Empty Land and nowhere else. She told me, for example, that our precious peddler is a wizard. She claims his was the other voice that cried out along with you."

"So there was someone else," said the Knurly Man. "I thought that there was help. I heard no one cry out, but I felt a new strength when mine was waning."

"Then you did get some help? No matter who it was or what it was, the peddler or someone else . . ."

"Yes, there was help for me."

"Yolanda may have been of some help. She chanted while you cried out against the Elder Ones."

"I knew she was there. And I wondered where she had learned the chant, for it was one that I dimly recognized; from far in the mist of time I knew what it was."

"We must watch her," Harcourt said. "Yolanda knows too much."

"We'll talk more of this later," said the Knurly Man. "I knew you must have wondered. I wanted you to know."

"There is one thing else," said Harcourt. "You knew about the mounds. You told us something of them . . ."

"In the olden days," said the Knurly Man, "we called them the Children of the Soil. A kindly name for them, for they were not kindly in themselves. They sprang from the soil like some obnoxious plant, although they were more than plants. We walked very wide around them. When I say we, I do not mean myself, but those old ancestors of mine from millennia ago. The Children were capable of mischief and, at times, of more than mischief. They were, I believe, the world's first evil, for there have been many evils, a long chain of evils. The Elder Ones came later, but very long ago. They were not children of the earth; they came from out of the Void. They flourished for eons, but they faded out. Today they lie in deep hiding, awaiting a day that we should hope will never come, when they can emerge again to ravage the world and all that lives upon it. What we faced on the island was a pale flicker of what they once had been, called forth in their relative weakness to ward off our invasion of their sanctuary. But the Elder Ones were not the first. The Children of the Soil were first. The Children were defeated by the plow and axe that destroyed and took away the places where they spawned. I do not know what happened to the Elder Ones. Perhaps no one knows. But they faded, too."

"And now we have what we call the Evil," said Harcourt. "As if they were the only Evil."

"There are fragmentary legends, not to be relied upon," said the Knurly Man, "that in the beginning our Evil was not evil as we know it now. There may even have been a time, in mankind's primal days, when they would have made companionable neighbors, strange in their ways, of course, but at times charming and entertaining folk. But as time went on, they learned their evil as a matter of survival. They may have learned from the Elder Ones, who saw them as an agency that could carry on the ancient tradition of malevolence, handing off the evil to them as they, themselves, sank into the torpor that was overtaking them. Even then our Evil might not have adopted evil ways had they not been caught up in events. They may have been forced into what they are when they were pinched between barbarians and Romans. By becoming terrible, they could protect themselves. Further hatred of the human race may have come about—I suspect it did come about—when this fumbling saint who is supposed to be prisoned in the prism that we search for tried to hurl them from this world into the Outer Darkness. One cannot blame them too much for the hatred that this act created. Since that day . . ."

"But our peddler-wizard said that their hatred and their rage seem to run in cycles."

The Knurly Man wagged his head. "The wizard may know what he talks of, but there's a chance he doesn't. It could be that the Elder Ones, who are almost gone, but not entirely gone as yet, may at times have some influence on them, may rouse them into rages, may . . ."

"But on the island the Elders killed the ogres who were trailing us."

"Perhaps no more than a blind lashing out," said the Knurly Man. "You cannot figure evil. There is no way we can. We cannot ever hope to think the way evil does."

"We stirred up the Elder Ones," said Harcourt, "and if what you conjecture can be true, then we may be facing a very bloody cycle."

"Don't worry over it," said the Knurly Man. "We have a full load of worry of our own. We cannot borrow other worries."

Then he was gone, scurrying down the hill to where the others were, leaving Harcourt to watch the land.

Harcourt scanned the skies; there were no dragons. Far to the west a glint of something was smudged against the sky, but it was too far off to make out what it was, only that it was something flying. He was sure, however, that it was not dragons. The flight pattern of these fliers was not the hurky-jerky flight of dragons.

An hour or so later a flight of fairies skimmed along the lower reaches of the hill, well below the timberline. The sunlight flashed off their gossamer wings in a tiny rainbow of color. They reached the river and followed it, swinging to the west.

He looked for the unicorns again, but they had moved off and he could not locate them. The wolves were gone as well.

Once the fairies had disappeared, there was nothing moving. He would have detected any motion to the north and west and southwest. There was little point in watching elsewhere, for anything that moved from the east or south would be concealed by forest growth. Nevertheless, he made regular checks in those directions to spot any flying creatures, should they show up.

Perhaps, he told himself, there was little need of watching. It was quite possible they were not being followed. By now the dead ogres would have been discovered on the island, and undoubtedly the assumption would be that the small band of humans had died when the ogres did. The fact that their bodies could not be found might give some pause to this belief, although it would seem unlikely they could have escaped. He had at first considered the possibility that it might be thought, when the ogres had been found, that they had been killed in battle with the humans. But now, as he thought about it, that seemed unlikely. It would be apparent that the ogres had not fallen before human weapons. They had died more horribly than that; theirs had been no clean death. Any Evil of this land probably would know immediately how and by whom they had been killed.

Perhaps for the first time since Harcourt and his group had set foot in the Empty Land, the Evil had no idea where they were. If they were careful and moved with some caution, they might, for a time, keep their presence and their movements secret.

Their luck so far had been greater than they could have hoped. If they had not happened on the place of the Elder Ones, they probably would have been tracked down and killed by the following ogres. It had been only by the most far-fetched circumstance that they had survived when they had faced the Elder Ones. If the Knurly Man had not dredged up from his ancestral memories the words that had held the Elder Ones at bay, if the peddler—if it had been the peddler —had not appeared to intervene, they would have suffered the same fate as the ogre band. And Yolanda—how much had Yolanda contributed with her chant?

He frowned to himself. Yolanda was a puzzling question mark. Jean, her foster father, he reminded himself, had been a loyal retainer of the House of Harcourt all his life, and his family before him for more than a hundred years, perhaps for several hundred years. Trying to think back, he could not recall how long. Jean had vouched for his foster daughter and had said she had some knowledge of the Empty Land. He had been openly honest about her contacts with the Empty Land. Harcourt could not doubt Jean, he knew, but how about the daughter?

She was a lithe tomboy who seemed scarcely a woman— one who scouted ahead and spied out the land, who located camping places for them, who found trails to follow. There was no question that she had performed all the functions and had been of the help that she had said she would be; she had served them well and faithfully. And yet she had led them to the peddler's cave, neglecting to tell them at the time that he was a wizard. She had led them to the island where the ruins of a seat of power of the Elder Ones had stood, not warning them of the dangers that they faced there. Although in all fairness, he told himself, it was possible that she had not guessed that, through some necromancy, they would come into confrontation with the Elder Ones. He puzzled over it and could not resolve the question—there seemed to be no solid answers.

The sun was higher now, in a cloudless sky, and the heat of the sun beat down mercilessly. The land to the north and west was beginning to acquire a shimmer, wavering lines of heat bouncing off the ground. There was something moving far to the north. A haze of dust hung over whatever it was that moved. Harcourt shielded his eyes with his hand against the sun glare in an attempt to make out what it was. From the distance of his viewing, it appeared that a number of dark spots made up the movement. From the cloud of dust it appeared most likely to be a herd of unicorns, but unicorns, he told himself, would be white, not dark. He shook his head, trying to shake the fuzz of sleepiness away; he rubbed his eyes. Still he could not determine what was out there. Perhaps, he consoled himself, it did not greatly concern him, for whatever might be out there was a long way north and moving in a northwesterly direction. Another flight of fairies showed up far to the west, recognizable only by the shimmer of the sunlight on their gauzy wings. Other than that, there was nothing moving on the land and, except for the fairies, nothing in the air.

He rolled over on his back, changing his position to ease his aching muscles, and stared straight up into the sky. It was high and blue and there seemed no end to it. Where did the sky end? he wondered, for somewhere it must end, as there must be an end to everything. He didn't stay long, lying on his back, pleasant as it might have been, but rolled back to lie upon his belly and continue the watching of the land.

The sun was just short of the zenith when the Knurly Man came creeping up the slope to stretch out beside him.

"You're early," Harcourt said. "I could have stayed a little longer and let you get more sleep."

"I had some sleep," said the Knurly Man, "and am much restored. Yolanda found some dry wood that makes no smoke in burning and brewed a pot of tea. When you go down, have some of that. It will help you sleep."

"There's nothing happening," said Harcourt. "A few fairies flying and some ground movement far to the north, which I can't make out. Otherwise the land seems empty."

"I'll take over," said the Knurly Man. "You go down and get some sleep. Ask Yolanda to rouse the abbot well before evening closes in so he can take his turn. All this time he's been lying flat upon his back and snoring, with his mouth wide open, catching flies."

Harcourt went sliding down the slope to where Yolanda squatted before the white-ashed, smokeless fire. She handed him a cup of tea.

"Get this into you," she said. "It will be a help. I'll put slices of cheese and meat between two slices of bread and warm them up for you. That's the best that I can do. At least you'll have warm food in your belly."

He took the cup and thanked her, sat down next to a large boulder, and leaned back against it. The abbot, as the Knurly Man had said, was flat upon his back, snoring and gulping, with his mouth wide open. The parrot strode up and down beside him, as if on patrol, muttering to itself. Sipping the scalding tea, Harcourt watched Yolanda use two long-handled forks to hold the slices of bread, which enclosed meat and cheese, above the fire. The bread took on a hue of brown, and the melting cheese ran down the crusts.

"That looks good," he said. "I've never seen anyone do such a thing before."

"I think you'll find it tasty," she said. "The Knurly Man seemed to enjoy it. I think it's almost done."

Finally she took the slices off the forks and handed them to him. "Handle this carefully," she warned. "It's hot."

He held the slices of bread gingerly, then took a bite. It tasted good. He had not known that he was hungry, but after the first bite, he was ravenous. He wolfed the food down.

She came over close to him and sat down with her legs crossed beneath her. The cowl of her robe hung down her back, and the golden beauty of her hair cascaded about her shoulders. The soft cornflower blue of her eyes looked steadily at him. But despite the beauty of the hair and the softness of the eyes, there was a hardness to her face. There was a certain boniness about it, and her lips were so thin they seemed to be no more than a slash. She was, Harcourt told himself, not really beautiful. Yet there was a compelling quality in the face: it was a face that one would look at more than once and would keep looking at. What is there about her? he asked himself. But he could not answer. Whatever it was escaped him.

Her lips scarcely moving, she said to him, "My lord, you do not trust me."

He was startled at her forthright manner. "Why do you say that?" he asked.

"You will not allow me to share the watch," she said.

"And you," he said, "did not tell us you were acquainted with the peddler. You led us to him, pretending you had stumbled on his cave. You did not warn us he was a wizard."

Since she has started it, he told himself, we might as well have it out.

"I could not tell you at the time," she said. "I'm not sure I should have told you ever. He is a secret wizard. He is known to no one and is not recognized. He dare not be recognized. All these years he has worked in secret, confounding the Evil in many different ways. If they should ever learn who he is, his usefulness would be at an end. He would be forced to flee. If he did not, he would be hunted down, and all his powers would not be great enough to save him."

"But he finally did intervene. He came to the island . . ."

"Otherwise all of us would have been killed," she said. "He weighed this, I am certain, against the risk of revealing himself. Although the risk might not have been great . . ."

"You mean because he was sure the ogres would be killed?"

"I can't be certain. Perhaps that. All I know is that the Elder Ones may hate the Evil far more than they hate humans. They hate everyone, but perhaps not equally. For the Evil stole much knowledge and ways of doing things from the Elder Ones. This was in the ancient days when the Elder Ones were growing weaker and the then-new Evil was creeping in, seeking to replace them. If the Evil had the temerity to set foot upon the island, the Elder Ones, though sleeping, perhaps almost dead, would rise to strike them down."

"I think I see," said Harcourt. "Yolanda, did you know that the ogres were trailing us? Is that why you led us to the island, luring the ogres there?"

Her face twisted. She started to say something, then caught the words and held them back.

"Tell me," Harcourt said.

"Please, lord," she blurted out, "I did not know, I did not even dream, that it would happen as it did."

"You gambled?"

"I almost got us killed. I thought the ogres would not follow us to the island. I could have found other places where we could have camped the night and be well protected should we be attacked. But I passed them by and led you to the island . . ."

"You did this, knowing we were being followed by the ogres. How did you know we were being followed?"

"The shell," she said. "The seashell."

"So that's why you listen to it. What does it tell you now? What should we do next?"

"Now," she said, "I hear only the sound of the sea."

"You mean it does not always tell you?"

"At the moment there may be nothing to be told."

Harcourt finished the meal she had provided him and sat brooding. There were some answers now, and he found himself inclined to believe most of what she'd told him. Some of what she had said was at variance with what the Knurly Man had told him. The Knurly Man had not hinted at any hatred the Elder Ones might have felt toward the Evil. In this case, however, Yolanda might be right and the Knurly Man wrong. Her version did explain why the Elder Ones had killed the ogres. There was still one question that he could not ask. Who was this bony tomboy who sat in front of him? He sensed that if he asked, she might not tell him, that there was a possibility she did not know herself what she really was.

"Well, thanks," he said. "Now I understand you better."

She said, "You should get some sleep."

She rose in one lithe motion and walked back to squat beside the fire.

"Yes, some sleep," he said.

The next that he remembered was someone shaking him. He put up an arm to shove away the shaker.

"Charles," someone said. "Charles, you must wake up."

He fought his way to a sitting position and scrubbed at his eyes with doubled fists. Blearily he saw that it was the Knurly Man who had been shaking him. Yolanda and the abbot were crouched beside the fire. The parrot perched on the abbot's shoulder, its head tucked beneath a wing.

"There's no one watching," Harcourt said.

"I came down just now. Soon the abbot will be going up. I want to talk with all of you."

"Trouble?"

"I don't think just yet. But something's happening. There is a great deal of movement out there. Bands of the Evil—ogres, trolls, gnomes, goblins—are on the move. All to the northwest. Harpies and banshees in the air, shoals of fairies, even a few dragons. The place is stiff with Evil. They're making no move toward us. I doubt they know we're here."

The abbot and Yolanda walked over, and Harcourt got to his feet.

"They may think we're dead, back on the island," said the abbot.

"That's possible," said the Knurly Man. "We can't stay here, however. Sometime we must leave. The way it looks out to the north and west, before too long this area should be empty of Evil. We should, I think, make a break for it. We probably can cover a lot of distance before they pick us up again."

"Should we start right now?" the abbot asked. "By the time we get off the hill . . ."

"No," Yolanda said. "We'd be traveling in the dark and at a disadvantage. Many of the Evil can see much better in the dark than we can. Some of them see best at night."

"Not only that," said the Knurly Man, "they're still out there; by morning they may be gone. When we leave, I think we should strike straight west. We should try to travel fast.

This venture is taking far more time than we had thought it would."

"The Romans?" asked Harcourt. "Do you think the Romans?"

"The thought has crossed my mind," said the Knurly Man.

"The one thing we don't need is open warfare between the Evil and the Romans. It would set this world aflame. The ogre whom we talked with . . ."

"We can place no reliance on what he said," the abbot told Harcourt. "He assured us we could proceed in safety as long as we watched our step. And yet we were trailed by ogres."

"I'm not so sure we should blame him," said the Knurly Man. "He may have been sincere, meant every word he said. He explained, you remember, that it was difficult to control the young hotheads. He said the raid of seven years ago would not have happened had it not been for them."

"The thing about it is," said Harcourt, "that the only trust we have must lie within ourselves. We can trust no other. We are on our own in a very hostile land."

Sixteen

The next morning the area to the north and west of their hilltop observation post was empty of movement. Not a thing stirred upon the land; nothing flew within the air. Full daylight had barely come when they started down the hill.

They pushed themselves all day and camped that night in a hidden cove beside a small stream from which they netted fish for eating. The night passed without incident, and the next morning they were on their way well before the sun was up.

It was a pleasant day, and there were no hills to climb. Yolanda, moving a short distance ahead of them, kept to the valleys that ran between the few hills they came upon, which made for easy going. Behind them the high hill they had used as an observation post sank lower and lower against the horizon, until, early in the afternoon, it was lost to view. Harcourt's calculations made out that they were going mostly west, although trending slightly to the north. Noting this, he hoped that Yolanda knew what she was doing and finally decided that probably she did.

After traveling for an hour or so, she stopped and waited for them. When they came up, she pointed to what apparently once had been a signpost, half obscured by undergrowth, close beside the trail. The sagging signboard, dangling from only a single nail, the others that had secured it having long ago rusted away, was only half a signboard. One end of it had decayed and flaked away, but the arrowlike forepart of it, although slightly canted upward, resolutely pointed down the path they followed.

Letters had been carved into it, but so long ago that they had weathered and were hard to read; furthermore, only a part of them remained, only the beginning of them. Harcourt stepped off the trail into the brush and stared up at the board. He was able to make out three letters—WIS—and that was all. The rest of them were gone with the weathering of the board.

"W-I-S," he said. "That is not much to go on. However, it could make little difference. The place the sign points to could be gone."

"It could be Wishing Well," said the abbot. "Did not the peddler say we should watch for the Wishing Well?"

"Of course," Yolanda said. "That must be it. He said if we looked into the water of the well, we could see the future."

"It's all blather," said the abbot. "One does not read the future by looking down a well."

"It could be worth a try," said the Knurly Man. "No four people in all of history need more to know what the future holds."

"I can tell you what you'll see," the abbot said. "You will see your own face staring back at you."

"Since we are traveling in that direction in any case," said Harcourt, "why don't we just keep on? If we find the Wishing Well, we can have a look. If we miss it, I rather think there will be nothing lost."

Somewhat short of a league they came upon the Wishing Well. It sat in the center of an extensive clearing. The well was marked by a circular curbing of stone rising about waist-high, the masonry still in place, the stones neatly set with fine lines of mortar. The post and pole of the well sweep sagged drunkenly beside the curbing, not yet fallen, but very close to falling. The rope that at one time had been tied to the end of the pole to lower a bucket into the well was no longer there. Beside the well, opposite the sweep, stood an ancient oak tree, and balancing himself on one of the tree's outreaching limbs was a troll. He was a sloppy-looking individual, very down-at-the-heels. He wore a pair of tattered shorts, and his coat of fur was most unkempt, the fur sticking out in tufts, mud-splotched and thick with brambles. He balanced on the limb and looked down at them with some surprise, his loose lips hanging open to reveal broken fangs. There was a rope about his neck, and the other end of it was tied to the limb on which he stood.

The abbot rumbled, "What have we here? So help me, a troll about to hang itself."

"We'll do naught to stop him," said the Knurly Man. "Go on," he said to the troll. "Do not let us interfere with you. Go ahead and jump."

"If the rope he is using was taken from the well sweep," said Harcourt, "he need have no fear. After all these years, it must be rotten. It will break beneath his weight."

The troll spoke to them in a high-pitched voice. "Stand back," he shrilled at them. "Do not try to stop me. Make no move to save me."

"We would not think of it," said the Knurly Man. "We are not in the business of saving such as you. Should it be necessary, once you are hanging, we'll do you the service of tugging at your feet to speed up the process. And that, Sir Troll, is the best offer you will get from me."

"But it's a sin!" the abbot protested. "It's a sin to take one's life. A life does not belong to the one who has it; it belongs to God."

"In the case of a troll," said the Knurly Man, "I would doubt that very much."

"I have no wish to live," the troll squeaked. "I have nothing left to live for. My bridge . . ."

"Unlike my friend the Knurly Man," said Harcourt, "I'll not urge that you jump, but, for the love of Christ, do one thing or the other. Either jump or climb down from the tree. Let's get it over with."

The troll jumped. He leaped high off the limb and came plummeting through the air, the rope trailing behind. His feet hit the ground, and, at the impact, he tumbled over and lay sprawled. A good length of the rope lay on the ground beside him. The four of them walked over and stood looking down upon the troll.

"He bungled it," said Harcourt, feeling disgust at a job very badly done. "He miscalculated the span of rope."

"He was faking all the time," said the Knurly Man. "He had no thought to hang himself."

The abbot shook his head. "No, I don't think that. I think he's simply stupid."

Harcourt stepped forward and grasped the dangling rope in both his hands and jerked on it. It frayed and came apart.

"As I thought," he said. "It's the rope from the sweep, and it would not have held him."

He tossed the end of the rope looped about the troll's neck toward the troll, who was struggling to sit up. "You can try it again," said Harcourt, "if you are determined, but there's not much point to it." The other portion of the rope dangled from the limb.

Yolanda screamed, "Dragon!"

Harcourt spun about, sword out of the scabbard and in his fist, and saw the monster that was sweeping in upon them. It was coming in at an angle and coming very fast, tilting on its side to avoid the tree under which they stood. The taloned claws were reaching for him, and the cruel, beaked head was darting in. The outside wing, he saw, almost touched the ground as the dragon banked.

He swung his sword, two-handed, with all the power he had, aiming at the beaked head. The steel rang on the armored hide, and something struck him in the side. He hit the ground and rolled out of the way of the outstretched claws.

Then the dragon was gone from sight, and Harcourt leaped to his feet. The abbot was running out beyond the tree.

"No!" Harcourt shouted. "Not out in the open!"

At the sound of his voice, the abbot turned and waved at him. Cursing, Harcourt ran toward the abbot. Someone, he told himself, had to protect the damn fool.

"There!" the abbot shouted, pointing.

Harcourt looked in the direction that he pointed and saw the dragon, no longer flying, but piled upon the ground, frantically flapping to regain its feet.

"He hit the tree," the abbot yelled. "He's grounded. Now we have him."

Harcourt sprang forward, leaping for the dragon. Off to one side he saw the Knurly Man running in the same direction, his battle-axe in hand. Behind him the abbot panted hoarsely as he attempted to keep up. There was no sign of Yolanda.

By now the dragon had righted itself and swung around to face them. It seemed to be uninjured. But, as the abbot had said, it was grounded. To take to the air, it had to have a running start. From its neck, Harcourt saw, hung a length of rope.

"This one's mine," Harcourt yelled. "I take this one alone. He belongs to me."

"The hell he does," the abbot shouted. "He belongs to the two of us. I claim a try at him."

The dragon reared up, its long neck striking out, its head poised high above them.

The neck was curving down, the beaked head snaking toward them. Something whickered above Harcourt's head. The whicker ended in a thud, and an arrow stood out stiff and straight from the dragon's neck.

At the arrow's impact, the dragon exploded into a frenzy. The head snapped up and then came flashing down, straight on top of Harcourt. The tail lashed out, its barbed point whistling in the air. The driving claws tore up turf and flung great gouts of it.

Harcourt threw himself to one side to escape the driving beak. The strike missed him by a hair's-breadth and his blade came slashing down, aimed at the outstretched neck. The edge, turning at an angle, caught the heavy scales at the back of the head and went skating off, nearly wrenching the weapon from his hand. The dragon turned its head and slashed at him, the beak grazing his leg and throwing him off balance. In front of him, as he staggered back, a great maul of metal caught the dragon squarely on the head. The head jerked back and hit the abbot in the chest, hurling him to one side. Sprawling on the ground, he scrambled after the mace that had been knocked from his grasp. In the tree, where it had sought safety, the parrot screeched.

Recovering from his stagger, Harcourt leaped forward to stand astride his friend, the sword raised high as the dragon's head struck down again. The sword caught the beak and sheared it off, and the blunted head struck, knocking him down on top of the abbot. Another arrow whickered and slammed into one of the dragon's eyes. Fluid gushed out of the socket and ran across the face. The head jerked up again, and there, astride the dragon's neck, was the Knurly Man, his legs locked around the neck, the battle-axe chopping down. It came down and rose once more and chopped again. The dragon folded in upon itself, toppling to the ground.

Harcourt, his left side a throbbing ache from one of the blows of the massive head, got to his feet. The dragon was down, its tail threshing, its neck half severed. The Knurly Man was trapped beneath the neck; Harcourt, reaching out, grasped him by the shoulder and pulled him free.

"That was a crazy thing to do," he said.

The Knurly Man made no answer, but moved off to one side, the bloody axe still clutched in his hand.

The abbot was getting to his feet. He had picked up the mace and now held it raised.

"No more need for it," Harcourt told him. "It's finished."

"I got in a lick," the abbot said. "A very solid lick."

Yolanda came walking out from under the tree, bow in hand, an arrow nocked.

Harcourt knelt to wipe the blade, although, truth to tell, there was little blood on it. It took him a while to get to his feet again.

"My lord, you're hurt," Yolanda said.

"Bruised," he said. "That's all."

The dragon was still quivering, but the upturned feet had ceased their clawing and the barbed tail was motionless. The trailing rope tied to the dragon's neck was laid out, rather neatly, on the ground.

Harcourt asked the Knurly Man, "Are you all right?"

"Just the wind knocked out of me," said the Knurly Man. "When I hit the ground."

"Why doesn't someone ask me how I am?" the abbot complained.

"All right," said Harcourt. "How are you?"

"I'm perfectly fine," the abbot said. "Somewhat knocked about, but fine. Although you could have asked."

"I did ask."

"But not until I reminded you," the abbot said.

"We all came out of it lucky," Yolanda said.

"Not lucky," said the abbot. "By the valor of our arms."

"Not our valor," said Harcourt. "It was the Knurly Man."

"One does what he may," said the Knurly Man. "Each one does his best."

"And thus it ends," the abbot said. "This thing of many years ago, when two boys of twelve tried to catch a dragon."

"Do you think it may have remembered all these years?" asked Harcourt.

"Who knows?" the abbot said.

The parrot flew down out of the tree and landed on the

fallen dragon. It pranced back and forth along the carcass; it squawked and chortled and sometimes flapped its wings.

"There is no need for us to celebrate our victory," said the Knurly Man. "The abbot's grotesque bird celebrates it for us."

"It is not my bird," the abbot said sourly. "Rather than its belonging to me, I belong to it. I am that bird's abbot. It rides me like a horse. It looks to me to feed it and it befouls my cassock disgracefully and with no respect."

"We should be leaving here," Yolanda said. "This disruption of our journey may attract attention."

"That's right," said Harcourt. "We should be moving on."

"You are limping," said the Knurly Man. "Can you withstand hard travel?"

"I told you I am only bruised and sore," said Harcourt. "Something hit me. I think it was the dragon's head, but I cannot be sure. Too much was happening, and too fast."

"Where is our friend the troll?" the abbot asked.

"He disappeared," Yolanda said. "As soon as the trouble started. The last I saw of him, he was skittering for the woods. The rope was still around his neck, and the trailing end of it he carried in his hand."

"Let us hope," said the Knurly Man, "that somewhere he finds another good, stout limb and that this time the rope will hold."

Yolanda started to walk toward the woods that hemmed in the Wishing Well. When she reached it, she waited for them. "We have been traveling steadily west, and the Evil know this," she said. "If some of them come upon the dragon, and in time they will—probably very shortly—they'll think we still are moving west and will seek us there."

"What you are saying," said the Knurly Man, "is that we should change direction."

"Not entirely," she said. "Not for long. But for a time, perhaps, we should travel north."

"But danger may lie in that direction," the abbot protested. "When we were watching from the hilltop, we saw bands of the Evil traveling north of west. We wouldn't want to become entangled with them."

"I'll run ahead and keep sharp watch," she said. "If there are Evil about, I can smell them out. And we'll not keep north for long. A day or two is all."

"Before we leave," said the Knurly Man, "there's one thing

else to do. We are at the Wishing Well. We should peer into it. We should make at least an effort to spy out our future."

"You peer if you wish," said the abbot. "As for me, I refuse to do it. This gazing into wells is all foolishness."

"While you're looking in the well," Harcourt told the Knurly Man, "I'll get the rope off the dragon's neck. The dragon has worn it long enough. It belongs to me."

He turned about and walked back to where the dragon lay. So long ago, he thought, and it was then so small, no larger than the boy of twelve who had tried to capture it, although even then a hissing, snapping thing and nothing one should fool with.

He stepped in close to the body and picked up the rope. The noose, he saw, was frayed. It was only by good chance that the dragon still wore it. One of these days soon, it would have parted and fallen from the dragon's neck.

He stood for a moment, considering, then dropped the rope and walked away. He told himself, Let the dragon keep it; it has worn it long enough to have established ownership. Although acting unintentionally, he had given it to the dragon, had made a gift of it. And he did not take back a gift once given. He, Harcourt, would not loot the dead.

The Knurly Man was coming from the well.

"What did you see?" asked Harcourt.

The Knurly Man grimaced. "I saw myself," he said.

Seventeen

They huddled in a cold camp through the night. They ate from their knapsacks and scooped up water from a small rill in their hands to drink. The place they had chosen to camp was a somber pocket of woods between two rolling hills. Great trees crowded close, and an owl kept hooting all the night.

Harcourt dreamed of Eloise. He was in a flower-strewn meadow of early springtime, standing beside the horse she sat and looking up at her. There were other riders gathered all around, and they were about to start out on a long journey

and were impatient to leave. But he could not let them leave,
he told himself, until he had caught a full glimpse of her face.
A soft spring breeze was blowing; it blew a strand of hair
across her face, and because of that blown strand, he could
not make out her features. Each time that he thought he was
about to capture them, the strand of hair would blow again
and he'd lose everything he had seen of her. She did not speak
to him, she did not smile at him, she did not lift a hand to
brush the strand away; she helped him not at all. "Eloise!" he
cried to her. "Eloise!" But even as he cried out her name, the
other riders started moving off, and she was moving with
them. He tried to run alongside her, but the horse she rode
was walking briskly, and there was something wrong with
Harcourt's legs. He could not move them as he ordinarily
would; it seemed as if he were wading through a stream of
knee-deep, rapidly running water. He pleaded for her to wait,
but she did not wait, pulling away from him. Finally he
stopped and watched the company of riders move away from
him, the horses breaking into a lope and pulling farther off.
He tried to keep his eyes on Eloise and the horse that she was
riding, but he lost her for a moment. When he tried to pick
her up again, he couldn't; she was only one of several riders,
and he could not tell which one. He stood until the riders had
disappeared, leaving the meadow empty. When he turned
about to go back home, he found that he was in unfamiliar
country.

There was a castle, but not the kind of castle that he had
known as home. This one was a dreamlike castle, scarcely
substantial, with the spires and turrets and slender towers
hanging about it, as if they were not part of the castle at all,
but were suspended in the air above it, hanging, as it were,
between earth and heaven. To his left stood a field of ripened
grain, with peasants building shocks while the reapers went
swinging down the field, their scythes glinting in the sunlight.
Beyond the field was an orchard, with people climbing the
trees to pick the fruit, their buckets and baskets scattered on
the ground, waiting to be filled and carried home. He heard a
shout far off to his right; looking in that direction, he saw
swineherds bringing in the hogs, waving sticks and shouting at
the hogs, calling back and forth to one another.

The land he stood on, which had been unfamiliar when he
first had seen it, now began to tug at him for recognition. It
was not as unfamiliar as he had thought; somewhere in the
past he had seen this very land. Then it came to him; this was

the miniature that was on one of the pages of the book of hours Eloise had given him—a painting come to life. His heart leaped up with gladness, and he started to run toward the castle. For, he told himself, Eloise was in the castle, and he would find her and, finding her, would see her face again. But he was running in place; hard as he tried to run, he did not move at all. The castle stayed where it was, no farther off, no nearer, hanging there, poised between heaven and earth. He had to get there, he had to reach the gate and climb the spires and towers, crying out for Eloise so that she would know he was there and would come to greet him. He tried to run harder, pumping his arms in rhythm with his legs, bending forward, striving forward as he ran, panting with his running.

He heard a cry behind him. Looking over his shoulder, he saw that the company of horsemen Eloise had ridden off with was coming back again. They were coming hard and fast. The horses were running full out, and their riders bent forward in the saddles, urging on their mounts. In the forefront of them rode Eloise, her hair streaming in the wind, urging on her horse and yelling with the others.

The company was headed straight toward him, and it was quite apparent they meant to run him down. Fear gulping in his throat, he made a superhuman effort to break whatever it was that held him running in one place. Breaking it, he fled, running and dodging like a hunted rabbit, while behind him the horses thundered, closing in on him, sharp hooves lashing out, bared teeth shining. His breath gasped in his throat, and a great hand seized his chest and squeezed.

He stumbled and fell, and as he fell he awoke, panting with his running, huddled with his fall.

The owl hooted at him in derisive tones. Somewhere in the darkness the abbot's parrot was chuckling to itself. Trees waved above him—he could feel their movement in the darkness—and now and then he could see, through the waving branches, the hard, cold glint of stars. The woods in which he lay were dark and dreary.

He elbowed himself to a sitting position. To one side of him, a short distance off, lay a lump of deeper darkness. More than likely, he thought, it was the sleeping Knurly Man. It couldn't be the abbot, for the chuckling of the parrot, which should be with the abbot, was coming from an opposite direction.

He tossed the blanket to one side and rose. Footsteps

shuffled and he turned to face the sound, his hand going to the hilt of the sword.

The abbot's voice spoke to him. "What is the matter, Charles?" The parrot grumbled at him.

"I'm all right," said Harcourt. "I woke from a dream."

"A bad dream?"

"A disturbing dream. I dreamed of Eloise."

The abbot moved closer, a blob of shadow in the dark. "Charles, you must not hope too much. Your uncle's story . . ."

"I know it is naught but a story. I have known all along. Stories come so easily from a land like this. But it gave me hope."

"You must be prepared for disappointment."

"I know that, Guy. But I cling so hard to hope. And yet . . ."

"And yet? What do you mean—and yet?"

"In my dream Eloise tried to ride me down. Not she alone, but others who were with her, and she in the forefront of them. They came charging at me, and I ran and ran."

"You have Eloise too much upon your conscience, Charles. You think too often of her. You blame yourself when there is no blame for anyone. You have tried hard to remember her, as if remembering her were some sort of recompense. Perhaps trying to keep hope alive by remembering her."

"In the fen there were many voices whispering. They spoke of Eloise."

"I heard them," said the abbot. "They did not speak of Eloise."

"To you they would not have spoken of her."

"Nor did they speak of her to you. It was your imagination and your guilt that made you think you'd heard her name. A guilt that you should not carry, that there is no reason you should carry. Charles, how long are you to continue torturing yourself?"

"I do not think of it as torture."

"No, you think of it as a deathless adoration for a woman whose face has fled your memory. You've lived a monklike life, doing penance when there was no penance to be done. You must try to drop this load you carry."

"Guy, you are a hard man. You have no . . ."

"In my calling," said the abbot, "at times I must be hard."

"Are we wrong, Guy?" asked Harcourt. "Were we swept away by our emotions into this journey? I swept by Eloise, you by the prisoned saint?"

"Perhaps we were," the abbot said. "That well might be

the case. But it does not mean that our purpose is the less. There's still good reason for our being here."

"Have you ever wondered how it might turn out? Can you foresee the end?"

"I have no foresight," said the abbot. "All I have is a steady faith in God. We must not question why we're here. Here, in the darkness of the night, as we watch against the Evil, perhaps are surrounded by the Evil, our thoughts are painted with a somber brush. One must not take counsel with himself in the dark of night. Then all thoughts are black; all hopes are dim."

"Perhaps you're right," said Harcourt. "Why don't you let me take the rest of the watch? I don't want to sleep again. I'd fear the dream coming back to me."

"If you would," the abbot said, "I would appreciate it. I am dead upon my feet. I carry too much weight."

"Awrrk," the parrot said.

"There is nothing going on," the abbot said. "That fool owl keeps chortling, and to the north there have been many wolves. I've heard them all the night, howling back and forth. As if they were gathering in force. But far enough away to be no threat to us."

"Off to your blanket, then," said Harcourt. "Take mine as well. It will help to keep you warm."

For a long time after the abbot had rolled himself in the blankets, Harcourt stood where he was, not moving, listening to the incessant chuckling of the owl. Now and then, far off to the north, he heard the howling of the wolves. The howling, he told himself, was unusual at this time of year. Wolves howled late in autumn and into the winter, but only occasionally in the spring and summer. There must, he thought, be something taking place to get them so stirred up.

His eyes became acclimated to the darkness, and he could make out the huddled forms of the other three. The abbot began to snore and gulp. The parrot grumbled. The owl, at length, fell silent. Light slowly began to filter through the woods. Harcourt paced up and down as quietly as he could in an effort to keep warm.

When the light strengthened somewhat, he roused his companions.

"It's still dark," the abbot complained. "It isn't morning yet."

"It's light enough to see where we are going," Harcourt told him. "We'll start without breakfast and get in an hour or two of traveling. We can stop later, after the sun is up, to eat. Perhaps we can take the chance of a fire and do some cooking."

He glanced inquiringly at Yolanda. She nodded. "I think we can. We'll not need to keep it burning long. We need hot food. Oatmeal, perhaps."

"And bacon?" asked the abbot.

She smiled at him. "And bacon."

The abbot brightened up. "That's more like it," he said. "Cold rations lie heavy in the belly."

Eighteen

That day and the morning of the next day they made good time. Travel was not difficult. Much of the land was open, spotted with groves of trees. A number of times they came upon abandoned homesteads, the fields gone to brush and weeds, the buildings sagging in decay. At one time this area had been filled with fruitful farms. There were no hills to climb; the land was a long expanse of swales. They kept close watch for dragons and other flying things, but saw none, not even a flight of fairies.

The Knurly Man, using his bow late in the afternoon of the first day, brought down a young boar that exploded out of a thicket as they came up. That night they built a fire and feasted on pork, extinguishing the fire after the cooking was done. Possibly there was no need of such precaution, for they seemed to be traveling in an empty area, but Yolanda insisted on it.

"One whiff of smoke may bring the Evil down on us," she said. "Sleeping in a warm camp is not worth the chance."

Harcourt sat beside her as they feasted on the pork. "What does the seashell tell you?" he asked.

It was a silly question, he knew. The seashell could tell them nothing; it had no faculty of foresight. Yet it was one of the few things they had, and besides, Yolanda believed in it. Her courage and devotion to the cause might be bolstered by talking of it, seeming to take it seriously. For she did seem to take it seriously; the shell, she had said, had warned her that the ogres were following on that day they had reached the island.

"It tells me nothing," she said. "That, I suppose, means the peddler has nothing to tell me."

"Or that he does not know," said Harcourt.

"Perhaps, although there's not much he misses. The peddler is a good wizard, a most efficient one."

"And he is working for us? In our interest? You can be sure of that?"

She hesitated for a moment before she answered. "As sure as I can be of anything. I've known him for a long time and I trust him."

"Then all that you are told by the shell comes from the peddler."

"My lord," she said, looking at him challengingly, "that also is something of which I cannot be sure. It is the peddler's shell, which he has loaned me, but I can't tell you whether it carries only the peddler's knowledge or the knowledge of someone or something else that may have even a greater knowledge."

Harcourt gave up. Further discussion, he was certain, would only lead him into metaphysical depths with which he could not cope. He had no wish to find himself floundering in a morass of wizardry.

"Well," he said, rather lamely, "by all means, keep on listening."

That night, just before morning, a brisk spring shower burst upon them, and they crawled out of their blankets wet and miserable. The sun, when it rose, was bright and warm, with the shower long gone and only a few fugitive clouds sailing across the springtime blueness of the sky. They soon dried out, although their blankets stayed wet.

"We'll have to stop," said Yolanda, "well before the setting of the sun and spread them out so they'll get dry."

Several times they sighted skulking wolves. Later on buzzards began flying across the skies in threes and fours. Shortly after midday, Yolanda came running back to them.

"We must be nearing the nest of harpies the peddler warned us of," she said. "There's a taint upon the air. That could be a sign of harpies."

"Whereabouts?" the abbot asked.

She pointed. "It seems to come from there. Slightly north of here."

"I think we may have more than a harpy nest," said the Knurly Man. "There have been too many wolves. They were howling in the night and we've seen them along the way. Also, there are buzzards."

Harcourt looked sharply at him. "You mean . . ."

"It could be," said the Knurly Man. "From the sentinel hill we saw a vast movement of the Evil. Hurrying north and west. A gathering of some sort."

"We'll have a look," said Harcourt.

"But cautiously," said the Knurly Man. "Very cautiously."

Taking advantage of whatever cover they could, never moving out into the open until they had taken time to examine the way ahead closely, they proceeded in the direction Yolanda had pointed out. They had not gone far when they caught the first faint whiff of the sickening taint of decomposing flesh. It became stronger as they moved ahead. They climbed a small hill, although somewhat higher than others they had been encountering. They went on hands and knees up the final slope; the stench had become stronger, and it was apparent they must be nearing its source. When they finally reached the top, they saw what they had been smelling.

The opposite side of the hill sloped down to a small valley, and in the valley and on the hillside lay huddled shapes. Vultures and other birds of prey perched on some of them. Over others of the sodden heaps wolves were feeding, snarling and snapping at one another to protect their meat. Scraps of fabric, caught on bushes, in some cases still attached to the dead, fluttered in the wind. A horse lay on its back, its four feet extended in the air. Many of the heaps were indistinguishable; others, they could see, were men, and still others of them Evil. There were places where the bodies lay in heaps; otherwise they lay scattered all about, up and down the slope and across the valley. Sunlight reflected off shields and swords. A fox, chased by a wolf snapping at its heels, ran for its life, dodging its way among the fallen dead. The whiteness of bare bones, stripped clean by the wolves and vultures, showed here and there among the heaps. Vultures, seething groups of them, fought among themselves over the heaps of the dead. And up from the valley came rolling the sickening, wretching stink of death.

The abbot said, his words choking as he said them, "There is a man down there. A man among the wolves, feeding on the dead."

"Not a man," said the Knurly Man. "I saw it, too, and have been watching it. It is not a man, rather it's a ghoul."

"I don't see it," Harcourt said.

Yolanda, lying next to him, grasped his arm. "Over there," she said. "See where I am pointing."

He looked and at first did not see the ghoul, then he did—a figure humped above a dead man, tearing at the body with its hands and teeth.

"It's not like a man," said Harcourt. "It is like a . . ."

At that moment it raised its head and stared up the hill toward where he was lying hidden. Apparently it did not see him, although for a moment he thought it had.

Its face was quasi-human. Its dank hair hung down in greasy locks about its face and neck. Its mouth was slack and loose, and sharp teeth gleamed inside the mouth. Even in the day its feral eyes seemed to shine with a hellish light. Its face was smeared with a greasy, dripping blackness.

Gagging, Harcourt put down his head, holding it against the ground to cut the stench of the battlefield, breathing in the scent of soil and grass—but still the gagging smell came through—clamping his eyes tightly shut to close out, even in his memory, the sight of the foully besmudged, almost-human face.

Scant days ago, he thought, he had sat his horse and talked with the centurion from whose helmet had floated scarlet plumes. Our tribune is out for glory, the centurion had said; he is apt to get us killed. Harcourt raised his head and looked down the slope, searching for the sight of scarlet plumes. If they were there, he failed to see them.

Decimus. But there had been more to it than that. It had been one of those long, proud names the Romans were so fond of bearing. Decimus Apollo . . . no, that wasn't it. Decimus Apollinarius Valenturian, that had been the whole of it. When you come back, Harcourt remembered saying to the Roman, stop by and we'll have a drink together.

But now, most likely, he would not be coming back and they'd not have a drink together. If I get back myself, Harcourt told himself. Although, he said, talking silently to himself, that is not the way to think. That's the way to get oneself killed. One must never doubt.

He whispered to the Knurly Man, not knowing why he whispered, "Now the fat is really in the fire."

"The Empty Land, right now," said the Knurly Man, also speaking low, "is not the place for humans."

"It doesn't look," said Harcourt, "as if many of the Romans got away."

"Perhaps none of them," said the Knurly Man. "This place must have swarmed with Evil. We saw them gathering and we had only one point of observation. They may have been pouring in from all directions."

"Where are they now?"

"There is no way for us to know. Probably all together somewhere for a victory celebration."

"The stench is too much for me," said Harcourt. "It brings back seven years ago. I'm leaving."

"We should go quietly. Not too visibly. Keep down."

"The battle's over. There is no one here but the scavengers and the dead."

"Nevertheless," said the Knurly Man, "keep low and back off quietly. One can never know what's here."

Harcourt started down the slope up which they'd climbed, bending down to keep his profile low. He saw the Knurly Man and the other two doing the same.

What rotten luck, he thought. Up to this point, they had been doing rather well. But once the victory celebration—if there were, indeed, a celebration—was over, the Evil once more would disperse, carrying with it again the ancient hatred for all things human. This renewed hatred, he thought, might result in fresh attacks upon the borderland. Certainly, within the Empty Land itself no human would be safe. What little tolerance that had until now existed between the Evil and the humans would have been swept away. It would be kill on sight.

Why the hell, he asked himself, did the Romans have to come messing in? A reconnaissance, Decimus had said. And maybe it would have been all right, maybe it could have been accomplished fairly peacefully, if it had been no more than a reconnaissance, quick in, quick out, to assess the situation. But there had been clashes, perhaps inconsequential in themselves, and the legion had stayed on too long. That was the trouble, he thought—they had stayed too long, allowing the Evil the time to mass against them.

Reaching the foot of the slope, the four of them stopped in the shelter of a small grove of trees. For a time they simply stood and looked at one another, shocked and sorrowed by what they'd seen, and worried.

Finally, the abbot asked the Knurly Man, "What do we do

now? Do we go on or should we turn back? Personally, I favor going on, but possibly we should warn the border."

The Knurly Man shook his head. "I can't tell you, abbot. It all depends on the Evil's cast of mind. I doubt if anyone can tell you. Who is there who knows the Evil well enough to say?"

"Yolanda may," said Harcourt. "She knows this place better than any of the rest of us."

They all looked at Yolanda. She answered with a negatory sign. "This is not my expedition," she said. "I'm simply along to help in any way I can."

"But you must have some opinion," said the abbot. "You should feel free to speak it. We're in this all together, you no less than any other of us."

"We're halfway to where we're going," she said. "Perhaps somewhat more than halfway. The Evil is always dangerous, more so at this moment because of the battle, but always dangerous. It has been a danger every step we've taken."

"Our first job is to find the cathedral," said the Knurly Man, "and talk with the priest whom Charles's uncle spoke of. We do not know where the cathedral lies. West of here, we know, but where west? We may have to do a lot of blundering around to find it. That would compound the danger. If we knew exactly where it was, we could make a straight run for it."

"Listen," Yolanda said softly. "Listen. I heard something."

They grew silent and listened. For a moment there was only silence, then they heard a moan.

"It's over there," said the abbot. "Someone in agony. Perhaps a survivor of the battle."

He stepped quickly forward, coming to a halt before a small clump of bushes.

"It's here," he said. "Whatever it is, it is in these bushes."

Harcourt leaped to his side, put a hand on his shoulder, and pulled him back.

"Go easy," the Knurly Man warned. "Be certain what it is before you go rushing in."

Harcourt bent down to peer into the bushes. Eyes glittered back at him. Shaggy brows bushed out above the eyes. Thick black hair, tangled by briars and small twigs, hung down about the face. The mouth beneath the hooked nose opened, displaying fangs. The face, not quite human, was thin and hard.

Harcourt stepped back. "It's a harpy," he said. "I'm sure it is a harpy."

"But it's hurt," the abbot said. "It has an arrow in it. It is suffering."

"Let it stay hurt, then," said the Knurly Man. "It crawled off to die, so let it die."

The abbot crouched down to peer into the bushes. "Knurly," he said reprovingly, "that is not the Christian way. We succor even our mortal enemies when they are in desperate need."

"Succor it," said the Knurly Man, "and it will do its best to kill you even while you succor it. Step clear. For the love of Christ, step clear!"

The abbot made no move to step clear of the bushes and the wounded harpy, so Harcourt, who had drawn back, stepped forward once again, reaching out to seize the abbot and haul him back. But even as he reached out for the abbot, the harpy hurled itself out of the bushes to land on top of the crouching abbot. It sprawled on top of him, its taloned feet slashing at him, its fanged mouth gnawing, seeking for his throat. Harcourt whipped out his sword, but before he could thrust with the blade, Yolanda hurled herself upon the harpy, her belt knife striking down, lifting and striking once again and yet again, blood spattering from its blade. The harpy went limp and tumbled off the prostrate abbot. Yolanda, kneeling beside the abbot, kept on striking at the harpy.

Harcourt gently pulled her back and set her on her feet.

The abbot sat up slowly and Harcourt knelt beside him. Blood was showing on the cassock.

"My legs," the abbot panted. "They burn like fire where the talons slashed me. And its teeth closed on my shoulder."

The Knurly Man was beside the abbot, bending over. "We'll take a look at you," he said. "See how bad it is."

The abbot chattered at them. "Its fangs were closing on my throat when I knocked its head away. If it had bitten me in the throat . . ."

"Yes, I know," said Harcourt, "but it didn't. Let us find out what it did."

He began untying the thongs that held the abbot's cassock closed.

"I have an ointment," said the Knurly Man, "we can use upon the wounds. It will smart, but you must bear it. A harpy feeds on foul matter, and it could be poison."

The Knurly Man came back with a jar of ointment he had taken from his pack.

"Now cease all that caterwauling," he told the abbot, speaking sternly. "We must tend to you, and you're not helping us."

Once the abbot was stripped of his cassock, it could be seen that his legs had been deeply gashed by the harpy's talons, while on his shoulder deep punctures, inflicted by the fangs, were oozing drops of blood.

"Hold him down," said the Knurly Man. "The ointment stings like the fires of hell. Try to hold him tight. I'll have to try to work it deep into the wounds."

The abbot howled and screamed and threshed about, but Harcourt, aided by Yolanda, held him down while the Knurly Man rubbed the ointment in.

When the two of them released their hold, the abbot sat up, grimacing.

"You could have been more gentle about it," he complained. "You manhandled me most irreverently. And you," he said to the Knurly Man, "were somewhat more energetic and ruthless than seemed quite necessary."

"I had to get it over with," said the Knurly Man, "as swiftly as I could. The ointment must be well rubbed in to be of any use at all."

Harcourt pulled the cassock about the abbot and began refastening the thongs. The abbot knocked his hands away. "I can manage that myself," he said.

"He makes an ornery patient," said the Knurly Man. "He has no gratitude for what we've done for him."

Yolanda picked up the knife that she had dropped and bent to wipe it on the grass, finishing the cleaning by wiping it on her robe, which was no longer white, but stained by grease and dirt. The blood she wiped off the knife made the robe seem more picturesque. She kicked the dead harpy, rolling it over on its back. A broken arrow protruded from its side.

"All this would have been unnecessary," said the Knurly Man, "if we had let well enough alone. The harpy would have died in any case if we'd had nothing to do with it. And we should not have concerned ourselves with it. You do not minister to a snake with a broken back." He said to the abbot, "I warned you. I told you to stand clear. But you, with your foggy sense of Christian ethics . . ."

"Ever since we started out, you have been making snide remarks about my Christianity," said the abbot. "And I tell you this—faulty as my Christian ethics may appear to you, they are better than any you may hold."

"I have no ethics," said the Knurly Man. "I'm a complete infidel from every theologic view, believing in nothing whatsoever. What I can't understand is how your point of view has changed. Back there, the first day we were out, you assailed a mound with that monstrous mace of yours, pounding it flat into the ground. Not knowing what it was, you obliterated it. And now, come what may and against all warning, you must need succor a known enemy, and what is more—"

"Stop it immediately," Harcourt said to the Knurly Man, speaking harshly. "You've been needling the abbot for days. Not for any good reason. Just to stir him up. What pleasure you get out of it I cannot imagine, but, for the love of God, make an end of it."

"The thing about it is that he doesn't mean it," said the abbot. "He says he has no ethics, but he has, although they may seem at times a rather funny set of ethics. He boasts that he is an infidel, and he's not an infidel, and furthermore—"

"You, too," said Harcourt. "The both of you shut up."

"Well," said Yolanda, "on such a brotherly basis, what do we do now?"

"We continue on our way," said the Knurly Man. "This area is dangerous. Once the word gets around, there will be sightseers pouring in to gawk at the battlefield. Looters, too, more than likely. There still is a lot of booty to be picked up out there."

"It seems to me," the abbot grumbled, "that we've been on the run ever since Jean took us across the river. Either something's after us, or we're afraid that something's after us."

"However that may be," said Harcourt, "I would judge that Knurly's right. We have to do more hard traveling. How about it, Guy? Can you manage it?"

The abbot heaved himself to his feet. "I can manage it," he said. "The worst of it is that cursed ointment that was smeared on me. It still smarts and burns."

"Those are deep cuts," Yolanda said. "Later on you will stiffen up. We'd best cover all the ground we're able to before you stiffen up."

"We should start, then," said the abbot. "The question is, which way do we go?"

"We continue west," said Harcourt, hoping he was right.

Nineteen

Well before sunset, rain began to fall, a persistent drizzling rain that gave no sign of stopping. It was the sort of slow, soft rain that promised to continue through the night and into the following day. Looking for shelter where they could hole up for the night, they did not find it. No cave, no tumbledown farmhouse, no ancient shed or barn, not even a dense pine thicket which, while not constituting an actual shelter, would still give some protection against the weather.

After a few hours, the abbot began to falter. At times his legs gave way beneath him; at other times he mumbled and seemed not to know where he was. While Yolanda ranged ahead, seeking some place where they could keep at least marginally dry, Harcourt and the Knurly Man helped the blundering abbot along.

"We have to find a place for him," said the Knurly Man. "He is hot and flushed. The man is burning up with a fever. I was right. The harpy carried poison in its talons and its fangs."

And that was not the whole of it, Harcourt thought. They'd had no opportunity to dry out the blankets that had been soaked in the storm of the night before. Now the blankets were getting even wetter, and there was nothing that could be used to wrap the abbot in to guard against a chill. They could have built a fire, of course, for even in the wettest weather dry wood could be found, but they needed more than fire. The abbot was a sick man and needed care, and there was no way they could give him care.

It's all wrong, Harcourt told himself. It all had been wrong from the very start. He and the abbot were chasing illusions. The other two were along because their help was needed in the illusion-chasing, Yolanda because her adoptive parents were retainers of the Harcourt fief since time immemorial, the Knurly Man because of his love for an old man to whom he was more than brother, because of a now grown-up child he once had trotted on his foot. Guy chased the Lasandra crystal in which, as legend had it, a saint's soul was imprisoned; but there was no evidence there ever had been such a crystal, no evidence that any soul, let alone the soul of a saint, had been imprisoned in it. And he, Charles Harcourt, chased the memory of a woman who, more than likely, had been dead these seven years and whose face he no longer could remember.

He had told himself earlier in the day that he must not doubt, and now he doubted. It was the rain, he thought, the persistent drizzle of the rain, the deepening of the chill that thickened in the air, the oncoming gloom of night, that made him doubt; still, when he tried with all logic to cancel out the influence of the rain, the chill, the gloom of approaching night, the doubt did not go away. It still remained.

I do not know, he said, talking to himself. I cannot decide. Am I right or wrong? Are we right or wrong? Should we all have stayed at home? Should we have plunged, driven by emotion and by hope, into this adventure?

The abbot staggered and fell. Harcourt tried to hold him erect, but the abbot slipped out of his grasp. The Knurly Man stumbled to his knees, still grasping the abbot's arm, but upset by his greater weight. Face down, the abbot mumbled at them. The parrot, dislodged from the abbot's shoulder, flew above them, screeching in distress.

The Knurly Man looked across the fallen abbot at Harcourt. "We must do something for him. We must find some place where he'll be out of the rain and be warm. Otherwise he'll die."

The rain slanted down, a stream of silver falling from the sky.

Whiteness flickered in the silvered air and Yolanda stood before them, drenched and slimmer than she had ever seemed before, the waterlogged robe she wore hanging straight, not billowing, clinging to her body.

"I've found shelter," she said. "A hut deep in the wood. Smoke comes from its chimney, light is shining from its window."

"Who's there?" the Knurly Man asked. "Whom does the hut belong to?"

"It matters not," said Harcourt. "No matter whom the hut belongs to, we take it for the night. Grab the abbot's legs, and I'll take him by the shoulders. We'll carry him."

He was difficult to carry. His huge weight bore down on them. At times his dragging bottom scraped along the ground. But they carried him, puffing and panting, stooped over, grunting with the effort. Now and then they were forced to let him down, but, after a moment's rest, picked him up again and lugged him a short distance farther.

At last they saw the light through the trees and arrived at the door of the hut. Here they let the abbot down and stood waiting while Yolanda knocked at the slipshod door. The hut, what little could be seen of it, was a poor thing at best. It was a ramshackle collection of logs and broken branches, and there was but one window in it. The window at one time might have been of glass, but some of the panes were broken, and tanned hides had been tacked over the broken panes. At one corner of the hut stood a rude clay chimney, smoke drifting from it.

Yolanda still was rapping at the door, and so far no one had come to open it. Then the door edged open, no more than a crack, and a face peered out. But the crack was so narrow there was no way one could tell what kind of face it was.

"Who's there?" a cracked and quavering voice asked. "Who comes knocking at my door?"

"Travelers," Yolanda said, "in dire need of shelter. We have a sick man with us."

The door opened wider, and now it could be seen that the one who stood there was an ancient crone. Her hair was white and her face so puckered that it seemed she had no teeth. She was clothed in rags.

"Why," she said, "it is a lass. Who would expect a lass to come knocking at my door? There are others with you?"

"There are four in all. One of us is ill."

The crone heaved the door wide open. "Then, my child, come in. And bring the others with you. Old Nan does not refuse to share her hovel with the needy and the sick. Come in and sit close against the fire, and soon there'll be a bite to eat, although I cannot vouch for its toothsomeness."

Harcourt and the Knurly Man picked up the abbot and carried him through the door. Old Nan pulled it shut behind them. The hut was small, but still somewhat larger than it had appeared to be when viewed from the outside. A blaze leaped in the fireplace, beside which stood a rack of wood. The floor was beaten earth, and there were wide cracks in the walls through which the wind was blowing, but the heat of the blazing fire drove back the chill borne on the wind. A lone rush-bottomed chair stood before the fireplace, and to one side was a pallet, close against the floor. In one corner was a large, stout table, and upon it were bowls and mugs and a spoon or two; piled on it, against the wall, were book scrolls, heaped one upon the other.

The crone, tottering as she moved, fluttered around Harcourt and the Knurly Man, indicating the pallet.

"Put him down there," she said, "and get his wet clothes off. I'll find sheepskins we can roll him in. Poor man, what is wrong with him?"

"Good dame," said the Knurly Man, "he was clawed and bitten by a harpy."

"Oh, those vicious things!" Old Nan cried. "They are worse than all the others. They are such filthy things that a touch of them is deadly, and they stink to the very heavens."

Harcourt and the Knurly Man placed the abbot on the pallet, and at the sight of him laid out, Old Nan exclaimed in wonderment.

"Why, he is of the cloth!" she screeched. "How comes a churchman here? This is no place at all for someone such as he." Swiftly she crossed herself.

"He comes on holy business," Harcourt told her. "He is the head of an abbey south of the river."

"An abbot!" she cried. "An abbot in my house!"

Harcourt reminded her, "You said something about sheepskins."

"That I did," she said. "I'll get them."

The Knurly Man divested the abbot of his clothing, and Old Nan brought the sheepskins; she used one of them to rub him dry, then wrapped him in the others.

"He's either asleep," the Knurly Man told Harcourt, "or out of his head. Doing a lot of mumbling."

The parrot had settled on the back of the chair in front of the fireplace. Old Nan, going to the hearth to stir something cooking in a kettle, brusquely knocked it off its perch.

"Where did that bird come from?" she demanded. "It was not here before."

"It came with us," said Harcourt. "It is the abbot's bird."

"Well, it's all right, then. But what would an abbot want with a gaudy bird like that?"

"I don't think he ever really wanted it," said Yolanda. "It was sort of wished on him."

The old woman bent to stir the kettle. "This is my night," she said, "for the taking in of strays. You," she screeched at something huddling in a corner, "you come out of there!"

The other three turned about to see what she was talking to. Slowly, seemingly reluctantly, the huddle in the corner stirred, came to life, uncurled, and stood up. Broken fangs gleamed in the wavering firelight. Mangy fur stood out in tufts, and a broken rope was knotted on the neck.

"Our troll," said Harcourt, astonished, "the one that tried to hang himself."

"It is a poor, befuddled creature," said Old Nan. "Cast out by its own people and with no friend in the world. It turned to me in lieu of any other. I tried to unknot the rope around its neck, but it pulled away. It wears the rope as a badge of shame. It will not have it otherwise."

The abbot mumbled on the pallet. The parrot, hidden somewhere in the shadows, mumbled back. The old crone took a bowl and spoon off the table and ladled some of the contents of the pot into the dish. She handed the bowl to the Knurly Man and said, "Here, get some of this into your mumbling friend. It will warm his gut against the pain."

"He's burning up," said the Knurly Man. "His face is flushed, his brow is hot. It's the poison from his wounds. I rubbed an ointment in them, but it did little good."

"You must fight poison from the inside, not the outside," said Old Nan. "Here, the rest of you get bowls and eat some of the stew cooking on the hearth. You, too," she said to the troll. "You need some of it as well. While the rest of you are eating, I'll fix a draught that will help the abbot fight the poison. You," she said to Harcourt, "take that stool over there and climb up on it, handing down to me from the rafters what I tell you."

Harcourt glanced upward at the rafters and saw that hanging from them were bundles of plants and grasses and roots all neatly tied together.

"I hang them there," said the crone, "to keep them from the mice that overrun the place, sharing it with me."

Harcourt hauled out the stool and mounted it, handing down what she pointed to.

"There," she finally said, "I think that these will do. I'll sing some little songs while I prepare the potion, and I pray you pay no attention to them. They are not the foolishness of an old woman, and I would not have you think so. They are part of the prescription, and while I have a suspicion they do no good, I am careful always to intone them on the chance there may be some value in them."

She got to work, kneeling before the hearth, scraping and kneading and thumping and bruising the various ingredients Harcourt had handed down to her, mixing them all energetically in a wide-mouthed jar to which, at times, she added liquid from tiny vials and powders from ornate boxes, all the while intoning chants or songs, whichever they might be. She set up a subdued clatter at her work. Her visitors, eating of her stew, watched her fixedly, fascinated by the performance she was putting on. Since they were hungry, the stew was eagerly eaten, although it could not have been said to be tasty. Gulping it down, Harcourt had some trouble in keeping from wondering if rats or mice or newts or toads might have been the basis of it.

At last the concoction that Old Nan was stirring up was finished, and she said to Harcourt, "You hold your friend up and I'll spoon some down him." The abbot still was mumbling and seemed not to know where he was, but he seized one of Harcourt's hands and hung onto it tightly. He fought rather weakly against the mess that the old woman spooned into his mouth, but finally was forced to swallow some of it, although by far the greater portion found its way into his beard when it dribbled from the corners of his mouth or he spit it out.

"I would guess that is enough," the crone finally said. "I got at least some of it down him. In a while we'll try again. By morning he should be better."

She and Harcourt went back to join the group sitting in front of the fireplace. The Knurly Man had put more wood on the fire, and it was blazing high. Yolanda was trying to make conversation with the troll, without much success. The troll sat huddled against the hearth and was playing with the end of the rope that was knotted on his neck.

"He told me something of his story," said Old Nan, "and it is very sad. You know that trolls can live only under bridges. I don't know why this is; it sounds ridiculous to me. But it is a fact that a bridge is the only proper place for them. This poor creature had just a small bridge, very badly built, perhaps in the beginning no more than a temporary log bridge over which a small ravine might be crossed. There was merely a trickle of water running in the ravine, and at times, during the dry weather of a hot summer, there would be none at all. His bridge was nothing like those great, grand bridges built of stone over a roaring stream that never would go dry. Our troll felt very bad about this. He felt most keenly that he was a very poor relation among all the other trolls. When he met them on occasion, they would condescend to him because his bridge was such a piddling one. Or maybe he only imagined that they did; that might be possible. He tried hard to keep his bridge in good repair; he even tried to make some improvements on it. Trying, you see, to make of it a home of which he might be proud. But that, on the face of it, was quite impossible. And I suspect, as well, that he was all thumbs when it came to construction work. He's not very bright, you know. No troll is bright, but he is less bright than the average. He is well below the norm. So, no matter what he did or dreamed, the bridge kept getting worse and worse. It sagged a little more each year, and the timbers were undermined by the eroding of the banks of the ravine. The logs of which it was built began to rot, for even good, honest oak, given time, will rot.

"A short time ago there was a heavy rain, and a mighty surge of water came roaring down the ravine to wash away the bridge. Our friend, huddling over there against the hearth, was left without a bridge, without a home. Had he been human, he would have known what to do about it. He could have cut down several oak trees—if he could acquire an axe, that is—and he could haul the logs and place them across the ravine, floor them with other logs, and have a bridge that would endure for several centuries more. But this, in troll tradition, is not the way it's done. No troll can build a bridge as his residence. Such a procedure would be—how do I say this?—perhaps quite immoral. A troll must not build his own bridge; he must reside beneath a bridge that is built by others.

"So here was this friend of ours, without a home, naked to the world. What could he do? For one thing, he could throw himself on the charity of others of his kind. That, in his weakness, is exactly what he did. He went to other bridges, all of them much grander bridges than the one that he had lost, and he said to those who resided there, 'Please take me in. Please share your bridge with me. If only for a day or two, please share it with me, giving me a chance to think what I may do. A respite is all I ask. A little time for thinking and for planning. A time to rest my bruised self and to recover just a little.' And they laughed at him, they hooted at him and drove him off. They had no mercy on him, no charity to extend. It was as if he were not one of them.

"And that is why you found him, standing in the tree beside the Wishing Well with the rope around his neck. And that is why he leaped, poor fool, with the rope too long. Oh, yes," she said, "I know who you are now. There have been rumors concerning you for days, and in time all rumors come to me. I did not know you when you came knocking at my door, but

I know you now. Since you have entered my mean hut, it all has come clear to me. You are the ones who slew the dragon, also with a rope about its neck."

"I had not noticed," said the Knurly Man. "Charles, did you note if that dragon had a rope about its neck?"

"I can't be sure," said Harcourt. "It seems to me it might have."

"There are those who call me witch," said Old Nan, "but I am not a witch. I have nothing of the supernatural about me, although I have an interest in it. I have some knowledge of the medical arts, common-sense knowledge of those arts, based on the properties of roots and barks and the leaves and fruits of plants. I have no magic and there is no magic in my medicines, although I chant the ancient words, telling myself that one must do all one can, even if some of it may be utter nonsense. So I do my little chants, although I have no doubt they have no part in curing, but are devised only to impress the ignorant."

Outside, the night had deepened to full dark and the wind was blowing a gale. Gusts entered the hut through the gaping cracks in the walls, but the heat from the fireplace beat back the cold. The trees just outside the hut moaned in the gusts; when the wind went down a little, from far off could be heard the howling of wolves.

"There was a battle a league or more from here just a few days ago," said Nan. "A Roman legion was slaughtered by the Evil. How could, in the face of this, four people be roaming in this land? To me it seems the height of foolhardiness."

"No more foolhardy," Harcourt said, "than living out here in the middle of it."

"Oh, I am relatively safe," said Old Nan. "I am perfectly harmless, and everyone knows I am. Also, my medical skill at times are useful to them. Were I not here, who would doctor them? For, as you know, the Evil have no doctor among themselves. If they use anything at all to help the sick or injured, it is no more than magic; and magic, used without deep and sophisticated understanding, usually is worthless. They come to me at times—oh, not many of them, but they do come at times, and I sew them up and patch them up and bind them up and purge them and do whatever else may seem the thing to do. Do not mistake me. I am not their friend. They do not love me and they have slight respect of me, but at times they need me. For that reason they allow me to keep on living. After the battle that I spoke of, I had several pa-

tients. One was a fairy with one wing shredded. I tried to put
it back together and succeeded after a fashion. Once I was
done, she could fly, albeit a bit lopsidedly. And there was an
ogre, a most ugly brute, with his tail cut off, carrying the
severed tail in hand, pitifully confident that I could grow it
onto him again. I had a hard time explaining to him why
that would be impossible, and he left, disgruntled, still carrying the cut-off tail. I think he thought that I could use magic
to rejoin the tail to him, and I tried to explain to him that
magic was imperfectly understood except in some of its
grosser aspects. I think that he doubted what I told him was
the truth, for he did a lot of grumbling and threatened me.
But I knew his threats were all idle and paid him no attention.
Although what I told him is quite true enough. There may be
much truth in magic, and one who understood it undoubtedly
could develop trustworthy methods for its use. But few have
examined it. No one has ever really tried to make sense of it.
To most people, even to most of its practitioners, it is no more
than mumbo jumbo. It does work, of course, in certain in-
stances, but that is only because, through trial and error,
applied through the ages, certain people have stumbled across
procedures that have worked and, having found these procedures, they and their descendants have faithfully transmitted
them through the ages. But these procedures are trial and
error; they work, although no one knows why they work. And
if we are to develop magic to its full potential, we must know
what makes it work. It is my hope that I can arrive at a little
of that understanding. I have labored at it for years, and I
work here because I want no interference. Should I work in
the human world and it was found what I was doing—which
would be the case, of course—I would have people lined up in
front of my door seeking help, bursting with ideas, intent on
helping me, or shouting against what I tried to do. This would
disrupt and slow the progress of my studies, and I need all the
time I have to try to make at least a simple start I can hand
on to someone else. You see those scrolls upon the table . . ."

"Yes," said the Knurly Man, "I did. And wondered what
they were."

"They are a collection of the most perceptive tracts and
treatises that I have acquired through the years. Some of
them, of course, are rubbish—rubbish at least in part. But a
surprising lot of them are the works of devoted men and some
women, who through the centuries have made a scholarly
approach to magic. It is my hope that by studying them I can

make that start I speak of—a good, solid approach to an understanding of magic, looking for certain underlying principles that may point to an effective use of it."

"How are you doing?" asked Harcourt. "I mean, are you making progress?"

"Some progress," she said. "I think I am beginning to see some chinks of reason. I do not fool myself that I'll live to see it done, but I'll have something to pass on."

The Knurly Man levered himself to his feet. The troll still crouched in a slump against the hearth.

"Look at the ninny," said Old Nan. "Even when I talked of him, even when I told his story, he did not speak a word. Never in my life have I seen such a nincompoop as he."

Somewhere, in some shadowed corner of the hut, the parrot launched into speech. "Nincompoop!" it screamed. "Nincompoop. Goddamn nincompoop."

No one paid attention to it. The crouching troll fiddled with his rope. The Knurly Man went across the room, picked up a handful of the scrolls, and brought them back. He squatted and carefully began unrolling them, bending close above them in the firelight to make out what they were. He looked up from them, astonished.

"Here," he said, "are works from some of the finest minds out of the past. I do not recognize the works, but I do the authors. How came you by all of these?"

"By years of work," said Nan. "By extensive correspondence with friends of mine. I spent years at it. When I had in hand all I thought that I could get, I came here and became a recluse in this land, where I could hide away, where there would be no interference, where I could work alone.

"For years I have sat there at that table, reading the writings and mentally digesting them, making notes and thinking. I go out into the woods to do much of my thinking, walking up and down, muttering to myself, holding conversations with myself, trying to correlate the thoughts of these other students, trying to weigh what they have said, accepting some of what they've said, although rejecting far more than I accept, trying to get it straight in my mind, trying to winnow out the chaff of superstition. The Evil spy upon me; I am sure they spy on me. And seeing me trudging in the woods, talking to myself, they must think that I am mad. This thought that I may be mad may help to save me from their fury, for they think, in their fuzzy minds, that madness may be sacred.

"But I talk too much of myself. I'm too wrapped up in

myself. Tell me of yourselves. Once your companion is well again, will you continue on?"

"We seek an ancient cathedral," said Harcourt. "It is somewhere in the west, although we know not exactly where nor how far it may be. Nor do we know its name. We know almost nothing of it except that it is there."

"Ours," the Knurly Man said quickly, "is a pious pilgrimage."

"Why," the crone exclaimed, "that must be the very place to which I go to obtain my medicines!"

"You say you know the place?" Yolanda asked.

"Yes, I think I do. It is the only cathedral that I know of, the only structure that is large enough and lordly enough to accommodate that name. Although I never knew it as a cathedral; I knew not what it was. All I knew was that it was a long-deserted place of Christian worship. There are crosses and tombs and an old cemetery . . ."

"You go there often," said the Knurly Man. "You would know the way?"

"I do not go often. Only when my supplies run low or at certain seasons of the year when some items are available or most readily gathered. I find good hunting in the cemetery and in a garden—at one time, I think, a very stately garden, but now gone to bush and bramble, although there still remain certain herbs that have lasted over from olden times."

She rose from the floor, on which she had been sitting, and picked up from the hearth the jar in which she had mixed the potion.

"It is time," she said, "that we give the abbot another dose of this."

The Knurly Man went with her, knelt, and raised the abbot from the pallet so she could spoon the potion into him.

"He seems less hot," said the Knurly Man, "and there's sweat upon his brow."

Nan knelt to lay a hand upon his cheeks and brow.

"You are right. The fever's broken."

She lifted the sheepskins in which he was wrapped and inspected the gashes on his legs. "The cuts are less angry than they were before, and they're beginning to scab over. Very healthy scabs. The ointment that you used on him must be a potent one."

"It has a long history," said the Knurly Man. "It comes from my people. Its origin is far lost in time."

"My potion helped, of course," said the crone, "but I'm

inclined to think much of the healing power came from the ointment. Is there a certain magic in it?"

"No magic, ma'am. An honest mixing of ingredients, some of which are very hard to come by, and meticulous attention to its preparation."

"He's sleeping now," said Nan, "and that is good, for he needs the sleep to gather strength and let the medication work. By morning he will be a new man, although the wounds will continue sore. Now, if you will hold him up a little higher ..."

The abbot sputtered and coughed as she spooned the potion into his mouth, but wakened only momentarily and then went back to sleep again.

Back at the fire, the Knurly Man said to Harcourt, "Nan says that he's vastly recovered, that he'll be a new man by morning."

"That's a quick recovery," said Harcourt. "Much quicker than I had hoped."

"The abbot has the constitution of a horse."

Harcourt said to Nan, "We intrude upon you, and I fear that we may endanger your safety. Would you say that we might be able to move on in the next few hours? By morning light, perhaps? The Knurly Man and I can help the abbot on the way should our help be needed."

"There is no need to leave," said Nan.

"But should the Evil learn that you have sheltered us ..."

"I had thought," she said, "that perhaps when you left, I might go along with you. It is the time of year when I can find in the cathedral gardens many of the herbs I need."

"You mean you'd show us the way?"

"You could find it in any case. It is not hard to find. But yes, if I went along with you, I could show the way. That might make it easier for you."

"If the abbot's up to it," Yolanda said, "I think we should move on as soon as possible. I've spread out the blankets, and in the heat of the fire they're quite dry again. I'll feel much better once we're at the cathedral."

"So will I," said the Knurly Man.

"The storm has ended," Yolanda said, "and the clouds are fleeing. The moon is shining between the clouds. If we leave, tomorrow should provide fair traveling weather."

"It all depends," said the Knurly Man, "on how the abbot's feeling."

The troll was crouched in the far corner of the fireplace

wall. The rope still hung around his neck, and he was busily counting his fingers, first one hand and then the other. His head was bent close above his hands to watch the finger counting, his loose lips hanging open, slobbering.

He looked up and saw Harcourt staring at him, then dropped his head, but stopped the counting of his fingers.

Harcourt looked around the small, shadowy room. The abbot was sleeping in one corner. He had quit the tossing and the mumbling that had marked his earlier sleep. Now he was breathing gently, his chest rising and falling with his even breaths.

"Thank God," Harcourt whispered to himself. Back there in the storm, before they had come upon the hut, he had feared for the abbot's life. Although that, he told himself, might have stemmed from his ignorance of medicine. If Yolanda had not found the hut, however, and if Nan had not been at hand with her knowledge of herbs, the situation now might be much different than it was.

He said to Nan, "In your visits to the cathedral, did you ever meet a priest?"

"One time," she said. "A little, scuttling man, a very gentle man. So old and feeble that a good puff of wind would have tipped him over."

"Did you talk with him? Did he tell you what he was doing there?"

"Only once. We passed a few words when I was digging in the garden. He observed that at one time the garden must have been beautiful. He said it was a pity there was no one there to take care of it. Then he scuttled off."

She hesitated for a moment, then she said, "As to why he was there or who he was, I have no idea. Certainly he was not there officially, not in a post to which he was appointed by the Church. The place—you call it a cathedral, and I suppose that is what it is—has been abandoned for years. Yet his being there is not remarkable. Throughout the Empty Land, one may find others such as he, clerics who come into this land, or self-ordained missionaries who feel that their very presence lends assurance that this place is not totally abandoned by the Church. Some of them, perhaps, in the thought that they can convert the Evil. That is a silly thing to think, for the Evil have no souls, which would make conversion no more than a hollow gesture."

"Yes, I know," said Harcourt, thinking of the dead old man and his water wheel.

Fingers plucked at his sleeve, and he turned to see that it was the troll.

"Please, sir," the troll asked in its lisping whine, "would you know of any bridge . . ."

"Get out of here!" Harcourt yelled. "Take your filthy hands off me!"

The troll shrank back into its corner.

"What happened?" Yolanda asked.

"It was that goddamned troll. He wanted to know if I knew of any bridge."

"Poor thing," said Nan. "He does need a bridge so badly."

Twenty

They did not leave the next day, as they had thought they might, but stayed throughout the day to give the abbot a chance to gain back his strength. He was up before the day was over and did full justice to a feast of venison the Knurly Man provided after a short morning hunt. Nan appreciated the venison almost as much as did the abbot.

"It is seldom," she said, "that I have meat upon the table. I'm the farthest thing from a huntress that you can imagine, and the Evil who come to me for doctoring and bandaging and other such services never give me gifts of food or otherwise. They take it to be their right to demand my services. At times they are barely civil; they've not been known to thank me."

"Which is all, milady," the abbot told her, "that can be expected of such soulless creatures. They are different in their sensibilities. They know none of the finer things of life. They are worse than animals. Even a horse, a dog, or a cat will develop love of its humans and be grateful for the food and care it is given."

"They do occasionally bring me scrolls," she said, "that they have found in the ruins of human habitations. I suspect they believe that my medical and magical knowledge is gained from the books I read and that by giving them to me they are helping themselves. Although few of the scrolls, almost none of them, are of any value to me. Mostly they are ballads or tales of ancient chivalry or other such nonconsequential things."

The day was spent pleasantly and they went to sleep early, after watches had been set, to get in a good night's rest against an early morning start. The abbot, although he complained of the terrible itching of his healing wounds, which he blamed upon the ointment used by the Knurly Man, seemed quite himself again and anxious to start once more upon their journey.

"How far away may the cathedral lie?" he asked Nan. "Charles tells me you have talked with the priest who lives there."

"Two days at the most," she said. "An easy two days. And yes, I have talked with the priest, but only once, and then quite briefly. Why do you ask of him?"

"We hope," the abbot said, "that he may have information which we need."

"I have not asked the reason for your dangerous pilgrimage," she said, "and I shall not pry. But you must view it as important."

"It is vital to us," the abbot said pompously. "It may be vital to the Church."

The next morning they set out, Old Nan going with them and the troll tagging sheepishly along.

The day was bright and pleasant, and the woods were dressed in the soft, fairy green of early spring with a carpet of wild woods flowers covering all the space between the trees. There was no path through the open woodland. Nan led the way and the others followed, thankful that she was there to lead them, for there seemed to be no landmarks by which they could have guided themselves.

There was no sign of the Evil. Could it be possible, Harcourt wondered, that they finally had broken free of it? He was reluctant to accept the thought and kept a constant and alert watch, but throughout the day there was nothing to be seen.

The abbot got along amazingly well. Harcourt and the Knurly Man kept their attention on him and called for frequent halts to provide him a chance to rest. He grumbled at them, "I know what you are up to. You are coddling me, and there is no need of it." But his protest advanced no further than that. Secretly, Harcourt guessed, he was grateful for the halts.

They stopped for the night in a grove of trees that surrounded a spring gushing from the foot of a hill. Nan and the Knurly Man set about the chore of making the evening meal. Harcourt climbed a short distance up the hill and sat down with his back against a massive oak, still keeping his close watch against the danger of the Evil.

He had sat there for only a short time when he heard a rustle in the fallen leaves. Turning, he saw that it was Yolanda. She stepped forward and sat down beside him.

"My lord," she said, "you seem deeply troubled. You have been troubled all the day. Is there aught that I can do to help?"

He shook his head. "No trouble. No single trouble, that is. All has gone too well today, and that worries me."

"Good fortune worries you?"

"We have fought our way across this land—well, not fighting, really, but running. Scuttering from one danger toward another. Always with the sense of being hunted. Today has seemed no more than a summer stroll."

"You are full of worries," she said. "You will let loose of none of them. You carry them most secretly. You will share none of them. Tell me one of your worries. Get rid of it by sharing it with me."

He laughed at her. "One worry and you'll cease your pestering of me?"

She nodded her head.

"All right, then," he said, "one worry and no more." And as he said it, he thought of something that had been nagging at him without his realizing it was there, something that he had pushed back into his consciousness and had, until now, given no room in his mind.

"You remember," he said, "that night we spent in the fen on the pile of rocks? Knurly and I climbed the rock pile to see what lay beyond."

"Yes, I do remember that. Foolishly, you took your lives in hand. The pile was not safe to climb."

"When we came down," he said, "Knurly told you what we found there, the skeleton of a crucified ogre chained to a rude cross of cedar. You and the abbot listened, the two of you, but paid the tale slight attention, as if it were not remarkable. The two of you accepted it as just another happening on the way, and Knurly seemed to think it was nothing of very great importance."

"It wasn't. Nothing of any great importance."

"But, don't you see, the ogre had died upon a cross."

"I recall that you sat there glowering while Knurly told of it."

"Then perhaps I'm wrong," he said.

"No, perhaps not wrong. It may be that I do not understand. Tell me of it. What about it bothered you? Not sympathy for the ogre. You have no sympathy for them. My father tells how, upon the castle wall, you rained blows upon them, shouting oaths at them, killing as you shouted."

"It was not the ogre," he said, "although he must have died a horrible death. He must have died of thirst. They chained him there and left him, and he dried up, like a leaf fallen from a tree."

"If not the ogre, what?"

"It was the cross!" he shouted.

"The cross?"

"Our Savior died upon a cross."

"And what of that? There have been others since who have died upon a cross."

"The cross is sanctified," he said. "We pray in front of it. We wear it on a chain about our necks. It is the pendant of our rosaries. It is a holy instrument of death. It is bad enough that others, as you say, have died upon it since. But an ogre? An Evil dying on a cross!"

She put an arm around his shoulders and hugged him close. "And you have suffered this," she said, "saying nothing to any one of us."

"Whom would I have said it to?"

"You've said it now to me."

"Yes," he said. "I've said it now to you."

She took her arm away. "I am sorry, sir," she said. "I meant a touch of comfort only."

He turned to face her, took her face between his hands, and kissed her. "It was a comfort," he told her, "and I needed comfort. I may be a foolish man, to be troubled so . . ."

"You're not a foolish man," she said. "You have an unsuspected softness in you, and all must love you for it."

"You must understand," he said, "that you are the only one I could have told it to."

Saying it, he wondered why he said it. For it was not the truth, he told himself. He could have told it to the abbot. There was nothing he could not tell the abbot. And yet, he had not told the abbot.

"There is something I must talk with you about," she said.

"Nan has been watching me, closely watching me. And she has tried to question me. Gently, of course, without seeming to. But there are questions in the things she says."

"You have told her nothing."

"Nothing. You, yourself, have not told me. But from what the three of you have said, from the chance remarks, I know."

Harcourt said, "I did not try to keep it from you. I only thought . . ."

"It's quite all right."

"Nan, you think, has tried to worm our purpose out of you?"

"I had thought so. More than that, she is not what she says."

"What do you mean?"

"She dresses in rags. She goes barefoot. Her hair is tousled; she never puts a comb through it. She wants us to think she is a crone. Yet what she is shows through."

Harcourt was amused. "What do you think shows through?"

"At one time she was quality, a woman of high quality. She is so much quality that she cannot hide it—ways of speech when she's not on her guard, little moves she makes, some of her mannerisms. On her finger is a ring she would like us to believe is a trinket of cheap glass. But I know it's not; I swear it's not. It's a ruby of the finest water."

"How do you know this?"

"Anyone would know. Any woman would know. Not a man. Men pay no attention to such things as rings."

"I'll try to have a look at it," said Harcourt. "I am glad you told me. Now let's get down to supper."

The meal was ready, the abbot already eating.

"I was too hungry to wait for you," he said. "Sit down and commence upon this food. Our friend Nan has extraordinary skillet skill. Who else would think of cooking ground meal with scraped cheese and bacon bits and greens gathered from the woods? All mixed up together. It is very toothsome."

Having said this, he greedily stuffed his mouth.

"The old goat," said the Knurly Man, "is almost himself again."

The abbot mumbled, "Except that I still itch abominably from that cursed ointment you rubbed into my wounds."

"Tomorrow we'll be at the cathedral," said Nan, "and then you'll have to dispense with me as cook. I shall be very busy seeking out my herbs and roots."

Late the next afternoon, from the top of a hill, they sighted the cathedral.

"There," the abbot said. "There it is at last, the cathedral that we've been blundering toward across this ungodly land."

It stood in a little valley through which flowed a winding, limpid stream, and all about were trees, great ancient trees that masked a full view of it.

"We'll camp here," said Harcourt, "and go to it come morning. I would not want to stumble about in it in the dark."

Twenty One

The cathedral was the largest structure that Harcourt had ever seen, a colossal pile of masonry topped by soaring towers, and even the towers were as solid as the massive stones that fashioned them. Segmented roofs sloped in all directions, highlighting the architectural puzzle that held it all together. Colored windows blazed red and green and blue in the light of the rising sun. There was an olden splendor and an everlasting wonder built into all the looming structure. Harcourt, staring at it, wondered how the hands and minds of men could have erected it and held it true to form.

A low stone wall, rather crudely laid—crudely compared with the magnificent cathedral itself—ran all about it. In places the wall was crumbling, and inside it grew many fruit trees, some of them in bloom.

Walking solemnly in line, one behind the other, they went along the south side of the wall, heading west. Near the point where the wall turned north, they found a break which gave them entrance to the cathedral grounds. Rounding the west end of the structure, they came out upon a stone-paved front with wide stone stairs leading to the entrance. At one time heavy oaken doors had closed the entrance, but one of the doors, fallen from its hinges, lay upon the stones, while the other sagged, half open. From the porch above the door, snarling or grinning gargoyles looked down upon them.

Staring up at them, Harcourt sensed, rather than saw, a

strangeness in the gargoyles. Some of them had about them a different quality, a somewhat smoother, softer appearance than the others. He looked a second time and was not as convinced of the differentness as he had been at first glance.

"Yolanda," he said to the woman standing beside him, "is there a wrongness about some of the gargoyles? It seems to me they do not look alike."

"They're not supposed to look alike," she said. "No gargoyle is like another. The sculptor uses his imagination, gives each of them a slightly different cast."

"That's not what I mean," he told her. "Not the expression on their faces, but the texture of them. As if they were made of a different kind of stone."

"That could be possible," she said, "and yet—wait, I see what you mean."

"There are a few of them," he said, "that remind me of the gargoyle I saw when you showed me your workshop."

She drew her breath in sharply. "You could be right. Some of them look as if they were carved in wood. Not stone, but wood. If that were true . . ."

"But that makes no sense. Why should some be stone and the rest be wood?"

"I would not know. As you say, there would seem to be no reason. Perhaps some of the originals were broken and were replaced in wood until someone could be found who could carve in stone."

"A temporary replacement?"

"Yes, but still it makes no sense."

The abbot said roughly, "Enough of this talk of gargoyles. We're not here to talk of the pretty conceits of this cathedral. Let us be about the finding of this priest of ours."

"He may be hard to find," said Nan. "He's a retiring sort. As if he might be afraid of visitors. He scuttles all about."

"That is strange," said the Knurly Man. "It must be lonely for him here. One would think he'd be glad of visitors, that he'd come out to welcome them."

Nan shook her head. "He is a funny little man. He talked with me but once. I had glimpsed him before, but only fleetingly."

"He's been here for years? He's no new arrival?"

"I think he may have been here long."

"The Evil must have known of him. Would it be your impression he was trying to hide from them? That perhaps he is afraid of everyone?"

"The Evil would shun such a place. The odor of sanctity is objectionable to them."

"It was no deterrent when they came against our abbey," said the abbot. "They killed everyone they could find and looted everything they could lay their hands upon."

The Knurly Man suggested, "Perhaps the odor of sanctity in your abbey was somewhat diluted by the many barrels of wine and the women whom you hid away."

"Let us not get into a squabble about odors nor argue about degrees of sanctity," said Harcourt.

"I shall let it pass," the abbot said with cold dignity. "I shall not attempt to answer."

And saying this, he strode through the open doorway. After a second of hesitation the others followed. Once through the door, however, they halted. Ahead of them, the abbot also had stopped. The nave, stretching out before them, lay in deep gloom. Only stray rays of sunlight entered through the stained-glass windows, and those rays, colored by the glass through which they passed, heightened the unreality of the place. The hollow, vast interior seemed to pulse with a faint booming sound. Harcourt found himself holding his breath, listening intently to learn where the boom might be coming from. It was, he told himself, like the gentle breathing of some monstrous animal. The abbot moved forward a step or two, and the hollowness of the nave caught up the faint sound of his tread and sent it, magnifying it, reverberating through the empty space.

Two rows of mighty pillars flanked the nave; between the pillars shone the ghostly whiteness of tombs, some of them very plainly made, others topped by carved recumbent figures, one of them with a kneeling angel, whiter than the tomb. To the right and left were archways leading into chapels.

As his eyes became accustomed to the gloom, Harcourt could see the interior more clearly, and yet the clearer seeing did not help him much, for all there was to see were the pillars and the tombs, a highly decorated font, and, at the end of the space, the high altar and the choir. Beyond that, it seemed to him, he caught the sense of the vastness and the emptiness going on and on. If the priest they sought, he told himself, should take it into his head to hide from them, there were a lot of places in this structure he could hide in. High on the walls were murals, at one time all full of color, but faded now and with the light too dim to make them out.

The odor of sanctity, Nan had said, and there was no

odor of sanctity in this place. The incense all was gone; no trace was left of it. All that was left was the haunting hum of emptiness in a place that had been abandoned centuries before.

The abbot shuffled forward again and the others followed, stirring echoes that ran all around them, a murmuring as if hundreds walked the paving stones.

They searched carefully and thoroughly, probing into even the most unlikely corners—the chapels, the vestries, the cloisters, the crypts, the open courts, the chapter house, the kitchen and refectory, the library where hundreds of scrolls filled cupboards to overflowing. Dust lay thick over everything. Their scuffing feet stirred it up, and it hung heavily in the air. Breathing it, they sneezed, and their sneezes set up chains of echoes that never seemed to end, as if a million ghosts were sneezing. To start with, they had tried calling out to the priest, not knowing what name they should call, for they did not know his name, but soon they desisted from the calling because it waked so many and such loud and persistent echoes that they could not have heard an answering priest had he been there and wished to answer.

The place was spotted with tombs, not arranged in any order, but tucked everywhere, some of them in unexpected and secluded corners. The stone lid of one of them had fallen off or been wrenched off, lying broken on the floor, with the moldering bones of its occupant still within the coffin. An angel on another tomb had been neatly beheaded, the head scattered in shards of the purest white. A font had been tipped over and much of its delicate carving smashed.

Except for the scrolls found in the library, there was nothing of value left. The altar had been stripped; cupboards that should have held vestments and the precious vessels and other items of worship were bare.

"The place has been most thoroughly looted," said the Knurly Man.

"Perhaps not," said the abbot. "The good fathers may have carried all of it away to save it from the Evil."

At the very end of their search, when they were beginning to run out of cathedral in which to search, in a tiny chapel at the far eastern wing, so cleverly tucked away that they almost passed it by, they found the man they sought—or what was left of him.

The dismembered skeleton lay scattered on the floor. Strips of black cloth, such as might be used in a cassock, lay tangled here and there. Shreds of flesh and gristle still clung to the bones. The Knurly Man picked up the skull and held it for them to see. The lower jaw was still attached, and four matching front teeth, two lower, two upper, were missing.

"This is our priest," said the Knurly Man.

Harcourt nodded. "My uncle mentioned the missing teeth. Their absence made the priest's words hard to understand."

"Ghouls," said the Knurly Man.

"Ghouls," said Harcourt. "Ghouls or harpies."

"I thought you said the Evil shunned places such as this," the abbot said to Nan.

"Ghouls you cannot tell about," she said. "What goes for the rest of the Evil might not apply to ghouls. All that concerns them is meat to fill their gut, however they can get it."

In one corner of the chapel a litter of blankets and sheepskins had served as a bed. A frying pan and a kettle sat beside a rude hearth. The wall of the chapel next to the hearth, which at one time had borne a mural, was smudged with smoke from the cooking fire.

"This is where he lived," the abbot said. "Here he spent his days in meditation."

"And here he died," said the Knurly Man. "They may have crept up on him while he slept. From the looks of it, not too many days ago."

"And here we come to a dead end," said Harcourt. "There now is no one who can tell us how to reach the villa."

"We seek toward the west," said the Knurly Man. "That much we do know."

"We can find it," said Yolanda. "I am sure we can."

"We have to lay our plans," said Harcourt. "We can't go running off in all directions."

Using one of the blankets from the bed, they gathered up the bones, carrying them to the garden. There they dug a shallow grave and laid the bones to rest, the abbot officiating at the burial rites.

"I did not know his name," the abbot mourned. "All I could do was call him our dear, departed brother, and that seemed, on the face of it, to be not quite sufficient."

"It went off well, I thought," said the Knurly Man. "You put your heart into it. You were properly elegant and filled with touching sorrow."

The abbot looked at him sharply. "You mock again?" he asked.

"But, my dear abbot, you know I never mock. I would not think of it."

Harcourt, pretending not to note the exchange, hoping it would go no further, led the way from the grave back to the cathedral front. Yolanda walked beside him while the others trailed behind.

"I somehow cannot get out of my mind the gargoyles carved of wood," Harcourt said to her. "They look so very much like the one I saw in your workshop. May I make a guess?"

"If you did, my lord," she said, "you would be very wrong."

"But at times you journeyed here."

"Not here; I've never been this far. And I was never gone for so long a time as to carve the gargoyles, if that is what you're thinking."

"It was what I had thought. You must understand why I might have been thinking so. The resemblance of your gargoyle to the ones above the door . . ."

She shook her head. "I couldn't do that kind of work. There is a touch of genius in it. Fashioned so well that to the casual glance they resemble stone. It takes a sharp eye to distinguish them from stone. Someday, perhaps, I may be able to equal the skill and feeling that are in them. But not yet. Even if I could, I have not the tools to do that sort of work. All the tools I have are the ones that Jean forged for me."

"I meant nothing," said Harcourt, "except a sincere compliment."

"I thank you, sir," she said.

They reached the western doorway and stood waiting for the others.

Arriving at the steps, the abbot sat down solidly upon them. He lowered his head into his hands and mumbled, "Now what do we do?"

"We keep on toward the west," said the Knurly Man. "We continue searching for what we came to find."

The abbot lifted his head out of his hands. "But we go so blindly. Not knowing where we're going. We could walk past it, not knowing it was there. It could be just beyond a hill we passed or hidden in a valley, and we would never see it. Lost babes in a thick, dark woods. That is what we are."

Nan asked them, "What is it that you seek?"

"A villa," Harcourt told her. "An ancient Roman villa. Some call it a palace, but we think most likely it's a villa."

"With that I cannot help you," she said. "I know of no such place."

"We'll be going on," said Harcourt, "and you'll be going home again."

"I have roots and herbs to gather," she said, "and when that is done, I'll go back to my hut. Although I must tell you that I have a strong compulsion to continue on with you. I know not what sort of pilgrimage you're committed to, but it has been long since I've been with people of my own and such pleasant company." She glanced toward Yolanda. "This sweet child," she said, "reminds me much of my own girlhood. I think that when I was her age, I was very like to her."

"That is a kind thought," Yolanda said.

"One thought haunts me," said the abbot. "Why was the good father killed? He had been here for years and the Evil had not bothered him. Was it because it became known to them that he had talked with Raoul?"

"It's possible," said the Knurly Man.

"Ghouls would need no reason for a killing other than that they hungered," said Nan. "I know them inside out. I know them for the filthy things they are."

Harcourt turned away from the steps on which the others sat and walked slowly across the stone-paved esplanade. He reached the gate that pierced the wall surrounding the cathedral grounds and stood there, staring out into the wilderness that lay beyond. In a short while, he thought, they would plunge again into that wilderness to continue their westward search. But this time, as the abbot had said, they would be traveling blind. The only thing they knew was to travel west, and the west contained too much ground to be searched as thoroughly as might be necessary to come upon the villa. Along the way there was a chance they might find someone, perhaps some hidden humans, who could help them in their search. But the chance might be small, he knew; so far in their travels they had come upon only three humans—the peddler-wizard, the old man with the parrot, and Nan.

The search, he admitted to himself, seemed just short of impossible. Yet, having come so close, having finally won their way as far as this cathedral, there could be no thought of turning back.

Someone tugged at his sleeve. When he turned to see who it was, the troll was standing there.

"Sir, you are wroth at me," it said.

"I do not like trolls, if that is what you mean," said Harcourt. "Of them all, I like you least of all. Not only are you vicious, but you are stupid, too."

"I am not vicious," said the troll. "I am the lowliest of my kind. I'm outcast among my fellows. They turned me away when I begged help of them. Before that, they belittled me because my bridge was so small and miserable."

"And now you have no bridge at all. I have no bridge for you. But wait a minute. Perhaps there is a bridge."

"You mean you would . . ."

"Hear me out," said Harcourt. "If I tell you of a bridge, will you no longer pester me?"

The troll nodded piteously.

"There is a bridge that spans a mighty river between the Empty Land and my fief on its southern shore. Built long ago by Roman engineers. I would suspect that trolls may live beneath its northern span, although I have not heard of them, but there are none who live in that area where it joins the southern shore. The bridge I tell you of would not be in the Empty Land, but on land that would be foreign to you. At times, hostile to you."

The troll's voice quavered. "Hostility I would not mind, if it were not too intense. My fellows in this land are hostile to me. But the bridge you mention must be a very grand bridge."

"It is a grand bridge on a mighty stream."

The troll shook his head. "I would find no comfort there. I would not feel at home. It would be too grand for me. I've lived all my life beneath such a tiny bridge and . . ."

"Well, then, the hell with you," said Harcourt. "I've told you of a bridge. Take it or leave it, and talk no more of it."

"But, sir, I need a bridge so badly. A very small bridge that I can call my home."

"That's too bad," said Harcourt. "If my bridge is too grand for you . . ."

"In this land," said the troll, "all bridges are taken and held by my fellow trolls. They will not let me in, and I am such a small troll and I ask so little and I sorrow so . . ."

"All right, then," said Harcourt. "It seems I must do something to get you off my back. I want to fix it so that I'll see no more of you, hear no more of you. I must satisfy you by some means to gain your freedom from you. Tag along with us and keep out of my way. No more whimpering . . ."

"Yes, sir," said the troll. "No more whimpering."

"If you get back with us," said Harcourt, "if we ourselves

get back, I'll build you a bridge somewhere. A small bridge, a miserable bridge, a crude bridge that will fit your crudity."

"My lord," the troll cried. "What can I do . . ."

"You can get the hell away from me," said Harcourt. "Stay out from underfoot. Speak no more to me."

"Thank you," said the troll. "Thank you, thank you . . ." And he went scuttling off.

Harcourt turned to face out into the wilderness.

That goddamn troll, he thought. Sniveling, scuttering, miserable, whining, pleading for a silly bridge. When he tugged at me, I should have knocked him flat and kicked him out of the way. Why did I offer him a bridge—for Christ's sake, to *build* a bridge for him? To get done with him, perhaps, although it was not entirely that. "Poor thing," Nan had said. "He needs a bridge so badly." But the troll was not the only one who had his needs. The rest of them had needs as well—the need to find the villa, the need to . . .

There was something moving out among the trees, at first only the flicker of something that dodged from one tree to another, and then a second flicker as something else darted from one tree to another. Harcourt stood tense, watching, trying to make out what might be out there in the trees. Perhaps, he told himself, no more than birds fluttering among the trees. You're too keyed up. You've been too tense for days, watching for the Evil, waiting for the Evil. He might, he thought, have reached the point where he saw an Evil behind every bush.

He waited and nothing happened. There were no more flickers. It had been, he decided, no more than his imagination. There was nothing lurking; he was seeing things. The cathedral grounds and the woods lay quietly in the warm sunlight of a dreaming afternoon.

He turned slowly around and paced back toward the steps where the others sat. They couldn't stay sitting for too long, he thought. In just a little while they must be on their way. It would be pleasant to sit in the sun all afternoon, but this was no time for sitting in the sun. Once this was all over, once the adventure had been finished and they were home again, there would be time for the wasting of an idle, sunny afternoon.

As he reached the foot of the stairs, the abbot surged upward to his feet, the mace raised in his hand, and the others sprang to their feet as well.

"Evil!" the abbot howled.

Harcourt swung around, sword out of its scabbard, and saw

the Evil coming through the gate. There were ogres and trolls, banshees and ghouls, harpies and goblins, the whole hell's brew of them, massed together and pouring through the narrow gate.

An arrow whickered above his head, and in front of him an ogre stumbled, clawing at its throat, from which an arrow shaft protruded, still quivering from the impact. The others came on, trampling over the ogre's fallen body, shuffling rapidly ahead, fangs bared, taloned claws reaching out and flexing. They came silently; except for the scuffing of their feet along the stones, they made no sound at all. There was more menace in the silence, Harcourt thought, than if they'd charged in roaring. There was in that silence a dread certainty of their purpose, as if they had a job to do and meant to get it done without a single wasted motion.

Harcourt took a quick step forward. On his left side someone brushed against him. Out of the tail of his eye he saw it was the abbot, huge and bulky, mace lifted high, moving steadily forward as if there were nothing that could stop him. Rushing out ahead was the Knurly Man, his axe a flash of steel in the sunlight as he whirled it above his head.

A troll off to the right went down with an arrow in its chest. Harcourt did not look back, but he knew where the arrow came from. Yolanda was standing on the steps with that deadly bow of hers, shooting methodically with no hurry and each arrow centering its mark.

There had been something out there among the trees, Harcourt told himself. I did see something there; there had been something lurking. It was not my imagination. I should have stayed a little longer, should have looked a little harder . . .

He struck with all his might at the ogre charging down upon him, the sharp-edged steel striking on top of its head. The face of the ogre came apart, divided into half, with a gush of blood and brains, and the steel was free, somehow, to strike again and yet again. A slobbering troll was reaching out for him; before he could make his stroke at it, a massive sphere of iron came down on top of it and smashed the slobbering into nothing. The abbot was whooping now as the mace smashed its way into the mass of Evil that came on and on without a sign of stopping. There were too many of them, Harcourt thought. No matter how many they might kill, the Evil would keep on charging forward and in the end would run straight over them.

A harpy leaped high into the air with its wings half spread, plunging down on top of him; but even as it fell, an arrow thudded into its outstretched throat, to go entirely through it. The harpy fell on top of him, and with his left arm he thrust it away, straight into the face of an ogre that was coming in from his left. Caught by the flung harpy, the ogre stumbled and went down. As it was going down, the abbot's mace caught it in the head, and it disappeared in the crush of its oncoming fellows.

Harcourt fought in a haze of red, the red of anger and of desperation, mostly perhaps of desperation, although he was not aware that he was desperate. Off to his right stood the Knurly Man, his axe as red as the haze in which Harcourt fought, its fine-honed edge slicing through the press that kept closing in on them.

And now, on his right, between himself and the Knurly Man, another man stood beside him, a fighter with a sword, a most true and deadly sword. And that was wrong, Harcourt told himself, for he was the only one among them who had worn a sword. He had merely an impression of the man, a sense that someone was there, for he had no time to turn and look, no time to wonder. If there was another sword beside him, fighting by his side, he was grateful for it, but there was no time for anything other than feeling thankful.

Harcourt flicked out his blade to slice the throat of an Evil that was piling in on him. Ogre or troll, he did not know, for all of them had come to look alike. They had become the faceless enemy at which one hewed and hacked. They were horrific shapes with gleaming fangs and merciless, ripping claws; all that one could do was strike out at them, as mightily and as often and as hard as one could manage.

He lost all sense of time. There was no past, no future, nothing but the steaming present. He stumbled on the fallen, squirming bodies and caught himself to keep from going down. The blood-drenched stones were slippery to his feet. It seemed incredible that it could keep on, that he and the others still stood against attack, that their singing, thudding weapons had not thinned out those that came against them. It seemed as if there were a funnel of some sort that fed in new Evil to replace the ones that they had killed, for there seemed no end to them.

Again and again, arrows came thunking in to take out of the fight a foaming horror that pressed too hard against them. Yolanda was still there, Harcourt knew, standing on the cathedral steps, winging in the arrows. None of the Evil as yet had reached her. Any that had tried, she had downed before they got near her.

The abbot still was to his left, and to his right, perhaps, was the Knurly Man, although since the fight had started, he had seldom seen the Knurly Man. The Knurly Man might well be down and he not know of it. To the right, still close beside him, stood the second sword.

Then, between himself and the abbot, a very solid something hurled itself upon the pack of Evil, boring into it, striking and clubbing as it went. All along the line the Evil press fell back, for there was more than one of these solid, massive somethings. Now, given a little room, Harcourt was able to see what they were—stubby, knotty gargoyles, advancing on bowed and rugged legs, swinging their mighty, clublike fists, beating back and beating down the Evil that confronted them. Skulls were cracked and arms and legs were snapped as the gargoyles plowed into the line of Evil that now was surging back, no longer fighting forward, but fighting to retreat, hampered in their effort by all the other Evil that had crowded in behind them.

Gargoyles! Whence could have come the gargoyles, and why had they come to assist the humans in their fight against the Evil? The only gargoyles that Harcourt knew of were those who had stared down at them from their perches above the cathedral door. Could these be the very same gargoyles? They must be, he told himself, for there were no others. He took a quick glance over his shoulder and saw that there were fewer gargoyles above the doors than once had been the case, that many of the places that had been occupied were empty. Standing on the steps before the doors were Yolanda and Nan, both of them with bows. How, he wondered, had Nan found a bow and the arrows to go with it? She had not had one earlier, and she had said that she was not a huntress. Yet there she stood, bow in hand, beside Yolanda.

One quick glance only, then he turned his head back to face the Evil. But now there were no Evil, or none that he could reach. The Evil were fleeing out the gate, and behind them came the gargoyles, smashing down all that they could reach, moving silently, making not a sound, deadly, inexorable, bent only on killing. All of them, he saw, were the wooden gargoyles, those that had been carved of wood to replace the stone ones that had fallen from their places.

As he had turned his head from looking at the diminished row of gargoyles above the doors, he had caught a glimpse of the stranger who had fought beside him. Now, as recognition flooded in upon him, he turned quickly to face the man.

"Decimus!" he cried.

The Roman raised his sword in a half salute. "Greetings, Harcourt," he said. "The two of us work very well together."

He was attired in light armor, and from the helmet that he wore, one bedraggled, broken scarlet plume hung down. The rest of them were gone.

The centurion chuckled at Harcourt's stare. "I am somewhat the worse for wear," he said. "Not quite the upstanding officer you met back on the river."

"I thought you were dead," said Harcourt. "We found the battlefield—that is, we viewed it from a distance. I looked for your scarlet plumes."

"I told you," Decimus said, "that our glory-hunting tribune would be the death of all of us."

"Yes, I remember that."

"Except for me, he was. I'm convinced I am the lone survivor."

The Knurly Man came limping up to them. The fur of his left side was bright with blood.

"One of the ogres raked me," he said in answer to Harcourt's stare. "They are scratches only. I got a little careless. I let the beggar get too close."

"You are limping."

"Something hit me in the leg. I don't know what it was. Maybe one of the gargoyles. Where did they come from, by the way? And who is this new recruit of ours?"

"You met him at the castle only a short time ago. One of the Romans who stopped by."

"I remember now," said the Knurly Man. "Decimus, was it not? I do not remember . . ."

The Roman bowed. "Decimus Apollinarius Valenturian. At your service, sir."

The abbot came stumping back from the gate. "They all are gone," he said. "The gargoyles still pursue them deep into the woods. It seems to me that the gargoyles are the ones that roosted there above the door."

"That they are," said Harcourt.

"God," the abbot said, "sometimes moves in most peculiar ways to protect His own." He said to Decimus, "You are the Roman, are you not? I was aware of you in the foray, but I had slight time to welcome you to our ranks."

"We all were busy," said Decimus.

Yolanda came down the stairs, followed by Nan.

"Are the Evil gone?" she asked. "Are they really gone?"

"Milady, they are gone," said the abbot, "and much of it is due to your marksmanship. And also, as well, to Nan, who has a bow, I see."

"It's your bow," said Nan. "When you sat down upon the steps, you slid the quiver off your shoulder, and it was lying there. I am no bowman. I did but little. A shot only now and then, when it seemed a shot might do some good. I tried not to waste the arrows. Yolanda made far better use of them."

All around them and extending to the gate lay the huddled bodies of the Evil, many of them with arrows bristling from them.

"We must retrieve the arrows," said Yolanda. "In case they should come back."

"They won't be coming back right now," the abbot said. "Perhaps later they will regroup and try again. But not immediately, I think. Nevertheless, I'll pull the arrows from them, and if there should be some of them who still show signs of life, I'll make sure they are dead."

"You," said the Knurly Man, "are the most bloodthirsty cleric I have ever known."

"Throughout all history there have been warrior churchmen," said the abbot. "I had not suspected that I had it in me . . ."

"You surely have it in you," Decimus told him. "In all my life, I've never seen so deadly a mace."

Nan said to the Knurly Man, "You have been wounded. You are all over blood."

"It is nothing," said the Knurly Man. "Scratches, that is all."

"Be sure, then," the abbot suggested, "to use that ointment of yours upon them. I'll be happy to hold you down while Charles, here, rubs it in."

"I don't think we should waste much time here," said Harcourt. "In a while the Evil will pull together and will be coming back. We left our packs piled just inside the cathedral door. We should pick them up and be on our way without too much dawdling."

"Again," said the abbot, "we are forced to run. We've been running ever since we came to this cursed land."

"There are times," said Decimus, "when running may be the better part of valor."

One of the gargoyles came through the gate and in a moment was followed by another.

"I saw them climbing down from off the cathedral front," said Yolanda. "I could not believe my eyes."

The gargoyle went clumping up the stairs, saying nothing, not looking at them, going straight ahead. Arriving at the cathedral front, he began to climb, deliberately and ponderously, clambering up the wall. The one that followed also went up the stairs and began to climb.

"I'll get those arrows," said the abbot.

"I'll help you," Yolanda said.

Harcourt stepped forward to the Roman and held out his hand. The Roman grasped it in a crushing grip.

"Thank you, Decimus," said Harcourt.

"It was my pleasure," said the centurion, "to fight in line with such men as you and the other two. I wonder, would you mind too much if I went along with you? Would I be intruding?"

"We need another blade," said Harcourt. "You wield a valiant one."

"Good," said Decimus. "At the moment, I have nothing else to do."

Another gargoyle came clopping through the gate. It advanced to the foot of the stairs, but did not go up them to climb the front. It planted itself solidly on the paving stones and waited there.

Nan had guided the Knurly Man to the steps and had forced him to sit down on them while she used a short shawl she wore about her shoulders to wipe away the blood that covered his left side. The Knurly Man bore a very pained expression.

"No need to fuss with me," he protested. "In my time, I have been much more grievously hurt and each time have survived."

"You shut up," she said severely, "and let me have a look. Later on I can stir up some potion that may help you with your healing, along with that ointment you have that worked so well upon the abbot. You say they are only scratches, and that is what they look like, but we must be sure."

"What about yourself?" he asked. "Do you intend to stay here to gather herbs and roots?"

She shook her head. "I cannot. They saw me standing on the steps against them, with a bow in hand."

"You can't flee back to your hut. They would find you there."

"I know that," she said. "The only thing that's left is to travel with you. I'll hurry. I'll try not to hold you up."

"Your pace, I'm sure," said the Knurly Man, "will match the abbot's. He's always puffing and panting and wanting to sit down and rest."

"The abbot," she said reprovingly, "is a holy man and a warrior to boot."

"He is all of that," said the Knurly Man.

Other gargoyles came back, and several climbed the facade to fit themselves into the niches they had left. Two of them did not, but ranged themselves alongside the one that stood by the foot of the stairs, all three of them standing, waiting.

The abbot and Yolanda returned to the stairs with the arrows they had torn from the dead. A few minutes later Harcourt and Decimus walked up to join them.

"How is he?" Harcourt asked of Nan, nodding at the Knurly Man.

"Exactly as he said," she told him. "No more than scratches. The bleeding's almost stopped. The medication can wait until this evening, when we halt to spend the night."

"She's going with us," said the Knurly Man.

Harcourt nodded. "I had hoped she would."

He looked around him. Except for the dead Evil sprawled upon the pavement, everything was as it had been before. The cathedral grounds still drowsed in the afternoon. The sun was several hours above the western horizon, and if they started now, they could cover a fair amount of ground before dark closed in.

He gestured at the three gargoyles still standing at the foot of the stairs. "What about these?" he asked.

"I don't know," said Nan. "They are the ones that did not climb back to occupy their places. I wonder what they're waiting for."

Harcourt said to the abbot, "Come and help me carry out our packs. Once we have them, we'll get started."

"I wonder where our troll is," Yolanda said. "Has anyone seen him?"

No one had.

"He probably went skittering off at the first sign of trouble," said the Knurly Man. "Personally, I don't blame him."

Another gargoyle came through the gate and up the esplanade, lining up with the other three.

Harcourt and the abbot came down the steps with the packs, and both began cinching them in place about their shoulders.

"Let me carry yours," Decimus said to the Knurly Man. "You must be slightly sore."

The Knurly Man hesitated. Then, finally, he said, "If you would. I can manage it tomorrow."

In a body, they started toward the gate. The four gargoyles that had not climbed the cathedral front trudged along behind them.

Twenty Two

The parrot, which had not entered the cathedral with them and either had not been present or possibly had remained silent and well hidden during the battle, now came back again. It rode the abbot's shoulder and did a lot of squalling and squawking. The abbot lectured it sternly and with little patience on the cardinal virtues of silence, but the parrot, perhaps not understanding, paid him slight attention.

The four gargoyles posted themselves, as if they might be guards, on the four corners of the marching group, two of them slightly ahead of the line of march, two bringing up the rear.

"Our company," the Knurly Man said to Harcourt, "has more than doubled since we began our venture. Not counting the parrot, we now have picked up six—Nan, the Roman, and the four gargoyles."

"One is missing," said Harcourt. "Have you seen the troll?"

"No, I have not," said the Knurly Man, "but he never really counted. He just trailed along."

"I have no great liking for the situation," Harcourt said. "The Evil band was scattered by the gargoyles, but we're now out in the open. We have no cathedral at our backs. In a day or two, if not sooner, they'll be on us once again."

"We mauled them well," said the Knurly Man. "We made them smart. They're out here somewhere, licking their wounds."

"They won't spend much time in licking wounds."

"I fear that you may be right," said the Knurly Man. "We must be ready for them. There is little use in running. If they start pressing us, we'll have to stand against them."

"I wish Yolanda would stay with the rest of us," Harcourt grumbled. "But no, she must be, ranging on ahead. It's dangerous for her to be out there alone."

"I think she is staying fairly close. I doubt she's going far. I caught sight of her just a while ago, off to the right."

"How are your scratches?"

"They smart to some extent. And my side is stiff. When we stop for the night, you can rub some of the ointment on me. I still carry a fair store of it."

"I could do it now. It would take only a few moments."

"We should waste no time."

"All right, tonight. The abbot said he would hold you down."

The Knurly Man snarled. "There'll be no need to hold me down."

The heavy forest was thinning out. At times they came to small stretches of open space. Even where the woods still stood, the trees were smaller and at a greater distance from one another. This was all to the good, Harcourt told himself. The Evil, if they came, could not now sneak up on them through the heavy woods.

The Knurly Man hurried ahead, drifting off to the right. Harcourt dropped back to walk with the Roman.

For a time they walked in silence, then Decimus said, "I can't tell you adequately how glad I am I found you. I had been floundering around for several days, not knowing where I was, expecting at any moment to be jumped by some frothing horror. I made slow progress, having to stop quite often to spy out the land and take a close look around before I dared continue."

"I, in turn, am glad you found us," Harcourt told him. "We are a pitifully weak force. We can use another fighting man."

"It was a great surprise to see you here," said Decimus. "Why didn't you tell me back at the castle that you'd be going into the Empty Land? If you had, I would have invited you to accompany us. As it turned out, it's just as well I didn't."

"There were too many of you, and you stayed around too long," said Harcourt. "You attracted Evil from the entire area. They were swarming in on you. That, I suppose, made it possible for us to get as far as we have come."

"I had words with the tribune," said the Roman. "I told him we should turn back. We hit the old Roman road two days before the ambush. If we had turned back then and followed it, with forced marches, we could have been back across the river in very little time."

"But he refused?"

"He was out for glory. One big victory was all he needed. My friend, he found that battle."

"And you?"

"I played the coward," said Decimus. "As a result, I am still alive and all the strong, brave men are dead. Including, I would hope, the tribune."

"You ran away?"

"Well, not exactly that. In the foray, I was hit on the head by something, maybe a misdirected blow by one of my own men—I would hope not intentionally. I was not a bad officer. Or I thought I wasn't. In any case, I was hit and went down. I guess I was knocked out. When I came to, I found myself in a pile of dead. A huge, loathsome troll, quite dead, was sprawled all over me. Peering out of that pile of tangled bodies, I could see the battle was almost finished. Our legionnaires were fighting to the death, in small groups, surrounded by the Evil. A few Romans were running to escape and were being pulled down. Others of the Evil roamed the field, killing the wounded men who crawled along the ground or lay gasping out their life."

"And you stayed there, among the dead."

"Roman tradition," said Decimus, "would have required that I leap to my feet and run out, shouting joyfully, to die with my faithful, heroic men. But I said to myself, 'Decimus, you have a God-given chance to get away unscathed, with no scratch upon you, only a bump upon your head, and you'd better take it gratefully.' So I stayed, not moving, as if I might be dead. There was a legionnaire within a hand's reach of me who was not dead as yet, but dying. I suppose I should have tried to help him, should at least have reached out a hand to him so he would know that he did not die alone. Although, in all conscience, except for that rather senseless act of compassion, there was nothing I could have done for him. If I had tried, I would have been noticed, and that would have been the end of me. He finally died, but he took a long time in his dying, and often it was piteous to hear. Finally the battle was all over and night fell, and a silence with the night. I crawled out from underneath that filthy, dripping troll and made my way cautiously from the battlefield, crawling on my belly mostly. And that is how I'm here."

He turned his head to look at Harcourt. "So judge me," he said. "Tell me I'm a coward."

"I judge no man," said Harcourt. "Least of all you. Under those circumstances, I could well have done the same. I do not pretend to know what I would have done, but I might have done the same. Any man might have."

"I'm warmed by your understanding," said the Roman, "if not by your admiration."

"Admiration has nothing to do with it. I've already said I am glad you're with us. Had you not stood with us, the Evil could have overwhelmed us before the gargoyles climbed down to join us in the fray."

"What, Harcourt, do you know about the gargoyles?"

"Not a thing. I remain as puzzled as you seem to be. I know only that the ones who came down to help us are carved of wood, not stone. Apparently, they were carved to replace stone gargoyles that had fallen and been shattered on the paving stones below. But who carved them or why they should have climbed down to aid us, I have no idea."

"I smell magic in it."

"So do I," said Harcourt. "But how or why the magic, I am afraid to ask."

"In any case, it was helpful magic. Which one seldom finds in this land."

"That is right," said Harcourt.

"I am one," said Decimus, "who always asks one too many questions, and the one I am about to ask may fall into that category. I am puzzled as to why you should be here at all."

"We are embarked upon a mission."

"That you do not want to talk about?"

"One we do not want to talk about," said Harcourt. "As you can see, there is danger in it."

"Except under exceptional circumstances," said the Roman, "I do not quail at danger. At times I may be stricken by sheer common sense. That's the worst you can say of me."

They stopped for the night at the first falling of dark, beside a tiny rill at the head of a small valley. Their camp was in the open, with bare hilltops standing stark about them. Here and there stood small clumps of trees.

They built a fire to cook flat cakes of wheat and to fry bacon. The four gargoyles took up guard posts. Harcourt

smeared ointment on the wounds of the Knurly Man with no
need of help from the abbot to hold him down. The abbot sat
by, watching the procedure, with the parrot grumbling on his
shoulder.

Nan and Yolanda, cooking at the fire, called them in to eat,
and they sat in a circle about the fire.

"This is a pleasant place," said Decimus, "a pleasant place
to camp. Not closed in by crowding trees or a noisome fen.
And it is good, as well, to have four gargoyles standing guard
on us."

"Maybe we, ourselves, will not be forced to set a watch
tonight," the abbot said. "With the gargoyles . . ."

"We'll set watches," said Harcourt. "I'll take the first and
Guy the second, with . . ."

"Let me take one of them," the Roman said. "The Knurly
Man should get a full night's sleep."

"You carried my pack today," said the Knurly Man, "and
now you must take my watch. I need not all this kindness."

"I think you should accept the kindness," Harcourt said,
speaking gently. "A full night's sleep won't hurt you. If you
don't mind, however," he said to Decimus, "would you take
the first watch, while I take the last, with the abbot in between
us?"

"What watch I take makes no difference to me," said the
centurion.

"There is one rule we have," said Harcourt. "We do not
prolong our watches to give the one who should follow us a
little extra sleep. We do not play the hero."

"I shall abide by your rules," Decimus said, perhaps a
shade too haughtily.

The moon was riding low in the western sky when the
abbot nudged Harcourt out of sleep.

"All seems well," the abbot said. "I have heard nothing,
and the gargoyles still stand guard. They're standing exactly
where they were when they took up their posts. They do not
move, they do not say a single word. I went out and tried to
talk with them, but they made no answer. You would swear
they had not heard me. They paid me no attention."

"That's the way it has been ever since they climbed down
from their cathedral niches," said Harcourt. "They do not
notice us, or they act as if they do not notice us—as if they
don't even know we are here. And yet they must know that,
for they go along with us and set up guards for us. They do
not speak; they may be incapable of speech."

The abbot lowered his voice. "What was all that mummery about changing the order of the watch? Don't you place full trust in our Roman friend?"

"I stayed awake and watched him," Harcourt said, "until he turned the watch over to you."

"You don't trust him, then."

"Look, Guy, I don't know him."

"Still, he fought most valiantly beside us."

"I know that. But to trust a man, he must be someone whom I know. We trust with our lives the man who is standing guard. He may be all he seems, but would you trust him with your life?"

The abbot puzzled over that. "I'm not sure I would," he said. Then he added, "Sometimes I worry about you, Charles. You are a hard man, and you have dark moods."

Harcourt made no response, and the abbot went shambling off, the parrot muttering on his shoulder, to find his blankets.

The westward-slanting moon shed a bright, soft light. The four gargoyles were lighted by its glow, their dark shadows stretching out beyond them. As the abbot had said, they stood stock-still, like so many posts planted firmly in the ground. A fair distance off to the right stood a small grove of trees, a dark blob in the moon-washed brightness. Not moving, Harcourt stared intently at the grove. There was no breeze and the trees were not moving. Nothing, it seemed, was moving. The night was silent and unmoving.

He walked a way beyond the campfire circle and crouched down. Somewhere out there, he told himself, was the Evil. Those who had attacked them at the cathedral and perhaps a greater force than that. The word would be going out, as it had gone out to call in all the clans against the Roman cohort. With the cohort massacred, this small band would now become the target for the Evil. Four able-bodied men, two women, four gargoyles, and a parrot—not much of a force, he thought, to stand against attack. At the cathedral they had had their backs protected by the cathedral itself, and the surprise factor of the gargoyle attack had been enough to spell out victory. But out here, and perhaps for leagues beyond, they'd have nothing at their backs; they'd face attack from every side, and in the end the force of Evil would sweep over them. The rush of the Evil might not come tonight, it might not come tomorrow, but somewhere along the way it would come, and they'd have to stand against it.

It was well enough, perhaps it was even brave and manly, to say quite blindly that they could stand against it, that they'd find some means, by the valor of their arms or by some unknown circumstance, to win free of it, to beat the Evil back, to save their lives and continue with their quest. But that, he told himself, was no more than foolish, empty thinking.

He fought against this kind of thinking, but there was no realistic answer that he could find to say that he was entirely wrong. We're all dead men, he said to himself, and dead women, too. It was no longer a matter of skittering around and hiding from the Evil. If not now, in a short time great forces of the Evil would be on all sides of them and closing in.

Was he, he wondered, placing too much significance on this small band of his? Thinking about it, he shook his head. This band might be small and unimportant, nothing to compare with a legionary cohort, but it was an insult flung into the face of Evildom. The Evil could be satisfied with nothing other than obliterating it. In answer to whatever kind of honor the Evil might subscribe to, they had to wipe it out.

A rustle jerked him around, and he saw that the rustle was Yolanda. She had come up on him silently and even now was crouching down beside him.

With a flood of gratitude that the rustle had not been something else that had sneaked up on him, he reached out an arm, encircling her and drawing her close against him.

"I'm glad it's you," he said.

She whispered to him, a trace of laughter in the whisper, "Who else could it have been? Who else can walk so noiselessly up to you? This is the second time."

At her words, he remembered that first time, when he had taken her face between his hands and kissed her. Now he felt guilty about the kiss, for who was he to kiss her? If he were to kiss anyone, it should be the long-lost Eloise.

"You're thinking," she said, "that it was wrong of you to kiss me that other time."

"How do you know that?"

"Because you have that guilty look about you. You think now of Eloise."

He gasped. "Eloise!"

"You think it is a secret, this grief-stricken, guilt-ridden obsession of yours? This personal path to Calvary that you tread? All in your fief are aware of it. And those beyond the fief. Your continual agony for a woman dead these seven years!"

Shocked, he fought to control his anger at her.

"It's tearing you apart," she said. "All your friends see it tearing you apart . . ."

"Yolanda!" he said, speaking sharply.

"I know it's no concern of mine. It is not for me to speak to you of it . . ."

"Yolanda, how much do you know of this mission we are on?"

"Only what I've heard and pieced together. You have never told me. No one has ever told me, but I know you seek Lasandra's prism, within which the soul of a holy saint . . ."

"It's not the prism alone. Not the soul of a saint alone."

"What else could it be?"

"It's Eloise. There's a chance we'll find Eloise when we find the prism."

Her eyes widened. "Can that be possible? I'd be so happy for you."

"It's possible, Yolanda, just barely possible. The priest, the one we found dead in the cathedral, told my uncle that someone by the name of Eloise had been mentioned . . ."

"That sounds incredible," she said. "But I hope . . ."

"It is incredible," he said. "I agonize over it. I tell myself at one time that it's not possible, that I am a fool for thinking that it could be. And then again I hope. I tell myself miracles can happen."

She said soberly, "You must live with it as best you can. You must not allow yourself to hope too much. The disappointment . . ."

Harcourt said, "I'm prepared for disappointment. I try to steel myself against it."

She pulled away from him.

"I did not come to talk of this," she said. "There is something else."

She hesitated then, and he waited for her to go on.

"I've been listening to the shell," she said. "The seashell . . ."

"The shell has some information?"

"Yes, a place of refuge. It tells of a place where we'll be safe. We must start toward it now. The Evil are gathering against us."

He asked, somewhat amused, "Did the shell tell you where this place might be?"

She paid no attention to the amusement in his voice. "Northwest of here," she said. "In a little valley."

"And we must start now?"

"The shell advises that it would be best to start immediately."

Harcourt rose to his feet and reached down a hand to help her up.

"Then we'll start right now," he said.

Down the slope, a running figure burst from the clump of trees Harcourt had studied so carefully. It ran at a reckless speed, head down, its body sprawling forward, flapping its arms. Harcourt gripped the hilt of his sword, but did not pull it free. Two of the gargoyles, springing into instant motion, lumbered swiftly toward the running figure. But there was no chance, Harcourt saw, that they could intercept it. He stepped forward, steel rasping as he pulled the blade.

Yolanda caught his sword arm. "No," she said. "Don't you see? It is our little troll."

Once she had spoken, he saw that it was, indeed, the troll.

He bellowed, "I thought we were shut of him."

He shouted at the gargoyles, "No, go back. He is one of us."

The gargoyles halted in midstride, turning to resume their posts.

"Well, at least," Yolanda said, "now we know the gargoyles can hear us. Even if they don't speak, they still can hear."

The troll came flapping up, skidding to a halt.

"I hurried hard," he panted. "I hurried to catch up."

He still wore the noose around his neck, still carried the free end of it in his hand.

"I could have wished you had stayed lost," said Harcourt. "We have no need of you. But now that you're here, stay close. But not underfoot. You understand? Don't get in our way."

"But I must catch up," the troll gasped. "I must be with you. You promised that you'd build a bridge for me."

Yolanda looked at Harcourt in surprise. "Did you tell him that?" she asked.

"I'm afraid I did," said Harcourt, turning on his heel to rouse the others of the band so they could get headed for the place of refuge the shell had spoken of.

Twenty Three

They had traveled no more than a couple of leagues when the Evil struck. The little band was toiling up a hill which rose out of the rolling countryside they had been traveling. The rising sun lay straight behind them. The Evil came boiling over the hilltop, which rose only a short distance ahead, and came charging down upon them—leaping, gamboling, hopping, beasts of prey closing in upon their prey.

The Knurly Man, the first to see them, shouted a warning. Harcourt, standing on the uneven footing of the hillside, saw three ogres leaping at him. All along the hillside, coming down the slope, were other groups of Evil, not coming in a mass as they had at the cathedral, but charging in small groups. The abbot was slightly to his left and somewhat behind him. The Knurly Man and the Roman, almost side by side, were to his right and a short distance ahead of him. Yolanda and Nan brought up the rear. The troll was in very rapid motion, running down the hill. The parrot, launching itself from the abbot's shoulder, flew in circles, squalling loudly. The gargoyles, leading the way up the hill, were out in front.

Harcourt, blade in hand, awaited the charge of the three ogres, trying to work his feet into a more solid, surer stance on the sloping ground. It was no way to fight, he knew, standing on a hillside and with uneven ground as footing. But there was nothing he could do about it; he must stand as best he could. It would be just their luck, he thought, to be caught out on a bare hillside.

The leading ogre was almost on top of him before he swung the sword, aiming at the juncture between the head and shoulder. Behind him he heard the joyous whooping of the abbot, but there was no time to see what was going on.

Head half severed and spouting blood, the ogre crashed into him. He tried to sidestep. A stone turned underneath his right foot and he lurched to one side, but not far enough to clear the falling ogre. Out of a corner of his eye, as he went down, he saw one of the gargoyles smash into the two ogres that had been grouped with the third, crashing into both of them, as a falling tree might crash, its clublike arms swinging as it came in contact. The two ogres went spinning off and falling.

The fall loosened Harcourt's grip upon his blade, and, on hands and knees, he went scrabbling after it, cursing underneath his breath, shoulders hunched against attack. But there was no attack.

Sword again in hand, he bounded to his feet and saw no Evil in front of him. Spinning around, he saw the attackers all downhill of him, downhill of everyone. The damn fools, he thought; they had planned to overwhelm us in a downhill attack, charging in a thin line to sweep us off the hill. But the attack, as the Evil should have known it would be, had been a failure; the downhill rush had carried the attackers through and past their objective, doing little damage.

Yolanda was kneeling, bow in hand, fitting an arrow to the cord. Nan was crouched beside her. A little farther up the hill, the abbot had dropped his mace and was reaching for his bow. The attacking Evil had turned around and were beginning to climb the hill, heading back toward them.

"We have them now," said Harcourt, talking to himself. "We have the bastards cold."

He slammed his blade into the scabbard and reached over his shoulder to pull the bow out of the quiver. A coward's weapon, he told himself, but that was quite all right. He'd use a coward's weapon if there was nothing else. It would be insanity to go rushing down the hill with sword in hand. From here, the Evil could be shot down like so many rabbits.

Down the hill, a troll went toppling over with an arrow in its chest. Another troll was toiling up the hill, reaching forward with its hands to claw its way up the slope. Harcourt raised the bow, began to bring it down, pulling the feather of the arrow back almost to his ear, then released it, reaching back to grasp another shaft. The troll sprawled, the feathered arrow quivering between its shoulder blades. Just behind the troll, an ogre flung up its hands and fell, a shaft protruding from its throat.

One of the gargoyles came down the hillside and planted itself alongside Harcourt. Another had taken its position just behind Yolanda. They were standing by, Harcourt told himself, just in case an Evil moved too close. In the meantime, they seemed to be content to see the attackers fall to arrows.

Some of the smaller Evil, mostly imps and goblins, were scattering down the hill. They had no heart, apparently, for this sort of battle. But the larger ones—the trolls, the ogres, and the harpies—still were coming on. One of the harpies launched itself heavily in the air, wings beating furiously to lift itself.

Harcourt flicked his gaze to the left. The Knurly Man was there, his bow bent, with an arrow nocked. Decimus stood waiting with his sword grasped in his fist.

The flying harpy folded in the air, turning end for end, its wings fluttering helplessly. When it struck the ground, it bounced.

Two ogres went down, and then a troll. The line of advancing Evil faltered. Arrows swept the line and more bodies huddled on the ground. Then the line broke, and the Evil began running down the hill.

Harcourt relaxed and thrust his bow back into the quiver. By now the retreating enemy was well beyond its range.

Decimus came over to him. "We did it once again," he said.

Harcourt shrugged. "A small party. A bunch of young bloods out to make a name."

Decimus nodded. "They used poor judgment. Bad tactics. They rushed straight through us. They couldn't stop the charge. Before they could, they were downhill of us."

"Next time, it won't be that way," said Harcourt.

"There may not be another time."

"There'll be another time," said Harcourt. "There's a lot of them out there, and they intend to kill us."

"Yolanda said there was a place of refuge."

"We can't count on it. Her information could be wrong. Even if there is a place, we could miss it."

Two of the gargoyles were down the hill, among the dead, retrieving arrows. The abbot and the Knurly Man came over to join Harcourt and Decimus. Yolanda and Nan came up the hill.

"Is everyone all right?" Harcourt asked.

It seemed that everyone was. Decimus had a gash on his shoulder where a falling troll had cut him with its talons, no more than a glancing blow. Nan had a bruise on her left arm, the result of falling on a stone. But other than that, there were no injuries.

"Let me look at that bruise," Harcourt said to Nan.

"It is nothing, my lord. I got it from a fall."

She reached out a hand to squeeze his arm, a gesture to emphasize her gratitude at his concern. He looked down at the hand and saw a brilliant red stone in the setting of a ring. A ruby, Yolanda had said. Not a cheap glass trinket, but a ruby of the finest water. The ring stone blazed in the sunlight, as if a deep and hidden fire burned in the depths of it. There would be no such hidden fire in a piece of glass, he told himself.

"All right, then," he said. "Let us get on with it."

They got on with it, climbing the hill. Nan trotted along beside Harcourt.

"What think you of our gargoyle friends?" she asked.

Harcourt told her, "I think nothing of them, but I am glad they're here. I've had no time to think of them."

"They are puissant allies," she said.

"Yes," said Harcourt. "They saved our necks back there in the cathedral skirmish."

"There is a magic in them," she said. "Whoever carved them put some magic in them."

"Perhaps you have some idea who might have carved them."

"No, I have not," she said. "For a time, I thought . . ."

She stopped and did not go on.

"For a time?" he asked.

She made a negatory motion. "It matters not," she said. "Old hopes are dead. They had best stay dead."

He hurried ahead to catch up with Yolanda.

"What does the shell tell you?" he asked.

"It has been silent for some time," she said. "The last it talked to me, just before we began to climb the hill, it said the place of refuge lay straight ahead of us."

"Far?"

"It did not say."

"I hope not too far," said Harcourt. "Unless I miss my guess, the Evil are swarming all about us. Next time they will come in force."

A gargoyle came lurching down the hill toward them. Reaching them, it grasped Harcourt's arm, pointing downward. Harcourt turned about and they were there, a massed line of Evil climbing slowly up the slope. They were too far away for him to make out individuals; they were no more than a clustered line of black bodies, moving slowly forward. About the line there was a sense of purpose and of power, a very deadly power.

Yolanda spoke softly beside him. "They're still downhill of us."

"This time," said Harcourt, "a few arrows will not stop them. Slow them, perhaps, but not stop them."

Decimus came trudging up. "That silly charge," he said, "was meant to stop us, to pin us down, to gain some time for the others to come up."

Harcourt nodded. "Probably that was its intent. There could be others coming up the back side of the hill. They could have us in a vise."

The abbot, who had followed Decimus, said, "In any case, we will make our stand atop the hill. In the face of this, there is no sense in running. We'd become separated and they'd pull us down, one by one."

"That is true enough," said Decimus. "We should get on top of the hill in time to choose with care the place we make our stand."

The crest of the hill was only a short distance above them.

The abbot was right, Harcourt told himself. It was the only thing to do. But this, he thought, was where it all would end. Their small band could not prevail against that massed rank of Evil. This time they'd not be fighting with the cathedral at their backs, but out in the open, with the Evil outflanking them and attacking from all sides. The cost to the Evil would be high, he was sure of that, but there was nothing that could make it possible for the humans to escape.

Above them a shout rang out, and when he turned to see where it might have come from, there atop the hill stood a man with a pack upon his back—a small man, shaven smooth of jaw and chin, his face tanned by the sun almost to blackness. In one hand he grasped a pilgrim's staff, which he was waving at them. His trousers were in tatters, and he wore a sheepskin vest with the wool side out.

Beside Harcourt, the abbot gasped. "The peddler!" he shouted. "For the love of Christ, the peddler!"

The peddler bellowed at them, "Up the hill! Run for your very lives!"

"Peddler," Yolanda yelled. "Peddler, why are you here?"

"Why, child," he said, "to save you. To save the silly lot of you from your monstrous folly."

They went scrambling up the hill, with the peddler waving his staff and yelling at them to hurry.

As Harcourt reached the crest, he saw below them a deep,

wild valley filled with boiling mist, morning fog that had not lifted with the rising of the sun.

Beside him, the abbot panted, "Another cursed fen. I will not wade through another fen."

"I assure you it is not a fen," said the peddler. "Run straight down this side of the hill and into the mists. There you'll be safe, but hurry."

Harcourt braked to a halt, protest on his lips. Here, on this barren hilltop, they had at least a chance to put a high price on their lives, but if they were caught running down the hill or in the fog-wrapped recesses of that hidden valley ...

"Get on, you fool!" the peddler bellowed at him. "Did you not hear what I told the abbot?"

"I will not run," said Harcourt. "I will stand and fight."

"Alone?" the peddler asked, and Harcourt saw that he was, indeed, alone, for all the others were running down the hill.

"Alone," said Harcourt. "Yes, if need be, I'll stand alone."

"You have little faith in me," said the peddler.

"I have no faith in you at all," said Harcourt. "Only in my good right arm and Almighty God."

The peddler frothed at him. "You raging imbecile! Do you not take my meaning? That is a refuge down there. Into that mist no Evil thing may enter. In it, you are safe."

Harcourt glanced down the hill up which they had climbed. The Evil line was nearer now, better than halfway up the hill, and coming faster. From it came a roaring of anger, a raging that made his blood run cold.

The abbot and the others who had run down the hill were almost at the edge of the mist that shrouded the valley.

"I am leaving," said the peddler, "and I am leaving fast. I pray that you go with me. It is a senseless gesture for you to remain here to face them, with no one standing by you."

Harcourt shrugged his shoulders. "I suppose that you are right." He grinned wolfishly. "But if that valley is not a place of refuge ..."

"It is. I tell you that it is."

"For your sake," said Harcourt, "it had better be."

The peddler started running down the hill, with Harcourt following.

Plunging into the first thin veil of fog, with the peddler going pell-mell down the hill ahead of him, Harcourt stopped and swung around.

The Evil was running toward him at full tilt, line after line of them, shouting, frothing at the mouth, closing in for the kill.

They did not close in. Before they reached even the thinnest of the fog, they skidded to a plunging halt, some of them falling and rolling, clawing at the ground to stop their slide. They fell over one another, and there were, in places, tangled groups of them, all struggling to stop before they touched the danger line of fog, crying and baying in their rage. They stood on the steep hillside and danced a rigadoon of anger, roaring out their lungs, waving clenched fists, raking the air with their gleaming talons.

Watching them, Harcourt felt a shriveling of his soul. It was this, he thought, that in his swollen pride he had proposed to face. No man could have withstood for a moment that massed force of viciousness. He would have gone down at the first rush, torn to bits, ripped and chewed and slashed, flung and torn. Within the ticking of a clock, there would have been nothing left in the semblance of a man.

The fog had stopped them. The fog and the enchantment, for he realized that the fog, in itself, meant nothing; it was no more than the manifestation of enchantment. How and why, he wondered, had so powerful an enchantment been laid upon this place—the last place that one would expect to find it, deep in the heart of this Empty Land?

The Evil were now beginning to drag themselves back up the hill, their steps slow, their feet shuffling. The first surge of rage and anger had drained out of them, and now they retreated to the hilltop, the kill snatched from their jaws, all their vengeance thwarted.

Harcourt swung about and looked down into the valley. It was a narrow place, studded with tumbled boulders, filled with ancient trees that wore a hoary look. Over it, like a blanket spread for protection, hung a heavy quietness.

The abbot was climbing up the hill toward him, grunting and panting as he toiled slowly upward. He planted himself squarely in front of Harcourt.

"You damn fool," he panted, "you would have stood against them. You would have stood and fought to cover our retreat. Did you not believe the peddler?"

"No," said Harcourt, "I did not believe him. What reason did I have for belief in him? He and his phony seashell, he and his talking of a Wishing Well and watching out for dragons..."

"The shell told us of this place," said the abbot. "The

peddler stood with Knurly and Yolanda in that place of the Elder Ones."

"Yes, I guess he did," said Harcourt. "But even Yolanda was not sure of that."

"Awrrk!" the parrot screeched.

"Come on, my friend," the abbot said. "Forget for the moment all your thoughts of contending with the Evil. For once, there is no need to contend with them. Be thankful that we are still alive."

"Yes, I am thankful for that," said Harcourt.

"Then come down with me to where the others are."

So they went down together, making their way around the boulders and the trees, to find the others all together inside a ring of open space that was formed by clumps of fallen boulders.

Yolanda came running up to Harcourt. "So you are safe," she said. "I was worried. I looked back and saw you, still on the hilltop. You seemed to be arguing with the peddler. Why should you have argued with him?"

"He was not arguing," the abbot said. "He only stayed behind to protect our rear."

"That's not true," Harcourt said bluntly. "I believed not a word the wizard said."

"You believe nothing that you do not hold in hand," the abbot told him. "Charles, you are filled with contradictions. A romantic and a cynic . . ."

"This, Sir Abbot," said Yolanda, "is no time for philosophy. We all are finally safe, and that is all that matters."

She took Harcourt by the arm and urged him toward the others of the band, who were gathered in the middle of the circle that the boulders formed.

"What I want to know is," said Harcourt, "what do we do now? Having reached this place of sanctuary, will we be forced to stay here, unable to move for fear of roving Evil?"

"That is something," Yolanda said, "that we can talk of later."

Decimus came up to them. "Have you ever heard of such a place before?" he asked.

"I still don't believe it," Harcourt said. "Any moment now, the enchantment will be lifted and the Evil will be howling down upon us."

"You need have no fear of that," said the peddler. "This place has existed for centuries. I have used it myself when the Evil went on a rampage and no other place was safe."

"But what is it?" Harcourt asked. "Why should it be here, in the middle of all this nothingness?"

"It is the burial place," said the peddler, "of that unknown and legended saint whose soul is supposed to be trapped within a prism. Even with his soul stolen, there still must be a place to inter his body. You know the legend, do you not?"

The abbot blurted out, "Then you must know the prism is hidden hereabouts."

The peddler looked at him in some surprise. "No, I had not known of that," he said.

"Guy, this is not the time to talk of it," Harcourt told the abbot.

Twenty Four

Darkness had fallen, the evening meal was done, and now, with wood piled on the fire to send it flaming high, they sat about the blaze. The four gargoyles had posted themselves on guard, standing between the boulders that encircled the campfire, facing out into the night.

Harcourt sat with the others in the circle, thinking, not paying attention to the chatter that went on around him. In the earlier part of the day, they had explored the enchanted valley. While it was narrow here, where they had entered it, it grew in width as the hills on either side of it spread out, coming to an end at a river into which flowed the small stream that ran through the valley. Along the foot of the hills on both sides of the valley were long lines of boulders that in ages past had weathered from the hillsides or fallen from the cliffs that in many places reared out of the hills. In the central area of the valley there were fewer boulders, but throughout it all grew the ancient forest, in some cases with the mighty trees so close together they crowded one another. There was little undergrowth beneath the trees, but in many places the forest floor was colorful with the blossoms of shade-loving plants.

The fog, never dissipating, hung over the valley, blocking

out any sight of the hills beyond. The sun brightened an area in the gray wool of the fog, but its disk could not be seen. There was a hushed quality to the land. All sounds were softened and muffled. The fallen leaves were damp and did not rustle underfoot.

At several points, the Knurly Man and Harcourt had climbed the lower part of the hills to reach a place where the fog thinned out, standing and surveying the landscape for any sign of Evil. There was none. "But they are there," said the Knurly Man. "They have not left. They are out there waiting for us."

"They won't give up soon," said Harcourt. "They know they have us penned in."

"We can try to outwait them," said the Knurly Man. "One day they'll grow tired of waiting."

"One day," said Harcourt, "we'll run out of food. We carried only a small supply to start with, and now there are three more mouths to feed."

"There are fish in the stream," said the Knurly Man, "and perhaps game. I have seen some rabbits. From time to time, deer may wander in."

Harcourt shook his head. "The day will come when we'll have to make a break for it."

"We can give the matter some study," said the Knurly Man. "Among us, we may come to see a way in which it can be done."

"I'm not sure I understand what is going on," said Harcourt. "The peddler gives us to understand that this is an enchanted place because the saint who tried to banish the Evil lies buried here. Does it make sense to you that the simple fact of burial would, in itself, create enchantment?"

"I am," said the Knurly Man, "not as knowledgeable on enchantment as might be many others, but no, it does not seem to me that mere burial would spread an enchantment so vast as this one appears to be."

"Then," said Harcourt, "it must be the work of several wizards or of one who was most talented, setting out a tract to protect forever the mortal body of our saint."

"Throughout all this land," said the Knurly Man, "there must at one time have been many wizards—some commendable, others bad in their intent. Perhaps, in the context of this place, all rallying together to pay tribute to one who was greater than them all."

"You're saying the saint might have been a wizard?"

"No, I don't say that at all. He must have been, forsooth, a very holy man. But at times it seems to me there may be no great degree of difference between holy man and wizard."

"There was one thing Yolanda said to me," said Harcourt, "that seems passing strange. She said that the peddler was a wizard of very low repute, intimating he might be much more than what he appears, that he is forced to seem of small powers in order not to attract attention."

"The wizard who travels with us," said the Knurly Man, "is a scruffy sort of person, or so he seems to me."

"It may be," said Harcourt, "only a part of his disguise."

"It may be so," said the Knurly Man, "although I would not want to wager on it."

Walking through the valley, Harcourt remembered, sitting now in the firelit circle, had somehow been unearthly. This was not, he told himself, an actual place. It was divorced from reality. Out there, beyond the curtain of the fog, the Evil waited and life was harsh. Here the Evil was held at bay, and one walked on a carpet of thick leaves that did not rustle to the tread. Here, before the campfire, some of the unreality was damped. The fire itself might have made the place more realistic; the circling boulders and the gargoyles standing guard hardened the reality, so that the limbo in which the valley lay drew back a way—but not too far; it still was only a few footsteps away.

Decimus was speaking. "It seems to me there are two problems—perhaps not problems, rather a problem and a question. The problem: How do we get out of here? The question: Why are we here at all and where might we want to go?"

The abbot said to Harcourt, "In all fairness, Charles, now may be the time to tell them. Yolanda, for a certainty, has gained some understanding of it, but neither Nan nor Decimus ..."

"Yes, I agree," said Harcourt. "Why don't you go ahead and tell them?"

For there was now, he knew, no reason they should hold their secret longer. Perhaps from the very first, Yolanda should have known. Now, committed as they were, trapped by the Evil as they were, Nan, Decimus, and perhaps even the peddler should know about the venture.

The abbot settled himself comfortably for his storytelling.

"It is a long tale," he said, "and I shall start at the beginning of it so you'll understand as I go along ..."

It was so like Guy, Harcourt thought, to start at the beginning, to string the story out and lay his premise carefully, to miss nothing in the telling. It was not, he told himself, the way he would have told it had he been the one to tell it. Perhaps, he admitted, the abbot's way was best.

The others listened intently as the abbot told the story, not stirring, not asking any questions. It took an incredibly long time, for the abbot left out nothing. He told the story fully and in detail.

"So that is it," he said, finally coming to the end of it. "I have told you all of it."

For a moment the silence of the listeners held, then Decimus said, "I take it that you do not know exactly where the villa lies—the place where you hope to find the prism and, perhaps, Eloise as well."

"We know only," said the abbot, "that it lies west of here, perhaps not too far away. We must be close to it."

"That is the nub of it," said Harcourt. "It can't be far from here, but we don't know where." He said to the peddler, "How about you? Might you know of it? Back at your cave, you told us little, nothing that we did not know ourselves . . ."

"I can't help," the peddler told him. "But there may be others here who can."

"Others? You must speak of Nan."

Nan sprang to her feet. "I do not know," she said. "I have heard about the prism—that there was supposed to be one—but all that the abbot told us here tonight was entirely new to me. I had no idea . . ."

"Lady Margaret," said the peddler, speaking gently, "why don't you drop the masquerade? It came to me some hours ago who you really are. Long ago I met you. Do you remember meeting me?"

"Yes, I do," said Nan. "It was at a fête."

"And we talked of magic. Even then you were very much concerned with finding logic in the magic."

"That is right," said Nan. "You were of no help to me. As I recall, you laughed at me."

"I had word from time to time," said the peddler, "of the mad witch who lived in the forest and was physician to the Evil. I never for a moment dreamed it might be you. Not the beautiful, dazzling woman I had met so briefly and so long ago. I meant at times to search out the witch, thinking we might have much to talk about, but each time circumstances intervened and I could not seek you out."

"This is all well and truthful," Nan told him, "but I have changed. I have greatly changed. I no longer am either beautiful or dazzling, if I ever was. I have become a hag. Certainly even a wizard of your skill could not see through the change."

"I saw the ring you wear," said the peddler. "The ruby full of fire. It is not a gem one would soon forget. You wore it that one and only time I saw you. Now, seeing it again, I sought for other things—for the evidence of your nobility. The way your head is carried—proudly, when no one is watching you. The evidence of a courtly way of speech . . ."

"You need go no further, wizard. I dispute nothing that you say. But I do not understand your interest in unmasking me. I see no advantage to be gained. It does not help you, nor does it harm me, although I cannot fathom why you should want to harm me. Given my wishes, I would have remained a mad old witch."

Harcourt spoke icily. "That's enough," he told the peddler. "There is no point that I can see in what you've done. She was contented as she was and . . ."

The peddler raised a hand. He spoke to Nan. "That day when I saw you, you had with you a daughter. A winsome little creature . . ."

"She is dead," said Nan. There was no emotion in her voice, no hope, no faith. "She must be dead. She ran off with a troubador who had the idea that he could sing magic songs that would charm the Evil."

"You have looked?"

"I have looked and asked. I have asked the Evil. They only simpered at me when I mentioned it. She came to the Empty Land with that troubador of hers. I am sure she did. With that scatterbrain of a troubador who thought he could entrance the Evil. I am sure that she was here."

"She is still here," said the peddler. "She and her troubador, who almost charmed the Evil. She lies here with her troubador and with our mystic saint and with many ancient wizards who were greater than the wizards of today. Ones I cannot hold a candle to. And all these are the ones, the moldering bones, the dominant and everlasting spirits, those who do not truly die, but live on and on, who can bridge the barrier of death to reach out and touch us . . ."

He paused for a moment, then raised his arms above his head, and from his outstretched fingers came the cracklings of lightning.

"These are the ones," he shouted, "who have the answer for us."

And the answer came. It rose out of the darkness beyond the campfire. It came with the shrilling of an orchestrated song. It rose into the air in a towering radiance that was lanced by lightning bolts and was full of thunder, and it struck the watchers to the ground.

Twenty Five

The fire was gone, and someone was weeping in the darkness. The flare of brilliance had vanished, and with it, as well, the flicker of lightning and the rumbling of thunder. Even in the dark, Harcourt could make out the looming shapes of trees against the starry sky, but these trees, he knew instinctively, were not the trees that had stood within the circle of boulders in the enchanted place, where they had been sheltered against the Evil. He was lying flat upon his back, and now, cautiously, he levered himself to rest upon his elbows.

The weeping still went on; he got onto his hands and knees and crawled toward it. A woman's sobbing. Yolanda, he thought, what could have happened to Yolanda? But almost immediately he knew that it was not Yolanda, so it must be Nan. His crawling brought him up to her huddled form; reaching out blindly, he took her up and held her head against his chest. He tightened his arms about her and rocked her back and forth, as one might rock a baby.

"Hush," he whispered. "Hush, everything's all right."

There were other voices now, and among them, the sharp tones of one who could only be the peddler.

"Shut up, everyone. Don't talk. Lie low and still. Be quiet, every one of you."

Hands clawed at Harcourt. The abbot's voice whispered hoarsely, "Charles, is that you?"

"Yes," said Harcourt.

"Where are we, Charles?"

"God knows," said Harcourt.

The enchantment, he told himself, had somehow hurled them from the safe sanctuary. For this, he knew, was not where they had been. It was quiet here, as it had been in that enchanted place, but the hush was gone, the sense of hush was absent. But where? he asked himself. A league away, ten leagues away, a hundred leagues away—perhaps farther now from their goal than they had been when they started out? Safe from the Evil, perhaps, hurled out of the Evil's clutches? But of that there could be no surety.

Nan was wailing softly. "Marjorie," she was saying. "Marjorie, Marjorie, Marjorie . . ."

No emphasis on the name. Just saying it. Saying it over and over.

A whiteness crawled out of the darkness.

"Here, let me," Yolanda's voice said. "Let me take her. She is grieving for her daughter."

Yolanda slid closer, nudging him away, gathering Nan against her. "There, there," she said. "There, there . . ."

His eyes, Harcourt realized, were becoming more accustomed to the darkness. Here and there were other moving forms—the others of the band.

"Awrrk!" the parrot screeched, almost in his ear.

"Strangle that damn bird," said the peddler. "Strangle him, wring his neck if that is what it takes to keep him quiet."

"Forsooth," the abbot said, "I'd much rather strangle you. What damnable mess have you hurled us into?"

Glancing up one of the hillsides that hemmed in the ravine where they were, Harcourt could vaguely make out trees and other indeterminate forms of blackness. Among them stood another form that he recognized—the hunched, awkward shape of a gargoyle.

So they're still with us, he thought. With us and already standing guard and watching. And what, he wondered, about the other member of the band—the troll with the noose about its neck? The last he had seen of it, it had been scuttering away, fleeing from the hillside fight. Perhaps, he told himself, it had good reason to flee. As a member of the human band, its life surely would have been forfeit had it been caught by any of the Evil. If it had known of the enchanted refuge just beyond the hilltop, it must have realized that the enchanted ground was closed to it, that it could not hope to enter.

Which raised the question: Had the Evil known of the place of refuge? Certainly they must have. And if that had been the case, why had they not thought to throw a force between the humans and the refuge? The answer, he told himself, was that they had. The band of Evil that had charged down the hill upon them had been that intercepting force. But something had gone wrong. Thinking of it, Harcourt believed that he knew what had happened. Disobeying orders, the intercepting force had attacked rather than lying in wait to trap the humans when the larger force had come storming up the hill. Glory hunters, this smaller force had hoped to gain a victory on their own, to snatch it for their own rather than wait for the main body of the Evil to come up. Young bloods, more than likely, out to gain a name for themselves. Their tactics had failed, as they should have known would be the case, if some thought had been given to the situation. Impetuous youngsters, he thought, seldom took the time to think a situation through. He smiled grimly—it couldn't have worked better for his group if he, himself, had planned it.

The peddler was whispering hoarsely. "Gather around. Come in close, as quietly as you can. I have word that you must know. I cannot shout it out."

Nan had ceased her sobbing, Yolanda still sitting close beside her. The abbot, who had been close to Harcourt, had moved off, probably pulling in nearer to the peddler.

Harcourt touched Yolanda's arm. "Come, the two of you. The peddler has something that he aches to tell us."

All of them gathered close around the peddler in the darkness.

"Be quiet," the peddler said, "and listen well. Do not interrupt me. If you must speak, keep your voice down."

Off to Harcourt's right, the Knurly Man grumbled in disgust.

"The Evil are still here," the peddler said. "They may be very close. We are in near vicinity of the villa that you seek, although, in relation to it, I cannot tell you exactly where."

"The Evil guards the villa," said the abbot. "That we know. Perhaps in heavy force. There are traps and ambuscades, and we must be wary of them."

"I am not about to be wary of them at the moment to the point that we stay penned in here," said the Knurly Man. "I, for one, do not propose to stay huddled here until morning, when we may find the Evil looking down our throats."

"How can you be sure we're anywhere near the villa?" asked the Roman.

"Our friends back in the refuge knew where we wished to go," the peddler said. "One can keep nothing from them. Before they acted, they looked deep into your soul."

"But why should they want . . ."

"You seek the prism, do you not?" the peddler asked. "In that sacred ground lies one who would be most concerned that you find it, and others who would be almost as much concerned. You are the first and only ones who have ever, in long centuries, taken up the quest they so devoutly desire, except perhaps for Harcourt's uncle. Why should they not help you in every way they can?"

"Granted," said the abbot. "That makes sense to me."

The peddler was talking about the saint, Harcourt told himself, and what he said was wrong, for if the saint's soul had been torn from him, then no more than the inchoate clay remained to be buried in the ground. He frowned, trying to puzzle it out and unable to get at the nub of it. Maybe, he thought, the peddler was talking as well of the wizards also buried there—although why should the wizards be so concerned? Unless, he told himself, it had been a joint effort, with the holiness of the saint not quite steady to the job of thrusting the Evil from the world, and requiring wizard help. Or could it be, he asked himself, that there had never been a saint, that the entire legend had been a storyteller's fantasy and there had been no saint and no soul trapped in a prism, and that all this great venture they were on was no more than a folly?

He crouched close against the ground, thankful that the darkness covered him and concealed his anguish from the others. He could ask the peddler, but he did not want to ask the peddler. He shrank from revealing his foolish lack of faith, and he could be wrong in everything he thought. Also, to ask the peddler might bring an answer that he did not wish to hear.

The abbot asked the question. "It makes sense to me," he said, "except for one tiny thing. Since our blessed saint had no soul, being robbed of it . . ."

"Others speak for him," the peddler said smoothly. "Others act for him."

"They were of help to him?"

"Of that I do not know. But there were very ancient men who knew of him and what he tried to do. They admired him greatly. There are those who say they loved him."

"It's not much of an answer," the abbot said gruffly. "I

suppose that we must be content with it. But the wizard Lasandra . . ."

"Lasandra," said the peddler, "is quite a different matter. A traitor to the brotherhood. There are those whom pelf and power may blind."

The Knurly Man tugged at Harcourt's sleeve. Turning, Harcourt saw that the Knurly Man was moving off and beckoning. Without thinking, he followed.

"I am climbing up the hill," said the Knurly Man. "I do not intend to stay here, like a grunting hog trapped in a sty, waiting for the butcher."

"I'll go with you," Harcourt said.

"At least one of the gargoyles is on the hill."

"Yes, I saw him. Just a while ago."

"I like not this sleek, smooth peddler," said the Knurly Man. "I am not sure at all that he speaks with the certainty that he would have us think he does."

"Nor am I," said Harcourt.

The Knurly Man started up the hill, moving like a drifting shadow, slowly, smoothly, noiselessly. Going as silently as he could, although not quite as quietly as the Knurly Man, Harcourt trailed in his wake.

They came up to where the gargoyle was posted; and the Knurly Man spoke to him. "Come with us," he said, "but no blundering, no crashing through the woods."

The gargoyle did not answer. It seemed he did not hear, but when they started up the hill again, Harcourt no longer trailing, but abreast of the Knurly Man, the gargoyle came along, moving as silently as the two of them.

Halfway up the slope, the Knurly Man drew to a halt, and Harcourt moved over closer.

"We came to earth between two hills," said the Knurly Man. "We're huddled in the narrow ravine that lies between the two of them. The Evil may be stationed on the hill above us or on the hill behind, perhaps on both of them. We can't let morning find us there. That dim-brain of a peddler, however, seems to stay quite content."

"He has no military training," said Harcourt. "He simply knows no better."

"He's a stubborn man," said the Knurly Man.

"If need be," said Harcourt, "I'll knock the stubbornness out of him."

"The worst of it," said the Knurly Man, "is that it's not all stubbornness. There's arrogance as well."

"Once we get to the top," Harcourt suggested, "we'll know what to do."

They proceeded up the hill, the three of them abreast, stopping frequently to smell out the land, listening for even the faintest sound, alert for any sense of danger.

They reached the crest of the ridge, and the two of them squatted down, the gargoyle standing, like a planted post, between them. At the foot of the ridge a broad valley spread out, and not too far behind it another hill loomed up against the sky.

"There's something down there in the valley," said the Knurly Man. "Can you make it out?"

"Very dimly," said Harcourt. "It is mostly dark. The night's too thick for seeing. What looks like a hump and a broken line of white."

"The line's a wall, I think."

"Uncle said there was a wall around the villa. What kind of wall, he never said. We never thought to ask. There were many things that day we never thought to ask."

"From all indications, there are no Evil on this ridge," said the Knurly Man.

"If that dark hump in the valley is the villa," said Harcourt, "then the white line could be a wall. But a wall of what?"

"Stone, perhaps. Probably thick and high."

"Uncle said that it was guarded and that he tried to get in, but he couldn't wriggle through. From that I take it the guard lines may not be very deep."

"Shallow, probably, but strong. Don't fool yourself. It will not be easy to penetrate. We'll have to study it carefully before we make a move."

"You stay here," said Harcourt. "I'll scout along the ridge."

"Take the gargoyle with you."

"I'll do better by myself."

"What will you be looking for?"

"I don't know. Anything at all."

Harcourt started off to his right, moving cautiously. At times he halted and stood, masked by undergrowth, to have long looks at the valley and the humped blob of darkness that could be the villa. He saw little more than he and the Knurly Man had seen. The dark hump persisted, as at times did the line of white, but at other times the line could not be seen. Undoubtedly, Harcourt told himself, when it could not be seen, it was blocked by heavy clumps of trees.

For the most part, the ridge top was forested, although here and there he came to open spaces that he crossed as quickly as he could. As he went along, he became convinced that the Evil was close by. He felt the oppressiveness, the tingle, the very sense of Evil. But there was no other sign, no rustle, no sound at all, no evidence that they were there.

Ahead of him the ridge dipped sharply, as if, he thought, a mighty fist had been swung against it, denting it, gouging out the smoothness of its course. He went down the incline that marked the edge of the gouge and found himself in a littered, broken place. Huge slabs of rock lay scattered, and above them rose a cliff, starkly white in the darkness of the night. In the face of the cliff was a cave—not too deep, not too broad, but a cave that ran back into the rock. Among the tumbled slabs of shattered rock in front of the cave reared massive oak trees, the largest he had ever seen, huge of bole, squat, not too high, and with spreading branches that grew close against the ground. Opening out beyond the trees was a broad view of the valley that lay below.

He walked out past the trees and stared down into the valley. He could barely make out the hump of deeper darkness that might be the villa. Only a few scattered segments of the white line could be seen. For a moment he thought he caught a glimmer of light in the vicinity of the hump, but if he did, it was gone so quickly that he could not be certain. It might have been, he thought, no more than a trick his eyes had played on him. Then it came again, not a glimmer this time, but a flickering light that flared up momentarily, then almost went out; gaining strength and flaring up once again, it finally died into nothing. He waited, holding his breath, watching for the light to appear again, but there remained nothing but the darkness. A signal? he wondered. Perhaps a signal to him, although that seemed quite improbable, for no one could know that he was near. Eloise might know, he told himself; somehow she might be aware that he had finally come for her. In his mind's eye he saw her dressed in flowing white, with a slender candle in one hand, shielding its flame against the wind with her other hand, staring out into the darkness as if, despite the darkness, she might make him out. Her hair blowing in the wind, a wisp of it across her face, as he saw her in his dreams.

"Eloise!" he said aloud, then held his mouth fast shut. He wanted to say her name again and again, but it was ridiculous. Although, in that moment, he knew that she was there—without a shred of proof, he knew that she was there.

Knowing this, not questioning how he knew it, but glad he did, the question rose as to how he finally could reach her. His Uncle Raoul had said the villa was heavily guarded. It was doubtful that a frontal assault, no matter by how great an army, could take it. His uncle had tried to slip through the screen of guards, but had been unable to, because there had been too many of them. His uncle, he reminded himself, probably was a good man at skulking, at sliding unnoticed through any sort of impediment, to arrive at his objective. He had never known too much about his uncle, for while this strange kin of his had told many marvelous tales, Raoul had been extremely reticent as to his actual operations. Standing now before the cave and looking out into the darkness where he had seen the light, Harcourt wished that he had known more of Uncle Raoul.

Behind him, a pebble clicked and he turned quickly. A small figure stood beside one of the canted slabs of rock just beyond the cave's mouth. For a moment Harcourt stood looking at the figure, gorge rising in his throat.

"So it's you," he said. "Am I never rid of you?"

The troll said, lisping as it spoke, "I reasoned you would reach this place in time. I hurried to get here, for I must be with you until you build the bridge for me. Without a bridge, I'm nothing, even less than nothing."

"Cease your chatter of the bridge," said Harcourt. "You knew I would be here?"

"I traveled far and very rapidly," said the troll, "and I am fair exhausted. First I must run around the horde of my fellow Evil, who no doubt are wroth with me for traveling with you. Then I must circle even wider to get around the enchanted place and . . ."

"You knew where we were going?"

"I heard certain whispers. I keep my ears wide open. I would have told you where this place was, but you were very angry with me. For what, I do not know. You gave me no chance to tell you. I tried, many times I tried, but you quickly brushed me off as if I were something of no consequence."

Harcourt walked up to the troll, jerked out of his hand the rope's end that he carried, and pulled it taut, the noose tightening about the troll's throat.

"Being here," Harcourt asked, "can you now tell me how to get through those who guard the villa?"

"Not you," said the troll. "You are too big and clumsy. But

I could sneak through. I am sure that I, myself alone, could reach the villa."

"And what good would that do?"

"Good sir, I do not know. Once I was inside, I might think of something. I must do what I can to pay you in advance for the bridge you are about to build me."

Harcourt flung the rope's end away in disgust, and the troll reached out quickly to grasp it.

"Come with me," said Harcourt, "and keep quiet. Not a word out of you."

Trailed by the troll, he went down the ridge to where the Knurly Man waited.

"I see you picked up a friend," said the Knurly Man.

"I did not pick him up. He hunted me down. He is all of a lather to be of help to us."

"As to that," said the Knurly Man, "we'll wait and see."

"I found a cave," Harcourt told him. "Gouged out of the rock below the ridge. Well screened by broken rocks and trees. It's better than hunkering down in that ravine down the hill. It overlooks the valley and the villa and will make a fine lookout. If the Evil should attack, it will give us protection for our backs."

"You stay here and keep the troll in check," said the Knurly Man, "and if he moves, cut his goddamn throat. I'm far short of trusting him."

"So am I," said Harcourt.

"We have a few hours until light," said the Knurly Man, "and we should be in position at the cave well before the sun comes up. I'll go down the hill and bring up the others." He said to the gargoyle, standing stiffly and only a little distance off, "You stay here with Charles."

Twenty Six

The first light of morning showed that the villa was in the valley, where they had thought to see it the night before. The white line, which Harcourt and the Knurly Man had guessed to be a wall enclosing it, was indeed a wall.

"Stone, I would say," the abbot said. "Thick and solid. And high. How high would you say?"

"It's difficult to estimate from here," said the Knurly Man. "I would think six feet or higher. Probably higher. I've been looking for a gate. Do you see a gate? There should be more than one."

Harcourt shook his head. "No gate that I can see."

The three of them squatted among the mighty oaks that reared up a short distance downhill of the cave.

"It seems to me," the abbot said, "that every now and then I can detect some motion. But it's hard to know."

"It stands to reason," said the Knurly Man, "that the place is stiff with Evil. What I hope is that the crowd that attacked us before we reached the sanctuary will not come pouring in to reinforce the people down there."

"That's not likely," said Harcourt. "They're still back there, waiting for us to make a break. They can't know that we are gone. They think they have us trapped."

"I think that you are right," the abbot said.

"Our troll told me last night that he could wriggle through the guard."

"What good would that do?" the Knurly Man asked.

"Probably none. I asked him that, and he had no answer. He said he probably could figure out some way to be of help to us once he got into the villa."

"I put no faith in him," said the Knurly Man. "My inclination would be to knock him on the head and be done with it."

"I'm not so sure," the abbot said. "Charles, you promised to build him a bridge?"

"Yes. In a moment of weakness, I did promise him."

"I think that might buy his loyalty to us," said the abbot. "If he had a soul, he'd sell it for a bridge."

The Knurly Man grunted in disdain.

The gargoyles had posted themselves among the trees. Decimus was seated on a stone a little distance off, using a small whetstone to touch up his sword.

The abbot nodded at him. "He's a strange one. Acts like an interloper. As if he's not quite welcome. He should be here with us."

"He's a good man in a fight," said the Knurly Man. "Which is not to be wondered at. Fighting is his business."

Harcourt said, "He probably feels like an outsider. He joined us, but still is not one of us."

"I'm willing to accept him," said the abbot.

"So are all the rest of us," said Harcourt. "But he can't let loose of his terrible Roman pride."

Nan and Yolanda sat just inside the cave, near where the packs had been piled. The peddler stood beside them, stiff and straight, leaning on his staff. The troll squatted at his feet.

"The peddler is another strange one," said the Knurly Man. "No matter what happens, he seems to be a problem. When I went back to tell the others about the cave, he wasn't as happy as he might have been. He seemed to think I was trying to take over."

"Did he have any suggestions?" asked Harcourt.

The Knurly Man shook his head. "He was just pigheaded. That was all."

"I take it," said the abbot, "that he does not like this business."

"It may be because he recognizes the danger of it," said Harcourt.

"If he does," said the Knurly Man, "why doesn't he trot out a spell or two that will be of some help to us? He called on the wizards or whatever powers may be in the enchanted sanctuary to get us from there to here."

"I'd say he may have lost his nerve," said the abbot.

"I don't like it, either," said the Knurly Man. "But we're here and we'll try to do something. We have to make a move soon. Some of that hidden crowd down there will detect us, and then we'll be fair game."

And the thing about it, Harcourt told himself, was that if, in some extremity, they should be forced to flee, to try to get away, the chances were that they would never make it out of the Empty Land. The Evil was aroused and would be out. Hunting bands, once it was suspected they might have left the enchanted sanctuary, would be roving in all directions.

The Knurly Man was speaking. "We must have a closer look at what's down there. A reconnaissance. I'll go, and so, I think, should Charles. Abbot, you stay here. You are not built for scouting."

"The two of us should go separately," said Harcourt. "That way there's less danger of our being spotted, and two lone men will see more than two together."

"Leave your blade behind," said the Knurly Man. "It clanks too much and might get in your way. Take a dagger. Decimus has one that he will loan you."

"What of Decimus?" asked the abbot.

"He stays along with you and the peddler. The Roman is accustomed to stand-up fighting. He's not cut out for sneaking through the bushes. And, for the love of Christ, keep close watch while we are gone."

Harcourt rose to his feet and went back to the cave, unbuckling his sword belt as he went. He walked up to Nan, who was sitting on the cave floor, with Yolanda standing behind her, beside the peddler.

"Here," said Harcourt, handing the belt and the scabbard to Nan, "keep these for me. I'm going out to scout."

"That's my job," said Yolanda. "I'm the scout."

"Not this time," said Harcourt.

"You'll be weaponless."

"I'll borrow a dagger from the Roman."

"I have one that will serve you better. I keep it honed. The Roman's is a clumsy thing."

She held out the dagger and he took it. It was slender, its point needle-sharp, the blade triangular, with three razor edges. He looked at it in surprise.

"It's been in the family for years," she said. "One of Jean's ancestors brought it back from an olden war. Booty taken from some heathen tribesman who, in turn, probably had taken it from someone else."

"Thank you," said Harcourt.

"You're sure you don't want me with you?"

"You're needed here," said Harcourt. "If there should be an attack, your bow would be needed."

He lifted his quiver from his shoulder and laid it on the cave floor. He looked at her defiant jaw. "Please believe me," he said. "You are really needed here. The Knurly Man and I will go. We'll be back as soon as possible. We have to know what is in front of us."

He looked around. "Where's the troll?"

"He was here just a while ago," said Nan.

"Goddammit, he's always sneaking off," said Harcourt. "I don't trust him. If he comes back, make sure he stays."

For a moment he stood in indecision, fighting off an impulse to take Yolanda in his arms and kiss her before he started down the hill. Instead he ducked his head. "I'm leaving now," he said.

"Good luck to you, Harcourt," said the peddler.

Harcourt did not answer. He had small liking for the peddler.

At the edge of the trees, the Knurly Man was waiting for him.

"Ready, Charles?"

Harcourt nodded.

"Right or left?"

"I'll take the right," said Harcourt.

"Not too fast," said the Knurly Man. "Remember what I taught you as a boy. Go slow. Take advantage of every cover. Look before you move. Be all eyes."

There was plenty of cover on the hillside. At times on hands and knees, at other times crawling on his belly, Harcourt angled down the slope. The sun was not up as yet. When it did rise, it would be behind him, and then the necessity of keeping down would be even more important. But at the same time, the glare of the sun would be in the eyes of anyone looking out from the villa at the hill and could make him more difficult to detect.

After each creeping, crawling movement he lay for a time, peering out through the cover toward the villa. Nothing moved. Heavy underbrush and occasional clumps of trees grew in front of the villa wall, and there could be any number of watchers hidden in them. But if there were, there was no sign of them. He closely examined that segment of the wall nearest to him, alert to the hidden form, to the slightest movement, and there was nothing. One would be almost tempted, he thought, to say there was nothing there. But he knew there was; there had to be. Uncle Raoul had ferreted out the watchers and had tried to elude them and get into the villa, but he had turned back when he realized that there were too many guards, that no man alone could work his way through them.

For years, Harcourt told himself, members of the guarding Evil had crouched around the wall, waiting for the threat that did not come, but keeping sentinel despite the fact there had never been a threat. Although, he thought, there could have been threats; that was entirely possible, threats that had been beaten off and not become general knowledge. The chances, however, were that there would not have been many of them. Could Uncle Raoul, he wondered, have been classified as a threat? Possibly not, he decided, for the best evidence was that his presence had not been detected.

Humans, Harcourt thought, would have become bored with the seemingly senseless vigil and would have relaxed the watching, going through the motions without really watching.

How about the Evil—would they have become bored as well? Would their attentions wander and their attitude be relaxed? He shrugged. How could one know? Who could tell about the Evil? It would not be wise, he thought, to wager that they had in any way relaxed their watchfulness.

He went on, crawling from bush to bush, bush to boulder, each time surveying the valley intently before moving on. Now, for the first time, he spotted watchers, one huddled group of blotted forms, so huddled that he could gain no impression of what their shapes might be, crouched beneath a heavy growth of shrubs close against the wall. At first he caught only a fleeting glimpse of them. He had to look hard for several minutes before he was able to pick them up again. They did not move; apparently they had not seen him crawling on the hillside.

He moved on, more cautiously than ever, angling down the slope. When he next stopped to have another look, he could not see the watchers. His angle of vision had changed, and they now were better hidden by the shrubbery behind which they hunkered.

Why should they be so hidden? he asked himself. Why did they not stand out in the open? Such a posture would be more effective in warning off possible intruders. Was it possible the Evil wanted to avoid any impression that the villa was guarded, that it had an importance that called for guarding? If it appeared to be no more than a deserted villa, perhaps plundered many times, there might be very little interest in it. The one thing the Evil might wish most fervently could be a lack of interest in it.

He came to a dense thicket and, full upon his belly, made his way through it, moving slowly. The thicket seemed endless, but finally he came to the end of it and lay prone, staring out at the villa, which now was appreciably closer than it had been when he had started through the thicket. It was a large structure, comfortably large, but not as big as he first had thought it was. The yellow and red of its tiled roof, the colors dimmed by years of weather, shone softly in the glare of the rising sun. Huge timbers outlined the structure's plastered walls. Before it and, presumably, all around it, the white stone of the enclosing wall went up, so high that it cut off the view of the lower part of the villa. Inside the wall was a park, in the center of which the villa stood. There were a few trees in the park, whose green lawn was spotted here and there with flower beds, blazing with color. The park, Harcourt thought, was a pretty place out of another time. Once Roman gentlemen had paced up and down the greensward, and Roman ladies, draped in the finest silk, had sat at tables underneath the trees, eating cakes and sipping wine, gossiping gaily among themselves. Now there was no one there.

A hand touched him softly on the shoulder.

Startled, gulping in sudden fright, he twisted over onto his back, Yolanda's dagger raised in his right hand for a vicious stroke.

And gazed into the face of the troll, the rope knotted on its neck.

Harcourt's left hand struck out and seized the troll by the throat and hauled it close against him.

"You!" Harcourt whispered, his breath hissing between his teeth. "You!"

The troll struggled, gasping, croaking in its effort to speak.

"Sir!" it croaked. "Sir!"

"What do you mean, sneaking up on me? Tell me."

Harcourt released the pressure of his fingers on its throat slightly.

"Danger!" the troll gasped. "Sir, I show you danger."

Harcourt turned back onto his belly, dragging the troll with him, holding it close against him and hard against the ground.

The troll pointed straight out in front of them.

"A trap, sir. A pit."

Harcourt whispered, "A pit? I don't see a pit."

"Just ahead of us. That patch of bare ground."

"There are a lot of patches of bare ground out here. I've crawled over some of them."

"Not this one. A trap. A pit, lightly covered. You crash through. Pointed stakes thrust up from the bottom."

Harcourt looked closer at the patch of ground. It looked all right to him.

"How do you know?" he asked.

"I know. I smell it out. I know my Evil kinsmen. I know how things are done."

Harcourt kept on staring at the ground. It still looked all right to him.

"That big boulder halfway down the hill," said the troll. "There's an ogre behind it. Hiding. On watch. He thinks there is something wrong. He peers out now and then."

Harcourt saw no evidence of an ogre when he looked at the huge rock down the hill from him. But there were other Evil hidden all along the villa. He had no trouble seeing them.

They were hidden, but, this much closer to the villa, he could make them out.

"Why don't you give it up, sir?" the troll whispered. "You never will get in."

Harcourt didn't answer. He continued his close examination of the area nearest to the wall. There were a lot of Evil down there. The longer he looked, the more he saw of them. And not all of them were against the wall. Some distance down the slope from the boulder where the troll said an ogre lurked, there was something hunkered next to the ground in a clump of hazel growth. For the love of Christ, he thought, they're all over the place. The wonder of it was that he had not been seen by any of them. The ogre was suspicious, the troll had said, but not sure as yet, most likely.

Harcourt nudged the troll and started sliding back into the thicket. The troll slid along with him, gulping in relief. Both of them got turned around and crawled back up the hill, going through the thicket and, once out of the thicket, keeping close to other cover.

Long minutes later, they halted, crouching in heavy undergrowth.

"Is it that way all around the villa?" Harcourt asked. "All around the wall?"

"As heavily guarded, sir, all around the villa. All around the wall."

"How do you know this?"

"I scouted it last night, sir. Well before first light. I went all the way around."

"In the dark you saw all that?"

"I see, sir, in many ways, better than you see. I know what to look for. I am an Evil One. I know where to look and how. I know the thoughts of Evil. Don't turn, don't try to look, but there are dragons in the air. In the hills across the valley, there are harpies."

"Troll," said Harcourt, "I am human. You are Evil. We are enemies. I did not raise a finger to help you when you would have hanged yourself. I told you to jump and get it over with. Why do this for us?"

"I would have thought you'd understand. The bridge."

"Yes, of course, the bridge. You'd better hope we get home so I can build that bridge for you."

"Also," said the troll, "I am an outcast now. I have walked with you. I have stayed with you. I am a traitor to the Evil. I am no longer of them. They'd hunt me down. With you or without you, they would hunt me down."

Harcourt nodded in understanding, then said, "There are guards outside the wall; are there none inside?"

"They do not intrude inside the wall," the troll told him. "They fear what is inside the wall."

"They guard something they are afraid of?"

"Only so that no one else can get in. They are afraid of it, but even more afraid of a human getting it."

"Do you know what it is?"

The troll shook his head. "There are tales. Too many tales. I can't perceive the truth among the many tales."

Harcourt crouched, considering. Why don't you give it up? the troll had asked, and he had not answered. Perhaps this was one of the situations, one of the problems that churchmen so delighted to debate, to which there were no answers. It was a dilemma, he admitted to himself, and also stark, raving foolishness—a small band of humans arrayed against all the forces of the Empty Land. They had not a fiddler's chance in hell, he told himself; there was no way to go forward and no way to go back. If they attempted to retreat, they'd soon find all the Evil of the Empty Land baying at their heels. All of the Empty Land might now be seeking them, quartering back and forth in search of them. If it hadn't been for the Romans, he thought bitterly, if they'd not come in—but no, the Romans had had to come blundering in to get themselves killed and to raise a war cry that rang across all the Empty Land.

To go ahead, to seek to break into the Roman villa down there in the valley, seemed as equally impossible as to retreat. There were guards along the wall and dragons in the air—although as yet he had not seen the dragons, taking the troll's word for it—and the harpies waiting in the hills across the valley. It's impossible, he thought—all of it's impossible. And yet, he reminded himself, they could not turn tail and run when they were within a stone's throw of what they had come to find. The prism enclosing a saint's soul was down there, and Eloise might be down there, and he could not turn his back on either the prism or Eloise. Especially, he could not turn his back on Eloise. Even if no one followed him, if all the others should desert him, he must go down this hill, his sword flashing in the sun, to do whatever had to be done. For him, he knew, there could be no other answer.

"Perhaps," the troll said, "we should continue up the hill."

"Yes," said Harcourt, "I think it's time we did."

They reached the cave, and the others were waiting for them. The abbot walked out and seized Harcourt by the hand. "Thank God you're back, Charles. I see you found someone."

"He found me," said Harcourt. "Before I could see who he was, I damn near choked him to death. Is Knurly back?"

"Not yet. The two of you have been gone a long time. We've been waiting for you, chewing on our nails. What did you find?"

"They're down there, all right. A hell's brood of them."

"You think we can break through?"

"I don't know," said Harcourt. "It won't be easy."

"Maybe Knurly can tell us something when he shows up."

"I hope so," Harcourt said.

Yolanda came running up to him. "My lord, I worried for you. You should have let me go along."

"How are things here?" he asked.

"As they were before. The Roman and the peddler are on watch. They swear they've seen nothing."

"They wouldn't. There is nothing there to see until you are on top of it."

He held out the dagger to her and she took it, slipping it into the belt sheath.

"I didn't have to use it. I didn't nick it, dirty it."

"We'll have to eat cold food today," she said. "We cannot build a fire."

"I wonder how they have failed to notice us," he said.

"Maybe they have seen us. Maybe they're just waiting to see what we will do."

"We, ourselves," he said, "don't know yet what we should do. All the way here I have kept wondering what we'd do once we found the villa. And I told myself that once we were there, we'd know. We'd look the situation over and we'd know."

"We've been here only a few hours."

"Yes, I know," he said.

He walked over to Nan, who still sat in the cave, in the same place she had been when he had left. The belt and sword still lay in her lap.

"You like that girl," she said.

"She is the daughter of a friend."

"A miller, who owes allegiance to your fief."

"He and his family, for many years. But Nan—or should I call you the Lady Margaret?"

"I was the Lady Margaret once. I am no longer. I shall continue as Nan. I could kill that peddler of yours. It was none of his business."

"Wizards have long noses."

"Yes, I know they do. I should have expected it."

The abbot came hustling up toward the cave mouth. "Knurly's coming in," he said. "I just caught sight of him. He is almost here."

Nan handed up the belted sword and Harcourt grabbed it in his hand. Yolanda said, "We're all together once again."

"Does he seem all right?" asked Harcourt.

"I saw nothing wrong with him," the abbot said. "You told me you did find the Evil down there."

Harcourt nodded.

"Any indication they might have spotted us?"

"Not that I could see."

"It does seem quiet," the abbot said. "Perhaps too quiet. All of us have been on watch. Decimus and the gargoyles, too. We have detected nothing."

The Knurly Man came around one of the massive oaks and started up the slope toward the cave. The parrot, perching on the abbot's shoulder, let out a squall at him.

"Can't you keep that bird quiet?" Harcourt asked the abbot.

"It's impossible. He is a mouthy creature. I think that he may hunger."

"I'll get him a slice of bread," Yolanda said. "That might keep him quiet."

"At least while he's eating it," said Harcourt.

The Knurly Man reached the cave and sat down heavily beside Nan. He looked at Harcourt. "I'm glad you're back," he said.

"I just got back."

"They're down there seven deep," said the Knurly Man. "Is that what you saw?"

"Exactly," Harcourt said.

"There's no way we can break through them," said the Knurly Man. "Or sneak through them. I didn't go all the way around the wall. I had no time. But I suspect the entire wall is guarded."

"The troll says so."

"What would the troll know about it?"

"He went out on scout. Last night. He was down the hill

with me. I guess you could say he saved my life. There was a pit . . ."

"I don't like it," said the abbot. "Why should he so much as turn a hand to help us?"

"He needs a bridge," said Nan.

"Oh, that again," the abbot said.

"Where is the Roman?" asked the Knurly Man.

"He's out with the gargoyles," said the abbot. "Watching."

"He should be here," said the Knurly Man. "The time has come for us to plan our move. He should be sitting in on it."

"He feels he is not one of us," said Harcourt. "He is just along."

"That's ridiculous," said the Knurly Man. "He helped us. He is one of us. He has earned his keep."

"He'd not be much good in our kind of a council of war," the abbot said. "He's a different sort of fighting man. A line-up fighting man, a face-to-face fighting man. That's the way he has been trained. We're too weak a force to do that kind of fighting."

"He has good military sense," said Harcourt. "He urged caution on his tribune. Had he been in command, the cohort would have been out of the Empty Land before the massacre could take place, and we'd not be in all the trouble we are in. I have my doubts that we should attack, but we can't retreat either. The entire Empty Land must be full of Evil bands that are hunting us. They would track us down."

"I don't like talk of retreat," said the Knurly Man. "We have come too far."

"There must be something we could do, if we could only think of it," the abbot said.

"Sooner or later, the Evil will nose us out," said the Knurly Man. "Sooner, I would think. We can't underestimate them. The worst thing anyone can do is underestimate an enemy. The Evil are smart. If they weren't smart, they would have been wiped out long ago."

"If we struck straight south," said the abbot, "we might be able to reach the river. Once across it, we'd be out of the Empty Land."

"The Evil might follow us across the river," Harcourt pointed out. "In any case, the river runs west for a distance and then turns south. From where we stand, it may be a long way to the river."

"I'm not ready yet to start running for the river," said the

Knurly Man. "There is too much at stake, and we've worked too hard to get here."

No one answered the Knurly Man. Each stood in silence. Yolanda walked over to the abbot with a slice of bread and gave it to the parrot. He seized it with a ready claw and began to eat it ravenously.

"There, you see," said the abbot. "He was hungry, as I said."

Nan rose. "I suspect we all are hungry, but it has to be cold eating. There is bread and cheese and a portion of a ham bone that has some meat still on it. It is getting slightly high, but still is edible."

Decimus burst around one of the big oaks and came running up the slope.

"The Evil are attacking!" he shouted. "They're coming up the hill!"

"It seems," said Harcourt, "that the decision is no longer ours. Yolanda, do you know where my bow and quiver are?"

Twenty Seven

There were not many of them as yet, but a few were moving up the hill, small groups of them, a dozen or so together. More of them were coming out of the line of trees and shrubs that grew before the wall. They were not moving fast; there seemed little purpose in them. They ambled and they shambled and, at times, they stopped and stood peering up the slope, as if they were not as yet convinced there was anyone up there.

The abbot nudged Harcourt and made a thumb toward the sky. When Harcourt looked, he saw the flapping dishrags, perhaps ten or more of them. They were fairly high, and they were not moving fast. They simply were flapping their way along, as if they might be looking for prey they could gobble up. And that was exactly it, Harcourt thought; they were looking for prey they could gobble up.

The gargoyles watched at the outer edge of the oaks, standing absolutely motionless. From down below, he thought, they probably appeared to be ancient stumps, although certainly the guarding Evil would know there were no stumps. They had looked at this hillside long enough to know there were no stumps.

The abbot said, "We can't hurry it. We have to wait until they are close enough. We can't take any chances of missing. Every arrow counts."

"Arrows alone won't stop them," Harcourt said. "When they get rolling, arrows won't stop them. They'll take their losses and come on. They've waited a long time to face this sort of situation. That place down there holds something of great value to them—something that has to be of value to be so heavily guarded."

"We know what's down there," said the abbot.

"We think we do," said Harcourt. "We can't be absolutely sure."

Although, he told himself, just a while ago he would have sworn he was sure. Uncle Raoul was no fool; he would have known what was going on. But now Harcourt found a new doubt creeping in. A man, he told himself, could not be sure of anything.

"You have lost your faith?" the abbot asked.

Harcourt shook his head, saying nothing. He was wrong, of course, he told himself, but how could a man be certain?

"We have kept the faith," the abbot said. "All these many leagues, in the midst of danger. We cannot forsake it now."

"I am not forsaking it," said Harcourt. "I find it forsaking me."

The parrot ate the last of the slice of bread. It settled itself more firmly on the abbot's shoulder, digging in its claws.

Harcourt glanced down the thin, defending line. He and the abbot formed the right wing, although, he thought, the line was far too slight to have either right or left wings. Next to him, on his left, stood Yolanda, calm and confident and waiting, the bow held lightly in her hand. Was there ever anything, he asked himself, that could ruffle her?

To her left was the Roman, without a bow but with his short sword drawn, standing stiffly erect, as if he might be flanked to both right and left by a line of fighting men, all standing ready with their blades.

And beyond him Nan crouched close against the ground, clutching an old tree limb that she had picked up, a length of wood that seemed too heavy for her frail strength to handle. Ranged beside her was the Knurly Man, spraddled on his bowed legs, set and ready with his bow in hand, the axe hanging from his shoulder by a thong. At the very end, at the farthest left, Andre the peddler leaned on his staff.

Harcourt looked for the troll, but did not see him.

Down the slope, there were far more of the Evil now. By some sort of accretive process, a line of advance had formed —late arrivals catching up with those who had gone out ahead or the early starters loitering for the others to catch up. The line was ragged in places, but it still was a line, and the pace of its forward motion had increased. Wherever the line was densest, the Evil were crowding one another, shouldering others aside to gain a place in line. There was a deadly purpose in them now; they were moving in, massively, to close and make the kill. And among them was not a single weapon —nothing but their talons and their fangs. It had been that way at the castle seven years ago, Harcourt remembered. The Evil did not carry weapons. They relied on what they carried in their jaws and claws. A disdain for weapons? he wondered; an overwhelming pride in their own sheer savagery? An over-riding confidence in their own prowess? An article of primal faith? Would any one among them be disgraced if he picked up a weapon?

Behind the line were bands of scurrying, scampering lesser Evil—elves, goblins, imps, sprites, pixies, and others; and in the air, clouds of fairies, their gossamer wings shining in the sun. Camp followers, Harcourt told himself, troublemakers, trick players, cheerers on, mischief brewers, a legion that had no particular weight, but that might make an impact on a less perceptive band than the ones who waited here for them with the arrows ready. Overhead, the dragons were circling lower and closing in, about to make their killing dives, long necks stretched out and swaying side to side, seeking out their targets. Coming in from the north, approaching the villa, was a long, ragged line of other fliers, smaller than the dragons, but no more tidy in their flying.

"Harpies," said the abbot.

A few arrows, Harcourt thought—and when it came to closer quarters, two swords, a mace, a battle-axe, the club clutched by Nan, and the staff of the peddler. That was all they had to face this host that came up the hill toward them. It was madness, he told himself, but there was no other choice. It was too late for flight—from the very first it had been too late for flight. From the moment they had arrived here, they had been boxed and trapped.

"It's time," the abbot said. Saying this, he drew the bow and let the arrow fly. In the line that was surging up the hill, an ogre stumbled, falling forward, clutching at the shaft that protruded from its breast. Along the line others were going down as well, but not enough of them, Harcourt thought. Four bows were not enough. No matter how well aimed and shot, no matter what the accuracy, they would not halt the Evil.

Down in front of the archers, the gargoyles moved out, stumping forward, their massive arms, like so many timbers, swinging. The line of Evil momentarily gave way before them as the swinging arms knocked it aside like a row of jack-straws, but even as it gave way, the line flowed around them as water would flow through a dam of piled-up rocks, going past the gargoyles and moving on, leaving the gargoyles in its wake.

Harcourt flung his bow aside and unsheathed his blade. The Evil had moved too close for efficient archery. To his left, he heard the howling wrath of the Knurly Man as he plunged into battle with his swinging axe, a scythe of death that mowed down everything it touched. Beside Harcourt, the abbot was laying all about him with the mace. Above him the parrot flapped in frantic circles, screeching horribly. Out of the corner of his eye, Harcourt saw the peddler, still standing where he had stood before, negligently—negligently!—leaning on his staff, staring out in stupid complacency at the collision that was taking place only a few feet in front of him. At least, Harcourt thought, in split-second contempt, the bastard had not run away; he still was standing firm for all the good that it would do.

Then time and space dissolved into a blur across which flashed momentary glimpses of what was taking place. Stroke and thrust and shove, duck and leap and plunge, and always the face of hate and savagery that stared out from many faces, one replaced by another that moved forward to take its place, to be replaced almost immediately by another grimacing visage, twisted by its fury. For a time Harcourt stood side by side with Decimus the Roman, a fighting machine that fought mechanically, saying not a word, wasting not a single motion, a man trained for such as this and who was an expert at it, who found no joy in it nor a thrill of satisfaction, who fought without the flame of hatred burning in him and was more efficient because he was not distracted by that hatred. Then the Roman was gone, and Harcourt neither had seen

him go nor knew what had happened to him, and he was with
the abbot, who whooped a battle chant of his very own while
he swung his mace two-handedly. Everything that stood in the
path of the mace went down, for there was nothing that could
withstand its twenty pounds of iron. And in the space of a
breath, the abbot and his mace were elsewhere and a slim
figure clothed in flowing white, a white streaked by the grime
and smudge of days upon the trail, stood with Harcourt, her
thin face grim and businesslike in the work that she was
doing, wielding a sword that could be none other than the
Roman's sword. Harcourt wondered where the Roman was,
that she should have his sword, but he had no time to ponder
on the question, for always the Evil came crowding in upon
him. Somewhere to his right, the abbot whooped his chant,
and above him the parrot flew and squalled. Off to the left,
the Knurly Man was roaring in a fighting rage.

Suddenly, with no warning, a tempest of wind swept the
battle line and black clouds boiled across the sky, low, black
clouds that dropped upon the fighting mass, as if to smother
it, roiling in a rage that matched the battle fury. As they
dropped closer, a dazzling bolt of lightning snarled across the
clouds. Harcourt threw up an arm to shield his eyes against
the searing brilliance of the bolt, and as he did, a thunderclap
so close and loud that it seemed to be on top of him knocked
him to his knees. He tried to struggle to his feet, but a second
bolt of lightning and another thunderclap that crowded close
upon the flash knocked him to the ground again. The air had
a strange tingle to his nostrils, and he gasped at the sulfurous
smell of it. Then there was a silence—a frightening silence
after all the turmoil of the fighting, an unnatural and unearthly silence, as if the lightning and the thunder had blotted
up all sound.

He rose shakily. As he did, some instinctive sense made
him glance back over his shoulder, and he saw the peddler
standing where he had stood before, but now with his arms
lifted high and his fingers spread. From each of his spread-out
fingers, tiny flickerings of light were writhing—tiny flickerings
that were miniatures of flaming lightning bolts. As Harcourt
stared in amazement, the flickers all ran down, and the peddler, sagging in the middle, slumped and fell upon the ground.

On the slope below, the Evil was running, retreating back
to the shelter of the villa wall. In the sky the flapping dishrags
that were dragons beat their way rapidly upward. There was
no sign of the harpies, and all the lesser Evil that had romped

behind the battle line had disappeared. The slope was littered with burned and twisted bodies, still smoking from the lightning bolts. Closer were the piled bodies of the Evil that had died before the lightning struck.

Yolanda, still carrying the short sword of the Roman, came walking around the piled bodies to make her way to Harcourt.

"Decimus is dead," she said.

Harcourt nodded. The wonder, he told himself, was that any of them still lived.

She came up close to him, and he put an arm around her and held her against him. Together they stood looking down the slope at the twisted, smoking bodies of the Evil.

"It was the peddler," he said, "and all this time I had thought ill of him."

"He's a good man, but strange," she said. "He is hard to know, harder still to love. Although I think that in a strange way I do love him. He is like a father to me. He was the one who took me out of the Empty Land and sent me across the river. He put me on the bridge and slapped me on the bottom and said, 'Cross the bridge, my little one. You'll be safer there.' So I went across the bridge and came to the miller's house, and there was a kitten there, and I sat down and played with it . . ."

"The peddler!" Harcourt cried. "I saw him fall. And then forgot . . ."

He spun around and started running up the hill to where he had seen the peddler fall, Yolanda running with him. But Nan was already there. She was kneeling beside the peddler. She looked up at them. "He is still alive," she said. "I think he is all right. He is quite used up. It took all the energy he had to call down the lightning."

"I'll get some blankets," Yolanda said. "We'll try to keep him warm."

As she ran toward the cave, Harcourt swung around to gaze down the slope. The abbot was plodding up the slope, the parrot perched upon his shoulder. Beside the abbot, the Knurly Man limped along, with the abbot's arm around him, half supporting him. A crimson splotch of blood seeped across the chest of the Knurly Man. Harcourt hurried forward, but the Knurly Man waved him off. "This meddling and officious churchman," he said, "is pretending that I need his help, and I am letting him because it makes him feel so good."

When they reached the peddler and Nan, the abbot lowered

the Knurly Man to a sitting position. "He's ripped rather badly," the abbot said, "but some bandages will stop the blood flow and protect his ribs. I think he'll be all right."

"I'd better be all right," said the Knurly Man, gesturing down the hill, "for we have our work cut out for us. The Evil are forming up again." He looked at the peddler. "What is wrong with him? Faint from the excitement?"

"He called down the lightning bolts," said Nan.

"So that was it," said Knurly. "I wondered what was going on. That was the fastest storm I ever saw. Clear blue weather one minute and a thunderstorm the next."

Harcourt took off his shirt and began ripping it into bandages. "You still have some of that ointment in your pack?" he asked the Knurly Man. "It would help the healing."

"I think there still is some. Remember, it has to be rubbed in hard or it doesn't work."

"I'll rub it in hard enough. Especially in the gashes."

"You'd better hurry," said the Knurly Man. "They'll be starting up the hill again, and I want to be well bandaged so I can use the axe on them."

Harcourt moved off a step or two to see better down the hill. The Evil did seem to be forming a new line, but he judged it might be some time before they started up the slope.

Yolanda came back from the cave with blankets, and a moment later the abbot showed up with the ointment.

Harcourt got down on his knees beside the Knurly Man. Using a strip of cloth torn from his shirt, he began to wipe the blood off Knurly's chest. It was a messy job. The gashes were more numerous and deeper than he had thought at first. The Knurly Man had not simply been slashed; he had been mauled. The Knurly Man did not flinch as Harcourt continued with the wiping. But he was impatient. "Get on with it," he said. "No need to wipe it clean. Just get some bandages on and pull them tight. Forget the ointment, too."

Harcourt looked up at the abbot and nodded. "I think we had better do what he says. We can't put on the ointment until we stop the flow of blood. The bandages will do that. We can use the ointment later."

"There won't be any later," said the abbot, speaking soberly.

"If that's the case," said the Knurly Man, "why bother with me at all? Get those bandages on and pull them tight. We'll stand them off, I tell you. We stood them off this time."

"We stood them off because of the peddler," said the abbot.

"The peddler's out on his feet. He won't be any help next time."

"Quit your moaning, Guy," said Harcourt, "and help me fix Knurly up. He's right. We will stand them off."

"We'll retreat to the cave," said the Knurly Man. "No more than ten feet to defend. The gargoyles will be with us."

"A last-ditch stand," the abbot said.

"This time we'll hold them," said the Knurly Man. "We'll make the price too high. They'll pull back."

"And if they come again?"

"We'll stand again. We'll bleed them white. We'll win out in the end."

"Sure we will," said Harcourt. And told himself, Sure we will. We'll win out in the end. If there are any of us left, we'll win out in the end.

One of them on each side of the Knurly Man, they worked together, wrapping the bandages around his chest and pulling them tight. Finally it was done, and the Knurly Man lumbered to his feet. "That feels better," he said. "You've got me stuck together."

Down to three, Harcourt thought—a sword, an axe, a mace, and Yolanda with the Roman's sword, if need be. And probably there'd be need. The gargoyles would be a help. The peddler and Nan would have to be counted out. They would be of little help, if any. Twice in a row the peddler could not be expected to pull a new piece of magic from his bag.

The Knurly Man stamped about. He reached down and picked up the axe from the spot where he had dropped it and swung it. With his left hand he patted his bandages. "I'm as good as new," he said. He didn't look as good as new. Spots of blood already were seeping through the bandages. When he'd swung the axe, he had winced with pain.

Harcourt walked down the hill beyond the trees. Down the slope, the Evil had formed up again in a line that seemed scarcely thinner than it had been before. Dragons and harpies were circling in the air. Closer at hand lay the piles of bodies scorched by the lightning bolts, tendrils of foul smoke trickling up from them. The four gargoyles, who had stationed themselves down the slope in front of the trees, now turned around and began lumbering up the hill. The line of Evil lurched into motion and started up the incline, moving slowly.

The abbot, close behind Harcourt, asked, "What think you of Knurly?"

"It's not good," said Harcourt. "Two of the wounds were

bubbling. There was froth at the edges of them. They're deep. Perhaps into the lungs."

"You said nothing."

"No need to say it. Knurly knows as well as I. There is nothing we can do. Even were we where we could reach a chirurgeon, there would be little to be done."

"What can we do?"

"We'll let him fight along with us. That is what he wants. We'd shame him otherwise. He'd resent it if we tried to coddle him."

"I'll watch him," said the abbot.

The gargoyles went past them and continued up the hill.

"We should seek out the Roman's body," said the abbot.

"There is no time to be seeking bodies. The Evil will be on us in no time at all."

"Some words should be said. Some compassion shown."

"The Roman was a soldier, Guy. He knew that he might die at any time and no words be said. He might not have valued final words as much as you do."

"You mean he could have been a pagan?"

"No, I didn't mean that. Although there still are some who are. Christianity has not taken as firm a hold upon the Empire as you seem to think."

The abbot mumbled to himself.

"Let's get back to the cave," said Harcourt. He turned about and stopped in astonishment. "Guy, do you see that?" he asked. The gargoyles were climbing trees, each of them shinnying up separate oaks, doing it laboriously.

"They're deserting us!" the abbot cried. "They're climbing up to hide." With a shout he started forward, but Harcourt grabbed him by the arm.

"Leave them be," he said. "If they want out of this, we're not about to force them."

"Without them we are dead," the abbot said.

"Even with them we may well be dead," said Harcourt.

They stood and watched. Once the gargoyles reached the lower limbs, which were, in all truth, low against the ground, they went up the trees more swiftly, disappearing into the foliage.

Harcourt started toward the cave again. Glancing back over his shoulder, he saw that the Evil were in full motion. They would soon be here.

The abbot plucked at Harcourt. "We'll face them, you and I together, Charles."

"And Knurly."

"Yes, Knurly will be with us."

But even as he said it, there was a rending, tearing sound to one side of them.

Turning toward the sound, he saw that one of the oak trees was swaying violently and that, as it swayed, its roots tore from the ground, great sprawling roots that clawed and strained, raising the tree so that there would be room for the roots to position themselves solidly underneath the tree. Now there were other tearing sounds, and some of the other trees were swaying, too, with the roots coming from the ground.

The abbot hastily crossed himself, mumbling in Latin. Harcourt stood speechless, watching the four trees up which the gargoyles had climbed wrest themselves free of the soil in which they had been planted. They stood for the moment, all four of them, still swaying slightly on their roots. Then slowly, ponderously, they lurched forward, moving down the hill.

The Knurly Man was hobbling rapidly down the slope toward Harcourt and the abbot, swinging the axe above his head and howling out a battle cry. Behind him came the other three, the peddler stumping along with Nan supporting him and his staff holding him erect.

Yolanda sped past the Knurly Man and reached them first. "What is happening now?" she asked.

"I'm not sure," said Harcourt, "but stay here in the center of the trees." For he saw that the trees were moving to form a ring around them, one tree in front, one on either side, and one behind.

"It's the gargoyles doing it," the abbot gasped. "The gargoyles climbed the trees."

The six of them clustered in a group, and the trees, walking on writhing roots like spiders with very many legs, closed in around them. When the ring was formed, the trees again started down the hill. There was little space in the center of the ring. The limbs hung low and the spraddling roots reached out.

The abbot swung his mace idly to and fro. "Not many of the Evil can break through," he said.

"Those that do," said the Knurly Man, "will find us waiting for them."

"Be careful when we reach the lower slopes of the hill," Harcourt cautioned. "There are traps and pits."

"What magic?" the peddler wailed in a scratchy, feeble voice. "What magic makes the trees march?"

Yolanda seized the arm of the peddler opposite Nan and took his staff away from him.

"My staff!" he wailed.

"If you keep it, you'll get tangled up in it," Yolanda told him. "You'll trip yourself on it."

And all this time, all this time of babble, the trees moved down the hill. Their upper foliage closed together above the heads of the humans, forming an umbrella that closed the sky to them. On all sides the meshed limbs closed together, and there was little room to walk. The roots reached out, writhing and crawling, large and heavy; there were times the smaller ends of them struck with stinging blows against the humans' legs.

"Keep your feet firmly under you," Harcourt warned the others. "Do not stumble, do not fall. If you do, the roots will walk over you."

The trees must have reached and pierced the Evil line, Harcourt thought, for on all sides of them inhuman rage rose up—the frothing frenzy, the murderous fury, the manic raving of a kill denied. He tried to peer through the foliage surrounding him, trying to find even the tiniest space between the intervening wood and leaves that would allow him to see what was happening. But there was no such opening. Looking, he did not watch his footing, as he had warned the others to, and now he stumbled against something that made him come very close to losing his balance. His right foot, stretching forward to correct the imbalance occasioned by his stumbling left foot, trod on something that was slippery and that twisted. As he jerked his gaze down to it, he saw that it was a mangled troll, a troll that had been caught by the crawling roots of the tree in front, caught and crushed and trampled and passed over by the roots.

To his left, another troll came crashing through a tree, a very battered, confused, and bloodied troll. Harcourt raised his sword against it; but before he could make his stroke, the axe of the Knurly Man chopped down against its head, and the troll collapsed into the roots of the tree, its skull split open and brains oozing out of it. Sprawled and broken, it rode the roots of the tree, rocking with their motion.

Although he could not see it actually happening, Harcourt conjectured, from the motion of the inner branches, that the branches facing outward were flailing furiously at the Evil as they rushed in upon the trees, a scythelike progression mowing down everything that stood in their path. With a situation such as this, he thought, few of the enemy would manage to plunge through the branches to get at those who marched within their circle.

Other dead or dying members of the Evil force, pushed and shoved into the ground by the marching roots, appeared underneath their feet. A few other ogres, trolls, and harpies made their blundering, savage, futile way between the lashing branches and were killed by the weapons that awaited them. They rode, joggling, finally dropping loose and being passed over by the crunching roots that moved forward with remorseless strength. Once the trees moved over a pit that gaped wide open, but, seeing it in time, the members of the human band skipped quickly to one side, clinging to the branches of the sheltering trees for support, and got safely past it.

Now the ground beneath their feet no longer sloped as sharply as it had and gradually became level. The screaming rage of the Evil lessened; in its place came a keening, a melancholy wailing that beat and reverberated against the hills that enclosed the valley of the villa.

"They are beaten," said the abbot. "They know that they are beaten, that we have prevailed over them. The guards of this treasure place have failed. We must be almost at the wall."

A moment later the trees hit the wall and came to a momentary pause, a shock shuddering through them as they struck the wall. Then the movement began again, and to Harcourt's ears came the crunching sound of falling, shattered stone. The trees rose slightly as they crawled up the slope of crumbled blocks, and, inside their circle, the humans had to crawl as well, clambering over the fallen, scattered blocks that had made up the wall.

Grass was underneath their feet, the smooth, clipped grass of a spreading lawn, and the trees moved out of their closed formation, opening up the crowded pen that had enclosed the humans, moving off a little distance. It was all over.

Harcourt looked back up the hill down which the trees had come. Leading from the grove standing before the cave, double windrows of dead and broken Evil lay, those that had been stricken down by the lashing branches of the marching trees. Standing outside the windrows were the survivors of the Evil guard, in ones and twos and in small groups. From them rose the shrill keening of defeat, the death wailing of a beaten foe.

Here we're safe, thought Harcourt, remembering what the troll with the rope about its neck had told him—that the Evil did not dare to cross the wall into the villa grounds because they had a deathly fear of what was sheltered there. There was some motion in the windrows—injured, crippled Evil who still had some life left in them, crawling free of the dead that lay on every hand.

We are here, Harcourt told himself; we have finally reached this place we set out so long ago to find. Just a few feet up this green, trim lawn are Eloise and the Lasandra prism. No doubt now, he told himself; no doubt at all, as there had been before. He recalled how he had stood upon the hill and had seen the glimmer of the candle, flickering for a moment in the wind and finally going out. And how he had wondered if the candle might be held by Eloise, shielding the flame with her left hand, knowing somehow that he was there, that he could see the candle's light, sending out a signal to him, telling him that she awaited him.

"Eloise," he said, speaking the word almost inaudibly and, as he said the name, wishing that he could recall her face. But there had always been that wisp of hair blown by the wind across her face, and he could not remember it.

The abbot, the parrot perching on his shoulder, moved up beside him. "Charles," he said, speaking quietly, "it's Knurly. He wants to talk with you."

"Knurly, certainly. How is he?"

"He's dying," said the abbot.

That couldn't be, Harcourt told himself. Not Knurly. Not that old friend of his. Knurly was indestructible; Knurly was forever. And yet, he remembered, the blood had frothed and bubbled when he had wound on the bandages, pulling them tightly as Knurly had insisted.

Heavily, he walked up the lawn with the abbot to where the Knurly Man lay upon the ground. His eyes were closed, but when Harcourt knelt beside him, they opened. Uncertainly, he reached out a hand to Harcourt, who grasped it and held it tightly.

"Knurly," Harcourt said and could say nothing further.

"One thing only," said the Knurly Man. "You must promise that you will not allow that sanctimonious churchman to do any mumbling over me. Restrain him by force if that is necessary."

"I promise," Harcourt said.

"Another thing. You must not mourn. I knew that this would happen . . ."

"How could you know?" asked Harcourt. "Surely, you do not think . . ,"

"You recall the Wishing Well? I wanted to look into it, but you had to go secure the rope from the dragon's neck."

"I didn't take the rope," said Harcourt. "All the years he'd worn it, it belonged to him. When I reached to slip it off, I knew it belonged to him."

"You did this while I went to look into the well."

"Yes, and when I asked you what you saw," said Harcourt, "you said you had seen yourself. Which was not surprising, for that is what you would expect to see when you gaze into a well."

"I told you true," said the Knurly Man. "I saw myself, but dead."

Harcourt tried to speak, but was unable to.

"It did not astonish me," said the Knurly Man. "I knew that death was close, that it walked beside me. I told you, remember, that the people of my race live much longer than humans and that we do not slide into old age and senility, but die before we start to age, still in the prime of life. We die before we start getting old."

"I do remember that you told me so."

"I knew when I saw the vision in the well that I would not see home again. And this way of dying is better than some ways I can think of. You will speak to your grandfather on this matter? He will understand, and he will not be surprised. He knew how it might be. The two of us were like brothers. We had no secrets from each other."

"He will miss you," Harcourt said, "and I as well. And all the others of us."

"I have no regret at leaving life, but I hate to leave you while you still face the long journey home. I had hoped that I might stay long enough to help you on the way."

Harcourt bent his head, remembering other days, the stories that the Knurly Man had told him, the birds' nests and the foxes and the flowers that he had shown and named for him, pointing out the stars and telling him how to use the Wain to find the north.

The Knurly Man had closed his eyes again. The bandages wrapped about his chest were soaked with blood. The grip of his hand on Harcourt's lessened for a moment, then clamped down in a fierce grip.

His eyes came open and he looked at Harcourt.

"The axe is yours," he said.

"I shall treasure it," said Harcourt, struggling to hold back the tears. "I'll hang it on the castle wall, to one side of the great fireplace."

"Do not bother greatly over me. No words, remember. None of the abbot's mumbling."

"No words," said Harcourt.

"Leave me as I am. Dig no hole for me. Pile rocks over me. So the wolves can't dig me out. I hate the stinking wolves. I do not want my carcass to be hauled, flopping, all about the landscape by filthy scavengers."

"There are slabs of rock at hand, fallen from the wall," said Harcourt. "I'll pile them over you. I'll carry them myself."

"One thing more . . ." But the eyes closed once again and he fought for breath, although his hand still held its grip.

Harcourt saw that the abbot was standing near and raised his head to look at him. "Not yet," he said. "He still hangs on. He has more to say."

"I heard him say that he wanted no words spoken over him," the abbot said. "I shall respect his wishes. I like this Knurly Man. I have always liked him, and on this trip he has proved himself a friend. When I, myself, was near to death, he hauled me through a storm to the hut of Nan."

The Knurly Man stirred. His eyes opened once again. "I heard," he said. "I heard as if from far away. The abbot is a good man, true to his chosen faith, a good comrade on the trail. I have learned to love him. You'll tell him what I say."

"He is standing here. He hears what you are saying."

"And Eloise," said the Knurly Man.

"What of Eloise?"

"Not Eloise," said the Knurly Man. "You've been blinded for too long. Not Eloise. She is not your love."

His hand loosened its grip and would have slipped away if Harcourt had not held it firmly.

In so far a place, thought Harcourt. To die in so far a place, so far away from home. He thought of his grandfather, sitting on the bench before the castle fire, and the look that would be upon his face when Harcourt brought the word to him. And the worst of it, he thought, was that there was nothing he could say, no word of comfort he could bring to him.

The abbot, stepping closer, reached down with both his hands, lifted Harcourt to his feet, and stood for a moment holding him. Tears flowed down the abbot's cheeks and into his bushy beard.

Then he stooped and picked up the battle-axe and put it in Harcourt's hand. "He gave you this," he said. "Hang tight onto it. It is yours to keep."

Twenty Eight

The abbot raised his mace and tapped on the door again, then waited. Nothing happened.

"They do not answer," said the abbot. "They must know we're here. They must know what happened. Why don't they open up?"

On his shoulder, the parrot grumbled in a grating voice.

"We've given them a chance," said Harcourt. "They have heard your rapping with that monstrous mace of yours. They could not help but hear it."

"I'll rap again."

"No, don't rap again," said Harcourt. "Break down the goddamn door."

"We've given them all the time that politeness would dictate," said the abbot. "Please stand aside a little."

Harcourt backed up and bumped into Yolanda, who had been standing close behind him. He reached out a hand to steady her.

"It seems a shame," she said, "to break the door. It is carved so beautifully."

The abbot paid no attention to what she said. He swung the mace and the door bulged inward, its wood cracked from top to bottom. He smashed the mace against it again and the door came down, a shattered, jagged fragment of it swinging on its hinges. Harcourt, kicking the broken sections to one side, walked into a small entry hall that led into an atrium.

The atrium was lighted by flaming cressets fixed into sconces all along the walls. The floor was paved in colored tiles that spelled out a woodland scene with trees and flowers and, in the center of it, a shepherd surrounded by his sheep. Along the walls, between doors that led off from the central hall into other rooms, stood display cases filled with the shine of precious metals and the gleam of jewels.

An aged man, dressed in a robe of rusty black, fumbled his way out of one of the doors that opened onto the atrium. His face was a blob of white. He shuffled forward a pace or two, then stopped, swaying as he stood. And there were others there as well, half seen, some of them only guessed, the faint sense of flickers on the walls, the shimmer of whiteness; from them came faint moanings, so low-pitched, so nearly out of the world, they could barely be heard.

"Ghosts," said the abbot. "This is a place of ghosts. Ghosts are wardens of this place."

And if he had not arrived to rescue her, Harcourt thought, in time to come Eloise would have turned into one of the ghosts flickering on the wall. Throughout a large space of time, perhaps forever, she would have been a moaning ghost, waiting against the day when some unforeseen circumstances might release her. It might be, he thought, that she and the old man in the robe of rusty black were the only living beings underneath this roof.

But where was Eloise? Why had she not answered the door when the mace had thundered on it?

He stepped forward, the abbot pacing by his side, their feet booming on the tiles, waking echoes in the hall.

The old man in black fled with thin shrieks back through the door by which he'd come. The ghostly figures still danced all along the walls.

A jeweled diadem in one of the display cases threw back fire at them, the jewels glinting in the flaring of the torches. A burnished sword lay on a swath of purple velvet, a circlet of gold, a standing cup bejeweled and bright with silver, a pair of gold-encrusted spurs, a gem-sprinkled bridle, a chalice, another standing cup with a husk of coconut for a bowl, a drinking horn of ivory carved most delicately . . .

"A treasure house," said the abbot. "Loot from many lands over many years. But I do not see the prism that we came to seek."

"It's here," said Harcourt. "It must be here. We have not seen everything. The Evil guardians feared this place, would not venture on the grounds. They would not have feared the treasures that we see here. The prism is the one thing they would have feared."

He had been looking at the cases, and now he raised his head. A woman stood in the doorway through which the man in black had fled. There was something about her bearing that he seemed to recognize, but when he looked at her face, he could not see it clearly. There was no wind to blow a wisp of hair across her face, but even without the wisp of hair, he could not see it clearly.

"Eloise?" he asked tentatively. "Eloise, is that you?"

She spoke in a high, clear voice. "Yes, I am Eloise. But how do you, a barbarian, know my name? And what are you doing here? You have no right to be here. You should have been stopped long before you reached the wall."

"Eloise, I'm Charles. Charles Harcourt. Surely you remember me."

Her voice was crystal ice. "Yes, I believe I do. I remember you faintly and far away. But a mere acquaintanceship gives you no right to come calling on me. Be gone! Take your mangy crew and go."

He still could not see her face.

"And touch not a thing," she said. "Lay not a finger on any one of them. Keep your grubby claws away."

The moaning of the ghosts rose in volume and filled the room.

"But, child," said the abbot, "you are acting strangely. I recall you as a girl, sweet and adorable and in love with Charles. We sought you at Castle Fontaine and we did not find you . . ."

"Now you have found me," said Eloise. "Now you are satisfied. Please turn about and go."

"But we came to rescue you. Having failed before . . ."

"I need no rescue. I am the guardian of these treasures. It is a sacred charge that has been laid upon me and . . ."

"Child!" the abbot pleaded. "Child, come to your senses . . ."

"My lord," Yolanda whispered, close to Harcourt's elbow. "The tools! The carving tools!"

She grasped his arm and pointed toward one of the cases. "They are beautiful," she said.

Eloise stepped quickly forward, threatening. "Keep your hands off them!" she screamed. "They are not yours to touch. They belong to me. Everything here belongs to me."

"You have a right to touch them," the peddler told Yolanda. "You have the right to take them. They belong to you. They are your mother's tools."

"No!" Eloise shrieked. "No one takes anything."

She leaped swiftly toward Yolanda, clawlike fingers reaching out. Harcourt jumped to intercept her, swinging his arm to block her leap. The swinging arm caught her in full stride and sent her crashing backward. Toppling, she fell to the floor, striking it heavily, and slid along the tiles. Harcourt took a stride and stood over her. "Keep out of our way," he thundered at her, his anger blazing. "Your guard is broken. There are heaps of dead and dying Evil out there beyond the wall. Your stewardship here is ended. We take what we wish."

She began to crawl away. She crawled on hands and knees, shaken with her anger, spitting like a cat. At the doorway from which she had come into the atrium, she stopped her crawling and, clawing at the doorway, pulled herself erect.

"You never will get home," she screamed at Harcourt. "You are dead. All of you are dead. I'll have my vengeance on every one of you. Your bodies will be torn into small bits and scattered. There will be small feasting for the wolves."

Harcourt turned away and held his arms out to Yolanda. She came swiftly to him, and he held her close against him. "She tried for my eyes," Yolanda cried. "She would have ripped them out. If you had not reached her . . ."

She collapsed, sobbing, against his chest. "The set," she sobbed. "The wood-carving set. It is something I have wanted all my life. Jean tried to make some tools for me, and he did the best he could, but they were awkward tools and . . ."

Nan said to the peddler, "You said those are Marjorie's tools. Then *she* carved the gargoyles. I wondered if she had, but said nothing. It seemed so improbable."

"Yes, Lady Margaret, she carved them. I was there while she worked on them. She and John, her troubador whom she ran away with."

"And you put the magic in the gargoyles?"

"I did my best. My magic is so small. John and I lifted them and fixed them into place. And I worked a magic spell, although I was not sure that it had taken."

"It took," said Harcourt. "It saved our lives this day. Peddler, you saved us twice today."

Yolanda lifted her head from Harcourt's chest. "You are my grandmother," she said to Nan. "I think I felt it all the while. I felt a closeness to you. And my mother worked in wood?"

"As you seem to work as well," said Nan. "Why did you

not tell me, minx? There was so much that you did not tell me. I felt for you as you felt for me, and I asked you questions, but you would answer none."

Nan walked the few steps across the floor to Harcourt and Yolanda.

"Young man," she said, "let me have my granddaughter for a moment. For a moment only, you can let her go."

The abbot's subdued bellow cut across the room. "Charles! Charles, look here! I've found it!"

Nan reached for Yolanda. Harcourt swung about to face the abbot's bellow and saw that he was holding high above his head a glittering rainbow that flashed in all the colors wakened by the flaming torches set all about the walls.

"The prism," Harcourt whispered. "The prism of Lasandra."

"In one of the cases," said the abbot. "I saw it and reached down and lifted it, and it flamed at me. It flames at all the world. It flames with the soul of the blessed saint."

The parrot launched itself from the abbot's shoulder, shrieking excitedly, flying in erratic circles.

"And so it all is finished," said the peddler, speaking gently. "The mission's finished, and those who rest in the enchanted sanctuary can sleep more easily."

The abbot started walking down the room, toward them, with the prism held aloft.

The parrot, still shrieking, still excited, dived for the prism, one of its claws striking one of the abbot's hands. The prism slipped from his grasp; he made a futile effort to catch it as it fell—and failed. Still standing by the door, Eloise screamed, as if in agony.

The prism struck the floor, splintering into a million pieces, none larger than a grain of sand. The flame in the rainbow went away, and the atrium was filled to overflowing with a glorification and a beatitude that surpassed all understanding.

Harcourt fell to his knees, suffused by a sudden holiness that pulsed within his very being.

"God bless my soul!" the parrot shrieked, still gyrating in the air.

"So be it," said a ghostly voice, and a ghostly hand stretched out. Then the saint, released after many centuries, was gone.

And a sudden, doleful wailing went out across all the Empty Land.

Twenty Nine

The Knurly Man slept beneath a cairn built of the great stone slabs from the broken wall. One half of the jagged villa door, still hanging on its hinges, flapped back and forth in the wind that had sprung up from the west. The hill beyond the villa, still littered with its heaps and rows of dead, was prowled by lurking wolves.

The abbot said, "It was for the best. Now that I think of it, it was for the best. What happened should have been our purpose from the very start—not to secure the prism as a holy symbol to glorify the abbey or any other place of worship, but to find and destroy it so as to release the soul within it. To have done otherwise would have been close to blasphemy. By all that is right, the moment I took hold of it, I should have dashed it to the floor so that the magic of Lasandra might be broken and a blessed soul set free. The parrot saw more clearly than did I, or any other of us. Why should I have been so blinded, so blinded by the glory that I wanted for my abbey? Charles, how can men become and stay so blind?"

Harcourt put an arm around the abbot's shoulder. "Always the philosopher," he said. "Always the digger after the truth that may be found in theology."

"A blind philosopher," said the abbot. "I am ashamed and humbled. I have many beads to tell."

"Awrrk," the parrot said.

"I cannot understand Eloise," Harcourt said. "She was once a lovely woman."

"People change," the abbot said. "Or are changed. There might once have been a time when Lasandra was a righteous and respected wizard, and then he fell into temptation. He was taken to the mountaintop and shown the world. It may have been the same with Eloise. The Evil seized her at Fontaine and, instead of heaping indignities upon her, offered her a post that dazzled her—all the power and glory that she had never dreamed of, a power and a glory greater than the heaven that she at one time yearned for. You must not blame her, Charles. You must not hate her."

"I loved her once," said Harcourt. "I loved her for years."

"In these later years a blind and guilty love," the abbot told him. "You used your love of her to inflict punishment on yourself for a crime that never happened. I saw what you were doing to yourself. Knurly saw. Knurly told you so in his dying moments, told you something that he could not have told you until he faced death and must tell it to you then."

"I tried to find her later. She was nowhere to be found. The ghosts were gone, and the man in black and Eloise as well."

"You must mourn no further. Forget the guilt that poisoned you. Wipe your soul clean of it. You have Yolanda now. I saw you when you took her in your arms. There is a great love between you, and it will become greater. She will help you to erase the guilt. As your spiritual adviser . . ."

"I know you too well to have you for my spiritual adviser. You shade the doubt in my favor every time. You are not harsh enough."

"I can be harsh if need be," said the abbot. "If you don't mend your ways."

"I have mended them, I think."

"If you haven't," the abbot said, "I'll boot you in the rump. I'll boot you hard. I am the man to do it."

"We must get going," said Harcourt. "It's a long way home."

"We'll move fast," the abbot said, "once we strike the Roman road. It is only a few leagues from here. And the trees will be going with us. The peddler said they would. With them along, the Evil will give us little trouble. In any case, I think the Evil are disheartened. They may well thirst for vengeance, but for the moment the heart has been taken out of them. The prism was always a bargaining tool that they thought they could fall back on if they were pushed too hard by the Empire. They could have traded it for some concession if they were ever pinned against the wall. But now it's gone, and some of their spirit has disappeared as well. It's a blow in the belly for them. They'll rebound from it, of course, but not for a little time, not before we can reach home."

The others were sitting on the lawn, and Harcourt walked toward them, with the abbot following.

Harcourt sat down beside Yolanda. "I never had a chance really to see the tool kit," he said. "Will you show it to me?"

"She'll display the tools most willingly," Nan said. "I've never seen anyone so pleased with anything. I remember when

I bought the kit for her mother. You know, of course, that my daughter worked in wood. That's how Yolanda got her inclination for it. Is she really good at it?"

"She is good at it," Harcourt said. "I have seen her work."

"The peddler told me how it was," said Nan. "Marjorie and John decided to replace the fallen gargoyles. As a work of piety. The porch seemed so empty with them missing and the cathedral incomplete. John, with his songs, had won over some of the Evil to him, and they helped with the gargoyle work. The peddler, too, was there. Yolanda was a babe in arms, and the peddler tended her and played with her while the others worked. He helped to hoist the gargoyles into place, but that was about all he did; he was so taken with Yolanda that he spent all his time with her. Then the work was done and he went back to his cave. Months later, two of the Evil who had worked with Marjorie and John brought Yolanda to him. They had saved her when my daughter and John had been killed."

"You knew none of this, of course . . . I mean, until right now."

"That's right. Although I came searching for my daughter, for some word of her. I was certain she had gone with John into the Empty Land. I told you earlier I had come here to have time for research, but that was really not the case. I could have done the research, perhaps better, without coming here. I stayed here and worked with the Evil, bandaging them up and giving them potions, always asking questions, but never getting answers. I had finally come to the opinion that I would never get an answer, but now I do have one, and it's what I expected. But Yolanda is unexpected. I never dreamed I might find a granddaughter where I failed to find a daughter."

"You'll go back with us? With Yolanda and me? The castle waits for you."

"For a time," she said. "There is a castle in the south of Gaul that I suppose still belongs to me. I left it in the care of a faithful steward."

"Your scrolls? Your notes?"

"We can't go back to get them. The country is too forested for the trees to travel through. The peddler will bring them all to me later."

Harcourt looked at the peddler. "You're not going back with us?"

The peddler shook his head. "I have work I still must do."

"I have the tools all spread out," Yolanda said to Harcourt. "Have your look at them. This one is a chisel and that one is a gouge and that one over there, a rasp . . ."

She reached out an arm and, putting it around his neck, pulled him down, and kissed him tenderly.

Thirty

They topped the rise and there was the bridge, with the road running down toward it and the chimney smoke from the miller's house rising in the air.

"Charles, we're home," Yolanda said. "Charles, we're finally home."

The abbot dug out a piece of cheese which he had hidden somewhere in his cassock and began to nibble at it.

"We should have stopped back there a way," he said, "and had a regular meal. Ham and bacon, maybe. This traveling on an empty stomach is detrimental to one's health."

"Glutton," the parrot screeched in a grating voice. "A vice, a vice, a vice. Awrrk!"

"I don't know what to do with this bird," the abbot grumbled. "It is becoming hard to live with him. He rides my shoulder and admonishes me. He will not let me be. Do you think there might be a possibility that he could have a soul, that he could have become a somewhat holy bird?"

"Forget it," Harcourt said. "You've been griping and wondering about it for the last few days. It is an unhealthy way of thinking."

"And yet," said the abbot, "when this foolish bird screeched 'God bless my soul' back there at the villa, someone said 'So be it,' and a hand stretched out in blessing. None of the others of us asked that our souls be blessed."

"There can be nothing to it," Nan told him, "but if you can't be talked out of it, at least it will give you food for theologic maundering in the dark nights at the abbey, when you are all alone."

"I need no extra thoughts to chew on," the abbot said. "The abbey has problems of its own."

The abbot finished with the cheese and wiped his hands upon the cassock.

"Glutton!" the parrot screamed.

As they approached the bridge, the trees wheeled, two to each side of the road, and, positioning themselves, began to dig their roots furiously into the ground.

The abbot stopped short to stare at them. "Now what is going on?" he asked.

"Probably they will stay here until there is further need of them," Harcourt said. "If there's ever need of them. Their job is now done. They have seen us home."

"And the gargoyles," said Nan. "I have not seen them for several days. Are they still with us?"

"They've become part of the trees," the abbot said. "The trees have taken them to themselves. Or they have returned to the trees. I don't know which it is. The bark has grown over them. I thought I had mentioned it when I saw it happening."

"I don't remember that you did," said Nan. "All that I've heard out of you for leagues is your quarreling with the parrot."

Leaving the trees, they started down the road to cross the bridge. Out of a thicket popped a woebegone creature with a rope dangling from its neck.

The troll, jigging in the dust of the road, squeaked excitedly at them. "I came early, traveling very fast. I've been waiting here for you. There are the most obnoxious trolls living underneath this end of the bridge, and I was hard put to hide from them, for if they had seen me, they would have done me harm."

"All right," said Harcourt. "So you're here. Don't make a spectacle of it. Come along with us."

"I suppose," said the troll, "that it is too late in the day to build that bridge for me. If it should be, how about tomorrow?"

"In a day or two," said Harcourt. "Don't begin pushing me."

Nan and the abbot started across the bridge, Harcourt and Yolanda following, walking hand in hand.

The troll skipped on ahead.

ABOUT THE AUTHOR

Clifford D. Simak is a newspaperman, only recently retired. Over the years he has written more than twenty-five
books and has some two hundred short stories to his
credit. In 1977 he received the Nebula Grand Master
award of the Science Fiction Writers of America and has
won several other awards for his writing.

He was born and raised in southwestern Wisconsin, a
land of wooded hills and deep ravines, and often uses this
locale for his stories. A number of critics have cited him
as the pastoralist of science fiction.

Perhaps the best known of his work is *City*, which has
become a science-fiction classic.

He and his wife, Kay, have been happily married for
more than fifty years. They have two children—a daughter, Shelley Ellen, a magazine editor, and Richard Scott,
a chemical engineer.

Dear Reader,

Your opinions are very important to us so please take a few moments to tell us your thoughts. It will help us give you more enjoyable DEL REY Books in the future.

1. Where did you obtain this book?

Bookstore	□1	Department Store □4	Airport	□7	5
Supermarket	□2	Drug Store □5	From A Friend □8		
Variety/Discount Store □3		Newsstand □6	Other_____		

(Write In)

2. On an overall basis, how would you rate this book?

Excellent □1   Very Good □2   Good □3   Fair □4   Poor □5   6

3. What is the main reason that you purchased this book?

Author □1   It Was Recommended To Me □3   7
Like The Cover □2   Other_____

(Write In)

4. In the same subject category as this book, who are your *two* favorite authors?

_____ 8
_____ 9
_____ 10
_____ 11

5. Which of the following categories of paperback books have you purchased in the past 3 months?

Adventure/		Biography □4	Horror/		Science
Suspense □12-1		Classics □5	Terror □8		Fiction □x
Bestselling		Fantasy □6	Mystery □9		Self-Help □y
Fiction □2		Historical	Romance □0		War □13•
Bestselling		Romance □7			Westerns □2
Non-Fiction □3					

6. What magazines do you subscribe to, or read regularly, that is, 3 out of every 4 issues?

_____ 14
_____ 15
_____ 16
_____ 17

7. Are you: Male □1   Female □2   18

8. Please indicate your age group.

Under 18 □1   25-34 □3   50 or older □5   19
18-24 □2   35-49 □4

9. What is the highest level of education that you have completed?

Post Graduate Degree □1	College Graduate □3	Some High		20
Some Post Graduate	1-3 Years College □4	School		
Schooling □2	High School	or Less □6		
	Graduate □5			

(Optional)

If you would like to learn about future publications and participate in future surveys, please fill in your name and address.

NAME_____

ADDRESS_____

CITY_____ STATE_____ ZIP_____ 21

Please mail to: Ballantine Books
DEL REY Research, Dept.
516 Fifth Avenue — Suite 606
New York, N.Y. 10036

F-14